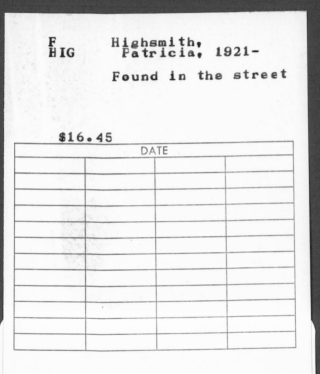

F   Highsmith,
HIG   Patricia, 1921-

        Found in the street

$16.45

DATE			

PKWY. VILLG.

© THE BAKER & TAYLOR CO.

FOUND IN
THE STREET

FOUND IN THE STREET

PATRICIA HIGHSMITH

THE ATLANTIC MONTHLY PRESS
NEW YORK

·

First published in Great Britain in 1986 by William Heinemann Ltd., London, England.

First American edition, October 1987.

Library of Congress Cataloging-in-Publication Data

Highsmith, Patricia, 1921–
  Found in the street.

  I. Title.
PS3558.I366F68   1987   813'.54   87-15287
ISBN 0-87113-208-7

Printed in the United States of America

First printing

For Kingsley

THE girl trotted, and leapt to a curb. She wore new sneakers, spotlessly white, black corduroy trousers, and a white T-shirt with a red apple design on its front. Dodging pedestrians, she swerved and disappeared into a shop whose window displayed lavender-colored items, scarves of shocking pink, beads, and was out within seconds, moving on, tempted by the other side of the street, but staying on the side where she was. Like a butterfly, she described a half-circle to avoid a shuffling clump of people, then hovered before another shop whose wares extended onto the sidewalk. Not this one either.

The white sneakers flitted on, the short yellow hair bobbed. She moved toward a spot of red, lingered, and entered. The West Fourth Street shoppers drifted in both directions on the sidewalk. It was nearly 6 in the afternoon of a late August day, and the air was cool and sunny. The blond girl emerged with a beige plastic bag in one hand. Her other hand shoved a small billfold into a back pocket of her corduroys. Her smile was wider on her unrouged lips, a happy smile with a hint of mischief in it.

She paused to let a car go by, heels together as she rose impatiently on her toes. A young black passed in front of her, made as if to tweak her breast, and she drew back, upperlip curling to reveal a pointed eyetooth. On again she went, lips parted for air, eyes searching for gaps to run through.

Several yards in front of her, beyond dumpy women and boys in blue jeans, she spotted a male figure with a rather side to side gait and with a dog on a leash. The girl stopped abruptly, and took the first opportunity to cross the street.

God's lifting his leg and all's right with the world, Ralph

Linderman was thinking as he approached the corner where Grove Street crossed Bleecker.

It was a lovely summer day, the low sun still poured from the west through certain of the crooked Village streets, and Grove Street looked prettier than usual to Ralph. Grove Street like Barrow and Commerce Streets was neat and tidy, and Ralph appreciated that. People polished their door-knockers and kept their front steps swept. Now Morton Street, just three streets southward, was a mess, scraps of paper in the gutter, ashcans in plain view at the curb. Ralph realized that he usually saw the uglier side of things and people too, but he considered this simply realistic, even wise, because to be suspicious of certain characters, before they had a chance to get at you, could save a man from a lot of mishap. New York for the most part was a sordid town. You had only to look around you at the littered streets to realize that people weren't pulling together, kids learning early that it was all right to toss paper cups right on the sidewalk, nuts of all kinds walking around muttering to themselves, usually obscenities and curses against their fellow men. Sick people and unhappy people! Then there were the muggers, one of them grabbing your arms from behind, the other fishing for your wallet, fleet of foot they were too. That had happened to Ralph once, coming home from work at around 5 in the morning. A curse upon *them*, muggers, the scum of the earth!

Ralph sometimes wished he had pulled out of New York twenty or more years ago, after he and Irma had broken up. Or rather, after she had gone off with another man, Ralph reminded himself without rancor now. He might have gone to Cleveland, Ohio, for instance, some place maybe a little more American, more decent. Might have met the right people or person who could have teamed up with him and made something out of Ralph's ideas. Ralph had a lot of ideas for useful inventions, but not enough training in mathematics and engineering. Then he'd had that fall about fifteen, no eighteen years ago, down the elevator shaft in a garage where he had been on daytime duty as security guard. In the bright sunlight, he hadn't seen that the floor of the elevator wasn't there, had thought the black square was just shadow on the floor, and he had fallen about seventeen feet. Nothing broken, amazingly, because he'd been in a heavy sheepskin coat that winter's day, but everything in him had been shaken up. That was what he had told the doctors, he remembered, and that was the way he had felt, as if his heart had come a little loose from its moorings, his brain too, headaches for a while and all that. They treated him for shock. They couldn't find anything wrong. But Ralph had felt changed ever since. He took care of himself now, he did, and made no apologies to anyone for it. He was lucky to be alive.

The black and white dog ambled at a leisurely pace, sniffing with interest at a car's tire, at a crumpled bit of tinfoil, lifting his leg now in a perfunctory way, having emptied his bladder minutes ago. The dog was about seven, and Ralph had picked him up at the city pound, saved him from death. God was a mongrel, but he had kind eyes, and Ralph valued that.

"God! God!" he said softly, tugging at the leash, because the dog had for several seconds been riveted to what Ralph saw was some other dog's excrement in the gutter. "Come along now."

Was this Elsie walking toward him? Ralph blinked. No. But quite a similarity from a distance, that perky walk, that head held so high, even the illusion of Elsie's smile from a distance, but Ralph saw as the young blond girl passed him that she was not smiling. Now Elsie—*there* was one who ought to steer herself in a righter direction before it was too late! An innocent and naive girl from a small town in upstate New York, and barely twenty! It certainly wasn't too late, and Elsie hadn't got herself into any trouble yet. But it was her attitude that was dangerous for her. She trusted anybody. She seemed to think drugged people and the crazily made-up prostitutes on Eighth Street and along Sixth Avenue were just as trustworthy as—ordinary people maybe, or himself! Everybody amused her, Elsie said. Well, at least she seemed to be earning her own living so far. Ralph had got acquainted with Elsie about six months ago in a coffee shop on West Fourth. Then she had disappeared for a while, and when he next saw her on the street, she said she had been working at an all-night place somewhere that served espresso and wine. Elsie took temporary jobs. Ralph never knew where she'd turn up.

God's stiff walk alerted Ralph to the fact that he was about to do his major business. "God—curb now, boy!" Ralph tugged the crouched dog until all four paws were in the gutter. Absently, Ralph observed that the dog's bowels were in order, pulled a plastic bag and a scoop out of a jacket pocket, and took up the pile. He carried the scoop with dirty end down in the bag to be

3

washed when he got home. Just as God ambled on at a brisker rate, something in the gutter caught Ralph's eye.

A billfold lay in the gutter just two yards from where God had defecated. Ralph bent and picked it up without quite stopping, and he and the dog—whose nose touched the wallet at the same time as Ralph's hand—walked on, Ralph with his eyes straight ahead. No one was rushing up behind him to claim it. Ralph had always wanted to find a wallet, a wallet full of money and identification, possibly. This wallet was fat with contents, its leather smooth and soft, calfskin probably. Ralph let the wallet slide into a pocket of his jacket. As was his habit, he walked left at Hudson toward Barrow Street, which led to Bleecker, where he lived.

Ralph and God entered a four-storey building and climbed the stairs to Ralph's apartment at the back. There had been the usual two kids insolently bouncing a ball right across the doorway downstairs, when Ralph had come in, the usual dark-clad figure of the Italian woman who lived on the third floor, and seemed always to be doing something with a bucket or a broom outside her open apartment door, and as usual Ralph had murmured, "Evening," to her, not caring if she replied or not, but these people did not irk Ralph now, because he had the wallet.

With his apartment door closed, Ralph removed God's leash, then his own jacket, and laid the wallet on a wooden table at his two back windows. He used this table for eating, reading, and making drawings with a long ruler, and sometimes for constructing models of things with moving wooden parts. The table was of pine wood and about five feet long, nicked with saw marks at the edges, and sleek with wear. Ralph sat down in a straight chair and opened the wallet carefully.

There were a lot of bills in it, lots of new twenties, and Ralph counted it all and arrived at the sum of two hundred and sixty-three dollars. Now the papers, the identification. Ralph discovered that the wallet apparently belonged to John Mayes Sutherland, who seemed to have at least three addresses, one of them a town in Pennsylvania that Ralph had never heard of, another in California, one on Grove Street, surely where he lived now, Ralph thought, and perhaps near where he had lost the wallet. One card with a signature of Sutherland had a photograph of a young man in a turtle-neck sweater stapled to it, and was an admission card to a French film festival as a journalist. The card was a year out of date, but it had Sutherland's date of birth, from which Ralph saw that Sutherland would be thirty this year. There were four plastic credit cards, and in a flapped pocket Ralph found three snapshots, two of a young woman with long straight blondish hair, the third of the same girl with Sutherland. In the picture with the girl, Sutherland had a happy smile, and he looked younger than in the journalist photo.

Ralph was not interested in examining every scrap of paper in the wallet, and there were many, cards, scribbled addresses and phone numbers. He was wondering if Sutherland was in the telephone directory? If he were home now? Ralph found himself smiling as he reached for his telephone book.

There were several Sutherlands, but Ralph found what he wanted, J. M. on Grove Street.

Now? Ralph hesitated, then decided to savor his pleasure, his victory over dishonesty, a few minutes more. He could even write Sutherland a note. Today was Wednesday. Prolong his pleasure until Friday. No, that was overdoing it.

Ralph spread the telephone directory on the table and pulled the telephone toward him.

"Aou-u!—*Woof!*" said God sharply, dark eyes fixed on Ralph, ready to lead the way to the fridge.

"All—right, you first, God," said Ralph, and put the telephone back in its cradle. Ralph was not on duty tonight until 10 p.m., so there was time to try to get in touch with Sutherland.

JACK SUTHERLAND had had what he considered a fine day. He had been to the supermarket in preparation for his five-year-old daughter Amelia's arrival tomorrow, then uptown to get some cash from his bank, then a pleasant lunch with his old college friend Joel MacPherson at a pub-like restaurant near CBS where Joel worked. Joel had liked Jack's four drawings, roughs, for *Half-Understood Dreams*, and his words had picked Jack up: "Just what I want! They look puzzled, discouraged—half-dead!" And Joel had laughed a bit madly. The book, eighty-two pages in length, was Joel's and the drawings, at least twenty, would be Jack's contribution. Jack didn't care for the title and had told Joel so, but a title could always be changed. The book was about a New York couple with college-age son and daughter, all of whom had dreams and expectations that they could not and maybe did not want to disclose to the rest of the family or to anyone else. So the dreams and fantasies were half-understood by the dreamers, and half-enacted in real life, and were misunderstood or unnoticed by the others. After lunch, and having left his drawings with Joel, Jack had walked to his favorite art supply shop on Seventh Avenue. Laden with a new portfolio and a couple of sketch pads and a bottle of Glenfiddich for Natalia (due day after tomorrow, Friday), he had treated himself to a taxi home instead of taking the IRT down to Christopher Street as he usually did.

What made him especially happy was that he would have Amelia to himself for about twenty-four hours. Amelia was arriving by bus tomorrow morning from Philadelphia, accompanied by Susanne, their informal nanny. Maybe he'd have Amelia a day more, since Natalia so often delayed her arrivals by one day.

And Jack also liked the Grove Street apartment, a floor through on the third floor of a well-preserved old town house. He liked it because he and Natalia had done a fair amount of work on it together, painted certain rooms and bought the kind of stuff they liked. They had been given the Grove Street place three or four years ago by a great-aunt of Natalia's who had gone a bit dotty in her old age. Natalia and Jack paid only the taxes and upkeep. The old great-aunt had a house somewhere in Pennsylvania, and since she was now in a nursing home, she would never set foot either in the Pennsylvania house or in the Grove Street apartment, everyone was pretty sure. Sometimes Natalia visited the old lady who half the time did not recognize her. She was ninety-six, and could go on to a hundred, Natalia said, as this was the habit in her family.

Jack and Natalia had had a wall torn down to make a larger living-room area, and put bookshelves against two walls. Jack's workroom was down a hall, closed on three sides with a curtain on the hall. He had a long table of the right height for standing at, and also a chair that swiveled up, if he wanted to sit while he worked.

For the last three months, Jack had been in Philadelphia, in a studio on Vine Street to which a friend of his had given him the key. In this way he had been able to visit Natalia easily on weekends at her family's house in Ardmore. He had of course been welcome to stay in the big Ardmore house too, as half its rooms were empty, but Jack preferred a place of his own, however crummy, to work in. Natalia's mother Lily was at the Ardmore house in summer, her mother's friends were always coming in, some of them staying a day or two, and meals were served by the butler Fred. Not Jack's cup of tea, not for more than two days at a time. He also thought it was good for Natalia to spend time away from him. She was the kind of girl, or woman, who would bolt and run off, perhaps forever, if she felt the marital harness chafing even a little. Natalia had been "sort of obliged", as she put it, to stay a few weeks with her mother, and her mother did sometimes make Natalia a present of a thousand dollars, even more, if Natalia or they both needed it or wanted it for something specific. But Jack knew that money was not the reason Natalia visited her mother so often. Natalia got more laughs and pleasure from her mother's company than she admitted.

In his workroom, Jack unwrapped his new gray portfolio, so

7

clean now, so free of the charcoal fingerprints, the ink spatters it would get in the next months, undid its three black bows and took a look at its empty interior, then closed it and laid it aside. He pushed the fixative bottle back among the ink bottles, jars of paint and cans of pens and brushes at the back left corner of his table, and laid his sketch pads on his work area.

He felt hungry. He had bought pastrami and cole slaw for himself at a delicatessen this morning. But first a nice cool drink. The drinks cabinet was of bamboo and had sliding doors. Natalia had chosen it, and it had been expensive, Jack recalled. He poured Jack Daniel's onto ice cubes, added some tap water, then turned on the TV. Before he sat down in the green slip-covered armchair, he touched his back right pocket, intending to take his wallet out. The wallet wasn't there. Then it was in the jacket he had worn today.

Jack lingered for a few seconds, watching the TV screen, before he went to the front closet. The inside pocket of the blue cotton jacket was empty, so were the jacket's side pockets. Funny. Jack wandered to the kitchen, looking, then to his worktable, then to the bamboo cabinet where he had stuck the Glenfiddich. No wallet. He opened the apartment door. The navy blue doormat's surface was clear.

What had happened? He'd paid the taxi out of the wallet, definitely. Had he dropped it on the taxi's floor? In the gutter? Jack grabbed his house keys and ran down the stairs. With fantastic luck it'd still be there. He recalled where the taxi had stopped. The gutter held nothing but a couple of filter-tipped cigarette butts, a ring from a beer can. Jack looked up and down, each way, then went back upstairs, eyes on the steps the whole way.

Well, *this* was a damned nuisance!

Maybe he'd meant to shove the wallet into his back pocket and missed. Served him right for being a little Western today, wearing levis and sneakers, carrying his wallet in his back pocket as he almost never did. Suddenly he remembered gripping the wallet between his knees after getting an extra dollar out of it for a tip. It must've fallen to the cab's floor, so there was no chance he'd see it again. The next fare would see it and quietly pocket it.

What pained him was the loss of his favorite snapshot of Natalia and him, just before they got married, and just about the time Natalia had become pregnant. Maybe she had been then. *I got married to get myself out of finishing school*, Natalia had said a couple of times to friends, smiling. They had also got married because Natalia was pregnant, and she'd been frightened and nervous about having an abortion, frightened of having to give birth too, but fortunately she had given birth, and it hadn't been too difficult. There were a couple of other snapshots of Natalia in that wallet, one looking so young and sure of herself at twenty-two, smiling, lips closed as usual, and with a bigger smile in her eyes. He'd never see the pictures again, and she would never look quite the same for any camera's eye either.

"Goddam it!" Jack got up from the armchair.

There were the credit cards too, Brooks Brothers, American Express and some gas company. Which one? He'd have to write the credit card people right away, and he hoped he had his account numbers here, that they weren't in the back of an address book that Natalia might have in Ardmore. Jack went to the kitchen, not quite as hungry as he had been. He'd have to go to his bank again tomorrow for cash, of which he had none now. Lucky he had some change for the subway.

Jack carried his plate of pastrami with dill pickle and cole slaw and a can of beer to the armchair in front of which he had set up one of the little folding tables that Natalia detested but put up with. "Dammit to hell," Jack murmured as a final remark on the wallet, before he took a bite of his sandwich. The TV was still on, though Jack wasn't interested. The TV was like another table in a restaurant, making a cozy noise.

The telephone rang and Jack got up, thinking it was Natalia, hoping she hadn't already decided to delay her coming. "Hello?"

"Hello. May I speak to Mr Sutherland, please?"

"This is Sutherland. Speaking."

"Can you tell me your first name?"

"Ye-es. John."

"Did you lose something today, Mr Sutherland?"

What was the guy—he didn't sound like a kid—up to? Money, of course, but Jack had a sudden hope of recovering at least the photos. "I lost a wallet."

The man laughed a little. "Well, I've got it. All safe and sound. You're the one in the picture? With the blond girl?"

Jack frowned, tense. "Yes."

"Then I'll know you when I see you. I wouldn't want to give it

9

to the wrong person. I'm not far away. Shall I bring it over? In the next quarter of an hour?"

"Yes, but—Look, maybe I can meet you downstairs on the sidewalk? There's someone asleep in the apartment just now, so I—"

"Very good, sir. Down on the sidewalk in about ten minutes? Eight minutes?"

For a few seconds after he had hung up, Jack felt as if he had been dreaming. Very American voice, that had been, rather like an old man's. Nevertheless, Jack thought it had been wise not to ask the fellow to come up to the apartment. There wouldn't be any money in the wallet, but maybe there was a chance of everything else, unless this man, or someone who had found the wallet first, had decided to lift the credit cards too. Jack glanced at his watch. Nearly half past 7.

Jack got the blue jacket from the closet, and went downstairs. On the sidewalk, he shoved his hands into the back pockets of his levis, and glanced in both directions. A lanky black youth strode toward him and passed him. Two women together, three men walking separate from one another walked by without a glance at him. The minutes passed. Here came a middle-aged guy with a dog, behind him a rabbi all in black with a beard, walking briskly.

"Mr Sutherland?"

Jack hadn't been looking at the man with the dog. At that instant, the streetlights came on, though it was still quite light.

"Yes, you are," said the man who was as tall as Jack or taller. He had black and gray hair, alert dark eyes. 'Well—" He shifted the dog's leash from right hand to left, and reached into the pocket of his old but rather good tweed jacket. "This I think is yours?" He produced the wallet.

"Where'd you find it? Right here?"

"Yes, sir. An hour or so ago."

Jack took the wallet, since the man was extending it, stuck his thumb hastily between its sides and saw the same chunk of new twenties, lifted a flap and saw the snapshots in their transparent envelope. And there was also the little clump of credit cards.

"Two hundred and sixty-three dollars," said the man in his husky but precise voice. "I hope that's right?"

Jack was smiling in dazed surprise. "Take your word for it.

I'm—bowled over! May I offer you a hundred for your kindness?" Jack was ready to count the money out. The man looked as if the money might be welcome.

"No, sir!" said the stranger with a laugh, a shy wave of his hand. "Gives me pleasure. Not every day a man finds a wallet and can return it to the *owner*! I think it's the first time in my life!" His smile showed a first molar missing.

Jack sized him up as a lonely bachelor, maybe eccentric. "But— when someone does a good turn like this—it's only natural to want to say thanks somehow."

"It's only natural to return something you find, if you can find the loser. Don't you think so?—That's if we lived in a decent world." Above his now faint smile, his dark brows frowned with earnestness.

Jack gave a laugh, and nodded agreement. "You won't change your mind and buy a nice twenty-dollar steak for your dog?" Jack pulled out a twenty.

"God? He eats well enough, I think. Fresh meat most of the time and not this old fatty hamburger stuff for animals. Maybe he eats too much." He tugged at the leash. "God, say hello to this gentleman."

"His name's God?" Jack asked, looking at the black and white dog who stood knee-high. The dog had ears that flopped forward, a tail with a curve, giving a pig-like impression, except that its nose was rather pointed.

"Dog spelt backwards, that's all," said the man. "I'm an atheist, by the way, so naturally I returned your wallet. I believe man makes his own destiny, his own heaven or hell on earth. For instance to spell God with a capital letter is ridiculous. There're so many gods. Did you ever think how absurd it would be to see in the newspapers that the President had asked for Jupiter's guidance? Or Thor's maybe? Make you smile, wouldn't it?"

Jack was smiling, uneasily.

"If we call our god God with a capital letter, makes you think we've run out of names, doesn't it? Africans at least have all kinds of gods, each with a different name." He chuckled.

A nut, Jack decided, sensing that the speech could go on all evening if he let it. Jack nodded. "You've got something there. Well—my thanks again to you. I really mean it." Jack extended his hand.

The older man gripped it as if he enjoyed shaking hands. "A pleasure, sir.—You're a journalist?"

Jack extricated his hand and edged toward his steps. "Sometimes. Free lance. Good night, sir, and thanks again." Jack went up his front steps with his key already in hand. He had the feeling the man was watching him, but when he looked back as he closed the door, he saw the man walking eastward with his dog, not looking back at him at all.

Funny incident, Jack thought. You could never tell what might happen in New York!

He sat down at the writing table in the corner of the living-room, and took a closer look at the wallet. Amazing to have it all back! He glanced at the three snapshots first, then checked the credit cards—all there he was sure, and there were four instead of three. He did not count the money, feeling sure every dollar was there. He returned to his cold supper with better appetite.

The TV was still on, and still uninteresting.

An odd man, the one with the dog named God. Jack had been about to ask his name, maybe what he did for a living, just to be friendly. Now Jack was glad that he hadn't. The fellow could become a bore, in his well-meaning way, and he apparently lived in the neighborhood. It would be a funny story to tell Natalia.

Less than an hour later, Jack was laying out his work for tomorrow, or even for tonight if he felt so inclined. Besides Joel's project, on which there was no deadline because Joel had no contract as yet, Jack had two book jackets to do, and they had deadlines about two weeks off. One was of a house front with three people at three different windows, a nineteenth-century house in New England; the other a scrambled scene of many people rushing, pushing, like a crowd coming out of a subway exit onto the street at 6 p.m. The editor had liked the preliminary sketches which he had posted from Philadelphia, and yesterday afternoon Jack had gone to the publishing house and they had decided on colors. Jack twiddled, dawdled, daydreamed, and experimented with the white he wanted for the housefront. White, pink and green it would be, with his pen line supplying the black and the outlines of the house. Tomorrow, with Amelia on his hands, he might not be able to work much. He disliked deadlines, preferred to think they weren't there, and if he could sustain that illusion, he could turn in his work ahead of time.

He put on a Glen Gould cassette for background music, though in fact, he listened, part of his mind on the music, and part on the colors and lines before him and under his left hand. The trick was the delicate balance between dreaming and trying, Jack thought, feeling happier by the minute.

JACK peered over the throng claiming luggage. How could so many people have been on one bus? Where was Susanne's long brown hair, her earnest face bending over Amelia who would be out of sight because she was so little?

"Take yer—"

"No, you won't!" replied a wisp of a man, addressing a fellow who had been about to seize his suitcases with the promise of a taxi. The little man gripped a case in each hand and seemed prepared to use a foot to ward off the bigger fellow.

Jack had worked that morning, and had exercised on his hand-rings in the tall hall of the apartment. Again he wore levis and the blue jacket, with his wallet in the inside pocket now.

"*Susanne!*" Jack cried, lifting an arm.

"Hi, Jack!—Got one more—to wait for!" Susanne meant a suitcase.

"Hello, sweetie!" Jack picked up the little girl in blue jeans and T-shirt. She had long straight hair like her mother's, only fairer.

"Hi, Daddy," replied Amelia calmly. "Put me down."

"You gained some weight."

"I'm taller." Amelia grabbed her small suitcase.

Jack relieved Susanne of a suitcase, and a knapsack he recognized as Amelia's. "How're things?"

"Everything's okay. Fine."

"Coming down to Grove with us or—"

"Well, not unless you need me, Jack. But if you do, I've got loads of time." Susanne was twenty-two, serious and rather pretty, though she gave no attention to make-up. She lived with her parents in a roomy apartment on Riverside Drive.

"No-o," said Jack. They were walking toward the taxis. "Thanks for straightening the place up this week." Susanne had looked in at Grove before his arrival to dust and put a couple of things in the fridge. "Natalia still coming up tomorrow?"

"I suppose." Susanne glanced at him with her easy smile, and brushed her long hair back from her face. "Didn't hear anything different."

If Jack needed Susanne for minding Amelia, or if he needed any shopping or cooking for "people in", Susanne said she would be available. That was the arrangement they had had since more than a year with Susanne Bewley, graduate of NYU and now working on her thesis since ages, it seemed to Jack.

"You take this one!" Jack meant the first taxi. "I insist!" He put Susanne's suitcase in for her. "We'll be in touch. Thanks, Susanne."

"Bye, sweetie! See you!" Susanne yelled to Amelia, as if to a kid sister.

Jack found another taxi at once.

"Glad to be in New York, Amelia?" Jack asked when they were rolling southward.

"Yes." Amelia sat up straight, looking out the window. "I like travelling."

"How's your mom?"

"She's okay. She's playing golf and she's—"

"Golf?" Jack laughed.

Amelia smiled too, showing baby teeth. There was a hint of knowing amusement in the smile, and the way she tossed her head to get her hair out of the way reminded him of Natalia. Natalia parted her hair on the right, Amelia on the left. "But you don't have to play golf to *go* there," she said.

Jack knew she meant the club. They were gliding past Twenty-third Street, down Seventh Avenue. "And Louis was there too?" Jack asked, not liking to ask it, but it would be the first and last question about Louis, he supposed.

"Oh, Louis wouldn't go to the *golf* club!" Amelia replied with a giggle.

But he's at the house, Jack wanted to say, and didn't. Don't quiz the servants, he remembered from his childhood, and it followed that one didn't quiz the children either. Louis was always hanging around Natalia, like a permanent fact or feature. Louis Wannfeld had a house in Philadelphia, and an apartment in New York in the East 60's which he shared with his friend Bob. Louis was a stockbroker or investment advisor and also in real estate, professions Jack understood little about. Louis seemed to have endless time on his hands. Louis could sit up till 3 in the morning talking with Natalia in Ardmore, or in a supper club in New York, and like Natalia sleep the next morning to make up for it, Jack supposed. Since Louis was gay, Jack realized that he had no reason for jealousy, but he was still a bit jealous, now and then. What in God's name did Natalia and Louis find to talk about from 10 in the evening until the wee hours? Why were they so attracted to each other? *He's my soulmate*, Natalia had said, more than once. Did you ever want to marry him, Jack might have asked, but he hadn't. Natalia would have replied, Jack was sure: *And ruin everything?*

And Amelia simply accepted Louis as she might an uncle she had inherited. And Louis in his way accepted Jack and Amelia, Jack knew, considering his own presence innocent and un-assailable, Jack supposed, because Louis had been a friend of Natalia's before she had met him, Jack.

They were turning west into Barrow Street to approach Grove, and Jack pulled his wallet out, mindful now of seeing that it got back into his inside pocket.

"I can carry it!" Amelia was saying about her suitcase, so Jack let her.

Upstairs, she announced, "I like this place!" as if she had never seen it before, though she had spent most of her life here. She walked from one end of the apartment to the other, and gazed out the front and back windows.

"Your room's here. Remember?" Jack was installing her bigger suitcase on an Austrian chest of pale blue with a pink flower design painted on it.

The telephone rang.

"Probably for you," Jack said. "Want to get it, Amelia?" He was hoping it was Natalia.

"Sutherland house," said Amelia. "Oh-h, hi, Penny . . . Yep . . . Don't know. I think so."

Jack was summoned to agree to a meeting time and place for Penny and Amelia tomorrow at Penny's mother's house at a cer-tain address in the East 80's. Jack wrote the address down in case it wasn't in an address book here. At 11 o'clock.

"I'll bring Amelia back around four," said Penny's mother. "Is Natalia there?"

"Due tomorrow," said Jack.

Jack turned to his daughter after he had hung up. "Busy girl." He hadn't the faintest idea what Mrs Vernon, Penny's mother, looked like, but he remembered Natalia mentioning her a couple of times. The kids knew each other from Amelia's school on West 12th Street. "What're you two doing tomorrow?"

"It's lots of us. Maybe four or five. Penny has some new video cassettes.—Can I have a bath?"

"Sure!"

Amelia wanted the blue pellets from the big glass jar tossed in, the bath salts Natalia sometimes used. Jack could smell its pleasant scent in the kitchen. To think I've helped create a miniature Natalia, he thought, smiling as he got the lunch ready. He set the white table with plain white plates, green napkins. Ham, potato salad, milk. Custard pie for dessert. Beside Amelia's plate he laid a long slender object wrapped in red-striped paper.

Amelia reappeared in white shorts, topless and barefoot. She pronounced it hotter in New York than in Ardmore, but she liked the air. Jack laughed, but he knew what she meant.

"What's this?" Amelia asked when she had sat down, picking up the present.

"For you. Open it."

The child pulled the slender bow undone. Her blond hair, darkened around her face by her bath, was the dusty gold color of Natalia's, her brows had the same unusual and unfeminine straightness and heaviness, but her mouth was rather like his, more slender than Natalia's, more apt to move and change. It seemed to him that Amelia grew, or became a little different, every time he saw her, even if the interval were no more than two weeks, and this was another reason why Jack never tired of gazing at her.

"Ooh, a rec—*recker!*"

"Recorder, honey. A real one. You can play something really pretty on that."

Amelia was trying it, frowning with effort.

"Takes all your fingers, don't forget. Nearly all. I've got a little book on it and I'll show you later. Come on, let's eat first."

By dusk that day, Natalia had not telephoned, which augured well for her arrival tomorrow. Amelia had practised for nearly half an hour with her recorder and the booklet in her room, and the toots had not bothered Jack while he worked. Then to his surprise, Amelia had taken a long nap. She awoke hungry, but Jack persuaded her to postpone eating for half an hour, because he was inviting her out.

"A place where they serve enormous plates of food. Like this." He spread his arms.

"Where's that?"

"Mexican Gardens. We can walk from here.—Didn't we ever go there? Seems to me we did."

Amelia couldn't remember. "You've got ink on your finger."

Jack glanced at the middle finger of his left hand. He often had ink there. "So what?—I've got a story to tell you."

He told her about losing his wallet, worrying because he'd never see the snapshots again, and there'd been quite a lot of money in the wallet too. Then the mysterious telephone call, and the meeting down on the sidewalk with the stranger and his dog who was named God. As he spoke, Jack picked up a pencil and the memo pad from the kitchen table.

"He looked like this, hair sticking out a little, sort of needed a shave—frowning and smiling at the same time. And here's the dog that looks like a pig—but a friendly pig, smiling too."

Amelia laughed, watching the pencil move.

"But he had my wallet and all the money was in it, and he wouldn't take even twenty dollars as a reward. Now isn't that a nice story? Isn't that a nice man?"

Amelia tilted her head and smiled thoughtfully at the cartoon. "How old is he?"

"Oh—maybe just over fifty, maybe fifty-five."

"Fifty-*five*?"

"Well, your grandma's maybe nearly fifty-five. Yes, sure. But this is more fun than a bible story, isn't it?" Jack asked, recalling that Natalia had told him her mother had been reading some bible stories from a children's book to Amelia, an effort that probably hadn't lasted long, because Lily wasn't the religious type. "And this is a true story."

"Aren't the bible stories true too?"

"Ye-es. Well, mostly. Anyway, Amelia, if you ever find a wallet or a handbag and if you can find out who owns it—I hope you'll do the same as this man did, take it back to the person who lost it."

Amelia tipped her head again. "If I found a purse with a *lot* of money?"

"*Yes!*" Jack laughed. "You should've seen how happy this fellow was when he gave my wallet back! It really made his day!"

4

NATALIA telephoned the next morning, just after Jack had returned from depositing Amelia at Mrs Vernon's apartment.

"I called before ... Oh, just what I thought, the Vernons," Natalia said. "I wanted to be sure you're home, because I can't find my keys—to the apartment, I mean. Maybe they're packed in a suitcase."

"I'll be home. Where are you?"

She was at a filling station, and she thought she could make it in about an hour.

"Don't rush it. Take care, darling."

Jack went back to his worktable. His house front drawing lay there, lightly penciled in, ready for ink. But for the next couple of minutes, Jack drifted around the apartment, tossed a cushion into place on the sofa, though Natalia didn't care if things were neat or not. There was food, and it would be lunchtime when she got here, but Natalia didn't care about regular mealtimes either, and there was never any telling whether she'd be hungry or not.

He was deep in his work, pulling a brush point delicately upward to create a tree branch, when he heard two notes of a car horn, different to him from other street noises. He went to the living-room window and saw Natalia across the street, opening the hatch of her red Toyota. The street's surface was dark with a light rain that Jack had been unaware of.

"Hey!" he shouted, and she looked up. "Be right down!" He saw her wave at him.

Jack grabbed his keys and ran down. "Hi, darling." He squeezed her arm in her old fur-collared raincoat, and quickly kissed her cheek. "You tired?" He pulled a suitcase out of the back.

"No, but it was raining like hell in Pennsylvania."

The car fenders were spattered with grimy dirt, Jack noticed. "This too?" He held a duffelbag.

"Yes. I'll take the bookbag." She locked the car door, then the hatch, after tugging out a burlap bag lumpy with books and bearing a Harvard University insignium.

Upstairs, it turned out that Natalia was tired, and from what she said, it sounded as if she'd slept only two hours or maybe not at all. She'd seen Louis and some of his friends for dinner somewhere, and then Louis had telephoned in the wee hours.

"I just got sick of it, so I took off pretty early."

But by then she was talking about people coming to the house, about a boring lunch at the golf club with her mother's friends, not about being sick of Louis.

"Get out of those shoes, at least. Relax."

She wore white sandals with heels, a summer skirt and a shirt with the tails hanging out. Maybe she hadn't changed since last evening, Jack thought.

"Want a shower? A drink? There's plenty of Glenfiddich."

"Yes," said Natalia, sitting on the sofa, removing her sandals. She lit a Marlboro, and leaned back.

Jack made a scotch on the rocks in an old-fashioned glass, because Natalia didn't like tall glasses. He inhaled Natalia's scent, faint and exciting. Even the whiff of her cigarette smoke was exciting.

"Thanks, Jack." She smiled at him, lips together, her gray-green eyes warm. There were tiny wrinkles under her eyes which make-up could conceal, if she ever bothered. Her eyes were not large, and their upper lids drew a bit over the inner corners. She seldom smiled broadly, unless she laughed, because she was shy about her teeth, which were not as white as she would have liked, though their color was not due to smoking. Her legs were not her best feature either, being just slightly too heavy. What was it that gave her her fantastic sex appeal, and not merely for Jack but for a lot of other people? Maybe her voice, which was full of humor, and intelligence too, though a little husky sometimes, and Natalia cleared her throat more than most people. Jack often thought that on the telephone, Natalia could simply cough, or clear her throat, and he'd know instantly that it was she. He very much hoped that he could put her into the mood of going to bed with him this afternoon before the return of Amelia at probably half past 4.

"How's your work going?" Natalia asked.

"Oh—tell you about that later. Show you. I'm on the book jackets." Jack was kneeling in the big armchair, forearms on the chair's back. He would have loved to leap over, crash onto Natalia, scotch and all, and make love to her on the sofa. "And your mum?"

"Oh, mum," Natalia groaned, looking at the ceiling, and laughed. "Teddie's coming Sunday. He'll keep her amused."

Teddie was Natalia's younger half-brother by a second marriage of her mother's. Natalia's father was dead, and Teddie's father was divorced from Natalia's mother. Teddie was twenty and in college somewhere in California. He had been raised by his father, who had custody.

Natalia remarked that the apartment looked in good shape. It was not a usual remark from her. Jack sensed that she was worried about something. Halfway through her scotch, she said she wanted a shower, and got up. While she was in the bathroom, Jack put her suitcase in the bedroom, undid the latches without lifting the lid. His heart was beating with a gentle and pleasant excitement. *How's your work going?* Jack had to smile. Half the time she didn't care, Jack felt. His work was just his way of amusing himself and maybe of earning a little money, he supposed, in Natalia's eyes. She thought some of his drawings were clever, but she was more interested in painting, needed to look at good art to stay alive, as if art were her vitamins or sunlight. Jack was not a fine artist. And for another thing, she didn't need his money, he well knew.

Natalia came out of the bathroom in her yellow terry-cloth robe that had been hanging on the door, blue fluffy houseslippers, her hair darker around her face, as Amelia's had been yesterday, and Jack averted his eyes, simply because he felt like gazing at her. Natalia detested slavish devotion, he reminded himself, even laughed at it.

"I might help Isabel out a little next week," Natalia said, recovering her drink from the coffee table. "She's got a Pinto show coming up." She sipped. "And he's a pain in the you-know-what.—You know?"

"Um-m." Jack recalled Natalia's tales of the nervous but self-assured Pinto, a newcomer from Brazil with a couple of shows behind him in Amsterdam and Paris. "When is this?"

"The show? In about a week.—I'll just help her hang and stuff. And she'll pay me something—which I can always use. We can, I mean." She laughed a little on the word "use".

"So she's dumping Pinto on you?" Jack's voice held contempt, for Pinto.

"Twenty-six years old and thinks he's it." She lit a cigarette. "Well, he isn't *rotten*. It's—" She shrugged. "He just isn't good."

Jack knew. It was a matter of getting some good reviews and getting his price up, Natalia might have said. Jack remembered Pinto's stuff, the couple he had seen reproduced in a brochure Natalia had shown him, reddish backgrounds and a lot of gray silvery circles of various sizes daubed on in what looked like heavy paint.

"Might go on into the fall—Isabel," Natalia added.

Jack knew, and in a way he was pleased. Natalia had worked at Isabel Katz's gallery before. She made a good receptionist, and could even sell pictures, and had. Natalia looked nice, she had pleasant manners, and a pushy saleswoman she was not. "Are you possibly hungry?"

"I bet you are. What've we got?"

"Sliced roast beef? And horseradish?"

"Yummy!" She danced on her toes and rubbed her stomach, like a child.

They laid out the cold things together, and there was also some ham and potato salad left over, and fresh French bread bought this morning. A sweet breeze blew through the open front windows all the way to the back of the apartment where windows were also partly open, and where green tops of trees showed higher than the sills. Jack had poured a glass of Chianti for himself, and Natalia had another scotch. She looked happier now, and a trace of color had come to her rather pale face. Natalia never made an effort to acquire a tan in summer. And she was looking sleepier by the minute.

Jack buttered a last piece of bread for himself. "I lost my wallet Wednesday evening, and a man returned it to me. Everything there, all the dough, credit cards, everything."

Her eyes widened with interest. "Lost it where?"

"Right in front of the house. On the street. I'm sure just after I'd paid off a taxi—about five-thirty in the afternoon. Anyway an hour or so later after I'd missed it and was agonizing, thinking about the credit cards—no, the photos, pictures of you, in fact—the telephone rang, sort of an old guy's voice, asking if I was so-and-so and had I lost anything. So I said yes, a wallet. He said he had it, and he'd see me in about ten minutes. Downstairs. And there he was, and he wouldn't take a reward, not a hundred, not even twenty bucks!" Jack slapped the table edge with his fingers and laughed.

"All the money was in it?"

"Yep, and I'd just been to the bank. Over two hundred and he knew—exactly. He'd counted it."

She gave a short laugh. "He must be a born-again Christian."

"Matter of fact he told me he was an atheist. 'So naturally I returned your wallet,' he said. Probably hates churches. Oh, and he's got a dog named God. Some kind of mixed breed, black and white."

"Dog named God." She smiled, shaking her head. "Dog spelt backwards, sure."

Jack sighed, happy. "Why don't you conk out for an hour? After that drive—it'll do you good."

But she got up for one more cigarette from the coffee table. "I will.—God, it's nice to be here!"

That made Jack even happier, but he said nothing. Slowly, he began to clear the table, letting Natalia do what she wished. She carried a couple of things back to the kitchen, went into the bathroom to brush her teeth, then disappeared into the bedroom, saying:

"See you. Wake me in an hour if I'm not up."

When Jack eased the bedroom door open a little more than an hour later, he found Natalia asleep with the sheet drawn nearly to her shoulders, face down with her profile clear against the pillow, her right hand curled under her chin. It looked an oddly thoughtful pose, and Jack smiled. An art catalog with a glossy white paper cover was splayed near her, with the word ART in big black letters on the front cover. A thick book by Irving Howe lay closed beside her left shoulder.

Jack folded his arms and leaned against the door jamb, making not a sound, but her closed lids fluttered and opened. "Are you—possibly in the mood?" he asked.

She turned over and opened her arms to him, smiling a little.

24

In a trice he had his clothes off, and had slipped in beside her. *Our own house,* he thought, *finally, after three months of Ardmore.* He loved the faint scratchiness of the fine blond hair on her thighs, her waist that was smooth and quite round, not flattish before and behind, like most women's waists. And she kissed him with enthusiasm.

But at the last, it wasn't the success Jack had hoped for. Feeling sure she was ready, he had let himself go, he had felt her breath in his ear. And afterward he had known from the way she breathed, that she hadn't reached a climax. He kissed her breast.

"Sorry. Dunno what's the matter.—'S nothing."

Jack raised his lips from the firm flesh under her breast. "Next time." He got up.

But the next hour held a curious heaviness for Jack. He was certainly not sleepy from the glass of wine or from having made love to Natalia, but his feet felt weighted. Amelia was due back. He and Natalia talked about her school on West Twelfth Street, the Sterling Academy for Young People, a name that usually made Natalia lift her lip with an amused and deprecatory smile.

"You really think it's good enough, considering what it costs?" Natalia asked in a somewhat irritated way.

They had been here before. It was a place to park tots and kids up to school-entering age and even up to nine years, and the Sterling Academy presumably taught them something too, like the three R's. It was within walking distance, and a schoolmarm would walk Amelia home, unless Jack or Natalia rang up and said they would fetch her. For two hundred dollars a week, a five-day week, Amelia got a good lunch too.

"I think you told me the Vernons thought the school's okay," Jack said, feeling that he'd said this maybe twice before, "and they come a long way to get here."

What was Natalia really worried about, he wondered? Something not serious, perhaps, but the slightest worry always showed on her face.

"What we need is a grandma taking over," Natalia murmured, "with the patience to teach them reading and arithmetic and all that."

"A grandma living at home?" Jack laughed.

"No, I mean some—" She jumped and shook her fingers with nervous impatience as the telephone and the doorbell rang at the same time. "I'll get this one," she said, moving toward the telephone.

Jack pressed the release button, left the apartment door ajar, and ran downstairs to say hello to Mrs Vernon and thank her.

But Amelia had been brought home by a girl of about twenty, whom Jack had never seen before, but recognized as the opposite number to Susanne.

"Hi," he said, "I'm Jack Sutherland, the father of this."

"Oh. How do you do? Here's Amelia." The girl smiled. "Everything's okay, I think. No skinned knees to report." This girl was English.

"Good. Thanks a million."

The girl nodded, said, "Bye-bye, Amelia," and was gone.

They climbed the stairs. Amelia was chattering, and Jack hardly listened. Natalia would have said something to Amelia about her not having said thank you and good-bye to the girl who had brought her. Rudeness.

"Afternoon, Mr Hartman!" Jack said to a middle-aged man coming out the door of his apartment on the second floor. "Yes, we're back—for a while."

"Glad to see you again. Hi, Amelia." With a friendly smile, Mr Hartman went down the stairs, carrying a neat plastic sack of garbage.

Natalia was still on the telephone, leaning against the wall by a front window, smoking, murmuring. Jack at once sensed that the caller was Louis Wannfeld, and rather switched off. The conversation could go on for fifteen minutes.

"Had a good time?" Jack asked Amelia.

"Yes. I'm thirsty." She pretended to reel against a wall. "We had LSD—Ooh!"

"Take some water," Jack whispered, repressing a smile. "LSD, f'gosh sake!"

"We did and I feel aw-w-ful!" Cross-legged, leaning against the kitchen wall, Amelia tried her best to look bleary-eyed.

"Quiet, your mom's on the phone." Jack drew a glass of water and handed it to her.

". . . *outrageous* . . ." Natalia was saying. "No. No, I wouldn't. Look, I'll call you back, there's so much—Ten minutes, maybe?— Okay."

"Mom, I've had *LSD*!" Amelia spread her arms and seized her mother round the thighs.

"Ow!" said Natalia as the child crashed into her. "I don't believe a word of it."

"Mom—Jack—Daddy, what did the mayonnaise say to the lettuce?" asked Amelia, changing her act, because the LSD had fallen flat.

Natalia groaned. "I don't give a damn. These awful kids' jokes, Jack. I get ten a day."

"I don't know. What?" asked Jack.

"Close the door, I'm *dressing!*" said Amelia.

"Oh-h-h." Jack feigned boredom and he was bored, suddenly. Or was he merely ill at ease? He wanted to go into his workroom and draw the curtain. He looked at Natalia. "I think I'll take a walk. You want to phone back—" He glanced at the white telephone.

Natalia started to say something, looked at the child, then beckoned to Jack to come into the bedroom. She whispered to him with the door almost closed, the knob in her hand. "That was Louis. He thinks he's got cancer. May as well tell you now."

Tell him now, Jack thought, as if it would break his heart? "Cancer? Of the what?"

She closed the door. "Stomach. Well, he *thinks* so. His doctor in Philadelphia—"

"Isn't it more likely an ulcer?"

Natalia gave one of her short laughs. "You'd think, with his nerves. And he's got some bleeding.—He mentioned it a couple of months ago. Pains. The doctor in Philadelphia wanted him to see a specialist here, so he did, this afternoon. Louis rode up with me."

"Oh.—Well, he can't know anything today, can he? Already?"

"Mommy!" On the other side of the door, Amelia wanted attention.

"He said they did some kind of scraping today. Sounds awful." Natalia winced, as if she were enduring it. She looked Jack suddenly in the eyes. "He's awfully brave about it."

That was something, Jack supposed. "I can understand that you want to talk with him.—Shall I pick up something for dinner while I'm out? Or we go out?"

"Let's have something here."

A couple of minutes later, Jack was down on the street, walking east toward Bleecker, turning right when he came to it, not left as he usually did. The stores he usually went to lay to the left. It was only just past 5, and it wouldn't matter if he didn't get back until 7. The brisk walking felt so good, he began to trot. In no time he was at Washington Square, where he slowed to an ordinary pace. Kids on bikes rolled up the gray cement hill, and down. It was a miniature hill, in proportion to what Manhattan could afford by way of juvenile recreation, Jack supposed, hardly four feet high and thirty feet in diameter, but the small fry loved it.

Depression dogged him now like a dark figure that he couldn't shake, that ran as fast as he. It was one of those moments, those periods of hours sometimes, when he felt that he and Natalia weren't really together and didn't belong together, and that the slightest jolt could sever them forever. The idea shattered Jack, because he felt that Natalia was the only woman he would ever be in love with, ever love. He could imagine being a little in love with some other girl or woman, even marrying her—though that was not a happy thought—knowing that she would be second best, nothing to compare with Natalia.

Or was he simply torturing himself? Weren't most marriages made up of anxiety as well as contentment? Was he different, or like all the rest, young or middle-aged, fat or skinny, rich or poor?

Ah, rich. His family wasn't as rich as Natalia's and the Hamiltons, that was for sure, but his father was a pretty close second. Only Natalia's mother might measure every last half million to make a comparison, and Natalia didn't give much of a damn. But Jack was sure she wouldn't have married, or maybe even let herself get pregnant by someone who was broke. That was true, much as she loved artists, and a lot of good artists were broke at the start of their careers, maybe at the end too. At any rate, Jack's family background, his schools, his social circle had matched Natalia's well enough. And then, no sooner had Jack finished Princeton, his majors having been English and Fine Arts, than he had made his third or fourth Grand Tour, this time on his own, and had ended up in a Yugoslav jail with two crummy pals for having been caught with heroin. There Jack had languished and scratched lice for four months, while his uncle Roger, a warmer soul than Jack's father Charles, had pulled every string he had in Washington to secure Jack's release. Jack's two chums had not been so lucky. They had also been sentenced to three years, and for all Jack knew, had served it. That was a dim and fuzzy past, even the faces of the other two fellows had become a blur of unshavenness, of silly or cocky smiles. He had met them somewhere in Austria, though they were Americans. Easy money they had said, carrying the stuff, and they would be paid at both destinations, more at the American end, of course, once they got to Canada, then America.

The awful thing, Jack realized as he walked downtown on Mercer Street now, bringing all shame down upon himself, was that he had begun sniffing and injecting too with his Austria-met pals. It had all been fun, hitchhiking, scanning maps, sleeping in the woods sometimes. Could have been healthy, Jack realized. Instead, he had behaved like a spoilt child, in a quiet way going wild, being uncivilized just when he had, he remembered, fancied that he was being more civilized, more real than ever before. His father had not let him forget that misadventure. And Jack had a scar like a dent about an inch long on the left side of his forehead up near the hairline, not from a blow struck by the Yugoslav police, but from bumping into a doorjamb on his first day in prison. His head hadn't been clear that day. *Lest you forget*, Jack often thought when he noticed the scar in a mirror. He meant, lest you forget you were once behaving like an asshole, there is the scar to remind you, and to remind you not to let it happen again. In a way, Jack's prison stint of four months had continued in his parents' house, his mother being cheerful and inclined to forgive, but his father ruled the roost. Jack had been subjected to a couple of lectures from his father, in private, and a promised twenty thousand dollars to start him off in New York as a freelance journalist or artist, or until he found a job in those two fields, had somehow been forgotten. Jack's brother Christopher's stock had risen, Jack felt, just because his father had set all his hopes on Christopher then. Christopher, three years younger than Jack, had fallen into line and joined his father's company after Harvard.

And then just before he had flown the nest or the coop to try his luck in New York, Jack had met Natalia at a party that Jack's mother had insisted that he go to, a black-tie affair, something to do with a charity. This had been at someone's house near Trenton. Jack's family had had a summer house near Trenton then, and Jack had come east with them. Out of the blue, out of the dulness, out of the shame that still haunted Jack, there had been Natalia, making a funny remark to him in her low, seductive voice as they stood with champagne glasses in some big room before the buffet supper began. Jack believed that he had fallen in love at first sight. There was such a thing, he was sure, and he had fallen in love at once with her voice. He had lost her for half an hour, found her again, and asked for her telephone number. I've got a car, he had wanted to say. *I've got a car*, Natalia had said. *Let's clear out*. Words that stuck in his memory.

How was it that he had said all the right things that night? He didn't recollect that he had been especially brilliant. They had laughed a lot, and on his part it had been due to repressed excitement. He had met the girl of his life. And wonderfully, as they said in the old songs, she had liked him. But he knew why, he was enough of a breakaway for her, and yet not too much. It might have been just an affair, but she had become pregnant. And Jack knew now, if he hadn't been sure then, that Natalia would have had an abortion if she hadn't wanted the child and by him. Her family had put up no opposition, because after all Jack came from the right stuff, a decent family with some money in the background, even if he hadn't yet found a career, and maybe he'd come to his senses and drop his art work and join one of his father's companies that made herbicides and pharmaceuticals.

Jack went into a coffee shop. He didn't know or care where he was, but he thought he was on the upper part of Greene Street. He ordered a coffee, white.

And now there was Louis in a crise. Cancer. Maybe. *He's awfully brave about it*, Natalia had said with a rare but fitting earnestness, Jack thought, considering that cancer was an earnest subject.

Now there was a bit of slumming for you! Natalia's best friend, her soulmate, from the Philadelphia equivalent of the old Lower East Side. Wannfeld wasn't quite his name, but the result of a slight change from some other name, Jack seemed to remember that Louis was half-Jewish. Louis didn't even read a lot of books, not the kind Natalia read anyway. Yet he was persona quite grata at Lily's, Natalia's mother's, house, even if he turned up with his boyfriend Bob Campbell. Was that because Louis had never presented a marital danger when Natalia had been twenty or so? Or because Lily—No, Lily didn't have to put on the tolerance or the broad-minded act. She wasn't that snobbish. Louis was quiet, almost self-effacing, and his manner was graceful, Jack had to admit, gentlemanly. The most formal company didn't daunt Louis, and he never lost his cool.

Jack drained his cup and pushed it back, annoyed with himself for going over the same old ground. What harm was Louis doing to him? None, except that he took an unconscionable amount of Natalia's time. But wasn't that all to the good? It left Jack with more time to work, and maybe it kept Natalia from being bored with him. He had been here before, too.

He paid, and left. Time to head back, time to keep an eye out for something interesting to bring home for dinner, maybe something Chinese, if he could find a take-away place. Amelia was always happy with pizza, but her parents could get tired of it. Jack ran into the unexpected, a Greek take-away, bought some oily boxes and bags, and walked on westward, feeling more cheerful. There was his work ahead, and the pleasant possibility of a contract for Joel and himself for *Half-Understood Dreams*, if his drawings could clinch it. A couple of publishers were interested, but wanted to see the illustrations to go with it. When Jack looked back on his total output, he felt he could have done better if he'd tried harder, as the prep school notes put it sometimes. His father, after the Yugoslav episode, had never set up the trust he had promised on Jack's finishing university, and Jack had not brought the subject up. The modest income from the trust would have given him enough to live on in New York and to study a few hours a week at the Art Students League, as well as to try his hand at journalism and drawing. Uncle Roger, by contrast, had gambled on him and staked him in New York with a few solid thousands, which Uncle Roger said was a gift. His father didn't approve of Jack's chosen profession or professions, but had approved of Jack's marriage. Predictable. In the last couple of years, Jack had spent more time on his art work than on journalism, which had been the occasional travel piece or kitchen gadget stuff or interior decorating reportage. Drawing was more fun, and more satisfying. Jack remembered with a warm pang of gratitude, that Uncle Roger had put up the money too for classes at the Art Students League, when Amelia had been a baby.

When Natalia opened the door to his knock, Jack felt suddenly happy and very lucky. The apartment looked lovely. What had

Natalia done to it in his absence? The white table was set. Amelia was sprawled on the floor in front of the TV, which was on not too loudly. In the kitchen Natalia raved over his purchases as if he were a hunter returned with something rare and difficult to bag.

"Your cheeks're all pink," she remarked as she sampled a black olive.

He put his arms around her, held her tight with his eyes shut, and breathed in her fragrance. Louis would never hold her like this, nor would he want to. Why did he doubt, Jack wondered, doubt Natalia, sometimes the wonder of his own daughter, the reality of everything? Maybe it was normal to doubt, even healthy, even wise? When would he ever come to any conclusion about that?

Natalia was saying that she'd get the supper on the table, and of course there was time for him to take a shower. And tonight they'd fall asleep in the same bed, Jack thought, and for an uncountable number of nights to come.

5

AT a little past 4 in the morning, Ralph Linderman went into the office of the garage where he worked, and without thinking pulled open a table drawer where lay two guns, one in a holster and on a belt. Ralph did not carry a gun on duty, but he was to know where the gun or guns were when he arrived, and when he left.

"Takin' off, hey Ralph?" said Joey Fischer, a lanky young man in mechanic's coverall who happened to be in the office just then.

"What else? What's new?" Ralph said as if he didn't expect an answer. He glanced at his wristwatch, then wrote the time and signed his name in a ledger on the desk. "No sign—"

An ambulance screamed by just then beyond the little glass-walled office on West Forty-eighth Street. A passing pedestrian turned to gawk after the ambulance, and collided with another man walking in the opposite direction. Then a car's bright lights swept Joey's young face and the office as a big car entered the garage.

"No sign of *Conlan* I was about to say," Ralph went on. Conlan, the next security guard on duty, was supposed to take over at 4.

"Ah, he'll turn up in a minute," said Joey, and went out of the office into the semi-darkness of the garage to take care of the car that had come in, show the fellow where to park.

Now if somebody wanted to do a heist on Midtown-Parking, any time before Conlan came on, now was the time, Ralph thought. Conlan to Ralph was an example of what not to be, as a security guard. The old guy must be sixty-four if he was a day, and he'd really let himself go, dragging around and looking as if it would take him five minutes to draw a gun if he had to, and always ten or fifteen minutes late. The least a man could do, Ralph thought, was haul himself out of bed or wherever in good time, extra time, to make it to a job he was being paid for. Now, for instance, while

Joey Fischer was dealing with this new customer who might be a crook himself, the office was unlocked and theoretically unmanned, except that he himself stood here, and a gun was within reach. You never knew who was passing by on the sidewalk just ten feet away outside, day or night, you never knew. Drug addicts needed their fix, needed dough, at any hour of the day or night. Ralph eyed the passersby critically, not really expecting any trouble, but intending to wait until Conlan got here. Joey returned with one end of the card he had given to the man who had just come in, and stuck it on a board.

"Still here?" Joey said, turning, lighting a cigarette.

"Not for long," said Ralph, having just seen Frank Conlan crossing the street from the uptown direction. "Here he comes. G'night, Joey." Ralph managed a rare smile. Joey Fischer was a decent young fellow, honest and hard-working, recently married too. "Morning, Mr Conlan."

"Hell-o-o," said Conlan breezily. "Little late, I know. I had a bitch of a wait for my bus this morning. How you, Joey?"

"Oh, just perky," said Joey with a smile at Ralph.

Ralph nodded a good-bye to Joey and left. He glanced at the sky which showed no promise of dawn, but would by the time he got down to Sheridan Square on the bus. He loved the very early mornings like this, walking God who was always so glad to see him after eight hours or so, breathing in the air that was a lot less polluted at 5 a.m. than it would be at 9 a.m., for instance. Be grateful for small things, Ralph thought.

He had got off the Seventh Avenue bus at Sheridan Square and taken a few steps into Christopher Street, when a yelp of drunken voices rent the air. Ralph saw them, three or four fellows and a couple of girls on the other side of Christopher, heading eastward, staggering, laughing, shoving one another. They'd been up all night, of course, in one of those sordid dens in Christopher Street, probably. Glancing at the group when they were just opposite him, Ralph recognized Elsie, and he felt a shock, a bolt of pain, as if she were his own daughter, or his precious ward at any rate.

"Ah-h—hah-ha!" That was *her* laugh as she collapsed backward, sank into the arms of a tall fellow behind her.

"Hey, Billy-o, where these girls *live*?" shouted a rowdy masculine voice.

More laughter. Babble.

34

Ralph had stopped dead. Appalled. He stared at the disappearing group as if he could annihilate them with his eyes—all except Elsie, of course. If only he had the guts to run after her! But he'd be mauled by the fellows. They'd shove him against a building and knock him out as soon as look at him. No, that wasn't the way. Careful counseling was the way to do it, not overdoing it, of course, but— Ralph felt suddenly helpless, hopeless. A swift sadness filled him, stilling almost his heart.

Ridiculous! He forced himself to walk on. He barely knew Elsie. He knew she thought he was silly, old-fashioned, maybe cracked. He had to put up with that, that was all. He might save Elsie yet, keep her from going down the drain, getting hooked on drugs, getting into casual prostitution by way of picking up extra money. She was worth trying to save, he told himself. Think about it. Think about the next move.

Well, God was waiting for him. And there was a hint of daylight in the sky now. And on Grove Street lived that nice young man who had been so happy to get his wallet back! That incident made Ralph feel happy every time he recalled it. He'd told Elsie about it, by way of illustrating what human beings *could* do for one another, if they wanted to live in a decent world. Elsie had looked at him open-mouthed for a few seconds. But finally, she had nodded, he remembered, as she wiped the counter in front of him. She was working at a place down on Seventh Avenue now, a snack bar. At twenty, what could she know about life, especially since she'd come just a few months ago from some tiny town in upstate New York? What was happening to her tonight? Where would she spend the night or what was left of it? Horrid to think about, horrid!

Ralph was now climbing the last of his four flights, and he already heard God's eager little yips, gasps of expectation as he pranced behind the door. Ralph had trained him, warned him firmly not to bark at the sound of his footsteps, whatever the hour.

"Hello, boy, hello, Goddy!" Ralph whispered, petting the leaping dog, but trying to calm him too. Ralph got the dog's leash from a hook.

Then they were down on the street, God peeing instantly against the side of a house. Ralph heard the clunk of a beer barrel hitting the sidewalk, out of sight around the corner. On 7th

Avenue the swish and hum of traffic was already starting. After a snack, Ralph thought, he'd have a shower and go to bed with the *Times*—yesterday's which he hadn't finished—and have a snooze for as long as he liked, maybe till 1 p.m., and then he'd walk down to the Leroy Street Public Library and change his books.

Ralph turned west into Morton Street, walking at God's pace, which was invariably slow because of his sniffing at everything. Ralph often took this route in the mornings, turning right into Bedford Street, crossing Commerce with its quiet and pretty housefronts, going on to Grove and turning right again at Bleecker. On Bedford was old P.S. 3, with heavy wire over its lower windows for protection against vandalism and flying objects, while a stone slab above the lower windows bore the statement in bold letters: CHILDHOOD SHOWS THE MAN. A truer word was never said, or chiseled, Ralph thought, and he liked to see it. A garbage can clattered somewhere. The streetlights had shut off. Ralph liked to look also at the few lighted windows in the private dwellings along Bedford, looking yellowish behind thin curtains, and wonder why people might be up so early—jobs, sickness, insomnia? A jogger was up and out already, running toward Ralph on the other side of Bedford, wearing a blue track suit with a white stripe down the pants, sneakers. On closer look, Ralph saw that the runner was Sutherland, John Sutherland, whose wallet he had returned.

Ralph repressed an impulse to hail him with a "Morning, Mr Sutherland!" John Sutherland was frowning a little, keeping his eyes straight ahead. Now that was nice to see, a healthy young man exercising before most of the city was up, keeping his muscles firm, lungs clear. John Sutherland's fair hair looked darker than Ralph remembered it, but there was no doubt the man was Sutherland. Ralph turned to watch the blue figure disappear on springy, silent feet around the corner into Morton, going west. Sutherland didn't run every morning, Ralph supposed, otherwise he'd have noticed him before. Ralph had been on his present schedule for two weeks now.

Ralph walked into Grove Street in the direction of Bleecker. Was Sutherland's wife still asleep? Probably. He knew what she looked like from the photographs in the wallet, but did not recall ever having seen her in the neighborhood.

The grocery store on Bleecker was just stirring, doors open,

Johnny in an apron tugging out wooden stands on which his wares would be displayed in a few minutes. Ralph went in. God walked in a circle on his leash, sniffing the aromas of mortadella, liverwurst, salami and cheese.

"Morning, Mr Linderman!" said Johnny, coming in. "You're the first customer. Gettin' to be a habit."

Ralph smiled a little, pleased, and stood taller. "Morning to you, Johnny. How's the liverwurst today?"

"Same as ever. Not sufferin', sellin' fine."

Ralph bought some, also some salami and cole slaw, and took a couple of cans of cat food off a shelf for God. Cats were fussier than dogs, so catfood was of better quality than dogfood, Ralph reasoned. God had still some liver and rumpsteak at home. Butter too, Ralph needed. Johnny totaled it all up on his calculator. He was a rather nice boy, Johnny, though Ralph in general didn't trust Italians, because they were Catholics, and because the Mafia was still mainly composed of Italians. Ralph remembered when he had hated Italians, as he had hated and still hated and mistrusted the blacks, as they called themselves. "Coons" Ralph called them to himself. Negroes certainly, with a capital n, but no, they preferred to be called blacks, a depressing word and color. Many hard-working Italians had made their way up in America, but he could never forget the Mafia, that family business, rich and tough, the epitome of evil, murderers and blackmailers, caterers to vice. The Jews had not changed, in Ralph's opinion, and by and large he didn't like them with their ingrown cliques, their money which they used to buy people, but the men who took their money were even worse, of course. Ralph paid, eight dollars and seventy-three cents.

"And how's God?" Johnny asked, leaning over the wooden counter to peer at the dog. "Howdy, God ol' pal!" Johnny laughed.

A pimple over Johnny's upper lip seemed to spread as if to bursting point. The down was turning to darker hair there. Johnny was perhaps seventeen, having quit highschool, but at least he was working for his parents, who were probably still asleep, Ralph thought, and well they deserved it, as they'd been minding the store until nearly midnight.

"God's fine, thanks," Ralph replied, taking up the brown paper bag. "See you soon, Johnny."

"Bye, sir. Have a nice day, God!" Johnny said, still grinning.

Ralph Linderman had a lovely day. At noon, the newsstand man at Sheridan Square had saved his *Times* for him, and he changed five books at Leroy Street, renewing Thomas Mann's *Last Essays*, because he liked to read something like that slowly. He read everything, or nearly everything slowly, letting it sink in, though some books that he borrowed he found had been a mistake, they bored him or they were worthless. Ralph liked to read fiction as much as non-fiction. He had wanted to read *1984* again, but the waiting list had been so long, he bought the paperback. He adored Robert Louis Stevenson, for pleasure. He took out a book on semeiology, because it looked interesting. And a novel by Iris Murdoch, whom he enjoyed because the English world she described, though contemporary and evidently realistic, was fantastic to Ralph, making him think of the plots of Richard Wagner's operas, somebody in love with someone impossible to attain, someone else hating someone for the slightest of reasons which became magnified. Ralph had never been to England, and he wondered if a fair number of English people kept falling in love like that, seldom if ever showing it under their calm exteriors?

He hadn't taken God to the library, of course, so Ralph was able to walk home briskly. Good exercise. The coffee shop where Elsie worked was south of Leroy Street, but Ralph had no desire to drop in now. Maybe Elsie was not even on duty today.

Later that afternoon, Ralph cleaned out the two shelves under his sink, got rid of old rags, useless paper bags, discovered some steel wool and a spare bottle of window-cleaning fluid that he'd been unaware of, wiped the shelving paper, and put most of the items back. Then he wrote a letter to his mother. She was nearly eighty and living in a small apartment in a town in New Hampshire. Ralph sent his mother money once a month, and wrote her maybe every three weeks. He was the only child.

Sept. 15, 19—

Dear Mother,

Things are about as usual, weather pretty pleasant and the worst heat seems over. Am still working at the parking garage way west on 48th St. $6.50 per hour is good pay, as $7 is about tops. Remember when I was making the $5.50 minimum not so long ago? I

*don't take such wages any more, as I don't have to. My work
record is sterling by the way.*

*How is your arthritis? Don't forget to get your woolies handy
with the fall coming soon. Not more than four aspirins a day, I
hope.*

God is fine and sends love to Tissy Cat.

Ralph paused for thought, and recalled black-and-white Tissy
Cat, who had long hair like a Persian but was quite ordinary, a
boring animal who looked at people from her pillow as if she
detested them.

Bless you and keep you. From your loving son
Ralph

His mother was a devout church-goer, protestant. That was why
Ralph had written "Bless you" to please her. Who and what was
to bless her? Fate? Luck?

6

By half past 8 the apartment had begun to fill up, and it looked like a party. People talked more loudly in order to be heard, and Sylvia Kinnock's laughter, a single shriek now and then, sounded muffled. Louis Wannfeld was here, and Isabel Katz, the old friend of Natalia's who ran the Katz Gallery. It was Natalia's twenty-eighth birthday, though she and Jack had not announced that fact when they extended the invitations, they had simply asked people to come for drinks after 7, and said maybe there'd be something to eat too. Only Natalia's closest friends might connect the date with her birthday. Natalia liked to do something on her birthday, but hated the idea of people feeling that they had to bring a present.

Joel MacPherson had come, and Jack had showed him four more roughs for the *Dreams* book, plus two finished with the pale pink, blue and green he would use on all of them. Joel was extremely pleased.

"Let's put 'em up—put 'em up all around the table like this." He demonstrated by leaning one against the wall at the back of Jack's worktable, daintily, as if it were precious, then his hands spread as he whispered, 'We'll ask the people in and see what they think.—Or don't you like that?" Joel's plump face beamed as if it were publication day.

Jack hesitated, not liking the idea. "But this is my private room, Joel!" he said with a laugh.

Joel's face fell like a disappointed child's. "I love the old grampa—looking like Jehovah or something. And his son—groveling." Joel pointed, smiling again, at the diminutive figure of the middle-aged husband Caspar, crawling on the floor toward his somnolent but dominant father-figure. "And the sex scenes—well—" Joel seemed at a loss for words of praise.

Jack jerked his head. "Let's go back."

As soon as he entered the big living-room where more people were standing than sitting, Jack's eye fell on Louis' tall figure in his dark blue summer suit, white shirt, the terribly chic blue bowtie, as Louis handed a small object in white tissue paper to Natalia. She opened it. They were both standing by a front window. Jack saw Natalia's lips part in pleased surprise, and she held up what looked like a silver chain of some heaviness with a red pendant stone.

"Jack, where's your drink?" asked Isabel Katz, looking at him with eyes whose upper lids were of a more intense pale blue than some in Jack's drawings. "Mine's fresh. I was going to toast Natalia's health. Just us."

Isabel's made-up face was in contrast to Natalia's, because Natalia had been doing something till the last minute, making the guacamole dip or simply shifting on her feet in feigned panic at the thought of "a party", and hadn't put even lipstick on before the first ring at the door. Isabel was smallish, slender, with dark hair done in a bun in back. She was at least forty-five, and needed some make-up, but underneath, as they said, she was not the made-up type. Isabel Katz was all art, not even business art or the kind that made money, just art. Isabel painted too, but was modest about her work. And what did she think of his stuff, his talent, Jack wondered, if she bothered to think about it? "I'm on white wine," Jack said. "I'll get some." He did, and lifted his glass.

Isabel raised her scotch and water. "To Natalia."

"To her," Jack said, and drank.

"Canapés," said a small figure suddenly beside and below them. Amelia held a plate of little hot sausages, each stuck with a toothpick. Amelia was diligent at parties, passing things around slowly and steadily, non-stop. "Ple-ease, Daddy."

Isabel didn't want any, and Jack took one to please his daughter. Amelia moved off to the sofa crowd.

"You look pale," Isabel said.

"Pale?" Jack was surprised.

"In the last seconds.—You feel all right, Jack?"

"Sure I do."

"Natalia's looking well, don't you think so? She looks happier—this last year."

Jack was pleased by this comment. "You should know. I hope so." Natalia was now working five or six hours a day, five days a week, at Isabel's gallery.

"Who's the girl with the long dark hair?" Isabel asked.

"Oh. Sylvia—Kinnock. Old friend of Natalia's. School friend, I think. Don't you remember, a couple of years ago, Natalia went away—well, to Europe—with Sylvia for a few months. I thought you knew her."

"N-no. I remember when Natalia was away in Europe.—The girl's got a wild face. Interesting," Isabel said with a smile.

Jack looked at Sylvia with new eyes. There was something gypsy-like about her face or her manner, though Jack remembered Natalia saying her family was Catholic and rather strict. Sylvia was Natalia's age, unmarried, and had a job that made her travel a lot, some kind of public relations. Odd that Isabel hadn't met Sylvia in all these years, but Isabel kept to herself in the evenings, and saw her best friends singly for drinks or dinner usually.

"Would you—" Jack had been about to introduce Isabel to Sylvia, but Isabel greeted someone with a warm "*Hello-o*," and Jack knew she was stuck for a while. Jack took a sip of his white wine, not wanting it now, even though it was excellent cool Frascati. Sylvia. Jack had not thought of her in maybe a year. He realized that he felt a faint resentment toward her, because Natalia had spent so much time with her on that trip when Amelia had been about two years old. It had been as if Natalia had wanted to kick over the traces of marriage, wanted to forget she was a wife and mother and feel independent again. Amelia had stayed with her grandmother in Ardmore, in the care of a nanny whose face Jack remembered but not her name. Natalia had been away for at least six months, and though Sylvia had come back to New York for a time, he remembered, Natalia had gone to Mexico and Sylvia had joined her there for a while. Natalia had come back in a more cheerful mood, but had been rather silent or laconic about her travels. *It's not the first time I've been either to Europe or to Mexico, after all.* Jack could still hear Natalia's voice saying that.

"Hello, Jack. You look thoughtful." Louis Wannfeld smiled affably at him. He had a broad mouth with full, pink lips, large teeth, a bald head. "It's a great party. I'm glad to be here."

What did one say to that? Jack murmured something with equal affability, and asked Louis if his drink was all right.

42

"Yes, thanks. Looks like a Bloody Mary but it's plain tomato juice," said Louis. "I hear you've got some new drawings. For a book." The spotlight behind Louis, focused mainly on the ceiling, made the crown of Louis' bare head look as if he wore a silver halo.

"Well—yes. Not yet ready for publication. Or inspection. In fact—" Now Jack smiled. "The book hasn't got a contract yet, but we have some strong interests, Joel and I."

"Yes, Joel," said Louis, and sipped. "You don't even use a pencil starting these drawings, Natalia said."

Jack replied. No, under ideal conditions, when he wasn't working for money. Jack was thinking, the latest was that Louis did *not* have cancer, though for three weeks Natalia had thought he had, because of what Louis had said. The New York doctor had saved him with a new verdict. What did Louis have? Something that made him watch his diet, cut out coffee, and preferably alcohol too. Jack had an unpleasant feeling that Louis was talking to him now to be polite, so Jack steered him toward Sylvia, who was talking with Joel in the middle of the living-room.

"Louis," said Sylvia, "are you a stuffed silk shirt tonight or a boiled owl?"

Louis laughed, his tall lean frame bent in a polite bow. "Not a boiled owl, anyway, I'm on the wagon."

Jack had not known that Sylvia and Louis were so chummy. He drifted away to the kitchen to see how Susanne was doing. Susanne had come to help out, and she was busy, but not too busy—she had a wonderfully easy manner—slicing the ham now with a very sharp knife, arranging it on a platter with pickles and olives and chunks of pineapple. Amelia hovered, eager for Susanne to hand her another plate of something that she could pass around.

"Darling, we're coming to the serious part now," said Susanne. "You'll get to put some of the stuff on the table."

"And *this*." It was Joel's voice, distant but loud.

Jack went down the hall and saw Joel and a couple of other people in his workroom whose curtain was pushed half open. "Hey, Joel," Jack said, advancing. "What's up here?"

"I just wanted to show Louis. He asked me about—I just showed him the couple lying here." Joel looked a little ashamed of himself, but not much.

And here was Isabel, smiling politely, Jack thought. And one other woman whose name Jack was not sure of. "Well, I did say—These aren't finished drawings. Not quite.—Of course they're not roughs either, I admit."

"You don't make roughs, I know," said Louis in his soft and careful voice.

Just sometimes, Jack thought, and who cared?

Isabel Katz' astute eyes narrowed as she gazed at the fine penline in the drawing Jack called, to himself, the masturbatory fantasies of the father.

"Well, that's enough, folks. Got to wait for the book." Jack wanted the people out of his workroom. "No more, Joel!" Joel had been reaching for more.

"Out! Out!" said Isabel, shooing people. "I like them, Jack."

That was a remark that he valued. Jack looked at the floor and turned. They were all leaving his room. Take it easy, Jack told himself, as he drifted deeper into the crowded living-room. Don't hold it against Joel, it was just Joel's extrovert nature, wanting people to share everything, even before it was finished. Jack poured a Jack Daniel's at the bamboo cabinet.

The serious eating had begun. Amelia was passing paper plates and napkins to everyone, looking like a little robot in her blue jeans and red-and-white checked shirt, moving among people without bumping, as if guided by radar. Natalia bent and squeezed Amelia's shoulders for an instant, and they looked like duplicates, one large, one small version of each other, due mainly to their blondish lank hair.

There was a sudden crack of thunder. Some people said, "Ah-h!" meaning that with rain it was going to be cooler. They were in a crazy heat wave, at the very end of September. Out the window it didn't look as if rain would come, it looked merely sullen, indifferent. Joel was getting a little high, Jack noticed, his face was pinker and he was talking a blue streak to a man who had arrived with Isabel, gesticulating. Joel was almost thirty, and he was still like a teen-ager, enthusiastic, optimistic for brief spells, downcast for longer spells, arguing with himself and aloud to Jack sometimes on the subject of "What am I doing with my life?" He wanted to quit his job and couldn't afford to. The money was too good. Jack felt suddenly *de trop*—the term came to him—but he really wanted simply to walk, to move on his own. It would be rude to slip out, even though Natalia and Sylvia and Louis, all standing in a corner, seemed to be engrossed in their conversation. Some people would notice that he was missing, when it came time to say good-bye. And when would that be? Three or four had already left. Some would stay until very late.

Amelia elected to bring her own plate over to join him, for which Jack felt rather flattered. Jack sat at one end of the sofa, Joel next to him, and Amelia was happy on the floor, where Jack told her her plate would be much safer. The abominated TV tables were up, all three of them. Joel had brought a girl to whom he was paying little attention. The girl, named Terry, had reddish hair. Jack had never known Joel to be overboard about any girl. Was there something just a little bit wrong with everybody, making them less than happy, halfway unhappy even?

"You're not sore at me," said Joel, chewing, but with an anxious look.

"About the drawings?—Na-ah. Forget it," Jack replied.

"Y'know—the sketch where the man, the husband, stands on that—cliff and he's about to fall off?"

"It's a building ledge. Yes."

"The ledge. How about having some little women down there—sort of laughing at him. Lots of little women, some with their arms out as if they're going to catch him and some—"

Jack laughed. "Yep. Gotcha." He was thinking that there was room for the little women in the drawing now, and it might be a good idea.

Natalia laughed, rising on her toes, closing her eyes. She was still with Louis and Sylvia, and Isabel Katz had joined them, but only to say good night, it seemed. She left with the man to whom Terry had been talking.

"Good night, Jack. Thank you," Isabel said. "Don't get up!"

Before long, Jack had managed his exit too. "I'm going down with Joel," he said to Natalia, and with a glance at Sylvia and Louis. "See you."

Joel and Terry, who worked at CBS too, had to watch a program at 11 tonight. Jack walked with them toward 7th Avenue where there was the best chance for a taxi.

"Can't tell you how I've enjoyed it, Jack," said Terry, beaming at him. "What a terrific apartment too! Bye!"

They had found a taxi. A wind swirled, and Jack felt the first drops of rain hit his face. The hell with the rain, he thought, he'd walk for half an hour, and come back and find Natalia and Louis ensconced on the sofa, probably drinking espresso, of which Louis was very fond, even if the doctor had banned it. Susanne would have gone home, after sticking all the glasses she could in the dishwasher and starting it. And Natalia would sit till maybe 2 in the morning, because it was her birthday and she could indulge herself with her soulmate, the whole sofa's length between them as each lolled back against a sofa arm.

Jack licked rainwater from his upper lip. His shoes were starting to feel squishy. Where was he? Way below West Houston now. He turned back and walked fast. The few people who were out in this downpour were either running or had umbrellas. Jack shoved wet hands into his pockets, lowered his head, and trotted uptown. In his right hand pocket, he felt coins, enough for a coffee somewhere, at least, to wait it out for a few minutes. The streetlights, shopfront lights made a glare on the surface of 7th Avenue. Jack crossed when a red shimmered. He had spotted a coffee shop farther up on the other side of the avenue.

Jack pulled his hands down his face, stomped his feet and went in. The place smelled of hamburgers, onions and steam and had a bright yellowish illumination, but at least it was dry. Jack stood by one of the stand-up counters fixed to a wall. Other people were coming in out of the rain, talking about the downpour. Jack finally went up to the counter which had a couple of curves to accommodate as many stools as possible. All the stools seemed taken. Jack ordered a coffee white when he got a waitress's attention, paid, and carried the mug back to the stand-up counter.

"*You* look like it's raining outside!" the blond waitress had said to him as she handed him his coffee.

Jack was still smiling at that. The girl had a friendly voice, not like a New Yorker's voice. Jack watched the blond girl whizzing about her tasks, serving a Danish on a plate, plopping ketchup down in front of somebody else, smiling, laughing, but he couldn't hear her laugh in all the noise. She had a word to say to nearly everybody. Her energy held Jack's eyes. He could see the other customers responding, smiling back at her. There were a couple of other girls working behind the long counter, not in the least eye-catching compared with this little blonde who looked about sixteen.

"*Whee-yoo!*" said a tall black fellow coming in with a pal, and they both stamped their feet on the now grimy tile floor. "*Man!*"

Both the blacks looked high on something. They drifted to the back of the place, chattering in shrill voices.

Jack sipped from his mug of weak coffee, and looked again for the blond girl. Now she was bent over the counter far to his left, pink lips parted. She shook her head quickly, then laughed again, started to move off, but looked back at the man who was talking to her from a stool. He was shaking a finger at her.

"*No!—No*, you're . . ." She flew off to the coffee machines.

Jack looked at the man she had been talking to, and recognized him. He was the man who had returned his wallet. Yes, certainly. There was his ugly dog on a leash. Now the man was getting up, ready to leave. Jack turned toward the wall, not wanting to be seen and maybe buttonholed. The guy was a bore, Jack remembered. Plainly he'd been boring the blond girl tonight too. Jack dared a glance, when the man reached the door, and watched him go out with his dog.

The rain was abating. Five more people departed.

Jack was curious about the girl, about the man, about what she thought of him. He sat down at a counter stool.

"Coffee white, please," Jack said to a waitress who was not the blond girl. The coffee arrived. The waitress was busy and didn't take his two quarters which lay on top of the check, but the blond girl swept by like a flying canary and did. Jack watched her, amused. She breezed back from the cash register with his partly torn check and his three cents, and as Jack slid his hand forward to take the change, their fingers touched, and the girl smiled at him. She had very white teeth, blue eyes that were not large but clear and intelligent. Her hair made him think of the word flaxen. It was straight, not thick, and cut carelessly and short.

"You're back again," she said.

"Yes. Say—that fellow you were talking with—with the dog." Jack gestured toward where the man had sat.

"Oh, him! He's nuts!" She gave a quick laugh.

"How so?"

The girl glanced around to see if she were urgently needed somewhere. "Giving me lectures all the time.—Oh, New York's full of screwballs." She was about to leave.

"I met him once before."

47

"Did you? He comes—Okay, Lorrie!" The girl went off. A short order was ready at the cook's window.

Jack lifted the hot coffee.

The girl came back. "He lives around here. He's a security guard, he says. You'd think he was getting paid to guard *me*. You'd think he was *tailing* me. Except I'm not the paranoid type, I hope.—How come you know him?"

Jack smiled. "He returned my wallet—after I'd lost it. I have to admit he's honest."

"Oh-h, you're the one!" Her eyes showed intense interest. "He told me all about that. He thought it was great, something like a miracle. He thinks *you're* great. He's blown all out of his mind by that wallet story.—Anyway, I'm glad to find out it's true. I wasn't even sure, y'know? He's so bananas. So now—" She looked off, for an instant dreamily, as if questing for words. "He keeps telling me that's the way I oughta be—honest and so on. Ha-ha!" She rocked back with laughter, holding to the counter edge in front of her.

"El-*sie!*" cried one of the waitresses.

"I'll come back!" Elsie dashed away.

Jack found himself smiling. Elsie could be an actress, Jack thought, or was her intensity confined to what happened to her?

"Goddam lamb stew," Elsie murmured, returning. "Well—this nut lectures me about my *sexlife*, f'Chris' sake, morals. He doesn't know what a clean life I lead! Does he think I'm a prostitute or something? And what about him, I often think. Or say. Sure, I say it to him. 'Weren't you ever young and happy?' Maybe he wasn't. In that case, he's just repressed and it's too late for him to do anything about it, isn't it?" She laughed without bitterness, with an amusement that brought moisture to her eyes. "He's weird! Especially since he doesn't believe in religion. And he calls his dog 'God', did you know that?"

Jack nodded. "I know."

"Say, is he following *you* around?"

Jack grinned. "I don't think so. Hadn't noticed."

"Watch out. He's out to improve the world.—He lives on Bleecker, I think. He said you lived on Grove."

"*El-sie!*—Get those burgers with! They're on your side!"

Once more she was gone.

Jack wished he had a ballpoint pen with him or a pencil. The

48

sharp angle at the corner of her eyes when she laughed was just what he wanted for Suzuki, the fantasy girlfriend of the adolescent boy in the *Dreams* book. Could he remember it? The angle was best seen in profile, and with the upturned corner of her lips too. Jack's left hand shot out and seized a short pencil that seemed to have materialized just for him, inches away on the counter. He drew rapidly on the back of his check, eyes as much on Elsie as on the paper. He had it. Whew! Good! He felt like a man who'd just captured a fish. Rapidly he drew the line of her neck, the back of her head.

"You're drawing me?"

"Finished. Thanks." Jack gave her a real smile, and stuck the folded check carefully into his back pocket.

"Are you an artist?" Elsie asked with a suddenly childlike curiosity. "Ralph said you were a journalist."

"Who's Ralph?"

"The guy with the dog."

"Oh. No, I'm more of an artist—I like to think. I wanted to get the corner of your eyes. Eye in profile. And I couldn't have asked you to come to my studio, could I? That'd have been like asking you to come up and see my etchings, no?" Jack repressed a happy laugh now, and there was something funny in the serious and thoughtful way the girl looked at him, as if she were pondering his last words. "Anyway, thanks—Elsie." He got up from the stool.

"Hey!—I'll come up if you need any sittings. No charge."

Jack's amazed smile was back. "Wh-where do I find you? Here?"

A laugh bubbled from her. "For the next week maybe. Sure. I'm around." She lifted a hand carelessly by way of good-bye, and turned back to her work.

The rain had diminished to droplets. Jack felt happy, rather as if he had just fallen in love. He was familiar with the sensation, though it had not come to him often. He'd had it a few times in art class on a good day, when a female model, not necessarily young or pretty, had inspired him to produce a good charcoal sketch or line drawing or whatever, and suddenly he had felt in love with the model, as if she had a special power, only she, to bring his talent out. It never lasted. But it was easy for Jack to understand why artists, Modigliani and others, had felt a desire to bed their models on completion of a good piece of work. Absurd, considering that his effort was a few lines with a blunt pencil on the back of a check that had faint blue lines on it. He had felt like embracing this girl Elsie, as if to make sure she was real, solid.

Elsie had worn a cheap ring on her middle finger, left hand, a skull surrounded by snakes. Bright red nail polish, neatly applied. Her hands were graceful and rather lean. A couple of boys, white, had stared at her, paid her wild compliments on her blue eyes, asked her when she was going off duty tonight, and Elsie had ignored them totally.

Jack let himself quietly into the apartment, heard the murmur of voices, slipped to the right, into the bathroom, where he combed his hair. His trousers were still slightly damp at the cuffs, but no matter. He went into the living-room where the air smelled of women's scent, cigarette smoke, where Natalia lolled back on the sofa, Louis on her right, Sylvia in the big green armchair facing them. Sylvia saw him first.

"Hi there, Jack! You were out?"

"Walking Joel and his girlfriend down." Jack saw his unfinished Jack Daniel's on a corner of the bamboo cabinet, and picked it up. Half an inch left. He felt as if he were returning to another world, one he had almost forgotten for a while.

"And then," Natalia was saying in her deepish voice, through a chuckle, "could I see about a frame for him at no extra charge. After all *that* . . ."

Louis listened attentively.

Natalia balanced an iceless scotch and water on her breastbone, or sternum as the art-school teachers would call it, and might not have noticed his absence or his arrival, Jack thought. He sat down on a straight chair. Now Natalia was telling another story from the Katz Gallery, about her sale of a Pinto whose price she had upped out of her head, unintentionally, and got. The price had been uncertain, said Natalia, it was the largest Pinto and not his best, maybe his worst even, but some idiot had bought it, and Isabel had been pleased, of course. Jack was happier now, gazing at Natalia, half-listening to the conversation of the three of them. When he had come into the living-room, he had thought: that trio, triumvirate in a way, closed to him. Old friends they were, for nearly ten years, Natalia, Louis and Sylvia, and he had known

Natalia merely six, even though she was his wife. Jack had felt a curious shock of anxiety, near-resentment at the sight of them when he had walked into the living-room. But he could forget this when Natalia, as she spoke, let her gaze drift toward him, linger without a change of expression, before it moved to Sylvia. He was hers, as much as she was his, wasn't that true? Belonging to each other, living together. Didn't that mean a lot? Yes, if Natalia were happy. Was she happy? That was the kind of question one did not ask Natalia. *Who's ever happy*, she would reply carelessly, and maybe with annoyance at the stupidity of the question. If people weren't happy, they didn't stay together, Jack supposed, unless both were masochists or sadists battling it out, or a convenient combination of the two.

Louis hauled his tall form up and excused himself to go and swallow some pills. "No, plain water, I'll get it, Jack." He went off to the bathroom.

When he returned, he kissed Natalia on the forehead, wished her many happy returns, and said good night. Sylvia was joining him. It was nearly 1 a.m.

"Buzz me," Sylvia said to Natalia. "I can manage lunch almost any day. In your neck of the woods, I mean. Or I'll bring sand-wiches," she said with an easy smile, "if Isabel doesn't give you a break."

The door finally closed.

Jack walked toward Natalia with outstretched arms, and loved it when she fairly collapsed in his embrace, so that he had to support her weight. "Darling—I love you, I love you."

"*Tonight?*" she asked in a surprised tone.

"What'd Louis give you? Looked like a chain."

"Something that belonged to his *maman*. He shouldn't have done it. Where is it?" She had left the box and tissue paper on a bookshelf. She lifted the chain. "This. A garnet. The silver chain's lovely, don't you think, Jack? But the garnet—" The garnet was rather large, making one think of an elderly Victorian lady letting it ride over a full bosom. The garnet was the size of a small lemon, but rather flat. "Looks like what you'd call an heirloom," said Natalia smiling. "He says his mother gave it to him years ago to give to a girl, in fact."

Jack burst out laughing. The idea of Louis giving it to his beloved, his betrothed! "'S beautiful," said Jack. "Hey! You have another little something." He went to their bedroom and took a plastic bag from his shirt drawer.

Natalia opened it. This was in addition to the brown calfskin letter-holder or "portfolio" from Dunhill that Jack had given her before the party began. He had written "For the serious executive" on his handmade card, a cartoon of Natalia looking pained and absent-minded at her Katz Gallery desk. In the plastic bag was a cassette of Prokofief sonatas for strings, one of which Jack knew she especially liked, and also a paperback, *The Unquiet Grave*, which Jack knew she missed, because someone had failed to return her old copy after borrowing it. These items were not wrapped.

"Ooh, perfect," Natalia said. "Lovely, Jack."

"Amelia's here? In bed?" he asked in a suddenly soft voice. Sometimes Susanne took her to her own house for the night, if they had a party, and delivered her the next morning.

"Amelia," Natalia said, as if just recalling that she had a child. "Yes, Susanne put her to bed hours ago."

Jack opened Amelia's room door a little and peered into the darkness. A couple of cars went by on Grove, covering the sound of breathing that he might have heard, but he could just see her form under the blanket.

"She okay?" asked Natalia.

Jack closed the door softly. "Yep." He wanted to embrace Natalia again, she was standing so close to him now, but he was afraid it would annoy her.

They looked over the living-room, carried some glasses and ashtrays out, but Susanne had already done a fair job of tidying. The dishwasher had finished its cycle. The sink could hold what dirty dishes there were. All was well. *And Christ, we're lucky*, Jack thought. To live in a nice place, not to have to worry about money, to be able to afford a reliable person like Susanne, to have a healthy kid!

Natalia was under the shower.

Jack took a deep breath. All was right with his world.

7

JACK emerged from Rossi's Fruit and Deli with both arms around paper bags. A cold bottle of Amelia's Coca-Cola was threatening to break the wet bottom of one bag, and Jack had his hand under it. Johnny Rossi wasn't delivering today, because his father was down with bronchitis, and Johnny couldn't leave the store. But the distance was short to Jack's house. *You're so naive sometimes, Jack.* Jack grimaced. Why couldn't he get the phrase out of his mind? Natalia had said it with a smile, but it had stung, maybe because Isabel Katz had heard it, and Jack remembered her faint smile, to herself. Natalia last evening, when they'd had drinks and dinner at Isabel's studio on East Forty-first, had mentioned "Sylvia's new girlfriend", who was a bio-chemist and quite attractive, Isabel had said, and both she and Natalia had remarked how much better and happier Sylvia looked since having met her a month ago. And Jack had said, "Girlfriend?" being genuinely surprised, and wondering for a moment if they were talking about Sylvia Kinnock, but they were. "You didn't know she was gay, Jack?" Natalia had asked with a quick laugh that was almost apologetic, for him, before she gave her attention to Isabel again. Jack had said nothing further on the subject, not even after they had got home. No, he hadn't known. Sylvia didn't look in the least gay, with her careful make-up, or in the way she dressed, which was rather on the feminine side, now that Jack thought about it. This revelation of Sylvia's sexual preference reminded Jack of the more than six months in which Natalia had breezed off with Sylvia to Europe and so on. Had they had an affair? Jack wasn't going to ask. The thought, the possibility, however, made him feel slightly shaky inside.

"Hi there!"

Jack was on Grove Street. The voice had come from behind

him. Instantly he recognized the face above the denim jacket, under the sailor cap, the blond girl from the coffee shop. Elsie. He smiled. "Hi. How're you?" He walked on, aware that the girl followed him, then was beside him.

"Hey, let me take one of those!"

"Right. Thanks. Just for a few steps." Jack held onto the collapsing bag, and let the girl take the other. "I'm here." He nodded toward his doorway. "If I can just set this one inside—" Jack worked his key with his free hand.

"I'll take one up," said the girl. "Is this where you live?—I'd like to see your drawings. Unless you're busy just now."

"N-no.—Okay. If you want to take a look."

The girl climbed the stairs with him, up to the third floor. Below the jacket she wore blue jeans and white sneakers.

"It's here." Jack used another key.

The girl looked around inside the living-room, still holding the big sack in her arms. "Gosh, what a place!—You live here too?"

"I sure do. You can set that thing on the table here.—Thanks a lot."

She did so, then went to look at a small gouache on a wall. "Is this by you?"

"Hah! Thank you. That's a de Kooning." And probably the most valuable thing in the house, Jack thought.

"Gosh, and that stereo!—This is really the nicest place I've seen in New York. And such high ceilings!"

"Yep, it's an old house." He put one big Coca-Cola bottle into the fridge for Amelia. The rest could wait.

She faced him, standing in the center of the living-room, hands in the slash pockets of her jacket. She was not tall, perhaps five feet five. "Where do you work?"

"This way." There was something odd, quite unusual, about brushing aside his curtain, seeing the girl walk into his sanctum sanctorum. Had he gone mad? Was he trying to risk something? If so, what? "Th—this," Jack said, indicating an old first sketch, just about the only one he'd abandoned of the many he'd made for Joel's book, against the wall at the left back corner of his worktable. "This is unfinished. In fact I'm not even using it. It's part of—"

"It's weird!" she said with admiration. "And this?—All these are *yours*?"

"Everything here, yes." All, all, the black and white pen and brush abstracts, the experiment with colored tissue paper pasted to a papier-mâché female figure, a small figure, to simulate a party dress, a large and not bad watercolor of the view from one of the front windows, which the girl spotted and recognized instantly as—right across the street from here.

"Gosh, you weren't kidding. You're an artist.—Where's the one you did of me?"

Jack smiled. "On that check?" He moved toward a wall against which stuff leaned, and pulled up an illustration board. He had paperclipped the little drawing to an upper corner of the board, the little gem, while the board itself was covered with twelve or fifteen line drawings of Elsie, three-quarter, profile, full face.

"Golly! That's really *me*!" Her blue eyes were wide now. "I think they're—" She shook her head, at a loss for words. "Say, I'll pose for you—like I said. No charge. If you do stuff this good."

Since the stuff she was looking at was rather unrealistic, except maybe for that corner of her eyes, Jack was surprised that she liked the sketches. "Well—maybe some time. Thank you for the offer." She was remarkably pretty, Jack thought, presenting her profile now as she gazed at the illustration board which she held carefully between her palms. Her nose was rather fine. She wore no make-up. He imagined her with some color at her lips and in a long pink gown. She'd look like a fairy queen come to life.

"Want to make any more sketches of me now?"

Jack shook his head. "No. Not just now." Just now he was not in the mood for sketching, only for looking at her. "You could just sit, if you've got a minute. In the living-room."

"Or maybe you want to work," she said, like a little girl trying to be polite.

"If I wanted to work, I wouldn't ask you to sit down."

She took the sofa, he the green armchair.

"Where're you from?" Jack asked.

"Upstate New York. Such a little town, nobody's ever heard of it, and I don't even want to say the name." She looked straight at Jack and laughed, revealing white pointed eyeteeth. "I ran away— with about fifty dollars. I got tired of the arguments at home. My parents wanted me to stick it out with a job in a five-and-dime. I

55

was so bored, I just couldn't. Selling spools of thread and stuff." She cringed as if in horror at the memory. "So I caught a bus to New York, got off at Thirty-fourth Street. *Wow!*—I had a friend living down on King Street. *Had.* We sort of quarreled—but she put me up when I first came, and I paid her something for sleeping on the sofa, but she didn't really like me. She didn't really know me, because I was just a friend of a friend of hers who lives in *my* town upstate, if you can follow all that, so—Well, there's nothing easier than finding part-time jobs in this town. Now I'm living on Minetta Street with a girl I sort of like. We share the rent." She shrugged. "But New York! I love it. It's better than a circus. You never know what kind of person's turning up next. Funny people—and bright people. People you can talk to and they'll let you alone too." She looked at Jack earnestly, pressed her palms together between her knees. She glanced at the pack of Marlboros on the coffee table. "Can I have one of these?"

"Sure." Jack got up to light it, picked up Natalia's jade lighter and held it for the girl.

"Thanks." She picked up the lighter quickly after Jack had set it down, rubbed her thumb along its flat side that was framed in gold, and set it down. "Beautiful, that is.—You don't smoke?"

"No. Those cigarettes are my wife's."

"Oh, yeah! Old Ralph told me you were married and had a little daughter too. Where is she?"

"How does he know I have a daughter?"

She smiled. "I told you he spies on everyone. He lives just here on Bleecker Street." She gestured with her left arm. "I try to stay clear of him. Ha! He knows it. He's always talking about my morals. *Morals!* What a laugh!—He doesn't seem to know that I tell people—fellows, anybody, '*Shove off!*' When I want to. And they do shove off!" Now she laughed, bubbled over with amusement. "I don't know what's so wrong about my morals, I swear!"

Jack had to smile too. "How long've you known this guy—Ralph?"

"Known him? I don't know him. He just walks around the area. He has crazy working hours like me. He's a security guard, he says. So—"

"He works around here?"

"I wouldn't know. I don't know.—But if I'm working at some

coffee shop or a bar—Oh, maybe he wouldn't go to a bar, but a coffee shop, in *he* comes, see, at any hour! Could be daytime hours too. This has been going on for—maybe five months! And a couple of weeks ago, it was so funny! I went to a disco on Christopher after work, after two in the morning, and then to someone's apartment, and I was walking home with my friend Genevieve and some fellows at nearly *dawn*, and old Ralph must have been coming home from work, so he saw me with these noisy people, even though it wasn't even light, and he was across the street. So he just stood there in the dark, looking. I had to laugh! Genevieve knows about him, because I told her.—He's harmless. He thinks we were all off to a sexual orgy or something, the three fellows and Genevieve and me. Or I." Another irrepressible laugh came at recalling it; she glanced at the ceiling and smoke burst from her lips. "I know what he was thinking, because the next time I saw him, he gave me a lecture about staying up all night, drugs and booze. Ha-ha! He doesn't seem to know I can sleep all day if I want to."

"How old are you? If I may ask."

"I just was twenty. Old enough to be seeing some of the world, don't you think?"

"Ye-e-es. And what's your last name?"

"Tyler. T-y-l-e-r. I hate it. Sounds so boring.—Do you ever go up to the Museum of Modern Art?"

"Sure."

"I like to go there. I sometimes go—"

"Do you do any drawing and painting yourself?"

"No-o. But I like it. I think I'd like to be an actress. I started acting classes at a free school—nearly free—at Cooper Union. Then I didn't attend enough. This was only a couple of months ago. I've been in New York about eight months now. I thought I'd look around for a year before I started working hard at something. I don't know what I want to be really." Again she looked straight at Jack.

A malleable girl, Jack thought, happy and free just now, and a pleasure to behold, naive, but he sensed a core: she wouldn't say yes to everything that came along. Thousands of young people drifted to New York to try their luck, he realized. What set Elsie Tyler apart was her energy, her clear face, her freshness. "You must have a lot of boyfriends," Jack said.

Another shrug. "I can take 'em or leave 'em. They bore me if they say they're in love with me. How long does that last? Two weeks? Or else they just want a lay. That's maybe worse. I don't want to settle down—to anything." She removed her cap suddenly, but sat up straighter, cap in her lap, with an air of departing.

Jack felt like making a sketch of her now. Could he remember the way she looked now? Blue thighs curved with young muscle, ready to spring up from the sofa, the singularly plain straight blond hair, doing little to enhance the beauty of her face except by its light. And the restless eyes.

"I better push off." She was up. "Got to go to work just before six. Same joint." She threw him a smile. "You really have a daughter?"

The doorbell rang. It was a little after 4. Susanne was fetching Amelia today from the Twelfth Street school.

"Yes," Jack said, pushing the release button in the front hall. "You'll see her now."

Elsie clapped her cap on. "Thanks for letting me up. I really enjoyed it—even though I did all the talking. Didn't I?"

She seemed to want to be assured that she hadn't. Jack didn't say anything, and went and opened the apartment door. He heard Susanne's and Amelia's murmurings as they climbed the stairs.

"Hi, Jack." Susanne released Amelia's hand.

"Daddy, I made a *bird* for you!" Amelia flopped against his legs, then handed him a blue paper bird of the kind that flapped its wings, the kind Jack had made for her many a time. "*I* made this one."

"Very good, honey. Thanks.—May I introduce Miss Elsie Tyler?" Jack said. "Amelia. And Susanne Bewley."

"How do you do?" Susanne smiled at Elsie, then went into the kitchen.

"How d'you?" Amelia looked up at Elsie. "What kind of hat is that?"

"Sailor's cap," Elsie replied. "English sailor's."

Amelia lifted one hand.

"No, come on, Amelia!" Jack said. His daughter was being herself, wanting to take the cap in her hands, to try it on.

Elsie let her. "Do you want it? You can have it. I know where to get more," she added to Jack.

Jack removed the oversized cap from Amelia's head. "No. You don't just take people's possessions, Amelia. Not done!"

Amelia, unhurt, looked at Elsie with curiosity.

Jack led the way to the apartment door and Elsie followed him. Then she ran down the steps ahead of him, and Jack after her, as he wanted to accompany her to the house door.

"What did you mean, the drawings upstairs were just practice?" Elsie asked as she opened the downstairs door. "Did you make another drawing of me?"

"I meant I made one finished drawing—finally." Jack was now walking down the front steps. "It's for a book I'm illustrating. I turned all the drawings in yesterday. At a publishing house."

"A book?"

"Book by a friend of mine. Not sure if it'll get published. But it's a nice drawing of you."

"You mean I'll see my face on the printed page?"

Jack laughed. "I'll let you know."

She lifted her right arm in good-bye, then turned and trotted toward the corner where Grove met Bleecker.

Jack shoved his hands in his back pockets and hopped up the steps. Now it was he who had to ring the bell for Susanne to let him in. Susanne had her keys, Jack had seen them in her hand. Sometimes she had them and pushed the downstairs bell, as if to warn them of her advent. Jack found the apartment door slightly open for him.

Susanne was washing something at the sink, and she had put away all the groceries.

Jack stood in the kitchen doorway. "How's the thesis going?" Jack suddenly remembered what it was on, though at other times it went out of his head: family ties and relationships in the Thirteen Colonies during the period of the American Revolution.

"Oh-h—don't ask me," Susanne said, squeezing out a sponge. "I *am* going to finish it by the end of November. I'm retyping now. But a book on this very subject just came out and I ordered—"

"Don't read it! How long is this going to go on?"

"But you should see the reviews of this book!—Oh, well—" She turned her freckled face toward Jack, and smiled, sadly.

Susanne just now was as unmade-up as Elsie Tyler, in sloppy brown corduroys, a cardigan over her blouse, brown loafers.

59

Susanne was all practicality, even if she hadn't yet finished her thesis. She intended to be a history teacher, and was aiming at a university place. She had a boyfriend named Michael, an assistant professor somewhere, and like her thesis the Michael affair had been going on quietly for at least two years.

"What's the latest about the 'Dreams' book, Jack?" she asked.

"I took the drawings in yesterday.—Nice of you to ask. The art editor's seen half of them, but yesterday I took the whole batch, twenty-four or so. This is Dartmoor, Aegis."

"I can see you're anxious," Susanne said in her calm, almost sleepy voice. "I think they're fascinating, Jack. They're funny and serious at the same time."

That was what he wanted, Jack supposed. He watched Susanne open a brown leather briefcase, the one she nearly always had with her, on the rectangular white table in the dining area. She slid out a couple of books and some papers. Susanne was staying for the evening, until Jack and Natalia got back from the theater between 11 and 12. Jack was to pick Natalia up at the Katz Gallery at 6.

When Jack arrived at the gallery, he had to wait while Natalia took a telephone call at the desk in the foyer. Then she went down the hall to wash her hands which were visibly grimy, because she and Isabel had been handling frames and wires and whatnot. Jack noticed two Pintos on the foyer's walls, both dominated by the bluish-red color which Jack particularly disliked, with superimposed silvery circles of varying sizes in both pictures. What did people see in such witless compositions? The maroon was tired, ugly and depressing all at once. Natalia with her bland salesmanship had raked in thousands of dollars in the past weeks by selling the stuff, even before the show. "The money from this stuff lets Isabel promote a good artist," Natalia had said to Jack. "Maybe a young guy or a girl who needs a show. Don't ask me why Pinto sells."

Jack watched Isabel, in limp jeans with frayed cuffs, emptying standing ashtrays, finally the wastebasket by Natalia's desk, putting out the lights in the big front room which had windows on the street. The Katz Gallery officially closed at 6 p.m.

"Had a good day, Isabel?" Jack was standing with a topcoat, which Natalia had asked him to bring, folded over his arms. Isabel was so busy, she hadn't noticed him.

"Hi, Jack! Yes, a good day, thanks, and I'm weary!" Isabel said cheerfully.

Natalia came back. "Ready!" She put on the coat that Jack held for her.

They took a taxi to West Forty-second Street, near where the play was, and went into the Blarney Rock Pub for a quick drink and a snack. Natalia ordered a cup of chile along with her scotch and water. She and Isabel between them had sold a picture by one Howard Branston, a name that meant nothing to Jack, and who Natalia said was "an unknown". Natalia had had it leaning against the wall rather near her desk, and someone who came in had happened to like it, and had asked the price.

"I just said—fifteen hundred dollars, off the top of my head," Natalia said, "and I went back to ask Isabel. She said, 'My God, for that thing? Well, try it.' So it went for that. Isabel said she'd been about to return it to this Branston, that's why she'd put it in the foyer today, to remind herself."

"Maybe Isabel should show her pictures leaning against the wall," Jack said, "so they'd look less intimidating." He was admiring Natalia's handsome, unpretty face, her special style in the black satin blouse which she'd taken from the house to wear tonight. He was thinking how much more interesting, important, consequently sexy Natalia was, than the child-faced girl called Elsie Tyler, exciting as she was in a strange way. He glanced at his watch. They had plenty of time, another quarter of an hour. They were going to see Sam Shepard's *Fool for Love*.

8

Two days later, on a Saturday morning, Jack received a letter from Dartmoor, Aegis. The typewritten initials above the logo on the envelope were T.E.W., so Jack knew it was from Trews, as he was called, the art editor. This was Trelawney E. Watson, whom Jack had met briefly with Joel weeks ago. Jack expected a letter saying that he liked the drawings, because Trews had liked the ones Jack had showed him so far, but that he had a few "suggestions for changes". Art editors always had.

Standing by a front window, Jack opened the letter.

Dear Mr Sutherland:
A note to say that I think your twenty-eight drawings are brilliant. Each has a freedom and freshness, and I wouldn't want to say add something or take something out—in short, do the drawing over, because you might not do it as well. These come out like doodles, personal and real. Well, they're certainly not real, but I mean they look as if you hadn't strained.

Congratulations.
Trews
Trelawney E. Watson

Jack smiled, looked around the living-room without seeing anything, and felt his heart beating harder for a few seconds. From *Trews.* Well, well, he was in! Should he call up Joel and tell him? No, cool it, Jack told himself. Joel might be getting a letter from Dartmoor, Aegis this morning too, in regard to a contract. Surely the drawings' approval would mean a contract.

It was around 9 a.m., and Natalia was still asleep. Susanne had taken Amelia off to the zoo earlier, and had charge of Amelia all day. And Natalia was due at the gallery by noon.

Jack had been up early, and had gone out for a run down Bedford Street, and over to Hudson and back again. He had spotted the guy called Ralph airing God, and if Jack hadn't been mistaken, he had raised a hand or a finger as if he wished to speak to him, but Jack had pretended not to see him. Imagine getting stuck at 6 in the morning in a track suit, having to listen to a lecture on human goodness, maybe, morals, as Elsie Tyler had said?

He looked at Trews' note again, and noticed a tiny "over" in the bottom corner of the page. The words on the back were in longhand:

I know of another project that might interest you. Call me soon.

The day was starting well! Jack went to his workroom and looked at his latest sketch for a painting. He was trying for a composition of balance, a look of floating tranquillity that he so admired in some of Braque's abstracts, and he was working with pencil, eraser and color pencils. Was it good to try hard, he wondered, or was it fatal? Out of perhaps twenty-five paintings that Jack had done and kept, four or five really pleased him. Should he stick to drawing? Would he be asking himself the same question ten years from now, still trying to paint? Yes, probably.

By the time Natalia got up, Jack had made fresh coffee and had set the kitchen table for a breakfast of croissants that he had picked up earlier. He showed Natalia the note from Trews.

Natalia pronounced it "marvelous". "I hope they do some advertising. That should be in the contract. What's the price again?"

"Someone there said sixteen ninety-five. Too bad it's a slender book. At *that* price."

"People pay for drawings," Natalia said calmly, biting into a croissant. "I'll tell Isabel—ask her to have a few of the books on a table in the gallery.—I think she already offered."

Jack was in his workroom when Natalia parted the curtains to say she was leaving.

"Back around six-thirty, I hope. I straightened up Amelia's room a little. Might inspire Susanne to do some more. Gad, what an untidy little girl!" Natalia said, emphasizing the last two words.

Jack laughed.

A couple of minutes after the sound of the apartment door closing, Jack yielded to his impulse to call Joel MacPherson.

Joel answered on the ninth ring, sounding breathless. "I was just going out shopping—had to open the door again."

"Can't you send Terry out shopping?"

"Terry's not here. You think she lives with me?"

"I don't ask rude questions."

"Then cut out your in-sin-uendos," Joel said.

"I'm calling because—I had a nice note from Trews. He likes my stuff. No changes."

"No kidding! No changes! That means a contract. Thank you, Jack."

"Show you his note some time. He's almost poetic about how much he likes 'em.—Go down and get your own mail."

Then all was quiet and Jack worked, oblivious of what the time might be. He was trying his colors, brown, pale green, dusty yellow, imagining them in oil. The yellow was an almond shape, floating. He propped the sketch up on the table, and stepped back to look at it.

The doorbell sounded, briefly.

"Dammit," Jack murmured. It could be kids playing tricks on a Saturday morning. He opened the apartment door, intending to go down to see who it was before he pushed the release button, and heard murmurs, then the soft but clear voice of Susanne, then Amelia's. Jack hadn't been expecting them back before late afternoon, and was a bit annoyed. He leaned over the hall rail, and when they were on the second floor, he called:

"Something the matter, Susanne?"

"No, Jack.—Amelia needs a coat."

It was getting cold out, Susanne reported. Amelia said she already *had* a cold, and Susanne told her she had not, and to stop exaggerating. Susanne had brought some lunch, something from her own house made by her mother, and asked Jack if he wanted to join them, and Jack declined.

"We'll shut the kitchen door, Jack, so you won't hear any noise. You probably want to work," Susanne said.

Jack did. The two were going to take off after lunch.

"Oh, something in the mailbox downstairs, Jack. I'd have brought it, but I haven't the key now, you know."

"I got the mail this morning. Does it look important?" The mailbox had a flower-shaped design in its front through which one could see.

"Can't tell. White envelope. Want me to go down?"

"No, no, I'll go."

Jack went down out of curiosity. The envelope had no stamp and was addressed in longhand to John M. Sutherland with street address and zip code. He was about to open it, when he saw Mrs Farley on the sidewalk with her little two-wheel trolley full of groceries, so Jack carried it up the front steps for her, then up the first flight, because she lived on the second floor. Mrs Farley was over seventy, and lived alone.

"That's very kind of you, Mr Sutherland! My, you've got strength!"

"Huff! Puff! A pleasure, Mrs Farley!" Jack grinned. He made sure she got the trolley into her apartment hall, then went up the stairs.

The letter was from Ralph Linderman, Jack saw, and was handwritten. He began reading with a puzzled frown that deepened as he went on.

Sat. a.m.

Dear Mr Sutherland,

I think a letter to you is less of an intrusion than a telephone call and maybe also I can be clearer. This is about Elsie—I am sure you know her name by now—whom I saw coming out of your house with you yesterday. I do not know what went on between you. Elsie is a very impressionable young girl, very soft in the sense that her character is unformed. She can easily be led astray and it has already begun. She has recently—very recently—come to this big city, does not know how to protect herself, and I know she has already fallen into what by anybody's standards would be called bad company. I believe the girl with whom she shares an apartment is a common prostitute, though very young also. Elsie has not much money and you know the temptations.

You are a married man but many a married man has gotten in trouble, and not because he wanted to. Two things could happen. Elsie could try, in her ways, to get money from you, or one of the hoodlums she associates with could for some reason decide to attack you. Nothing is impossible in this huge city in which so many half-insane people live. I am thinking of the best interests of you and Elsie both. If I may say so, with no intrusion meant or offense meant, I think it is best if you and she do not see each other again.

I would like to say a few more words to you on the subject, if you are willing to listen. If not, please take my words here as they are meant—kindly, constructively, hopefully.

> *Yours sincerely,*
> *Ralph Linderman*

The old guy was full of wild imaginings, with a salacious slant to them. The letter made Jack feel uneasy, somehow menaced. It was on two sides of a sheet of typewriter paper, which most people didn't have in the house, Jack thought. Was Ralph Linderman writing fiction in his spare time? Essays on morals? His handwriting was smallish, legible, all letters in each word connected.

The thing to do was ignore it, Jack thought. Attention, more talk was just what the old guy wanted. But it irked Jack that Ralph Linderman seemed to be patroling the neighborhood, even to Jack's very doorstep. Jack had no plan to ask Elsie to come and sit for him, but suppose he had? Who was this nut to make a fuss about it? Ralph Linderman had not put a return address on the envelope. Jack went to the telephone book and looked up Linderman. Rather to his surprise, since he hadn't expected Linderman to have a private telephone, he found a Linderman, Ralph W., on Bleecker Street, where Elsie had said he lived. It gave a degree of respectability to Linderman, and Jack didn't like even that.

Jack had thought of telling Natalia that evening about Elsie and her surprise visit, and her connection with the man who had returned his wallet, but he hadn't told her, because they had talked so much about the play *Fool for Love*, which Natalia had liked more than he. But Jack felt that if he told Natalia about Elsie, and then about Linderman's letter of this morning, it might be only disturbing to Natalia, and not funny enough to warrant telling for amusement value.

He remembered a morning about three weeks ago, when he and Amelia had gone out together to buy something at Rossi's, and Amelia had suddenly pointed a finger and said, "Look! There's that man you *drew*, Daddy! With the dog!" And so it had been, Ralph Linderman across the street (Bleecker) watching God lifting his leg. "You're not going to say hello to him?" Jack had replied, no, not now, and had tugged his daughter along.

Ralph kept odd hours. That was an added nuisance, making

66

Jack think of a three-man, round-the-clock, eight-hour-shift eye on him. The girl Elsie kept odd hours. But matter of fact, so did he, working sometimes till 2 a.m., and if he felt hungry, he went out for a hamburger at some all-night place in the neighborhood.

Jack decided to ignore Ralph Linderman, pretend not to see him or hear him, if Linderman tried to talk to him on the street. Linderman would tire of the game, maybe switch to someone else Elsie might be seeing.

Since Ralph Linderman seemed to walk God along Bedford, Jack began to avoid that street on his morning runs, which he did not take every day anyway, and head west for Hudson on Grove. And sometimes Natalia was in the mood in the early mornings, came half awake and awakened him with a slide of her arm across his waist, a part of his body—of all places—which was the most erotogenic for him, at least at the beginning of things. Often Natalia fell into sound sleep afterward, which pleased Jack because it made him think he had pleased her, and he would awaken her later with a cup of black coffee, if she had to get up for some reason, and otherwise let her sleep until she awakened.

The following week brought a small disappointment and a small note of cheer. The disappointment was that the book offered to Jack to illustrate was vulgar, strained and unfunny, in Jack's opinion. This was from another publishing house called Flagship. It was nothing more than a joke book—Joel's *Half-Understood Dreams* was a novel by comparison—so Jack declined politely. A glance at the manuscript or joke pages in the office was enough. One of the jokes had a crude pun on the word cockpit. John Sutherland's drawings were supposed to make and sell the book, Jack supposed. Surely Trews hadn't known what junk it was. Jack did not like the editor with whom he had to speak either, or maybe by association with the joke book did not like him, so Jack wildly elevated his prices. "I'm asking a thousand a drawing now, plus royalties to be adjusted, and . . ." Did the editor believe him? His eyes went wide, anyway, and perhaps the news of his price would get around, which, as Natalia would say, wouldn't hurt. Jack decided not to mention this hiccup to Trews, unless Trews asked him about the Flagship interview.

The bright spot was a postcard from Elaine and Max Armstrong, their favorite neighbors, who lived on West Eleventh

Street. They were coming back from Paris in early November and wrote that they hoped Natalia and Jack would be on Grove. Max was a lawyer, nearly forty, and had been sent to Paris for four months by his firm. The Armstrongs had a six-year-old son, Jason, a fact which had led to their meeting the Armstrongs at the Little People's Theatre in the Village. Elaine worked for an interior decorating company, and was several years younger than Max. It was Max's second marriage.

"I missed them," Natalia said a few minutes after she had read their postcard. She said it in the earnest way she had sometimes, frowning a little, not looking at Jack, as if she were thinking out loud. At such uncomplicated moments, Jack adored her.

She had made an equally simple remark about the Shepard play, *Fool for Love*. "I can see how a half-brother and half-sister could be in love more intensely than people who aren't related." Natalia thought there was a strong drive toward incest in everyone, which was why a tabu had been put upon it. She spoke of little siblings crawling around on the floor together, and Jack remarked that in the play the two hadn't met till they were about fifteen. "They still knew then that they were half-brother and -sister," Natalia had said, "and what I'm talking about is as primitive as sibling kittens mating as soon as they're able to." Jack understood her words, but did not understand the emotion she was talking about, not when it was attached to people. That often happened to him with Natalia.

Natalia spent as much of her spare time away from him as with him, Jack thought. There was always Louis Wannfeld on business trips to Philadelphia and New York, so that when Jack thought Louis was in one city, he might be in the other, and maybe Natalia was too, and seeing Louis not deliberately but because Louis happened to be around. Natalia came home at 2 and 3 in the morning after evenings with Louis "out somewhere", or at Louis' apartment, but if she felt tired the next morning, she could call Isabel, who was usually at the gallery by 10, and say she didn't feel like coming in till 2 p.m., and Isabel was never annoyed as far as Jack could tell. Jack could have accompanied Natalia on the Louis evenings, he knew, but he also knew that Louis' group was mainly all men, and that meant homosexuals, with whom Jack felt a bit odd-man-out.

"We don't talk about sex—or tell jokes," Natalia said rather defensively to Jack. "In fact there's more talk about sex and more advances made at straight parties, if you ask me."

They talked about everything but sex, according to Natalia. But they (the boys) always liked a girl or two around, or an older woman. Natalia an older woman at twenty-eight! On the other hand, Jack had learned that some of the boys were twenty. Jack was not really annoyed, or resentful, because the terms of their marriage had been that both should show respect for independence, avoid "feeling stuck together," as Natalia had put it. Intellectually, logically, Jack did agree that this was a good idea. For one thing, it staved off boredom with each other, and might prevent it entirely. Before their marriage, Jack had made a promise about this kind of independence, and he was not going to go back on it. Another element, which Jack could not complain about, was that it left him more time alone in which to work.

Unbeknownst to Natalia, who respected his creative efforts and never demanded to see what he had been doing lately, Jack was trying his mostly elongated weirdo personages on canvas in acrylic. They looked rather good in pale, pastel colors, with the finest of black outlines, sometimes incomplete outlines. Of course he could not even with a fine brush get the speed of a pen. But his ten or so efforts were not bad, he thought, and he especially liked one he called "The Suicide", which depicted a figure of indeterminate sex bending over a nearly full bathtub and clutching a rope, a straight razor, and a bouquet of flowers.

Even avoiding Bedford Street, Jack spotted Ralph Linderman one morning as he, Jack, was loping around the corner of Hudson into Barrow Street. Linderman was just then crossing Barrow, with God on the leash, of course, toward the north side of Barrow, saw Jack and called from the sidewalk, "Oh, Mr Sutherland! May I have a . . ."

Jack ran on up the clear sidewalk opposite Linderman, as if he had heard nothing. It had been two weeks, maybe more, since Linderman's letter, which Jack had torn up and thrown away.

9

THE latter part of October and early November brought nothing but unpleasant shocks in the life of Ralph Linderman. In October, he received a telegram saying that his mother had died of a heart attack and that his "services were needed". He was to communicate with "undersigned Mabel Haskins", who had sent her telephone number. Ralph recognized her name, had even met her, he thought. She was his mother's closest neighbor and best friend in the last years. So Ralph telephoned and learned that his mother had lain nearly twenty-four hours on the floor of her living-room before she was discovered by Mabel and the house superintendent who had a key. Ralph should come at once, if he wished to attend the funeral.

Ralph didn't want to attend the funeral, but he notified the Midtown garage of his sudden call of duty, and went to New Hampshire, only to find that his mother had been buried six hours before. The coroner came especially to see him at his mother's apartment. Her funeral arrangements had been taken care of according to her insurance and health policies. The funeral had been done nicely, said Mabel Haskins, who was with Ralph when the coroner arrived. Ralph had papers to sign, which he did. What Mabel Haskins knew of his mother's affairs was little, but better than nothing. She knew where his mother had kept her checkbook, and it seemed there were only a couple of little bills to pay in the neighborhood. Ralph had to arrange for his mother's furniture—none of which was worth much—to be auctioned or given to the Salvation Army. Mrs Haskins kindly invited him to stay the night at her house—she was a widow too and had a spare room—so Ralph did. He could not get to sleep for his thoughts, the strange room, the fact that he was not used to sleeping at night anyway, but no matter. He had requested an extra day to wind it all up. Somehow he still owed eleven hundred dollars on his mother's expenses for the funeral, toward which he signed a two-hundred-dollar check, with a promise to pay the rest within a month. There was a little jewelry, and Ralph hesitated, then decided to keep a ring he remembered, and for which his mother's fingers had probably grown too knobby in the last many years. Ralph emphatically did not want any of his father's jewelry, no tie pin, no cufflinks. He gave various things to Mrs Haskins, whatever she could use or even sell. She was a bent but spry little woman. One of her brown eyes was clouded over, due to an injury, she said. In the end, he was grateful for her help. After two days, he hadn't even visited his mother's grave, because he didn't want to. In the two (almost) sleepless nights, Ralph had stared at a dark and creamy ceiling corner of his room, and recalled that when he had been ten and twelve, he had loved his mother, had been even jealous of his father, because of his mother's affection for his father. Then his mother had seemed to spurn him when he was about twelve, and Ralph had been deeply hurt, and had kept the hurt to himself. She had continued to take care of him, preparing his meals and all that, but Ralph had sensed a terrible coldness. He had got over this by pretending to hate his mother for a while, though he had never really hated her. When he had become eighteen, and had gone to college for a while, he had realized his mother's limitations, and then he had decided to accept her as she was, and to do his duty by her also, when his father had died. But love her? Not any more. She had forced him to go to church, too, prodding him even when he had been fifteen and more. Even his father had begged out on many a Sunday, with one feeble excuse or another. His mother had contributed to his hating the church, which had been all to the good. Only when his father had died, and Ralph had had to leave college and take a job, had he refused to set foot in church again, any church. What had the church to do with morals? Very little, and that more honored in the breach than in the observance. Ralph could see that the church gave people a nice funeral service when they died, made the people attending feel they were doing the right thing, showing respect for the dead. Well and good. But the church throughout history had twisted right and wrong to suit itself, had usually sucked up to the powers-that-be, which meant the church had been anti-poor a lot of the time, to maintain social order.

Now the well-to-do in America were all church-goers, proper looking WASPS, and God was a sandwich-man advertising the Republican party. Filthy business! Only Poland seemed different, where the church was a fighting faction. Such thoughts ran through Ralph's head in the wee hours when the winter dawn broke dismally and late through the unfamiliar windows.

"I don't believe in an afterlife," Ralph said after some particularly boring remark from Mrs Haskins. "And it's barbaric to embalm corpses and put 'em in thick coffins, when they won't keep anyway and—fire is more sanitary and ashes take up less room."

Mrs Haskins told him he was just a bit upset.

The next jolt had come one night at the Midtown-Parking garage, when two blacks and a third fellow who looked more Hispanic than black, had opened the door of the glass office where Ralph had been standing. One had pointed a gun at him.

"Open the cash box or you'll get it! Now!"

Another had giggled nervously, but they had stood like three statues, each with one sneakered foot forward, concentrated on him, and it wouldn't have been wise to open the drawer and pull out one of the guns then. Joey had just gone to the mid-point in the wall of the long garage where the toilet was, and the trio must have observed this. Ralph had backed a step toward the desk, where the desk met the wall, and pressed a button with his right hand. The bell was the silent one, which summoned the police.

"Don't move!" another of the youths said, jutting his pocket forward as if he had a gun in it.

"I didn't move. There's the cash," Ralph had said with a nod at the cash register that stood on another table more to the front of the office, and if they all focused on the cash register, or shot it open, Ralph intended to pull a gun on them.

Then Joey came at a run, the trio looked at him, and Ralph picked up a gun and pushed the safety off. The three fled like lightning out of the office and around to the left, as a police siren sounded.

That was that. Nothing had happened. The police took Ralph's story. Joey had seen them too. How did one describe apes? Short curly black hair, all about eighteen maybe. Not even their blue jeans, sneakers and black plastic waist-length jackets provided any useful clue, because their clothing was like a uniform. Their gun might have been phony, Ralph thought, but didn't bother saying so, because lots of phony-looking guns were real, and vice versa.

Nothing had really happened, yet that incident seemed more real to Ralph than his mother's death and absence now. The cops' arrival—that too—had been real. Ralph had not been praised by anybody, perhaps he didn't merit praise, but he had done the right thing. The invasion had been real, or at least he realized that it had been real.

But his mother's death, no. She was just someone he would not have to write to once or twice a month. He would miss her, though she had so seldom written to him, and her letters had been all alike and boring when she had. The eleven hundred dollars that he had to pay were not a nuisance to him; rather he felt a bit ashamed and heartless when he wrote the check for the nine hundred that remained due, as if he were paying off something, saying farewell to his mother in a cold way.

Another worrisome thing in his thoughts now was the girl Elsie and to a lesser extent the young man John M. Sutherland, whom Ralph had thought so highly of just a few months ago. Elsie might already have sunk to the depths, probably had, but she was rescuable, because of her youth. He only hoped that she did not become pregnant, and did not contract some awful venereal disease like syphilis (said to be curable, Ralph knew) or herpes which was incurable, Ralph thought, or the latest called AIDS, which homosexuals could pass on to normal people. These days everything was mixed, homosexuals often had wives, few people seemed to love anybody or stay with any one person. Take John Sutherland. Ralph was not sure about his promiscuity, but he had a flashy and egocentric look, in Ralph's opinion. He had not replied to Ralph's letter—though Ralph realized after he had dropped the letter into Sutherland's box that he had not written his address on the back—and Sutherland had purposely ignored him when Ralph had tried to get his attention on the street. Ralph had taken pains with his letter, and the letter had been courteous. If Mr Sutherland were not up to something with Elsie, why hadn't he said as much, been willing to speak with him on the street? Or he could have opened the telephone book and found his name and communicated somehow, but he hadn't.

These matters of Elsie's and of John Sutherland's welfare presented problems of differing sizes, Elsie's being by far the larger,

Sutherland's like a little cloud no bigger than a man's hand, as the good book said somewhere. Elsie he had seen twice in the past three weeks, though even glimpsing her had been difficult. She was still working at the coffee shop down on Seventh Avenue, though her hours seemed to change all the time. Not only that, but she could duck back in the kitchen when she saw him come in, or she would ask another girl to serve him coffee or whatever. *Oh, knock it off!* she had said with a frown the first of the two times he had spoken to her, and she had avoided serving him then. Ralph had noticed the two other girl waitresses exchanging smiles, and he wondered if they knew more than he did about Elsie's nocturnal or anytime activities? The second time, when he had repeatedly and softly called her name, trying to get her to pause for half a minute, she had finally stood in front of him and said across the counter, *You mind your own business or I'll get the cops. This isn't funny any more.* And she had said something else about speaking to the manager who was back in the kitchen (Ralph didn't believe there was any manager in the kitchen), and seeing that he was not allowed into the shop. That was regrettable. But people who needed guidance, a word of advice, always put up a stonewall resistance. If he'd been preaching Jesus' footsteps or some such, he could have understood her telling him to get lost, but what he had to offer was commonsense. She was so vulnerable! Ralph felt angry when he thought of her behind that counter at all hours, 5 or 6 p.m. till 2 a.m., or 8 a.m. until 4 p.m., young and pretty, radiating health and innocence. Innocence! Always the magnet for the sexually sick boys and men who ogled her. Ralph had seen the leers by day and by night! He had seen Elsie pause to laugh with some of these characters, seen her flip the wet cloth she wiped the counter with into the faces of these boys and men who would nearly fall off their stools with delight at her attention. All of them trying to make dates with her, and Ralph had no doubt she did make a few dates. If she finished work at 2 a.m., it was easy to imagine her going for a drink somewhere with one of the toughs, who would want to walk her home. And then? Ralph had discovered where she lived, on Minetta Street, and had seen the girl with whom she lived. Ralph had seen Elsie and another girl coming out of the supermarket on Sixth Avenue one Saturday when he hadn't been working, and he had followed them to the Minetta Street house. The other girl looked about twenty-

74

five, was taller than Elsie, had dark reddish hair and her garb made her look like something out of a Turkish harem, billowy pink pants tied in at the ankles by chains, golden pointed slippers—in October—and the general look of a whore. Maybe the long-haired young woman ran a call-girl business on Minetta Street, and Elsie picked up extra money as one of her girls. Ralph recalled seeing a horrid green on the harem girl's eyelids, or had it been purple? Perhaps left over from the night before. Anyway, she had looked unwashed, and Ralph couldn't have cared less about her. Elsie was different, had been different that Saturday, bouncing along in her white tennis shoes, even though both her arms had been full of grocery bags, engrossed in conversation with the Turkish-harem girl. Ralph had thought Elsie might hand the girl the sacks and say good-bye at the door, but Elsie had gone into the house with the girl and with the air of living there. Before this, Elsie had lived on King Street, he knew from having followed her a couple of times, and then somewhere on Eighth Street for a couple of weeks, at someone else's apartment, of course. A man's or a woman's apartment on Eighth Street? Ralph had never learned. How could a young girl have any sense of home, respectability, security, hopping around like that?

To cap all this negativity, this long season of wrongness, Ralph discovered that someone had scooped him on one of his inventions. This was a cheap and simple way to take salt out of sea water. There was a diagram in the *Times*, much as Ralph had drawn his own four or maybe six years ago in his notebook. An inlet of *warm* salt water, yes, indeed, from near the surface, this passing through a heat chamber which converted it to steam, the vacuum which Ralph had thought of, of course, to decrease air pressure and make the water come to a steam point sooner. Of course, it required a generator and a turbine, which Ralph had included also, and these were in the drawing in the newspaper. Ralph's own drawing and notes were in one of his unruled, blank-page notebooks on a shelf above his table. He could have found the sketch easily, if he guessed the year. Ralph didn't bother. His fault, of course, for not making a little model, however faulty, and sending it into the patent office in Washington. How many times had this happened? Five, six? Ralph didn't care to reckon. It would only have made him angrier.

He had some white paint in the house and he bought more,

enamel paint. On his two free days in the middle of the week, he repainted both his bookcases, and dusted his books and notebooks and old magazines, and while waiting for the paint to dry, cleared out his upper shelves in the kitchen and washed them, and was about to repaint them completely, too, but did only the outside. These shelves were fixed to the wall. He must still have looked rather grim, because Johnny at the grocery store said when he walked in: "Don't give me no lectures this afternoon, Mr Linderman. I ain't in the mood. And I been good, I swear!" Laughing, Johnny made the sign of the cross on his breast. "No foolin' around with girls, I swear!"

"Who said anything about a lecture, Johnny?" Ralph replied, trying hard to smile too.

"Ah jus' believes in God. *God!*" Johnny laughed again, leaning over the counter, watching the dog strain at the leash and wag his tail.

10

"WELL, we did sit through it," Natalia said as they came out of the Waverly Theater 2 at close to midnight.

"Yep. Bad idea of mine," Jack said. "Sorry."

"At least there was some action in the last ten minutes.—I was so bored with that woman, the wife! You can't care about the story if the main character's a weak fish. D'you think?"

"What story, in fact?"

They were strolling toward home. They had just seen a German film, touted to be good, whose story was about two women who developed "a sustaining friendship".

"You notice that the husbands were all dimwits?" Jack asked. "Just backdrops labeled 'husbands'?"

"That was deliberate. Gad, all this crap about the sex war—or rivalry. It's so old hat." She was walking tensely, glancing at him as she talked, looking away.

"Want a nightcap somewhere?—Big evening!" Jack laughed. Susanne had their little one in charge at her family's apartment on Riverside Drive tonight, so they didn't have to rush home.

"Dunno," said Natalia, as if she were thinking about something else. "Let's just walk a little."

A couple of minutes later, Natalia said with the frown with which she often proposed something cheerful, "Let's go in here. Have a drink or something."

She had stopped at a depression in the sidewalk. Steps led down, disco music throbbed. They went in. Jack read BIRD'S NEST in green letters on black above the curtained door. The place was small, darkish, and rather full of people. A purple light pulsed off and on, and during its off second the place was totally dark.

"Sit?" Natalia shouted. "Let's stand up!" She headed for the bar to the left. She wanted a Ballantine's.

Jack yelled her order. "And a beer! Bud!"

The dancing was lively. Young people in blue jeans, a black couple, a pair of gay boys, two figures dancing on their own, and two or three swingers who were not so young. A red-headed girl in tight white trousers was blowing her energy like a bomb. The red hair was Afro-style, big as a pillow.

"Dance?" Jack asked Natalia.

"In a minute." She sipped her drink.

"You picked a good place!"

"Didn't I?— Look at *that!*" Natalia crumpled with laughter, and pointed toward the door.

A young man was being ousted in classic manner, the bouncer having grabbed the seat of his pants in a way that looked as if it hurt, while his other hand gripped the back of the fellow's sweater. Hard to throw a fellow *up* the stairs, Jack thought.

"That redhead—" Natalia leaned toward Jack, though she watched the dancers. "What do you think she's high on?—She's a *very* good dancer."

The girl was dancing with a slender boy who was a good dancer himself and looked Puerto Rican. Some of the crowd was watching them, clapping in time with the music. Something about the girl's profile reminded Jack of Elsie, though she spun so fast, he couldn't really see her.

"*Go, boy!*" someone yelled.

A male dancer fell, rolled into a couple of chairs and nearly upset a table, and did upset a couple of drinks.

Wau-wau-wau ... The electronic music meted out its beat, and like the film they had just seen, showed no sign of ending, and had no discernible direction. Natalia succumbed to it, and they moved onto a clear place on the floor. Natalia still wore her top-coat. It didn't matter. Jack leapt straight up several times, because it felt good. The redheaded girl was swinging her head from side to side as she danced, hard enough to break her neck, it seemed to Jack. Suddenly, when she was just four feet away from him, he saw that she *was* Elsie with a crazy wig on. Elsie's blue eyes spotted him, she nodded quickly and her parted lips spread.

The music grew fainter. That particular number was over, though the beat, like a heart machine that couldn't stop or even slow down, kept on and on.

78

Elsie was stopping. She walked off on high heels, smiling, with one arm casually around the waist of the dark-haired boy who tried to kiss Elsie's lips and made it to her cheek. Elsie whipped off her wig as she moved out of the dance floor's lights into the shadows of the tables by the walls.

"She's a blonde," Natalia said, gazing at Elsie. "Cute as can be!"

"Isn't she?" Jack found his heart beating hard, not entirely from dancing. Funny. Elsie just might come over and say hello, he thought. That would be like her. Maybe it would be like her, he wasn't sure. In that case, he would tell Natalia that he had met the girl in a coffee shop on Seventh Avenue. Jack realized that he didn't want to tell Natalia, now in all this noise, that Elsie had been up to their apartment.

Their drinks were standing where they had left them.

Jack wondered if the Latin-type fellow were Elsie's latest heartthrob? Small wonder old Linderman had his worries!

"What're you smiling at?" Natalia asked.

"That girl," Jack replied, as the music boomed up again. "She works at a *hamburger* place down on Seventh. I've seen her before." He had to shout.

Natalia nodded, then stepped closer to Jack and the bar counter. "*Hamburger* place!—She's a show-stopper!"

Jack said nothing. He saw one black fellow at the table where Elsie sat, and one girl who had long dark hair, unless that was a wig also.

"Shall we push off? Or do you want another beer?" Natalia asked.

They left.

That same week, on Friday evening, Jack and Natalia were invited to the Armstrongs' for dinner. Jack liked the Armstrong house, a long semi-basement apartment with a garden in back in which Max and Elaine grew vegetables, if they felt like it. The garden had rosebushes, and a couple of apple trees, and a terrace of modest size where the Armstrongs could do barbecues. The house—it merited the name—looked as if it had been lived in for decades instead of the three or four years the Armstrongs had been here. The sofa was sagging a little, so were the armchairs. Max and Elaine had bought most of their stuff second-hand.

"After what I have to work with all day, I prefer to look at

79

orange-crate bookcases,'' Elaine had said once, referring to her interior decorating work.

Their fireplace in the front room, where the sagging sofa lived, worked beautifully and had not been built yesterday. The Armstrongs had a fire going, and potatoes in foil baking near the embers. The kids played, yelling at each other in Jason's room, where Elaine said Jason had laid out his train tracks on the floor. Jack heard, over the yelling, the bleep of an electronic game. The four adults had drinks in the fireplace room. Max had put charcoal on for the steaks, and the meal was up to him, he told Jack, so Jack went with him into the kitchen. Natalia and Elaine seemed deep in conversation on the sofa.

"How do they always find something to talk about?" Jack asked.

"Who?"

"The girls." Jack gestured behind him. "Sometimes I wish I had the knack."

"Really do you?—I don't. It's exhausting." Max picked up salt and vinegar and pulled a salad bowl toward him.

Jack got the lettuce from the sink, stuck it into a lettuce swinger and went out onto the garden terrace.

"Hey, Daddy, my cassette player won't start!" Six-year-old Jason stood in the kitchen door, brown hair tousled, frowning.

"Well, Daddy's not going to fool with it now. How much noise are you trying to make, anyway?"

Jason turned and ran like a soldier, as if his father had given him orders.

Max was now stirring his dressing. "How's Natalia liking the gallery job?"

Jack said very much, and reminded Max that she had worked for Isabel before.

"And Louis? I forget his last name. Natalia's old friend."

"Wannfeld. He's fine. Natalia sees him now and then." Jack wasn't going to mention the cancer scare, because it seemed to have blown over. Louis hadn't cancer after all. Max never talked about his own work. "My little company protects big companies," Max had said once with a smile, wanting to get off the subject. Max did like painting, music, and Jack's cartoons and drawings too, and was more forthcoming on the arts.

Now Max was settling the steak between the two sides of the

steel grill which had a long handle. "And old Mrs Farley?" he asked, smiling. "Isn't that her name? Lives on the floor below you?"

"Yep, she's still there. Remember that afternoon when we lifted her over the snow? Out of that taxi?" Jack laughed. Max and he had been shoveling snow from the front steps, when a taxi with Mrs Farley inside had arrived at the curb, and they had carried her, packages and all, over a barricade of curb snow and up the front steps and deposited her safe and dry in the front hall.

"Sure I remember," Max said. "Loved it!"

In emergencies, such as snowfalls, Max and Jack helped each other on their respective properties. Max was over six feet and strongly built, with Irish good looks, Jack thought, though he was only half-Irish. He had long eyelashes, a strong jaw, and was the type of man Jack assumed women would label sexy, though when he had asked Natalia once if she thought Max had sex appeal, she had said, "Max? Not for me." Funny, Jack thought. *You're sexy*, Natalia had added. *Not that you look so sexy, you* are *sexy, which is more important.* Yes, it was more important, if it came from Natalia. Jack suddenly thought of Elsie, the whirling dervish on the dance floor, and of the oddball Ralph Linderman. He wished he could forget the name, but it stuck in his memory.

"Say, Max—"

"Can you bring the salad in, Jack?"

Jack carried the salad bowl and set it on the table as they walked through the dining room. Max had the big steak.

"And turn the spuds if you can do it barehanded. What were you going to say?"

They sat on their heels before the fire.

"Have you possibly noticed a guy in his mid-fifties in the neighborhood, walking a black and white dog?"

"Dalmatian?"

"Maybe part, but this one's a mongrel. This fellow walks his dog at six or so when I go jogging sometimes, or it could be at any hour, because he's a security guard. Anyway he's slightly nutty. Avoid him if he tries to talk to you. He lives down on Bleecker, so maybe he doesn't get as far up as Eleventh."

"Tries to talk to you?"

"Yeah," said Jack with a grimace. "The funny thing is, I lost

81

my wallet getting out of a taxi in front of my house, and this guy called me up and returned it about an hour later and wouldn't take a reward."

Max took his eyes from the steak. "With the money in it?"

"Every dollar. He said it was normal to return something you'd found." Jack gave a laugh. "Then he launched into a speech about—old-fashioned honesty and all that. But he's very anti-church, anti-religion."

"Very odd," Max said, turning the steak. "But lucky for you."

Elaine and Natalia were out of hearing on the big sofa, still talking, feet drawn up on the cushions.

"I suppose the guy enjoyed getting your wallet back to you," Max said, smiling.

"Oh, definitely. I could see that." Jack felt better, having told Max the story and having warned Max to keep a distance. It was like shedding part of a burden. Yet what was the burden in Linderman?

"Penny for your thoughts, Jack," Elaine said.

Jack was standing with a platter of hot potatoes in foil. "Just daydreaming," he said.

Jack hadn't seen the women move, but an oilcloth had been spread on the living-room carpet, plates and cutlery set for the two kids, mugs of milk.

"You can see all the spill problems this solves," Max said to Jack. "Anyway anything else that happens to that carpet won't matter much."

The four of them went into the dining room. Jack stood near the table, watching Natalia, adoring the tone of her voice. She had brought the rest of her scotch and water with her.

"And you there, Jack, as usual," Elaine said, pointing to a chair. "Sit down, you two!"

"HEY!—Hello!" Elsie was suddenly beside him.

"Hi!" said Jack, surprised.

They were walking on Seventh Avenue, and Jack was heading for the drugstore on Grove and Seventh.

She came into the drugstore with him, hands in the slash pockets of her jacket, a U.S. Navy pea jacket today. "I was going to call you up."

"Oh?—Mind if I pick a toothbrush?" Jack chose a red one, small size, for Amelia. He also had to buy aspirins.

"Yes," Elsie went on. "It's about that pest—Ralph. It's getting worse. He keeps coming into the place where I work, and Viv, the manager, can't throw him out because he's not drunk or anything." She went on talking as Jack paid. "We got rid of him once, because Viv laid down the law about not letting him in with his dog."

Jack was listening. They drifted toward the door.

"I was going to ask you if you'd *say* something to him—about this. Ask him to leave me alone. I could lose my job over this. And I don't want to lose it because the hours are nice and the people're nice.—He'd listen to you. He thinks you're great. Oh! And he knows I went up to your place once! How's that for spying on me?" She stamped a foot with impatience. "If you could just tell him I'm not a—a house-hopping hooker—" She looked straight at Jack, frowning.

Jack nodded, trying to envisage a quiet word with Linderman the next time Linderman wished to engage him in conversation. "Okay, Elsie, I'll try. I promise."

"Thanks. Thanks a lot.—Come with me, I just want to show you!" She took Jack's arm impulsively, and turned him in the downtown direction.

"Show me what?"

"I live just down here. Not far. Got five minutes?"

"Yep." Jack went with her. They crossed Seventh, walked past Jones Street in the direction of Father Demo Square, finally into Minetta Lane.

"Here's my street. Minetta Street."

They walked to a three-storey house with a front step, a brick house painted red. Elsie drew keys from the pocket of her blue jeans.

"Come up for a minute."

"No, I can see. It's a nice looking house."

"Nobody's home now.—I came up to *your* place," she added on a challenging note. "I just want you to see! You don't even have to sit down!"

Jack relented, smiling. "Okay, Elsie."

They climbed stairs, and she opened another door with a key.

"Here's where I live now with Genevieve," Elsie said, going in first, turning in the middle of a somewhat overfurnished living-room.

The ceiling was low, the two windows looked out on Minetta Street. There was a sofa with a dark red drape of some kind over it, modern armchairs with the black paint scratched as if by cats, though Jack didn't see a cat. The small fireplace looked as if it were never used, and had a skull-and-crossbones poster propped up in it. There were lots of books.

"And here's the bedroom," Elsie said cheerily, leading the way through a hall past kitchen and bathroom to a room at the back. This room was more than half taken up by a bed that looked like two double beds put together. Several Indian print counterpanes covered this, and the walls were papered with posters of pop singers, female nudes, a VOTE FOR somebody whose name and face Jack did not recognize.

"I see," said Jack. "Very cozy."

"And the kitchen—Maybe you saw it." Elsie gestured. "I ask you, does this look like a whorehouse? Genevieve's got a nine to five job! And I go to work before six today. Does this creep think we lie around doping ourselves all day, screwing men for dough!" Her resentment seemed to have mounted with the showing of her apartment. "Talk to him, tell him to fuck off, would you?"

84

Jack gave a nod. "I do promise. I will."

She relaxed visibly. "You mean it."

"I do." He was near the apartment door now, and he turned to say good-bye.

"Otherwise I'm thinking of getting the police after him," Elsie went on. "Any boys or men who come to our place don't stay the night. Fellows visit, sure, but Genevieve's my girlfriend just now. We don't fool around. She doesn't even like boys."

"Um. Girlfriend," Jack said matter of factly, recalling his visible surprise about Sylvia, and not wanting to repeat it. "Yes," he added.

"Yes, she's gay. So'm I—just now. I used to like boys a little, but not just now." She made an impatient dismissing gesture with one hand that Jack had noticed before. "Maybe I won't like Genevieve for long, but—while it lasts, I mean." She removed her jacket and tossed it onto the sofa, making a complete turn on her toes as she did so. Her happy smile was back, her brow clear. "I just want to enjoy my life! You know?"

"Yes." Jack knew. "Thanks for asking me up." He opened the door.

She came down the stairs with him. "Was that your wife the other night at that disco?"

"Yes," Jack said, smiling.

"She looks interesting. Different—y'know?" Elsie spoke as if she meant it. "Is she a writer?"

"No. But she reads a lot.—Bye, Elsie!"

Jack took a homeward direction. Elsie could look so intense, so earnest! Those trembling, thin blond eyebrows, the pale-blue stare! Very soon Jack was in Linderman's street. Linderman's house number had gone out of his head, and so much the better. If he encountered the old guy now, at ten to 4, he would have a word with him and get it over with, calmly and politely. Jack kept an eye out for Linderman, and when he neared Grove Street looked also for a girl or woman who might be approaching, walking Amelia home from the West Twelfth Street school, though it was a bit early. It was an extra service that he and Natalia paid for, the walking home of Amelia, though he or Natalia, usually he, took her in the mornings more or less at 9 o'clock. Sometimes Jack telephoned the school at half past 3 and said he would pick Amelia up. By the time Jack got to Grove Street, he had not spotted Linderman or Amelia with her warden, so he went on home.

Yesterday and today he had been working on pen and ink spots. He had done five yesterday and two so far today, in his preferred manner with no pencil preparation. His spots looked different to him now, and not bad. A couple of times a month, Jack peddled his portfolio to magazine offices, left some of his stuff, and returned a week or so later to get the results. Now suddenly he was not in the mood to do another spot.

So Elsie was gay! Amazing. Even more amazing when Jack thought of the closet he had just seen in the bedroom on Minetta Street, three yards long and crammed with frothy dresses, long skirts of every color imaginable. The floor of the closet had been full of high-heeled shoes, gilded slippers, sandals with straps that appeared to go up to the wearer's knees, sexy high boots. A lavender ostrich feather had leaned in a corner of the bedroom. Gay. Was Linderman onto *that*? Jack certainly wasn't going to enlighten him. Linderman seemed to be warning Elsie against prostitution. Jack now saw Elsie's enormous bed in a different light. Elsie and the girl called Genevieve made love on that broad Elysian field.

From a corner of his worktable Jack pulled out a rectangle of sleek red paper. Jack had a small collection of such paper which would not take ink or pencil, but would take grease pencils. Such paper came from the covers of company stock report magazines that arrived addressed to Natalia usually, though Jack got a few. Jack tore off the glossy covers, some of which had blank sides. Now he took a yellow grease pencil and drew a dancing female nude composed of curves and near circles. The hip curves turned inward at the waist, the head was a curve inclining left, the figure stood on one foot, while the other foot touched nothing. He drew the shoulder and arm on both sides in curves that made breasts. Tight and hot, Jack thought, pleased. While the yellow grease was wet and even removable with his thumb, if he had wished to remove it, he rubbed the tip of his forefinger along every line, softening it. It was like sculpting. Now it was finished, a portrait of Elsie, dancing. He propped it up at the back of his worktable. In fifteen or twenty minutes, it would be quite dry. The hint of short hair was good, flaring out with the swirl of motion. No facial features. Still, it was Elsie.

The doorbell sounded. Amelia had arrived.

12

IN the next several mornings, Jack did not happen to see Ralph Linderman when he went jogging. Jack was doing his jogging or running later, because the dawn came ever later, and maybe Linderman was earlier than he, airing God after he got home from work when it was still dark.

In November, Jack began work on an assignment that Trews had offered him. This was an account of a long hike in Tibet and over its mountains by a young American who had camped out among peasants and survived dangerous days alone and lost in freezing temperatures. Jack went to the Public Library on 42nd Street for picture research. Trews wanted his fantasy figures, his oddball types, but Jack still had to find out what a cooking pot looked like in Tibet, and even a yak, not to mention what the local clothing looked like.

Jack had not thought of Linderman in days, when he suddenly saw him at close range in Rossi's grocery store, with a couple of cans in one hand and God's leash in the other. Miles away in thought at the time, Jack felt a small shock, and moved his head in a way that was not quite a nod when Linderman saw him. Jack concentrated on the display of cold cuts behind the glass. There were a couple of other customers in the store. Linderman seemed to be waiting his turn to pay.

"Afternoon, Mr Sutherland," said Linderman.

"Good afternoon, sir," Jack replied. He remembered his promise to Elsie. He gave his order to the elder Rossi: a half-pound of gorgonzola and a quarter-pound of salami sliced as thinly as possible.

Linderman assembled his purchases on the counter, and Johnny Rossi took his money. Then Linderman came over to Jack, carrying his brown paper bag. "I did want to have a word with you, Mr Sutherland. I'd like to explain myself better." Linderman's voice was soft and serious.

Jack felt boredom already, swift and paralysing. Get it over with, he told himself. "Yes. Well—I'll be through here in a minute." Jack did not like the two Rossis even knowing that he was acquainted with Linderman. Jack paid.

Then they were out on the sidewalk, in the cool sunshine.

"I don't think I made myself very clear in my letter to you," Linderman went on. "Maybe I offended you. I really didn't mean to, but I must have or you would have answered. I realized later that I hadn't put my address down—on the letter—"

"You didn't offend me. Certainly not." Jack glanced at Linderman's heavy face, the creases down both cheeks, the self-righteous brown eyes. Linderman had shaved today. "The girl you mentioned—Elsie, she has a job, you know. She's not wasting her time—in the way you seem to think. If she's up late, well, she's just enjoying herself. Like all young people."

Linderman shook his head as if Jack were quite off the track. "I realize she's young. That's why she's worth trying to help.—Oh, excuse me, please."

God was going to do something, and Linderman carefully tugged him into the gutter. The fat, hunched back made the dog look more than ever like a lop-eared pig.

Jack took a breath. "Since you're interested in her welfare, Mr Linderman, I'm sure you wouldn't want her to lose her job. She might lose it, if you come into the coffee shop and talk to her. Her boss is annoyed about that."

Linderman's eyes widened with an amazement that did not look feigned. "She told you that? It's absurd! I have a cup of coffee there now and then. Of course she tries not to hear what I have to say!"

Jack hung on, staring as if fixated at Linderman scooping up the dog's mess, dropping it into a plastic sack he had brought with him. "Let the girl lead her own life, Mr Linderman. I thought you were anti-church, anti-stuffiness." Jack attempted a smile.

"I am anti-church. What I'm talking about is reality, something you can see and touch." Linderman scowled.

Indeed, Jack could see Elsie's fair face and body very clearly now. He could draw her exactly from memory. He recalled her face when she had spoken to him in her apartment, the moisture in her eyes when she had begged him to get Linderman off her back. "The girl has the right not to be lectured to, though, don't you think? She's not your daughter. She feels very strongly about this."

Ralph Linderman looked miserable at Jack's lack of understanding. "What does she know about life at twenty? She's on the way to ruining her life now. I say that and I stand by it!"

Jack noticed a male passerby glancing at Linderman, who had spoken forcefully. Jack looked toward home, at the corner of Grove Street behind him and to his right. How to wind this up? "May I say I don't think you're going to get anywhere talking to her the way you do. You might even make things worse. Have you thought—"

"But who else is going to talk to her? Her family's not here in New York. She's a girl all alone!"

Jack wanted to say that Elsie was on the brink of going to the police about Linderman, but he thought that might be unwise. Linderman's extremism was something deep and unchangeable. Suddenly Jack felt disgust, a hatred of Linderman's fixed stare, which struck Jack as obtuse. "Well—she's not the only girl alone in New York, you know," Jack said, ready to walk away.

"Are *you* protecting her now?"

Jack smiled. "No, and I don't think she needs protection. So long, Mr Linderman."

"Mr Sutherland!" Linderman sprinted forward and buttonholed Jack, almost literally, seizing a lapel of his jacket.

"Hey, cut it *out!*" Jack jerked back, and bumped into a girl who was crossing the street with a shopping trolley. The girl might have fallen, if Jack hadn't grabbed her elbow. "I *am* sorry. Excuse me." Jack saw the girl glance at him, annoyed.

"I haven't yet explained myself," Linderman said.

"You have. Just cool it, would you?" Jack realized that he clenched his teeth as Elsie had done, that his free hand was now a fist.

"It's not easy talking on the street," Linderman said more gently. "My place, my apartment's here a few steps away. If you'd be willing to come up for just two or three minutes—"

The idea was depressing, but would it be worse to show unfriendliness? Maybe Linderman fed on opposition. Jack gave a short nod. "Okay. Fine. Maybe I can make myself clearer too."

Two or three minutes later, Jack was climbing the stairs—four storeys of them—to Linderman's apartment, through darkish halls full of old cooking smells, dusty carpets. The dog looked at Jack with his apologetic smile, maybe with curiosity, as Linderman unlocked his apartment door.

13

At Linderman's cordial gesture, Jack preceded him into a smallish living-room that seemed crammed with bookshelves and tables. It was all neat, worn out, and old. Two windows gave onto the backyard or open area between the old apartment building and the back of the houses beyond. Linderman was hanging his dog's leash somewhere. A kitchenette had been installed in the back left corner, and there was a half-open door on the right, which might lead to Linderman's bedroom, since the couch in the living-room hadn't the look of being slept on.

"Please sit down, Mr Sutherland," said Linderman, gesturing toward his only armchair.

The dark blue plush-covered armchair also suggested the 1950s and though faded looked hardly used. The center of activity seemed to be a long wooden table near the back windows on which lay notebooks, pens and pencils, rulers and a couple of books from the public library.

"Not fancy here, but it's home—to me. Has been for more than ten years now." Linderman spoke with satisfaction and pride, as he pulled a straight chair from his wooden table so he could sit facing Jack.

"Nice place," said Jack pleasantly. He was now in the armchair. "Has Elsie been here?"

"Certainly not," Linderman said, shaking his head. "No, I never invited her. She's always in a terrible hurry, anyway." He smiled, almost chuckled.

Jack supposed Linderman seldom, if ever, had a guest. He watched Linderman wrestling with something he wanted to say.

"Is it you Elsie's visiting lately? Is that why you told me not to speak with her any more?"

"Me?" Jack gave a laugh and shook his head. "She helped me

carry some groceries in once. Must've been the time you saw her—coming in or going out, because it's the one time she's been to our place." Had Linderman seen her going in and waited to see how long she stayed?

"How did you meet her?" Linderman asked.

"Um-m. Yes. I went into the coffee shop where she works. Several weeks ago. Rainy night, I remember.—I remember you were there too with your dog. I saw you talking to Elsie. So— when she served me coffee, I asked her how she knew you, and I told her you'd found my wallet. She said she'd heard about that."

"You started talking with her."

"Don't know who began," Jack said with a smile, remembering Elsie's first words to him when he was standing, unable to get a stool, that he looked as if it were raining outside.

Linderman crossed his arms. "And you made a date with her?"

"No, indeed! Didn't see her again till the day one of my grocery bags was breaking at the bottom, and Elsie happened to be on Grove—and she carried a sack in for me. That's when you saw her come into my house—or go out."

Linderman's gaze might have been the same, if he had not believed a word of what Jack had said. "Do you realize, Mr Sutherland, that she is a little—ideal? Like a—"

"Ideal?"

"Young and perfect. She is a beauty just now."

Jack waited.

"She is what some people call 'a dream girl'. You must realize that."

Jack said, "She's very pretty, yes."

"And she's alive. She's not a statue."

"Very true."

"Consequently she runs a risk."

Of losing her virginity, Jack supposed. "Of what?"

"She is a temptation to others."

Jack smiled. "Like all pretty girls." He loosened the muffler around his neck, but hitched forward as if he would soon leave.

"Such a female is dangerous," Linderman went on. "Such a girl leads to unhappiness, to—destruction of others and of herself." He frowned and bit his underlip. "But I'm more interested in protecting Elsie than the men and young boys who may lust after her."

Jack thought of saying that Elsie preferred girls just now, but again decided not to. "Well, sir, I don't know what I can do to help Elsie. She has a job and she looks quite healthy.—I believe in live and let live."

"But she could be destructive to *you*. If you allow it. If you see her again a few more times."

"No, sir.—I've no particular intention of seeing her again." He picked up the grocery bag he had set on the floor. The dog had begun sniffing it, but at a firm "*No*, God!" from Linderman, the dog went back to where he had been before, an empty area of carpet near the door, where Jack saw him lie down again with chin on paws, listening.

"Such small and simple encounters can ruin marriages," Linderman continued, "and you're a respectable married man, Mr Sutherland."

Jack said amiably, "Happily married too. I'm not interested in other women." He felt naive saying it, as if he had made the old guy a gift of something.

"But don't you see how she flirts with everyone?"

"No. I don't. Matter of fact I don't think she flirts at all. She's unusually straightforward, says what she thinks and that's that.— I saw her giving fellows the brush-off in the coffee shop that night. And no mistake about it."

Linderman's face wrinkled with displeasure. "You should hear some of the things men say to Elsie in that coffee shop. That *scum* reaching out to grab her!"

Jack stood up. "Why take it so seriously, Mr Linderman? Elsie can take care of herself." But he knew why Linderman took it seriously, because in his sick and mystic way, Linderman was in love with Elsie. Yes, mystic, Jack thought, because Linderman had said Elsie was an ideal, a dream girl.

Linderman's frowning eyes stayed on Jack. "Because Elsie does not realize what we're talking about—now—doesn't realize her power. *That* is what is dangerous. Elsie has this power simply by being pretty, even beautiful. Then our society makes it worse by—by urging girls to wear make-up, anything eye-catching, high heels. The more ornamental and helpless they look, the sexier. Reached a peak maybe with the Chinese foot-binding in the old days, women were just sex objects that men carried to bed because they couldn't walk properly. Now it's hair over one eye some-

93

times, so women can't see where they're going. Sexy. It's conditioning.—Do you realize that, Mr Sutherland?" Linderman bent forward, dark eyes straining with more to come.

"When I've seen Elsie, she was wearing sneakers."

"I even think it's in women's genes," said Linderman, as if he hadn't heard the remark about sneakers. "And society and advertising—don't forget that—add to it! Nail polish—"

"Girls like to look nice."

"Who tells them what's nice?" Linderman retorted as if he had Jack now, pinned to the floor, defeated.

Yes, the old question, did women dress for themselves or for men? Jack couldn't go on with it. He turned in a circle, and noticed a blue-and-green flower design that someone, maybe Linderman, had painted in a clumsy manner on a white lamp base, and noticed also a photograph of a woman's head in profile in a round frame that stood on Linderman's bookshelf top. The woman had an old-fashioned bun and was young. Linderman's mother?

"You've been married, Mr Linderman?" Jack asked, not knowing what on earth to expect as an answer.

"Once, yes. My wife deserted me for another man—oh, twenty or more years ago.—Typical. Women are fickle. Fond of their powers. Don't you think so, Mr Sutherland?"

Jack was silent. And men were fond of falling in love with girls with those powers. Had Linderman been badly burnt? It was hard to imagine Linderman young, attractive to a girl. Just what was Linderman's problem? Impotence, maybe?

"That photograph you were looking at," Linderman went on. "It's not my wife, it's my mother. She died a few weeks ago." His tone was matter-of-fact.

"Oh? Sorry to hear that.—Where is your wife now?" Jack was curious.

"California? Florida? I don't know or care. I have no contact with her. We had no children." Linderman said the last sentence with an air of smug satisfaction.

It crossed Jack's mind, again, that maybe Linderman had never made it in bed.

"Too many children in the world," Linderman said. "Just look at the Pope. Anti-birth control! How *can* he be? He's even *seen* these shanty towns in South America—teeming, hungry people and kids, and he says, 'Bless you! Keep it up!' Flies back to Rome in a luxury jet."

"Yes, they say—" Jack forced words out to be congenial. "—he's a Third World Pope. Catholics in the Western World practise birth control if they want to."

"Thank goodness," Linderman said.

Jack took a breath. "What was your wife like?"

Linderman's eyes grew more alert, his mouth turned down at the corners. "How should I describe her?—Empty-headed. We were both about twenty-four when we married. Too young. She talked about being a writer. Fiction. But no discipline. She never got anywhere with her short stories—or a book she never finished." Linderman chuckled bitterly. "Normal for a wife not to have to work, I didn't mind that, but she couldn't even run a household. Frivolous, you know? Thought she was pretty. Well, she was sort of pretty. So she met another idiot who fell in love with her and she just flitted off. Like that! Like a butterfly. No loss to me, I assure you." Linderman waved a hand, then ran a thumb under the waistband of his trousers. His waistline was rather flat.

Jack waited for more that didn't come. Linderman's underlip was firmly set now, as if buttoned. "And your mother? She was living in New York?"

"No. New Hampshire. My family's from up there."

New Hampshire people were said to be stubborn and conservative, Jack had heard. He sought for some compliment to pay Linderman before he left. "I see a lot of serious books on your shelves here. Engineering stuff."

"Ah—yes." Linderman smiled. "I suppose I'm a failed engineer. I wanted to be an inventor. But an inventor doesn't amount to anything unless he's patented something. I'm scooped half the time. Haven't got the training or the equipment to make proper models.—I dropped out of college, because I had to support my mother. Then I—I tried the furniture business, custom made stuff. Couldn't make enough money at it. This was when I was married. Well—I'm a security guard now, lots of night work which I prefer. I try to protect buildings and people and their money from the evil that's walking the streets. A thankless task and a hopeless one. Most people will steal, given the opportunity.—Finding a wallet with a name in it, and *not* returning it, I consider—" Linderman sought for words of opprobrium.

"Yes." Jack was glad to thank Linderman once more. "I don't forget that, sir, never will." He moved toward the door, and noticed a framed picture on the wall. This was a reproduction of a pre-Raphaelite painting, but it had no color. It showed a pale young woman with long dark hair, wearing a long white gown. One of her hands rested on a rock, and she was barefoot, like a sleepwalker. Jack had the feeling that this was Linderman's ideal, the dreamy sylvan beauty that never was, that nobody ever talked to or went to bed with. Jack did not gaze long, lest Linderman start a conversation about it. "I'm probably keeping you from sleeping. Thanks for asking me up, Mr Linderman."

"Sleeping?" Linderman got to his feet in a surprisingly agile way. "I don't have to sleep till about eight o'clock. We must get together again. I'm not sure I made myself clear about the complicated things we were talking about, girls and women. Ha-ha!" The laugh was light, but still a real laugh. "I can't express myself properly in a few words—so what I said may have sounded lopsided."

"No, indeed. I'll think about what you said." Jack made himself grasp Linderman's extended hand. Linderman hung on, shaking and shaking, as he had the evening he returned the wallet.

At last Jack was descending the stairs, picking up speed as he went. Best to be on cordial terms, he reminded himself, better than sulking, better than pretending not to see Linderman on the street. Next time, on the street, he'd nod to Linderman.

Back at home, Jack felt that he saw Linderman in a clearer light. His hunch had been right: Linderman in an odd way was enamored of Elsie, and consequently resented all rivals. Linderman saw Elsie as a symbol of young womanhood, purity, so he had to protect her. She was both attractive and dangerous because of her charms, yet plainly an object of fascination to Linderman, maybe obsession. All women in one. Jack had read about such things in mythology.

He drifted toward his worktable, steering his mind back toward the yak, its longhaired ears, its overall shagginess that suggested gloom as well as friendliness. Jack dipped his crow quill into India ink and tested it, then hovered over the blank illustration board. He was thinking that it was odd Linderman had made Elsie Tyler

96

into an abstract, a symbol of all women, and thereby erased her as a real girl aged twenty. All this maybe because he couldn't get her. This was the opposite of what men in love usually did with objects of their affection, believe that their girl or woman was the one and only in the world, an individual alive and tangible. No doubt Freud had described Linderman's type in detail somewhere, but Jack hadn't read every word of Freud. Natalia probably had. He might tell Natalia about Linderman's attitude toward Elsie some time. It might amuse her.

Jack brought his pen down to the paper.

14

"GAD, what a way to hold a meeting!" Natalia said two minutes after she was home, having deposited her boots and also Amelia's on newspaper inside the apartment door.

Jack had been delighted to escape the downpour and also the parents' meeting—he had forgotten the name of the organization—but he listened to what Natalia had to say about it. Elaine Armstrong had been there with son Jason, but not Max, and the chair-person, a Mrs Cova of whom Jack had heard before, had tried to get the kids to vote separately, then along with their parents on the question of a gym room versus a table-and-chair room for the second room in an apartment on Bank Street. This apartment, two rooms in it, was to be a parking place for kids in the afternoon interim between school closing and when their parents got home from work. Supervision was to be voluntary and rotary, and no parent could use the facility unless he or she offered supervisory service one afternoon in ten, or one afternoon in however many kids would be accommodated.

"This Madeleine Cova," Natalia said, coming back into the living-room, having changed her slacks for pajama pants, "is sick-makingly sweet, listening to everybody, never making decisions, oh no. That's why these damn things take so long."

"A scotch, madame," said Jack, handing Natalia a Glenfiddich.

"Oh, thanks, Jack. Well, I know, I won't face being a chair-person myself. 'S matter with a chairman, I'd like to know." She sipped and laughed. "But here it is nearly half-past eight!"

"Wah!" Amelia took a run and hurled herself face down on the sofa, then looked at her parents, grinning. "Yackety-yack!"

"And what've you been doing while I was representing parenthood?" Natalia brushed her hair back from her face.

The rain had made darkish stripes in her hair, giving her a savage look that Jack had seen before, and he liked it, liked watching her hair fade back to its normal color which was indescribable, something like gold with a rough surface, unpolished. "I wrote to Uncle Roger," Jack said. "Told him about the yak book and—the *Dreams* book coming out for Christmas. They're hurrying it and I should get some copies in a couple of days."

"Oh? Nice. When'd you hear this?"

"Dartmoor, Aegis called up this afternoon and told me.—Is anybody getting hungry?"

"*I* am hungry!" Amelia yelled.

It was one of the evenings Natalia was to cook, and she had made spaghetti sauce that morning before leaving for the Katz Gallery. Finally, they both got dinner. The kitchen was big enough for two to work without bumping into each other. The telephone rang when the spaghetti was almost done, and it was Louis Wannfeld, Jack could tell when he leaned an ear into the living-room and heard Natalia's laugh, her slow voice. Of course it could be Sylvia, Jack realized, though Sylvia didn't phone as often as did Louis. Jack put the salad on the table, then went to Natalia.

"Spaghetti's *done!*" he whispered.

Jack served. Amelia in a shrill voice demanded her pillows to be put on her chair, she couldn't find them. Natalia did sign off, pleading that the spaghetti was done, and came to the table smiling.

Louis' friend Bob, she said, had got himself into a mess at Berlitz where he was taking French lessons. It was a story of mistaken identity between Bob and a teacher of Italian, resulting in Bob's being taken to the podium in a room full of Italian students. Jack barely hung on and rather missed the punch line, but gave a polite smile. Then Natalia had to look for Amelia's bib, spaghetti being a messy dish, and found it on the back of the kitchen door.

Jack had just made espresso coffee when the phone rang again. Natalia answered.

"Jack?"

"Who is it? Joel?"

"It's a girl."

"Hello?"

"Hello, Mr Sutherland, this is Elsie. I guess you spoke to the old creep?"

"I certainly did, yes. A few days ago."

"Well, he's laying off the shop here, thank you for that, but he's bugging me around my *house* now."

Jack heard a clatter of dishes in the background. Elsie was phoning from the café. "Hanging around your house, you mean?"

"Yes, and trying to talk to me. Now I'm wondering if I *should* talk to the police? What do you think? One of our friends, a fellow, nearly socked him the other night. But that just seems to make him madder. I'm not afraid to talk to the police, because I think I'm justified. But what do you think, really?"

Jack tried to think. It didn't seem wise to say, "Sure, go ahead." There ought to be some other way.

"You still there?"

"Yes," said Jack. Then he heard a crash like that of a metal tray falling, and a female voice saying, ". . . where you're *going*?"

"Wow!—Ha! Soup all over the floor here! I'm sorry to call you from here, but we had our phone cut off at home. Mistake about the bill . . . paid it, so the phone'll be back on in a . . ." Her voice faded in another din, this time that of a machine grinding.

Natalia set Jack's espresso on the bookshelf near the telephone base.

"Elsie, I'll talk to my wife. I promise. I'll think about it. Don't do anything in a hurry. Can you phone me again after—"

"Later tonight?" she interrupted. "Sure. Till how late?"

"Midnight. All right?"

That was all right.

Jack picked up his coffee and walked toward the table. Amelia passed him and switched on the TV.

Natalia sat at the table, and she looked a bit tired. "What was all that?"

"That," said Jack, sitting down, "was the girl we saw dancing that night."

"What night?"

"In that disco. The blond girl. The good dancer."

"Really?—How does she know our number?"

"It's because of this old guy on Bleecker, the one who found my wallet. He's been pestering this girl—for months, it sounds like."

Jack told Natalia about going into the Seventh Avenue café the night of Natalia's birthday, when he had taken a walk, and seeing Linderman talking to a waitress whose name he had learned that night, Elsie. And that night, Elsie had mentioned Linderman's moral lectures to her. Jack told about running into Elsie near the Grove Street drugstore, and her insisting that he take a look at her Minetta Street place, which she had shown him as if it were a model of respectability. He finished by telling Natalia about his rather painful conversation with Linderman in his apartment on Bleecker.

"Why didn't you tell me all this before?" asked Natalia, amused.

"Because I thought it might worry you.—Linderman. The old guy lives so close by." Jack said as if to himself, "I really don't want to make an enemy of him.—Have you ever seen him, do you think, with his black and white dog? He looks in his middle-fifties, about my height."

Natalia shook her head. "Don't think so."

"Just as well.—Elsie's going to call back tonight. She wants to know if I think it's a good idea if she speaks to the police about Linderman—bugging her.—What do you think, darling?"

Natalia turned in her chair. "Amelia, dear, just a little less loud? Please?"

"Yes, Mummy!" Amelia turned the volume down.

"I can imagine it's annoying," Natalia said. "But why's she asking your advice?"

Jack picked up the gold-rimmed lighter and lit the cigarette Natalia had put between her lips. "Well, I'm older—and maybe the only person she knows who knows this guy. Not that I *know* him, but—"

"But?"

"Well, it crossed my mind—what kind of cop Elsie might talk to. Might be the kind of cop who'll say she must be provoking the old guy."

"Provoking?" Natalia said in a throaty voice, and she chuckled. "Does she, do you think?"

"I'm absolutely sure she doesn't." Jack was smiling too. "However—what do you think I should say to her about the police when she calls back?"

Natalia raised her eyebrows, her shoulders. "Since it's been going on so long, maybe she should talk to the cops. A couple of cops."

While Natalia tidied up, Jack urged Amelia in the direction of bed. Sometimes he had to read something to her, though Amelia was a fair reader herself now. But to be read to was a luxury that Amelia relished. Tonight Jack read to her out of a wide thin book about ducks, and he put on his droning, sleepy voice which sometimes put Amelia to sleep and sometimes gave her the giggles. Tonight his somnolent voice worked. Jack dared to bend and touch her round cheek with his lips. Her long fair hair spread in a lovely, abandoned way over her pillow. Jack straightened and stretched, and looked around Amelia's room in the dim light of the bedside lamp. At least five art exhibit announcements were propped up on her small chest of drawers, all with color reproductions of a painting. He or Natalia, sometimes both of them, took Amelia to galleries, and Amelia was never bored. But she didn't like Rembrandt, Jack remembered from a recent trip to the Met, and he smiled at the thought. Amelia's own artistic efforts were thumbtacked to the inside of her room door. In one water color two figures were having cups of something at a table—clumsy in form, perhaps, but a well-balanced composition all the same—all in red. He put out the light.

"I'll talk to that girl when she calls back. If she does. I'd sort of like to hear what she says." Natalia sat on the sofa in pajamas now. The TV was still on.

"Would you?" Jack smiled, surprised. "Thanks, honey, because I swear I'm not sure what to say about the cops. Wish we knew a cop personally."

"Unless you think she'd mind talking to me," Natalia added.

"No. She's not that type, shrinking violet. Not at all. She remembers you from that disco. She said she thought you looked interesting—different, she said."

"Interesting! Ha!"

Jack was in the kitchen, tying up the garbage bag, when the telephone rang. He let Natalia answer it. It was not quite 11.

"Yes, Jack told me," Natalia was saying on the telephone.

Jack deliberately didn't listen, shook out another plastic garbage bag, fresh and noisy, and stuck it into the metal bin. He went down the hall to his workroom, turned on the light, and his eyes fell at once on the yellow-on-red drawing of Elsie on his table, propped against the back wall. Nice action in those curves, he thought. He could hear music when he looked at it, drums and a pulsing beat.

"Jack?" It was Natalia behind him.

Jack had jumped. "What?"

"Well, I must say Elsie talks a blue streak! And she *is* funny. Of all people for that old nut to pick on, *this* girl!" Natalia laughed. "She's the free-as-the-breeze type."

"Isn't it true—as Louis would say. So what did you advise her?"

"Oh. We didn't get into the police business. I suggested that she get some friends together and they all follow Lindman home and heckle *him* for a change. Scare him just once."

"Linderman."

"Linderman. Anyway, it might do the trick. Elsie told me he's scared of her punk friends even now. She calls them punks."

"Mm-m. But the police, no, eh?"

"She thinks the police might not discourage him, and he might tell the police she's living in a whorehouse or some such. Bet she's right. I also said, why not find another young girl who's about to lose her morals or whatever, and see that Linderman meets her."

Jack smiled. "But Elsie's so attractive."

"True." Natalia looked at Jack's worktable. "Is that Elsie?" She moved toward the drawing which stood among several others. "It is, isn't it?"

"Yep, I did it after the disco evening. Clever of you to recognize her."

"That's a good drawing."

Jack said nothing, but he appreciated the tone of Natalia's voice, not a tone she used often. Jack felt pleased.

"I'm having coffee with her tomorrow morning at eleven. At that place on Sheridan Square with the glass front. You know?—Want to come?"

Jack knew the place with its enclosed front terrace. "No, you go. See what you think." He smiled. "I don't think she'll bore you."

15

VERY early one weekday morning, Ralph Linderman rode homeward on a Seventh Avenue bus that was nearly empty and abominably overheated. Twice he changed his seat, trying to avoid gushing hot air that he thought might even singe his clothing. The heat intensified the stink of captured air in the bus, the stench of dirty woolen clothes, stale grease, body odor, even garlic. It was worse, Ralph thought, than what blew up from subway grills in the sidewalks when a train ran underneath, a gust like a belch of an ugly dragon monster, long dead and putrefying. That subway smell was of old metal-on-metal, of oily dust moist with human breath, the semi-trapped air of hundreds of subway cars and tunnels whose atmosphere had never been completely changed since the subway cars had started running. He could throw in the smells of chewing gum and discarded cigarette butts, spit, vomit and piss down there. Ralph hated the subways. They were dangerous as well as being hideous.

"You might allow people to open a window," Ralph said to the bus driver just before his stop, "since you've got the heat up so high!" Ralph hadn't been able to open a window, though he had tried two of them.

"Then we'd have complaints about a draft," said the black driver.

"Must be ninety in here. It's roasting!"

"Exit at the rear, sir, and no talkin' to the driver."

The driver stopped with deliberate abruptness, nearly throwing Ralph off his feet.

The cold December air felt good, and Ralph inhaled deeply. He had been thinking, on the bus, about buying a new overcoat, and his thoughts returned to this pleasant prospect. He had ample money, he reminded himself, but he was thrifty by nature, which he didn't consider a fault, in the long run. Was not the world full of people who overspent and made themselves miserable, lost their friends by borrowing and so on?

Ralph aired God in the pitch dark, making it short this time, and promising God a longer walk later. He kept his promise at 11 a.m., when he went out to buy some groceries and the *Times*. He might have walked down Seventh to the coffee shop where Elsie worked, since he fancied a coffee and Danish just then, but they wouldn't let God in (did that apply to other dogs as well?), and besides Elsie's shift started around 6 p.m., Ralph thought. It was a pleasure merely to look at her, Ralph realized and admitted to himself. He didn't have to talk to her, or lecture her, as Elsie put it. Goodness, no! And at least once he had gone into the café, without the dog, and said absolutely nothing to her, not even nodded a greeting, not even made an effort to sit where she might wait on him. This served two purposes in Ralph's opinion: one, he could enjoy being near her, watching her moving, smiling to people, talking, and two, he imagined himself the image of her conscience, sitting on a stool at the counter. Yes, seeing him, she would recall the things he had said to her about guarding her character and her health while she still had them. Cheerful things he had said to her, and why did she scorn them?

A couple of hours later Ralph was walking south from Fourteenth Street, where he had taken the crosstown bus westward, carrying a rectangular box with his new overcoat in it. At home, Ralph spoke to God and aroused the dog's interest before he opened the tissue-lined box.

What a beauty it was—for a hundred and sixty-seven dollars and thirty-eight cents! The overcoat was dark blue with dark blue satin lining, flaps on the two side pockets, an inner pocket, and a loop at the back for hanging. Ralph put it on in front of his largest mirror, a swinging mirror that sat on his chest of drawers.

"What d'y'think, God? Pretty neat, isn't it?"

The dog barked and pranced around, sniffed at the overcoat's hem.

Ralph put on all his living-room lights, and tilted the mirror to have a look at the lower part. Finally, he undid the stiff buttons and hung the coat carefully.

In the afternoon, he awakened in what was for him the middle of the night, and recalling his overcoat, felt no desire to go back to sleep. The winter sun came thin and bright through his bedroom window. Ralph never drew his curtains. Daylight did not affect his sleep. Sutherland's questioning him about his wife, *ex*-wife Irma, had upset him, and he realized the upset had even led him to buy the overcoat—*something* nice, something to make him forget the silly woman, in a way. How she'd prided herself on her cuteness, her prettiness so ephemeral! What did she look like now? In her mid-fifties? Men wouldn't flock now, just because she gave them the eye. Sex-obsessed too, he had thought. But no. Ralph had come to the conclusion that her sexy demands—she had meant them to seem sexy, at any rate—had been only another of her ways to annoy him, put him down. Indeed, it had! Of course he'd read about women having five orgasms to a man's one. But they could also fake it. As for Irma—Well, it might have worked out, if she hadn't been so shallow, so like a spoilt child, with no need to work, no need to do anything but keep house and go to the beauty parlor, and manicure her toenails. Why had he taken her writing aspirations so seriously? Out of a misguided courtesy, respect? Ralph reproached himself here: he had been stupid to marry such a silly woman, and for that he had no one to blame but himself. And of course he'd become impotent, for the simple reason that he hadn't even liked Irma after five or six months, certainly hadn't been enamored of her any longer. He wasn't impotent, as he had been able to prove to himself by masturbation, an activity he didn't really enjoy. Pleasant for moments, to be sure, but in the abstract, as a pleasure or as a substitute for something—well, was it necessary? He never imagined anything, any woman, when he did this, certainly not centerfold girls with big breasts, the usual arousers. No, indeed. He never imagined Elsie either. Unthinkable! He felt just the opposite, about Elsie. He couldn't conjure up in imagination a Prince Charming worthy of her. No, he thought only of himself during this activity, which he indulged in maybe once or twice a year, he wasn't at all sure about how frequently. He thought only, yes, I can make it, no problem. Irma had been wrong. He wasn't a freak with some kind of block in his head about this. If Ralph wished to be bitter or vindictive, which he didn't, he could "blame" Irma, because she had let him down as a person, as the twenty-four-year-old girl he thought he had married. He had thought there was some substance to her. She had had a job in a real estate agency as secretary when they met. Her parents had a house in town, respectable people, one older married brother, Ralph remembered Irma had had. Ralph didn't want to recall all that, because it was all negative, and he always got back to blaming himself. He'd been in love, to be sure. Dangerous state, a state to make bad mistakes in.

How had this train of thought started? With the conversation with Sutherland, of course. Irma. Impotence. Masturbation. Ugh! Ralph felt a vague shame about masturbation, which had nothing to do with his childhood, when a parent might have said, "Stop that!" and in fact Ralph could not recall his parents ever having said that to him. Ralph realized that Irma had planted a bitterness in him against all women, a fear of them, though he quite realized that not all women were like Irma.

Ralph got out of bed, having decided to test his overcoat against the elements, in this case, now, nothing more than a chill day. He shaved with his safety razor, annoyed still by the memories of Irma in her pink dressing gown at 7 in the morning when he shaved before going off to work. He'd probably have made his own breakfast on most of those mornings. Often she taunted him, because he had not been a success in bed in the morning. Hard to make love with your mind on the clock. And who'd have earned their living if he had let the carpentry shop slide? Damn her! Wisps, mere wisps, these memories, little pale ghosts like the lather bits he flung from his razor into the basin.

Ralph dressed and put on his overcoat. From a shelf in his front closet he took a round fur cap which he had bought a year ago and hardly worn since. He tried it on. Black rabbit fur, it was, with ear-flaps, rather Russian-looking.

Thus attired, and without God who could wait for his airing around 7, Ralph strolled off southward on Bleecker. He was tempted to walk through Minetta Street past Elsie Tyler's house. It was half past 5, she might be coming out of her house on her way to work, and he might see her. And then he might not. He realized that he wanted her to see him in his smart new coat. If he did see her, he intended to say in a friendly manner, touching his cap, "Afternoon, Elsie!" and walk on.

Yet another irritating matter crossed his mind as he waited to cross a street: the electricity people in his mother's town were dunning him about a bill he had paid by check long ago, but sent to the wrong branch office, it seemed. And her town church expected him to honor "a pledge" his mother had made to contribute a hundred dollars a year, and could he, etc. which amounted to seventy-three dollars still due for this year. Ralph had neither sent it nor replied, but the church's requests kept coming. If such a misguided pledge were not kept, it was no reflection upon the family's honor, in Ralph's opinion.

But why pain himself by thinking of all that on such a nice afternoon? There was Elsie's three-storey house, dark red like some of the others, yet special to Ralph because Elsie lived there. Its door was closed. Ralph kept his eyes on the house as he walked along the sidewalk on the opposite side of the street. The street was short and narrow with a crook in it. Once there had been Minetta Brook along here, and Ralph fancied that there was a depression where Minetta Street ended in Minetta Lane, which crossed it.

Suddenly Elsie's house door opened, voices male and female mingled, and someone laughed. A young girl and two boys came out, and Elsie was behind them, turning to pull the door shut.

"There!—Look!" Elsie cried to her friends.

There was a whoop from the others, and Ralph realized that he was the center of their attention. Ralph walked faster.

"Creep!" said a girl's voice behind him.

"Hey! Let Elsie alone! You hear us?" roared a male voice.

"Sex maniac! . . ."

"Who've you screwed lately?"

"Ha-ha! He can run! Look!"

Ralph felt both shame and fury. He wasn't running, just walking as fast as he decently could, and the few paces in Minetta Lane to Sixth Avenue seemed endless. A boy in sneakers had loped in front of him with arms outstretched as if to block him.

"Fuck off, ol' motherfucker, we're gettin' the cops onto you!"

Where was Elsie in all this? A boy struck Ralph's shoulder with the heel of his hand. "Cut it out!" Ralph yelled. "Leave me alone!"

"Leave *him* alone!" cried a girl's shrill voice, and this was followed by laughter.

"Yee-aye! Skit! Skit, y'bastid!"

"And don't come back! Don't come around again, see?" A boy with rouge on his face, with lipstick, said this to Ralph straight into his face. The boy danced backward and looked at Ralph through nearly closed eyes whose lashes bore black dust or grease. "Fuckin' *creep*!"

Ralph lowered his head and plunged uptown on Sixth Avenue. "Hah! . . . Ha-ha-haa-aa! . . . Run, boy! Beat it!"

The voices mingled. An ashcan lid slithered past Ralph on the sidewalk, making a horrid grating sound. Passersby stared.

But he had finally put some distance between himself and them. Ralph slowed his pace, breathed deeply, looked straight ahead, and as soon as he had a red light, he crossed to the west side of 6th.

Ralph walked right into them. The three—not Elsie, where was she?—had somehow crossed Sixth too.

"Where you headin'?" asked the unmade-up boy. "We're goin' with you! Ain't we?"

"Yeeow," replied the rouged boy.

Ralph strode toward home, but the boys, both of them, kept leaping in front of him, brushing his shoulders and sides as he headed toward Bleecker. But why go to his house, Ralph thought, and ducked into a restaurant, went through its storm door and through its second door.

"We're not serving yet, sir," said a waiter.

"The telephone—"

The waiter looked reluctant, but made a gesture toward the telephones at the back.

Ralph walked between empty tables, looked behind him, and saw one of the boys coming in. Words were exchanged, the waiter fairly hustled the boy out, supported by another waiter. And outside, they lingered, Ralph could see them. Ralph pretended to be making a telephone call, to talk. When he looked at the glass door again, they were still outside. They weren't going to leave, he realized. With the telephone against his ear, his lips mumbling nervous nonsense, Ralph suddenly saw Irma laughing at him as she withdrew a cigarette from her dark red lips, eyes closed with laughter at him, long wavy hair down to her shoulders, shaking. Bitch!

He hung up, started for the door again, knowing that it was inevitable that he face them, raised his head, said, "Thank you," to the two waiters, and went out.

"Here he comes!" cried a boy.

Now Ralph saw Elsie smiling at the other girl, apparently saying good-bye, near the downtown corner: Elsie had to go to work soon. Elsie's smiling eyes met his before she turned and trotted away. His shoulders back, Ralph walked uptown, the direction of home.

And it was the two boys who kept pace with him, who banged his shoulders from behind, who walked on either side of him.

"You leave Elsie alone, you hear? Or we'll fix you, man! You *bananas!*"

"Fuckin' creep, fuckin' creep!" This boy laughed merrily, as if he were doing a pleasant job now.

When Ralph turned into West Fourth, the boys were still with him. Their words were horrid. Ralph glanced around for a cop. Where should he go? He was not going to be pursued to his very doorstep! To the point of having to close the first front door against them, when in fact that door didn't or didn't always lock, and Ralph knew that the boys would push it open behind him, follow him to his apartment door and through it, if they could.

Ralph was suddenly beside the glass-enclosed terrace of the café-restaurant near Sheridan Square, hesitating. The newsstand by the subway entrance was nearby, the man there knew him.

"Hey, you!" The girl suddenly reappeared in front of him, a figure of lipstick, long hair that was plainly a wig, powder-pale face, under a garment that might have been a curtain or a counterpane. "Lay off Elsie, if you know what's good for you!—Got the idea now?"

"You tell 'im, Marion!" yelled one of the boys.

The boy with the make-up spat at Ralph and missed him. Naturally, no passerby did a thing to help. A couple of men and a woman only glanced from the unruly trio to Ralph and back again.

Ralph turned to the newspaper man. "I'll take a—"

"Y'bought your *Times*, sir," said the man in the kiosk. "Hey! Snazzy coat you're wearing today!"

Ralph turned. The light was red, he could cross. Was even the newsstand man, whom he hardly knew—was he mocking him too? Ralph went into United Cigars, a corner place where he never went. It was triangularly shaped to fit the corner, and smelt of sweetish tobacco, chocolate bars. Ralph stared at racks of paperbacks. The trio was not coming in. He dared to relax a little. There were other customers in the shop, so Ralph did not feel conspicuous. He stared at a horizontal display of magazines, then strolled to the door, through whose glass top half he could see. He thought they were gone. He *thought*—remembering the last time, when he had crossed Sixth Avenue and found them confronting him.

Ralph at last went out briskly, turned into Christopher Street and went on toward Bleecker. True, they were not following him. They'd given it up, it seemed. No cries sounded behind him as he reached Bleecker and crossed the street toward his house, reaching already for his keys.

Upstairs, he felt suffocated with a vague shame that sat more heavily on him than his anger. Worst was the memory of *Elsie*, of her amused and heartless smile, her departure, leaving him to his fate at the hands of those hooligans.

Those hooligans were her friends, he reminded himself. Horrid, horrid and wrong!

Once more Ralph undid the buttons of his overcoat, put it onto a hanger, then brushed the shoulders with a clothesbrush, brushed down the arms where those boys had touched the coat. For all Elsie had noticed the coat, he thought, he might not have had it on at all, might have worn his old soiled-looking gray tweed.

"Wretched, wretched, wretched!" Ralph said to himself between clenched teeth.

16

ON a Wednesday in December, Jack's six complimentary copies of *Half-Understood Dreams* arrived, with a congratulatory note, short but nice, from Trews. The jacket front was his drawing of the businessman father in the family, seated at his desk with an arm flung across his eyes, while a trio of figures, perhaps mama and papa and some unholy ghost, gazed at him with disapproval. All the figures were greenish, the title was in black script done with a brush in freehand. He flipped through one copy and felt a thrill of pleasure, and even pride. It was his first book. And about time, Jack thought, since he was thirty.

Joel MacPherson had collapsed about a week ago, Jack remembered, and smiled. Joel had telephoned to say that he had collapsed from Angst about *Dreams*, and was taking a few days off from work, at least four days, on doctor's orders. Dartmoor, Aegis was giving a little drinks party this coming Friday for *Dreams*, and Jack and Joel, Natalia and "some media people" and Trews were lunching together afterward.

This was the same week that Natalia had had a coffee with Elsie. Natalia's impression of her had been different from what Jack had expected. Natalia had found her extremely ambitious, and said that they had spent more time talking about the theatre and art exhibitions and painters than they had about Linderman.

"She loves the Guggenheim. And Kandinsky! She's trying to take in all of New York in one gulp—and she's had only a highschool education, you know? I suppose it's admirable—if it lasts."

Natalia had been staring at her closet as she spoke, pulling out things that had to go to the cleaners. Jack had to pry out of her what she had concluded about the Linderman situation.

"Oh, he'll surely knock it off," Natalia said. "He's just a lonely old bachelor who likes to look at pretty girls."

"Yeah. I'm sure he's lonely," Jack said.

The question of speaking to the police about Linderman evidently hadn't come up, and Jack didn't mention it. Then later the same day, Natalia said:

"I asked Elsie if she wanted to come to Louis' party and she said she'd love to. Louis' Christmas do next week, you know?"

Jack smiled, surprised. "Elsie's coming. Good." It was funny to imagine Elsie in Louis' quietly swank apartment, among Louis' decidedly quiet chums.

"Elsie asked if she could bring a girl called Genevieve with her. I'll tell Louis. He always likes new faces."

The Dartmoor, Aegis party took place in Trews' big square office whose windows overlooked the East River. There were eighteen or twenty people, some of them other editors of the house, who came in for a minute to shake hands with Jack and Joel. Joel had recovered, though he looked a bit pale. Trews had said to Jack, "Bring your child. It's a girl, isn't it? The press likes to see a family man." So the Sutherlands had brought Amelia, along with Susanne so that Susanne could take Amelia home before the lunch. Natalia circulated smoothly. For this sort of thing she was schooled, and Jack knew that when he next talked to her, she would be able to tell him who was important and who wasn't among the men and women she had spoken with.

"Do you have analytic dreams yourself, Mr Sutherland?" a journalist asked Jack.

Amelia, as if she were in her own house, was passing plates of canapés around, a feat the others found amusing and Jack pretended not to see. Jack and Joel signed several copies together, one with a special greeting to Trews. Out of that day, Jack and Joel netted one brief radio interview, which was taped in another room before lunch, but no television spot. Jack had not expected a TV offer, nor had Trews, though Trews said he had tried.

Louis Wannfeld had strung red and green crêpe paper streamers from the four corners of his living-room ceiling for his party. "An old-fashioned touch, I thought," Louis said. It was the only sign of Christmas, except for a long fir branch on the white-clothed table that held bottles and glasses and plates of caviar and olives and the like.

Isabel Katz was present, of course, as was Sylvia Kinnock who had brought a willowy boy named Ray, who Sylvia said was a dancer with the New York City Ballet. Even Max and Elaine Armstrong had been invited, though they were not close friends of Louis' or of Louis' friend Bob Campbell. There were lots of people Jack had never seen before, presumably friends of Bob's, and there seemed to be as many women as men. Louis, looking almost formally dressed in a royal blue silk suit, white shirt, and black patent leather slippers, pointed out to Jack the bottle of Jack Daniel's on the buffet table.

Jack was grateful and touched. "How's Bob?"

"Oh, he's—over there," Louis said, not having heard Jack correctly in the noise of conversation. "On the sofa."

One thing about Louis' parties, Jack thought as he moved off with his drink, the oddest assortment of people mixed, and all seemed to enjoy themselves. The size of the living-room helped. No one had to stay in one place all evening. Sylvia's boyfriend or boy companion looked as thin as a rail, and it was hard for Jack to imagine him with the leg strength to be a dancer. Pipe-stem legs in narrow black trousers. Pipe-cleaner legs, even.

"Oh, Mr Sutherland, I saw your book!" said a sturdy young woman whom Jack didn't know from Adam or Eve. "I know it's a joint effort, but the drawings will sell it first. They're funny and they also haunt you—and scare you. Maybe not you but *me*!" She laughed.

Jack nodded. "Haven't seen any reviews as yet."

"You will. I work for the *Post*. Hazel Zelling's my name. I just met your wife and she pointed you out to me. I wrote something favorable about it today, but it won't appear for a couple of days."

"Thanks," said Jack, smiling.

It was more comfortable talking to Isabel and the Armstrongs. Susanne had brought a copy of *Dreams* to the Armstrongs' house, and they thanked Jack for it and for what he had written in it.

"Here's to *Dreams*!" Max lifted his glass.

"I'm sick of it already," Jack said. He was thinking of the copies he had sent off to his Uncle Roger and to his father, one each. He wondered if he would ever hear what his father thought of it?

"Where's Bob?" Jack said softly to Isabel. "I'm always forgetting what he looks like, and I wanted to say hello to him."

"The plump bald one on the sofa over there," said Isabel with a smile. "With the glasses."

Of course. Jack recalled him now, a little less bald than Louis, gregarious and talkative, and apparently in the middle of a story now, grinning and gesticulating. Small wonder that he and Louis had been together for an uncountable number of years. Bob looked like the type who would understand and forgive everything. Jack advanced.

Jack never got to Bob, because Natalia pinched his jacket sleeve and said, "Go say hello to your friend."

Jack had glanced around earlier for Elsie, and here she was suddenly in the middle of the room, and Louis was bending attentively over her. She wore a black satin evening dress, slit to mid-thigh. Louis was smiling broadly, beaming with hospitality. Elsie put her blond head back and laughed. She looked extremely pretty. And eye-catching.

"Hi, Elsie," Jack said. "I see you've met your host."

"What may I get this young lady to drink?" Louis asked.

"Good evening, Mr Sutherland," Elsie said. "And this is my—"

"F'gosh sake, call me Jack, Elsie."

"—my friend Genevieve," Elsie said, gesturing with a black-gloved hand toward a young woman in yellow with long and slightly wavy red hair.

Jack and Louis took the girls to the drinks table. Elsie wanted tomato juice, which Louis had in a big pitcher. Genevieve was only medium pretty and looked like a bore, Jack thought. Her hair was the color of baked sweet potato. Could that be real? He wished he could get colors out of his mind tonight, because they jolted him like noises.

"Isn't Natalia here?" asked Elsie.

"Right here," Jack said, seeing Natalia two steps away behind Elsie, watching them.

The Armstrongs had drifted up, and Jack did the introducing. ". . . and Genevieve—"

"Perusky," Elsie supplied, plainly making an effort to be polite and to do the right thing tonight.

Jack didn't bother repeating Genevieve's last name. Max and Elaine were looking at Elsie. Elsie had some kind of grease on her hair, streaks of pink rouge on her cheeks, very red lipstick.

Anyway, she was spectacularly attractive tonight, and her energy or anima, or whatever it was, radiated from her even when she stood still.

"Sit down?" somebody said.

Nobody did. Elsie and Genevieve did not stay together, yet they were never far apart. Elsie went near the big east windows, standing straight, very cool looking. Her greased hair had begun to look chic to Jack.

"Do you know that girl? Or does Natalia?" asked Max Armstrong.

"We both do. She's—" Jack hesitated. "She's one of our neighbours."

"Awfully pretty. Is she a model?"

"I think she's aiming to be an actress. She's just twenty."

Max smiled a little. "I'd have thought even younger."

Jack heard faint harpsichord music, and straining his ears, he could just identify it as the Goldberg Variations. Typical of Louis or even Bob to put on a cassette of Bach. Later, during or after the major eats, someone would put on rock and there would be some dancing. Louis had rolled his rugs back.

"I thought this was a formal party," Elsie's voice said nearby in an uncharacteristically shy tone.

Elsie had said this to Natalia, Jack saw. Natalia shrugged and replied something that Jack couldn't hear.

"Hey, Jack, I just had an idea." This was Joel at his side, bright-eyed and gesturing. "Double lives, some real, some imagined. People who have *real* second families, second jobs in other towns. A bank director could be a thief in his spare time!— Does it sound promising?"

Jack winced. "No. To tell you the truth."

Joel's face fell, then Jack laughed, and so did Joel. "Okay," said Joel, and drifted off.

Joel wasn't hurt, Jack knew. They had known each other too long, had had similar exchanges too often. Joel would torture himself by wanting to quit his job, and not quit it, by dreaming of a different life that he thought he wanted, but perhaps didn't want. And out of this might come a few more good ideas.

When Jack next saw Elsie, she was sitting on an arm of the sofa and Louis was standing beside her. Louis extended a hand, Elsie took it, and they crossed the room and disappeared down a hall.

People were starting on the buffet, and Jack joined them. He saw the yellow-clad, red-haired Genevieve near him with an empty plate, looking a bit lost.

"Like some of this?" Jack asked her, because he had a slice of turkey on a fork just then. He laid it on Genevieve's plate. "Are you an actress?" He didn't know what to say to Genevieve.

"No. I sell cosmetics. At Macy's."

"Oh." She was a bit loaded with cosmetics herself, bluey-green eyeshadow, brick-red nails. Her yellow dress, tightly belted and resembling in front the back of an Arab's pants, must be one of the ones he had glimpsed in that closet on Minetta Street. Did Genevieve know that he had been in that apartment for a few minutes? "And how's the old guy these days? Ralph?"

The vagueness suddenly vanished from Genevieve's eyes. "Oh, *that's* a little better! Did Elsie tell you she and a couple of her friends scared the—scared him so, he ran off? They chased him up Sixth. He'd been hanging around in front of our house."

Jack grinned. "Chased him. Good!—You mean he's staying away now."

"Well, since that day. Of course he can still turn up at Viv's."

"Viv's?"

"The coffee shop where Elsie works."

Jack nodded. "So you didn't talk to the police?"

"We decided against it. The less you have to do with the police—If they started investigating some of *our* friends—They are our friends, but I'm not sure the police would like them."

Jack nodded understandingly. "Your friend Elsie's making quite a hit tonight."

"Doesn't she look great? I dunno how she does it on no sleep. Last night—well, maybe two hours. And she's got to work Sunday to make up for tonight she's taking off."

"What was she doing last night?"

"SoHo. Oh—" Genevieve shook her head and the red tresses stirred a little. "Some new nightspot. Guitar music.—I can't take the late hours, because I have to be at work by eight-thirty and not half asleep either. But then I'm three years older than Elsie.— You've been very nice to Elsie. You and your wife. She likes you both."

Jack bowed. "It's been a pleasure." He was ready to drift away, and he thought this a good time.

"And what did you glean from Genevieve?" Natalia asked Jack a couple of minutes later.

"She works at Macy's in the cosmetics department."

Natalia smiled, lips closed. "I knew that.—Elsie's doing all right for herself tonight. Louis thinks she's divine."

He and Natalia left early, because Susanne wanted to go back to her family's apartment tonight. Elsie was staying on, and when they left was sitting on the arm of a big chair, surrounded by Louis, Sylvia and her friend Ray, and also Isabel. In the taxi going homeward, Natalia said Elsie had wanted to see more of Louis' paintings and drawings, so Louis had taken her into the hall and the two bedrooms. Louis had a Goya of which he was very proud, Jack remembered.

"Pity Elsie's friend's such a drip," Jack said in the taxi.

"Isn't she.—Did Elsie give you one of those flyers about the guitarist?"

"No."

"I'll show you at home. A girl guitarist Elsie thinks is pretty good. Named Marion. Elsie wants us to go hear her. Some bar in SoHo."

Jack wasn't keen on SoHo nightspots, and as far as he knew, neither was Natalia. "Okay. If you're ever in the mood."

Natalia said, "Ha!" since in the mood had another meaning for them. "I don't think Elsie's going to be with Genevieve very much longer. It's Genevieve's apartment, and I suppose a Minetta Street place has its charms, but—"

Jack waited. He took Natalia's hand, gloved as it was, and put his head back. He liked long, rolling taxi rides, when the driver was clever enough to miss all the reds. Tonight the dark scene out the window had spots of blue and silver for Christmas.

At home, all was quiet and in order, Susanne reading a book in the living-room, and Amelia asleep. They all whispered, so as not to awaken the child. Jack offered to telephone for a taxi for Susanne, but she said one was easy enough to find at Sheridan Square at this hour. Susanne's occasional taxi fare was repaid to her by the Sutherlands.

Natalia took a shower, and Jack followed her. She was in the mood tonight, Jack didn't have to ask, and that was nice.

An hour later, as they lay naked and sleepy in bed, Natalia with a cigarette, she said:

"What'd you think of Sylvia's dancer friend tonight?"

"That skinny fellow? Looked like a drip."

"Sylvia says he's a dynamo on stage. Ray Gibson, his name is."

"I'd like to see him jog two miles. He also looks brainless. Why's Sylvia interested in him?"

Natalia drew on her cigarette. "She probably doesn't find him *interesting*.—She told me he wants to do a little social climbing, so she brought him."

"Social climbing at Louis'?"

"Well, a different gay set, maybe.—I can't believe it, but I'm hungry again."

"Good. So'm I."

Quietly they explored the fridge, and ate at the kitchen table. They discussed the rather important problem of what to get Natalia's mother, the woman who had everything, for Christmas. Natalia's half-brother Teddie was not coming east after all, so it was imperative that they go to Ardmore, where her mother had decided to spend Christmas, instead of at her Philadelphia apartment, because she was giving a Christmas Eve buffet party and needed space. Maybe the latest *Times* world atlas would be a good present, Jack suggested, because he happened to have seen an ad for it, and because her mother loved looking at maps of where she had been and were she might go next.

"Brilliant, Jack darling!" Natalia whispered. "I'll pick it up at Rizzoli."

They would have two Christmasses, one at her mother's and one here at home.

"By the way," Jack said, "Elsie's friend with the long hair— she said Linderman's leaving them alone lately. Some of Elsie's friends chased him out of Minetta Street and had him on the run!" Jack smiled.

"So Elsie told me—Have you seen him lately? I never have, but I must say I don't look around for him."

"No. Oh yes, once this week, I think. He didn't see me. He was sporting a new overcoat and a Russian fur cap. I wouldn't've recognized him if not for the dog."

17

Prayer is a form of betting, Ralph wrote in his notebook and underlined it. He continued:

> *It is another way of saying, "I hope," and the person praying doesn't count on it. Only when something works out do we hear anyone say, "I knew my prayers would be answered!" What rubbish and cant!*

Enough! Ralph could have gone on. The entry above the prayer entry read:

> *When will the United States get it through its head that the Likud party doesn't want peace? That peace would ruin all its plans? They are Artful Dodgers of peace, hating and fearing the meaning of the word.*

He sat at his wooden table thinking, being quiet. It was the day after Christmas. Ralph had had only God for company yesterday, but his dog was enough. He had thought of dropping a Christmas card into the Sutherlands' box, and he would have written, "A pleasant holiday season and good health to you." He would not have sent a card saying "Merry Christmas," that most banal of phrases, and connected with the presumed sanctity of the virgin-born Jesus. Christmas, a season dragged down by the very people who screamed it every year, was too dismal to contemplate, dismal for the poor, an obligation for others, a happy season only for children of well-off parents, and for people who sold things at prices seasonally adjusted higher—yes, and in stores where signs were put up saying: This is also pickpocket season so be careful. Ralph had worked Christmas Eve day and Christmas Day night, and he would work again this evening at Midtown-Parking. Business was brisk there, and the FULL sign was usually on display in front.

He had not delivered a card to the Sutherlands, but he could send or bring one for New Year's, he thought. Just a friendly gesture. He would address it to both, of course, though he sensed a great difference between the two: Sutherland was a finer man than his wife was a woman. Ralph believed that Mrs Sutherland was sly and secretive, possibly also snobbish and spoilt. She apparently went out to work, but she didn't work every day, Ralph thought, and not at regular hours, because Ralph at least twice had seen Mrs Sutherland going off at 11 or 12 noon toward Sheridan Square to look for a taxi to wherever she was going, though once he had followed her, and she had gone into the Christopher Street uptown subway entrance by the newsstand there.

And she too had made Elsie's acquaintance now. The day before Christmas Eve, Ralph had been buying his *Times* around 1 in the afternoon, he had walked past the glass-fronted café-restaurant near Sheridan Square and seen Mrs Sutherland and Elsie in lively conversation at a table, having lunch with wine. A cold day, that had been. They had perhaps been talking about him, Ralph thought. Naturally, John Sutherland would have told his wife that the man he had thought was honest and decent because he had returned Sutherland's wallet, was now "annoying" a young girl named Elsie, who had actually sought out him, John Sutherland, for help. Ralph Linderman could imagine the conversation, once a woman got hold of the story! Ralph detested remembering that instant when he had seen Elsie and Mrs Sutherland so vigorously tête-à-tête, but the image kept returning to him, as if something in him wanted to torture him by repeating it like a flashing light: Mrs Sutherland on the left, her long streaky blond hair down to her shoulders, smoking a cigarette as usual and gesturing with the hand that held it, and Elsie leaning a little across the table, fresh-faced and fair-haired, smiling her delightful smile, the smile she never gave him.

Ralph had been wearing his old tweed overcoat and a cap that day, hoping in fact to catch a glimpse of Elsie, maybe shopping on West 4th, without her instantly spotting him. If she did see him, she always turned the other way or crossed the street, which pained Ralph.

Just what were Elsie and Mrs Sutherland up to? If he had seen them once together, very likely they got together at other times. Ralph imagined that they were fashioning some bulwark against him, some way of preventing him from speaking to or even getting near Elsie again. Yet how could they? Had he yet broken any law, written or unwritten? Hadn't Elsie's hooligan chums been guilty of harassment and disorderly conduct in public when they had pushed and shoved him on Sixth Avenue? Was there any law against anyone walking through Minetta Street, pausing for two minutes to contemplate one of the interesting old houses there? Ralph's sense of injustice brought the dreary Lebanon situation to mind again. He had watched that creeping horror since how long? More than a year, anyway, when Israel had rolled its tanks in with the avowed intention of getting the PLO out, and Ralph had at once thought "more land", which was their eternal objective. Ralph read things the Israeli government said backward, such as "peace" and "security" and found it useful. The truth was, they preferred insecurity, enemies around them. Then the massacres at those two Palestinian camps, the dirty work done by someone else, of course, the Christian Phalangists, while the Israeli soldiers who controlled the territory looked on, pleased as Spaniards at a bullfight. Irksome that America financed all that. Then to cap all the wrongness, America had sent Marines as a "peacekeeping force" to Beirut, as if America could be seen as anything but the ally and financer of Israel, and of course the inevitable had happened, a suicidal truck-bomb attack on the Marine quarters, which killed about two hundred and fifty Americans, most of them nineteen-year-olds who hadn't a clue why they were in Lebanon in the first place. Wrongness and wrongness! All sick-making and phony! What had Reagan said to the parents of those boys? Nothing but more fuzziness, as the Americans crept out of the mess as quietly as possible, ships fading over the horizon. Ralph liked to think that American public opinion would not have stood for any more rubbish, any more lies as to objectives. Ralph still had faith.

He still sat at his table with his ruled notebook beside him, but he stared at a wall, and his heart beat faster with his angry thoughts, and he hated that. He went into the bathroom, where he was trying out some small wooden boats in the tub.

These three boats looked like floating top hats, though their brims were disproportionally wider than the crowns, and the boats were of different sizes. The crowns represented superstructures where the controls would be. One boat was made of a cigar box lid which he had rounded with a knife, the others of slightly thicker wood which he had found in the street and rounded. The superstructures were cylinders of wood. Ralph had a collection of metal rings, wood scraps, small steel springs that he picked up from the floors of garages where he worked, and from dump carts. He was trying out the little boats, when weighted with teaspoons and forks, to see how closely they might approach a shore, which he had simulated by leaning dinner plates and saucers around the edge of his tub's bottom. Not ideal, as sand would be, but maybe he could learn from it. The tub had about seven inches of water in it. As far as Ralph knew, no such boats were in use at ports and river docks in primitive places where not enough dredging had been done. His objective was to get the little boats as close as possible to the shore for unloading. The boats should be able to rotate on their own axis and be able to fit into a semi-circular floating dock. Ralph sloshed the water observing drafts, recovering teaspoons, imagining heights of waves that a storm might throw up, imagining a round boatside touching shore.

God's prancing and whining, his yelp of impatience, reminded Ralph that it was time for an airing.

"You're my clock, God." Ralph stood up. It was nearly noon, indeed time for God's airing, after which Ralph intended to sleep a little. He might play with the boats later, depending on when he awakened, if he had a few minutes to spare before work.

With the New Year, Ralph's hours changed at the Midtown-Parking Garage, and he was on the 4 p.m. to midnight shift now. He could keep almost normal hours and enjoy the daylight. Midnight seemed early to him, the streets were still lively at Sheridan Square, when he got off the bus by half past midnight or so. After airing God, Ralph sometimes walked down to the coffee shop where Elsie worked five nights a week until 2 a.m., though the nights varied, from what Ralph could see, and he was never sure she would be on. If she was, she managed never to serve him, and put up a good show of not seeing him. Ralph sipped his coffee, hardly took his eyes off Elsie, and ignored the nudging and whispering among the other girls behind the counter. He wasn't drunk or drugged, he wasn't spilling his coffee on the counter or the floor, as some of the other clients did. Ralph knew, however, that he annoyed Elsie by turning up at close to 2 a.m., and lingering till the place closed, till there was some awkwardness that Ralph could see through the kitchen window of the place, because Elsie wanted him to go before she went out the door, and the other workers knew this. Elsie had merely to walk up Seventh, through Carmine Street and across Sixth to Minetta Street. He had followed her one night, when she hadn't been aware of him, he was sure, and he had seen her make a beeline for home.

Ralph Linderman walked downtown on Seventh Avenue at a leisurely pace toward the slit of light where Elsie was, or he hoped she was tonight. It was half past 1 a.m., he would have just the proper time for a coffee, and he had brought the *Times* with him and was going to pay Elsie no mind, not even glance at her, so that she might leave for home in a normal manner, and he might— if he felt like it—follow her at a distance.

Twenty paces or so before the coffee shop door, Ralph slowed and almost stopped. A man and woman had crossed Seventh downtown from him, were now walking toward him, and the woman was Mrs Sutherland. A light had fallen on her hair, which Ralph would have known anywhere and at any distance at which he could have seen it: parted on the right side, some of it often falling over her left eye, and now he heard her short laugh which struck him as familiar, though when had he heard it before? The man with her was not John Sutherland but a more slender figure and he wore a top hat and a dark coat.

Near the patch of light in front of the coffee shop, the man swept his hat off in a graceful way. They were going in!

Ralph waited, curious, wondering if it were wise if he went into the place now. He advanced cautiously, stood to one side of the glass door and peered in. He saw Elsie talking to Mrs Sutherland, who had taken a stool and was sitting sideways on it. Elsie was smiling broadly. The man with Mrs Sutherland was bald-headed, though rather young looking, grinning, restless on his feet, standing near Mrs Sutherland with his top hat in his hand at his side. Elsie pulled the bow that fastened her apron in back, and disappeared through a door. Other patrons in the place glanced at Mrs Sutherland and at the man's top hat and patent leather shoes.

A moment later, Elsie appeared in a polo coat, walked around the end of the counter and joined Mrs Sutherland and the man, who looked at Elsie with a toothy smile. Ralph stepped into the darkness as the trio approached the door. He walked uptown, slowly, listening to hear, if he could, which way they were walking.

When Ralph paused, he heard nothing but the traffic's hum, and he turned. The three of them were walking downtown. Ralph followed. It was a cold night, windless but sharply cold. Ralph wore his older and thinner overcoat, and he had brought no gloves, and wore no hat. He turned his coat collar up, and he kept his hands in his coat pockets.

What were they up to, walking downtown at 2 a.m.? Two empty taxis passed, and the tall man showed no interest in them.

They turned east on Houston Street, and their laughter floated back to Ralph, though he was too far away to hear a word of what they were saying. Then they crossed Houston and entered a street going south. Ralph had to wait for the next light. When he got to the street, they were out of sight. They must have gone into the single place with a light, Ralph thought, the restaurant or bar ten yards away on the east side of the street. Ralph approached this place, which had a crude sign saying STAR-WALKERS above the door.

"Bah—de—dah—bah—de—dah ..." A girl's voice came through the closed door and dimly lit window. "Woo ... oo ... woo ..." There was a stringed instrument with the voice. A placard propped against a rail in front of the place showed a girl with curly hair clutching a guitar. MARION GILL and her talking guitar. Jazz. Rock. Rhythm and Blues.

The place looked as if it had formerly been a grocery store or some kind of shop that had had a display window. Dark red curtains hung behind the window, and through the glass top half of the door Ralph could see candle-lit tables, a raised section at the back where the guitar-playing girl sat, the girl on the poster outside, Ralph thought. Hadn't one of the hooligans who had followed him shouted that name, "Marion"? The hooligan girl had had long hair, but that might have been a wig.

This thought was a small blow to Ralph: for that tramp of a girl who had pursued him to be singing and playing before the public gave her some status—at least it was a job—though in truth

Ralph held such forms of entertainment in contempt. Untrained voices! Empty-headed people, the dregs of society frequented such holes-in-the-wall as this, poisoning their already sick selves with alcohol and tobacco, marijuana and cocaine. So Elsie had been seduced by this kind of entertainment, and Mrs Sutherland liked it too? Ralph could imagine that John Sutherland did not want to go to such a place, if his wife had even told him that she was going here. And who was this new man in the picture? Was he Mrs Sutherland's secret lover? Or was he possibly after Elsie? He looked as if he had money. That would be tempting to Elsie. Everything tempted Elsie, that was the problem, the danger. Ralph again peered, but could not see far into the place. He could not see Elsie, but he felt she was there. He believed that her presence, anywhere, had a magnetic effect on him, whether he could see her or not.

Ralpn blew on his hands, stepped into the shadow of the housefronts, and walked slowly to keep his circulation up.

"Mah . . . puddy . . . bah . . ." said the female voice.

Insane words, if they were words!

A young man and a girl, chattering away, walked briskly past Ralph and turned in at the door of Star-Walkers. Ralph looked in as they opened the door. He saw Mrs Sutherland in profile at a table against the left wall, leaning forward toward the bald fellow, and behind her and beside her sat Elsie with her eyes fixed on the guitarist.

Ca—*lumph!* The door closed again.

Ralph shut his eyes, turned uptown, rubbed his hands together and stuffed them back in his pockets. Misery! Unhappiness ahead! Ralph felt the sting of tears, might have wept, except that anger and shock dominated his feelings. Why hadn't he done better by Elsie? How had he failed, when he had meant so well? Ralph imagined drug-peddlers in such a place as Star-Walkers, and the top-hatted man would have the money to buy anything— for Elsie.

Well, he had not failed, he thought as he walked faster, as he turned left on Houston toward Seventh Avenue. If she damaged her health with these late hours, she was not yet wasting away, not yet even ill! He would keep trying.

Was Mrs Sutherland deliberately leading Elsie astray for her personal amusement? And did John Sutherland know about it?

Ralph would have liked to linger until Elsie and Mrs Sutherland and the man left the place, but that might not be for two more hours.

Should he write John Sutherland a short and discreet note or speak to him? Speaking struck Ralph as wiser. The possibly dangerous and crucial information would then not be on paper.

18

"Oh, Mr Sutherland!"

Jack whirled around. He had been walking fast.

"Good afternoon!"

Jack recognized Linderman, dogless now, smiling, with creases in his cheeks. "Hello."

"I have something—I'll be brief. I know you're busy."

Jack made a gesture with the portfolio under his arm. He had just come from a conference with Trews.

"I am, in fact."

"It's about your wife."

"Oh? What about her?"

Linderman spoke more softly. "I don't know—or maybe you do know that she's seeing Elsie Tyler lately and—one evening I saw your wife with Elsie and with another man—I can describe him if you like—going into a nightclub in the SoHo district.—I should think you'd be concerned."

"Mr Linderman—my wife's an independent woman. I like things that way. So does she."

"If she goes out with another man?—Perhaps it's quite innocent. But with Elsie? Elsie's so much younger!"

What was the old fool getting at? Jack suddenly recalled the evening that Linderman must be talking about. Natalia and Louis had gone down to SoHo to hear a certain girl guitarist whom Elsie knew. "Was it a tall man?" Jack asked. "Sort of bald on top and—"

"Yes!"

"Friend of the family," Jack said. "My wife's known him longer than—He's our daughter's godfather!" Jack said with a smile.

Linderman's mouth turned down a little, maybe with disappointment.

"You're worrying unnecessarily, Mr Linderman. I assure you. I've got to push off now." But Linderman's thunderous stare held him.

"I don't like Elsie meddling with these sophisticated people—older than she is. She can be led astray."

"She's—" Jack shook his head in exasperation. "My wife, for instance—Thanks to my wife, Elsie's going to a school now. Studying. Art and literature. I ask you, Mr Linderman, is that corruption?" Jack gave a laugh, though he had the feeling, as he had had before, that he had better try to end this encounter on a friendly note.

"What school?"

Jack pretended to think. "Forget the name of it. Uptown. Got to go now, sir. Busy day for me." With a wave of his portfolio arm, Jack strode down the sidewalk toward his house.

As he unlocked the front door, he did not look back at Linderman.

Jack returned to his own problems. A few of his yak book drawings were not quite right yet, and the meeting today was his second with Trews about them. First Brian Kent, the author of the book, had liked the spirit and atmosphere of the drawings, but had wanted more Tibetan detail in the huts, the costumes. This was easy for Jack, as he still had photographs from the public library. Now Trews thought he had overdone it. The details conflicted with Jack's dreamlike style in the first place, but Jack had added them. Now what it came down to was doing five drawings over, because the details could not be whited out. Jack hated doing drawings over, trying to duplicate the freedom of the first, and he was in a bad mood five minutes after he closed the apartment door. But he decided to make one stab this afternoon and not just call it a day at 3.45. He'd make some tea for himself when Amelia arrived in half an hour, he thought, keep her company while she had her snack, which was usually peanut butter on soda crackers with a glass of Coke, though Jack always proposed milk.

Jack laid out his work on his long table. Which drawing first? The cooking pot scene, he thought. This was the author, dark-haired as he actually was, his straight hair in need of a trim, hunched beside his clay pot which hung over a fire, as the author had described, on a horizontal stick supported by a heap of stones on either side of the fire. The details in this were genuine: mountain flowers, the narrator's Tibetan leather knapsack or huge purse, bedding roll, water canteen—Well, a few would go, but Jack would keep the sweet little flowers, which he had come to love. Jack was glad that Trews had passed on the encounter scene: the author and a small boy on a mountain slope in the chill morning mists. In the book, Brian Kent had heard pebbles rolling, and then the boy had slowly become visible, shrouded in a cape, his dark eyes round and amazed. Each had frightened the other to a rigid halt for a few seconds.

He would not tell Natalia about today's encounter with Linderman. What the hell had Linderman seen, after all? Natalia going into Star-Walkers with Louis Wannfeld about two weeks ago. Jack hadn't yet been to Star-Walkers, but he could imagine the place. Natalia had thought Marion, the singer-guitar-player, rather good. And Elsie seemed quite hung up on her, according to Natalia, and it was a mutual thing. Marion was twenty-one or -two, Jack remembered, and had an apartment on Greene Street, or had been lent the apartment. And where was Genevieve, Elsie's old girlfriend, in all this? Hadn't Natalia said something about Marion throwing out her own roommate so Elsie could move in? Or was it Genevieve who had thrown Elsie out? Jack couldn't keep track of such things. More interesting was the fact that Elsie was going to get some work as a fashion photographer's model, which would certainly beat shoving mugs of coffee across the counter at that place on Seventh Avenue. Natalia and Louis had managed this, and with the minimum of effort, it seemed. It had been Natalia's idea that Elsie might earn some money as a model, and Louis had introduced her to a fashion photographer friend or acquaintance of his. The photographer had been interested enough to invite Elsie to his studio to take some shots of her, and Natalia had heard from Louis that the photographer was going to try her on a job, and maybe he already had.

"Dad-dee-ee!"

Jack was startled by his daughter's voice within the apartment. "Hi, Jack? You there? It's Susanne."

Jack walked down the hall. "Well, hi. What a surprise!" Jack had expected a school employee to ring the downstairs bell.

"I was visiting a friend on Bank, so I thought I'd call for Amelia." Susanne looked her usual unmade-up self, rust-colored trousers and brown loafers in need of a shine, dark brown winter coat. "Amelia, I'll help you with that."

Amelia was starting on her crackers and peanut butter. "I don't want any butter with 'em!"

"Okay, but you do need a plate," said Susanne.

Jack reached for the kettle. "Can I interest you in a cup of tea?"

He could. They sat at the kitchen table. Susanne asked about the yak book, and Jack told her of his latest difficulties. Susanne had bought five copies of *Half-Understood Dreams* at five different bookshops to give to friends at Christmas, though Jack had offered to get them for her at his author's discount price. Amelia kept interrupting with events of Her Day, and Jack was happy to let Susanne chide her for rudeness.

"Don't just interrupt, Amelia. Now if you have something interesting to say, we'll listen. Won't we, Jack?"

"Sure," said Jack.

Amelia's lips parted, she looked sideways at some spot on the table, her well-defined brows frowning a little. "I read the best in class today."

"Is that true, Amelia?" Jack asked with respectful surprise.

"Probably is," Susanne murmured.

As if hit by sudden shyness, Amelia got up and fled to her room, whence, a few seconds later, they heard a recorder's tootling.

"Natalia's still working hard?" Susanne asked.

"Well—noonish to six or so most days. She likes it. Meets a lot of people, you know. All kinds," Jack added with a smile, because art galleries did attract all kinds.

"Whatever happened to that blond girl I met here once? With the sailor cap. Remember?"

"Oh, Elsie. Natalia's met her too. She's—she was working at a coffee shop around here. Now she's trying out as a fashion model. For photographers. I hope it works out."

"She is pretty. I remember that."

"Yes." Jack stared at his nearly empty cup, then picked it up and finished it. He didn't want to say any more about Elsie just now. Susanne knew about the old guy in the neighborhood who had returned his wallet. But Susanne didn't know that Linderman was pestering Elsie.

"You look thoughtful today, Jack." Susanne was clearing away dishes from the table.

"Me work," said Jack, smiling, getting up. "I have to get back to it.—Want to stay for dinner with us?" He knew Susanne could either read until dinnertime—she always had her brown briefcase with her, and she had it now—or she could find some task to do in Amelia's room.

"No, thanks, Jack. I'll be heading up to Riverside. Unless there's something you want me to do? Natalia hasn't lost a button lately?"

Jack laughed. Natalia detested sewing on a button, and would rather wear a suit or a coat with a missing button for a week than pick up a needle. "I don't think so, no."

Susanne called a good-bye to Amelia who was watching TV, then said to Jack, "Oh, how's Louis doing?"

Jack could tell from Susanne's tone that she had heard something about Louis' cancer. "Now it seems he's not in any danger. That's the latest. Must've been a suspicion—or Louis' fearing the worst."

"Isn't that great?" she said in an awed voice. "Natalia's so fond of him. Well, it's mutual, I know. She'd be really broken up if something happened to Louis."

Jack nodded. "True."

Susanne left.

Jack was still working when Natalia arrived at half past 7. It was Natalia's night to cook, they had agreed that morning, though she hadn't brought anything that Jack could see, except a bunch of chrysanthemums in green tissue.

"Elsie gave me these," Natalia said. "Aren't they pretty? I had a drink with her just now."

"Oh?—Nice." Jack meant the flowers. They were yellow and pink-red, fresh and starlike. "Shall I get a vase?" he asked elegantly, pronouncing it vahse, and went into the kitchen.

"Elsie's going to have a photo in *Mademoiselle*. Berkman clenched it today and Elsie called me at the gallery to tell me. It's a sweater ad. She's on top of the world.—Put them on the white table, Jack.— Funny—" Natalia stared at the flowers.

Jack set the clear glass vase in the center of the table. "What's funny?"

"In France chrysanthemums are for funerals. You bring them

only when somebody's dead—you know? I'm sure Elsie doesn't know that." Natalia glanced at Jack, smiling.

"Elsie has a lot to learn.—I'm pleased about the sweater job."

"Berkman wants her hair longer, but that's no problem."

"Who is this Berkman? Did we ever meet him?"

"No, he's one of Louis' acquaintances.—Elsie's given notice at that coffee shop where she works. I hope she's not jumping the gun, but there's no holding her right now.—Like a drink, Jack?"

"Yes, please. Can you do a Jack Daniel's?—And what's for dinner, ma'am?"

"Oh." Natalia turned from the bar cabinet, looking lost. "Oh! My God, it's outside the door! I'm losing my mind!" She went to the apartment door and opened it, and came back with a largish bag. "I went to that delicatessen on Sixth. Got some barbecue stuff."

"Ah-h.—Have I told you, my darling, that I love you in that dress?"

"Ye-s-ss," Natalia said over her shoulder as she unloaded things onto the kitchen table. "Thank you."

The dress was a dusty pink with long triangles of red coming up from the hem to mid-thigh. Natalia had bought it, then said she hated it, though now and then she wore it.

"Just what do you like about this dress?" she asked, back at the bar cabinet now.

"It's different. Like you.—Oh, never mind."

She handed him his drink. Then Amelia came into the living-room, having just finished something she wanted her parents to see. This was a watercolor showing red housefronts with several yellow windows and a green street running horizontal in the foreground. Amelia held the still wet drawing flat on her palms, and was at pains to point out to her father that the yellow windows didn't touch the red houses, so the colors did not run together.

"I did notice that," said Jack.

"That was a lot of work," said Amelia.

"And you did well. Not a single mistake." Jack cupped his hand against the back of her head, then she ran off, happy.

Jack joined Natalia in the kitchen. "Susanne brought Amelia home this afternoon. She said she's home this weekend if we need her. And she asked about Louis. She didn't use the word cancer. I told her he was doing fine now. That's right, isn't it?"

Natalia frowned at the kitchen door, as if at Amelia, but Amelia was back in her room. "He's not," she said softly to Jack. "Since you ask. He has got cancer of the pancreas. He told me a couple of months ago, November maybe. But he prefers to—you know, not talk about it. I don't know how Susanne heard anything."

"Are you talking about something fatal? Can't they take part of the pancreas out?"

"Yes, well—everybody's heard of doing that, but Louis' doctor thinks it might make things worse. Something about its leading to spreading."

Jack suddenly saw Louis in a more gallant light. A gentlemanly light, anyway. Louis had been his same old self at his pre-Christmas party.

19

IN the middle of February, Ralph Linderman lost his job at Midtown-Parking. A new mechanic-manager came on to replace Joey, the friendly and human Joey Fischer, who had gone off to work at a garage farther uptown and nearer where he lived, and at once Frank Conlan, the guard whose duty usually followed Ralph's and for whom Ralph had had to wait so often, blew his top against Ralph to the new manager for no reason, Ralph thought, except that Conlan was ashamed of his own work, and knew Ralph disliked him. Conlan told tales, apparently, about Ralph's unwillingness to cooperate, his surliness, and Conlan invented mistakes, and the new manager—a dumb, bored-looking fellow of forty or so—had listened. Not that Frank Conlan had said all this in the open, oh no, but behind Ralph's back after Ralph had gone off duty.

"What's this about you pulling a gun on a customer?" asked the new manager, who was called Roland something.

"Never," Ralph had said.

"Frank said you did. Frank said . . ."

Frank said this and that, and Roland had told Ralph all this with a nasty and suspicious smile, as if he might be expecting Ralph to deny these charges, but as if he, Roland, believed them.

"Conlan might've said these things to my face," Ralph had said. "He won't, because he knows they're not true."

"Plenty of other guard jobs in New York," Roland had said with a wave of his hand, walking off.

On his last day of duty, Ralph had lingered—Frank was even that day late—in order to say to Frank Conlan's face: "You're a nasty customer, Conlan. Backbiting and bitchy as a woman!" And Ralph had walked off, out into the sullen daylight, holding his head high, shutting out the filth that Conlan shouted after him, trying and succeeding in not hearing it.

Such warped characters as Frank Conlan were best erased from memory, thought Ralph. The world was full of them, but why dwell on them? The world was full of beautiful things too, though they were rarer and fewer. Ralph went to an employment office to say he had been fired for no particular reason, or if there were a precise reason, he would be glad to learn it. No questions were asked at the office, Ralph was offered another place, which he declined because of its location, way up on the East Side. Ralph said he would come back in a few days.

Meanwhile he had unemployment benefits, and he meant to enjoy a couple of weeks of leisure, even though it was the dead of winter and dirty snow lay around the city, covering nasty patches of ice in the gutters.

Oddly, in just these days when he had ample time to find Elsie on the streets, to watch her from a distance, follow her at any hour of the day or night, he lost her. It was amazing. He went to the coffee shop on three or four days and evenings, and she wasn't there, and he almost asked one of the other girls—three or four now, so it looked as if Elsie had been replaced—if Elsie were sick or if she had quit, but he knew the faces of two of the girls, and knew they did not like him. So he didn't ask even the new girls.

He walked through Minetta Street at 1 in the afternoon, at 6 p.m., sometimes at 2 a.m., and he never saw Elsie, though the third floor windows, where he knew she lived, were often lit behind their drawn curtains, and once he had seen the girl with long dark red hair, the girl with whom Elsie shared the apartment, Ralph thought, coming out of the house, alone. He even went twice after midnight to the street where the Star-Walkers bar or nightclub was, spent perhaps half an hour walking down the block and back again, without seeing Elsie.

Had she moved from Minetta Street? Mrs Sutherland would know, Ralph thought, but he could hardly ask her. He saw her occasionally in the neighborhood, but she seemed never to see him, and always looked as if she were daydreaming, or thinking only about where she had to go, to a taxi or the Christopher Street subway. "Excuse me, Mrs Sutherland. May I ask if Elsie is all right or is she sick?" Ralph might have dared ask, but he did not want to chance being rebuffed or ignored by Mrs Sutherland.

Once he had seen Elsie on the east side of Seventh, running

uptown, meeting Mrs Sutherland on the sidewalk. They had walked off into that triangle part of Sheridan Square that went into Waverly Place, talking away. Why wasn't Elsie so free with him, as happy with him? Ralph could have followed them, but hadn't. He realized that he hadn't wanted to be seen by either of them, when both might have turned on him, made some kind of fuss in public. When had that been? January, Ralph thought, when Elsie had still been working at the coffee shop.

Now, on the fifth day of his leisure, his freedom, Ralph realized that he was unhappy, confused, and somehow frightened. He had walked the familiar streets so many times, prolonging his shopping expeditions, prolonging God's airings. He had stared at corners where he had once glimpsed her, by that bookshop on a corner of Sheridan Square, along the rows of cheap shops on Christopher Street, and on lower Seventh Avenue, of course, on that stretch between the coffee shop and Downing and Carmine Streets, either of which Elsie would probably walk through to get to Minetta Street.

He wondered if she had gone back home, to that small town in upstate New York? But that seemed unlikely, since Elsie was so enamored of New York City. Had she been kidnapped, was she being gang-raped somewhere, mouth gagged? This thought made Ralph squirm, made his hands shake. But you never knew! In New York what seemed extremely unlikely could happen.

"Could happen," Ralph said aloud, when he thought of the gang-rape, and he stood up and looked out his window. It was dusk, nearly 5 in the afternoon. Dreary hour! He could see yellowish lights in windows in the back of houses. Ralph felt very alone, deserted, lost. He could not analyse his emotion. Elsie had not been a friend or companion, far from it. She had been a dear little thing, like a godchild or a daughter, a beautiful little sprite, whom he glimpsed now and again—not often, perhaps, but he had counted on the joy of those glimpses—and now she had vanished.

A couple of days later, Ralph mustered his courage, put on his good coat and black rabbit-fur cap, and an air of calm politeness, and walked without God to the coffee shop. It was around 5 in the afternoon, the place was half full, with mostly young people devouring hamburgers. Ralph ordered a coffee from a solemn-faced girl with brown hair. When she brought the coffee, Ralph said:

"Excuse me, miss. Do you happen to know where Elsie is working now?"

"Elsie?" This girl was one of the new girls here, Ralph was sure.

"She used to work here. A blond girl. Could you ask?" He indicated, with a nod of his head, another waitress nearby.

The girl went over and spoke to the other waitress, who Ralph recognized as one of the old stand-bys. She looked at Ralph, then shook her head as she murmured something to the other girl, which might have been: "Don't tell him anything."

"We don't know, sir. Sorry," said the new girl when she came back, and she wiped some drops of ketchup from the counter.

Ralph saw the second waitress go through a door to the kitchen. Had she gone to report that he was here and had asked a question, a *polite* question, about Elsie's whereabouts? An instant later, an older woman, who Ralph had learned before was the manager or owner, and who also wore a white and blue uniform, stuck her head around the kitchen door and saw him. But she did not come out, she ducked back with a negative gesture of her hand, and the second waitress turned and went back to her duties.

John Sutherland had said that Elsie was going to school now. But what school? New York was full of schools. Art and literature. Art appreciation? Or had Sutherland been lying to get rid of him, to try to snatch Elsie, in a way, beyond his grasp? Ralph did not like to think of John Sutherland lying. It didn't go with Sutherland. Sutherland was the kind of man who looked you in the eye. If Sutherland had told him, and so firmly, to stay away from Elsie, it was only because Sutherland misunderstood his attitude toward Elsie. A great pity.

Would Elsie stick with a school course? Not long, if Ralph read her temptations aright. That was why the girl needed such watching over! But Ralph sensed that Mrs Sutherland might make Elsie stick with it, since it had been Mrs Sutherland's idea, it seemed. Elsie had looked as if she were quite fond of Mrs Sutherland.

20

JACK approached the Hotel Chelsea smiling with anticipation. He had walked up from Grove at a fast clip but slowed as he turned the corner east into Twenty-third Street. No sign of Elsie or a cameraman out in front as yet. This was Elsie's first big job. She had called up last night, sounding nervous and happy, and had asked if Natalia or he, or both, could come around noon to the Chelsea, because Berkman was taking pictures out in front starting at 11. Natalia said she couldn't, because of work and a lunch date with Isabel and some buyers. It was another damned cold day with a wind kicking up dust and grit, hurtling litter of all kinds along the sidewalk on Twenty-third. Jack pressed his gloved hands against his ears, and entered the Hotel Chelsea.

He spotted Elsie at once in the back left corner of the lobby, standing near one of the black bench seats, surrounded by a few curious people, mostly male, and there was Berkman, Jack assumed, a plump dark-haired man with his camera on a tripod. Elsie stood in a black sleeveless dress with hand on hip, wearing a wide-brimmed hat, and with a huge white flower like an oversized chrysanthemum fixed above her right breast.

"Back, please!" said Berkman, motioning to the little crowd, and stepping back himself with his camera.

Elsie looked up at the ceiling near the door, but she had seen Jack, who was standing between her and the front door, and had given him a quick smile.

"Ser-rious," said Berkman. He took two or three shots.

"Ho-ho!" said a young man in levis and sweater, and clapped.

Other men clapped, smiled, and some drifted away while others, coming in through the front door, lingered to watch.

"Where's her coat, Hester? We're going out," said Berkman.

Jack stepped nearer a wall of the lobby.

Berkman carried his camera outdoors, accompanied by Hester, a lanky young woman in a long skirt, and Elsie came over to Jack, carrying her polo coat. Elsie had good make-up on, Jack saw, a line of dark at her eyes which was just right. Her lips seemed slightly changed by the red lipstick and for the better, or the more glamorous, anyway.

"You look just—terrific," Jack said.

"Thanks for coming. Thanks." Elsie glanced nervously at the glass front door. "It'll take him a minute to pick the right background. Whew!—Where'd Marion go?" Elsie looked around, then gave a wave to someone sitting among other people at a side wall.

A girl with shortish dark brown hair, soft and wavy around her head, came toward them rather shyly. This was the guitar-player Natalia had told Jack about. She had no make-up, and wore blue jeans, fur-lined boots and a denim jacket lined with imitation sheep's wool.

"Marion Gill," Elsie said. "This is Jack Sutherland."

"Oh!" Marion had a big smile. "How do you do, Jack? I heard about you."

"Hi," Jack said.

Elsie had suddenly acquired poise, Jack thought. Or if she were feigning poise today, she was doing a good job. Two or three fellows strolled around, looking Elsie over, but they might not have existed for Elsie. Jack was reminded of her indifference to her admirers in the Seventh Avenue coffee shop. She held her head high. Her hair was longer than when Jack had seen her last.

"You're the one who sings. With the guitar," Jack said to Marion.

"Yes. I'm here today just to give Elsie moral support." Marion shifted slowly from one booted foot to the other. "Don't you have to change, Elsie?"

"He wants one more in this dress outside," Elsie replied.

The Berkman assistant called Hester summoned Elsie.

"Put your coat on till he's ready," Marion said to Elsie. "It's freezing out."

Elsie drew her coat on as she walked toward the door. Jack followed. Berkman had his tripod on the sidewalk west of the Chelsea's doorway. Elsie was to stand ten feet to the west of the awning also, and Berkman was waiting for the right passerby for

140

background, and both Marion and Hester stood ready to take Elsie's coat.

"Not *behind* her, please!" Hester shouted to some of the curious, motioning them away.

"Okay!" said Berkman, focusing.

Elsie removed her coat and Marion took it, and stepped aside.

"Arm up!—Behind your head! Right leg!" shouted Berkman, and Elsie stood on her right leg, right hand on hip, left hand behind her head.

"Ah-h!" said someone in the crowd, half-mockingly.

She had to do more. Nobody who was bundled up against the cold should be seen in the background, so it was slow work.

Jack caught Marion's eye, and pointed to the Chelsea's door to indicate that he was going in. He wanted to look at the art work on the walls. There was a big picture of *Le Déjeuner sur l'Herbe* done in monochrome dots like a blown-up newspaper photo, which Jack thought was rather amusing. Another that he liked was a trio of heads and shoulders made of curving brushstrokes of varying colors: a pleasing composition on human imbecility, maybe, because the trio looked quite witless. Jack had told Elsie on the telephone that he would like to invite her to lunch today, and now it seemed that Marion might be coming along too. Jack didn't mind. Marion was Elsie's new girlfriend, according to Natalia.

The minutes passed. It became a quarter to 1. Elsie came into the lobby with Marion near her, and said to Jack:

"I have to change now in the ladies' room. If you're getting bored—"

"I'm not bored," Jack said.

The clientèle of the Hotel Chelsea was not boring. There were young people, the middle-aged and the elderly coming and going, whose faces Jack did not attach a name to, but he liked to imagine them writers, painters, poets, maybe. He knew that some painters paid their bills here by donating a picture for the lobby's walls. There was a table of brochures—flyers—about New York night spots, about a crafts sale for needy artists and sculptors. Elsie was back in the lobby again in no time in a different outfit, a white linen dress with short sleeves and a black patent leather belt. Marion dropped the polo coat over Elsie's shoulders.

After a few minutes, Jack went out to watch. This shot included a taxi, Elsie stepping out of the taxi's open door under the

Chelsea's awning, and they had been lucky in the taxi driver, a chunky fellow in a cap who looked as if he enjoyed smiling. Elsie had to do it three times, opening the door, stepping out in a natural way. It pleased the crowd, which applauded.

Marion got the polo coat onto Elsie again. She had been holding the coat over a radiator in the lobby. "She's cold as hell," Marion said to Jack.

Then Elsie disappeared with Marion, and returned in blue jeans, polo coat and sneakers, Marion behind her. Elsie looked pale, as if flour covered her face.

"Let's go get something hot," Marion said, mainly to Elsie.

"May I invite you both to lunch?" asked Jack. "I know a place very near—"

"I think Elsie's got a chill," Marion said.

They were walking out onto the sidewalk. Jack could see Elsie's jaw trembling.

"Take my gloves," Jack said, because Elsie seemed to have none. "No, I insist! Let's go to my house. Come on, I'll get us a taxi." He went to the curb, and luck was with him, as a taxi was just arriving with someone.

A few seconds later, they were rolling downtown.

Elsie sat huddled. "I had this once before. Ice-skating up where I lived."

Jack exchanged a glance with Marion, who looked worried.

Upstairs in Jack's apartment, he told Marion to get Elsie to lie down under blankets in the bedroom, opened the bed and added still another blanket. Then he got a couple of hot water bottles from the bathroom and filled them out of the tap, which was quicker than the kettle.

Elsie's lips were colorless, and her pallor was frightening. She hugged one hot water bottle with both hands close to her chest. She was lying on her side. Jack shoved the second bottle under the covers between her ankles.

"It'll take a few minutes," he said to Marion. "Don't worry."

Marion seemed speechless. She pulled the covers up to Elsie's ears and higher.

"A hot toddy's a good idea." Jack used hot sink water on top of a goodly measure of Glenfiddich, and handed the glass to Marion in the bedroom.

Then Jack started a fire in the living-room fireplace. When he had it going, he went back to the bedroom. Marion was sitting on a straight chair, holding the toddy which was half gone.

"She's better," Marion said with a glance at Jack.

Her lips looked better, Jack saw. Elsie's eyes were closed, and her brows had drawn together, making her look puzzled.

"Elsie?" Marion held the toddy glass toward her, Elsie took it and sipped carefully and looked at Jack.

"Thank you," Elsie said.

Jack gave a laugh. "Okay! I'll see about some food."

He chose lambchops, fresh from this morning's shopping. In a couple of minutes, the chops were on a grill over the fire. Then he lit the oven and opened a package of french fries.

Marion came into the kitchen. "I think she's pulling out of it.—Gosh, what a spread you've got here! And it's all so tidy!"

"You call this tidy?"

"Compared to my place.—Elsie says you're an artist. Or an illustrator."

"Yep." Jack put forks and steak knives on the kitchen table.

"Can I help you? We eat here?"

"No, in the big room. The white table. There're the napkins, those orange ones."

Marion set the table. "Ah, does that smell good!"

Jack checked his chops and put them aside, because they were cooking too fast. "Like a drink, Marion? Glass of wine?"

Marion preferred wine.

"You're playing at a place in SoHo?"

"Star-Walkers. But not since last week. The place is folding. But all that means is new management coming in." She looked at him with a frank and easy smile. "I play here and there, different nights. Sometimes at a place on West Thirteenth."

"What kind of songs? I haven't been to the Star-Walkers."

"Sometimes ones I've written, sometimes a little folk. All kinds.—I know, your wife was there a couple of nights. I like her. So does Elsie."

Jack looked at the french fries and turned them off. "We can eat in a couple of minutes. I hope Elsie's up to it."

Marion went into the bedroom, and Jack followed her.

Elsie sat up. "I think it's gone.—Wow! I was *scared*!" She gave Jack and Marion a wide, happy smile, and reached for a sneaker from the floor.

143

Color returned to Elsie's cheeks as she ate. "What a crazy day! It's like a dream. Even sitting here."

Marion looked at Jack and murmured, "Elsie says this same thing almost every day."

It was an odd day for Jack too, and in a happy way. He didn't want to ruin the atmosphere by inquiring if Linderman was letting up, even if the answer might be that Elsie hadn't seen him in weeks. It was enough to watch Elsie polishing off a brace of lamb-chops, splashing ketchup on her french fries. She chattered away to Marion. Did Marion think the taxi pictures would be better than the lobby pictures? Elsie thought so, because she thought she was better in action.

"Don't go to that school this afternoon," Marion said, wrinkling her nose. "You can afford to miss one session. Let's just go home, okay?"

While Jack was making coffee, Elsie asked where the bathroom was, and Jack showed her. Then Jack took the coffee into the living-room, and raked the fire.

"Are you from New York, Marion?" Jack couldn't tell from her accent. She spoke rather slowly and distinctly, as if she might be practicing good diction for her singing.

"Me?" Marion smiled. "Where I'm from I'd rather not say. From all over Pennsylvania, various towns. I'm more or less an orphan. My father—left, and my mother dumped me somewhere. At an orphanage when I was about five. I don't remember much."

This sounded sad to Jack. "You seem to be doing all right."

"Lots of people have had it worse. Old cliché, but it helps and it's true. I don't feel sorry for myself. I've been working since I was seventeen," she said with a roll of her round, light brown eyes, "and never was a hooker. I can tune pianos. I learned. I could also be a librarian, if I needed a job, because I took a course and I have a diploma.—Hey, where is that Elsie?" Marion stood up. "I don't want her to faint or something. The bathroom's back here?"

The bathroom was empty.

"Elsie?" Jack called in the direction of the bedroom.

"She's gone," said Marion with resignation. "Her coat's gone. She went to that four o'clock class."

Jack felt jolted. The apartment seemed suddenly empty, even with Marion Gill in it. "What class is this?"

"I think it's English today. Literature—grammar.—Typical of Elsie. I should've hung onto her every minute."

"Could you have?" Jack laughed. "Come on and finish your coffee."

"Don't you want to work?"

Jack shook his head. "No.—Tell me about Elsie. How'd you meet her?"

"In a bar. How does anybody meet anybody? Not the Star-Walkers, another place where I was playing one night. Elsie's just a kid. But she has something. Drive, I think. I hope."

Jack again thought of Linderman and decided to ask. "I hope you and Elsie—especially Elsie—aren't being pestered any more by this old guy with the dog."

"Oh, Ralph!—No, we scared him once. On Minetta Street. Maybe he's still interested, but thank God he doesn't seem to know where we live."

"Where do you live?"

"Greene Street. The SoHo part. A friend's in Europe, and he rented me his studio, cheap. It's not one of the big lofts, but it's still a studio-type thing, big enough for two, and I was living alone when I met Elsie, so—I invited her to move in." Marion glanced up from her coffee cup.

Jack was thinking that Elsie and Marion must be very happy just now. And wouldn't Ralph Linderman flip! "This school—"

"Oh, yes! Natalia recommended it. Elsie loves it and now she can afford it, with the money she gets from modeling. It's ten hours a week and plenty of homework in the reading department."

"You think she'll finish the course?"

Marion hesitated, then her calm lips smiled. "Not sure. But she'll get something out of it. It'll help her shed some of her inferiority complex—some of her shyness. She's not really shy when you come down to it. She's tough as nails and she knows what she wants."

Jack slumped in the armchair and put a foot up on his knee. "And what's that?"

"She wants to experiment with everything. Sometimes she talks about being an actress, but I don't believe that. It's just that an actress, for a time, plays a lot of roles.—Elsie could be a dancer, for instance, while she's still young."

"Boy, could she!"

"Well—" Marion got up. "I better split. Thanks for having us. Thanks for being so nice to Elsie."

Jack said nothing as he got up.

"I love your apartment. And the pictures." Marion gazed at the de Kooning, not for the first time. "You work here too?"

"Yes. Want to see?" Jack said on sudden impulse, maybe because Marion seemed now so close to Elsie. He led the way down the hall. "This is it," Jack said, pushing the curtain to one side. "My salt mine."

"Well! This looks like a busy little spot!"

She didn't enter the room as had Elsie, just gazed at his worktable, rimmed with clutter as ever, at the portfolios leaning against the walls and laid on racks. "Is that Elsie? It is, isn't it?" Her smile grew wider as she looked at the yellow drawing on red paper. "You did that?—Brilliant!" She took a breath as if she might be going to ask if she could have it, or have a photocopy, perhaps, but she said nothing more.

Jack didn't want to make a copy of that drawing, he realized. He walked with Marion toward the apartment door. "What happened to Genevieve?—Or do you know her?"

"Oh, Genevieve. I met her once. Maybe twice.—You've met her?"

"Elsie brought her to a party around Christmas time."

"Oh, at your friend Louis'.—You asked what about her, I don't know, but I hope she gets back with her old girlfriend. Fran, I think her name is. I heard Fran was very upset by Elsie. When Elsie came on the scene, I mean." Marion turned as she reached the apartment door. "Genevieve's the motherly type and I suppose Elsie liked that for a while.—Fran looks like a tough cookie, but I heard she and Genevieve had been together for two or three years before Genevieve met Elsie." Marion gave a laugh and opened the door. "Who cares? Thanks very much, Jack. See you again, I hope."

"Hope so! Thanks for coming."

Jack decided that he liked Marion Gill. She looked honest, she didn't take her guitar-playing too seriously, and maybe she was the best kind of girl Elsie could have run into.

The telephone rang around 6, and it was Natalia. Louis wanted her to have a drink with him, and would Jack mind if she wasn't home till around 8?

146

"Of course not, darling.—Just a drink?"

"Well—I think so. If not, I'll call you again in an hour or so. Anything new?"

"No.—Elsie and her friend were here for lunch."

"Marion too? That's nice.—Talk to you later, Jack."

Jack returned to a novel about arson, but not with the same pleasure as before Natalia's phone call. He hadn't any idea when Natalia would be home, maybe at 10, maybe not until later. But she'd call him, and that was something. Not like, Jack recalled, several dates he had had with her before they married, when Natalia had either stood him up because she forgot, or had been so fantastically late, you couldn't call it being late. Natalia at twenty-two hadn't known night from day. He had never been angry, only anxious, puzzled, walking the floor, or lingering in a restaurant, if the date had been at a restaurant. At first he had suspected that she wanted to tease him, but this was not so. Natalia was quite uncalculating. She had simply been being herself. She still was, but she had improved slightly, because of the teamwork necessary to bring up a child, Jack supposed. "I can't believe *I've* had her," Natalia had said a couple of times with a near grimace as she looked at Amelia. Jack remembered Natalia's terror of giving birth in the last weeks of her pregnancy. He didn't like to recall that. He had felt guilty, and had feared that she might turn against him, and then at the birth, at which Jack had been present until Natalia had shouted at him to leave the room, she had been quite brave, Jack thought.

"Ah, Christ," Jack said with a sigh, and tossed the book onto the sofa. He put his head back and closed his eyes. He'd scrape up something to eat for Amelia, and maybe there was something on TV to amuse them both before he got her to bed, he hoped, by 9. He could call up the Armstrongs and take Amelia and himself over to West Eleventh Street very likely, and stay for dinner, but he didn't want to go to the Armstrongs'.

Natalia called just before 8, and said that Louis wanted her to stay on for a little while.

"Where are you?"

"We're in a bar on East Fifty-fourth. It's a restaurant too. Louis is sort of depressed—you know? Wants to talk for a while."

Jack knew. Sometimes he thought Louis was rather unconcerned, rude, in regard to him. But now Louis had a fatal

147

disease. Or that was the latest, and Jack had to believe it, had to act as if he believed it. "Yep. I understand. Eat something. Don't be too late, honey. Tomorrow's not Sunday.—My love to Louis."

"I'll tell him. Thanks, Jack. Bye now."

Jack felt gloomy for a few seconds. Once he had been annoyed, even slightly angry, when Natalia had stayed out late two nights in one week. Had she been with Sylvia or with Louis? Jack couldn't remember, but he remembered that Amelia had been small, still crawling more than walking. He had said something to Natalia, and she had replied, "We can afford a baby-sitter, if you want to go out. Or come out with me and (whoever it was). I'm not going to be cornered, Jack, by a household." He remembered those last words, spoken with a rare flash in Natalia's eyes, which seemed to illuminate a landscape in her that he hadn't been aware of before. Well, *cornered*, and *household*. Jack had to agree. They weren't living in some primitive society in which a woman certainly and a man probably were trapped and fated to live forever on a small patch of territory. If Jack had pressed too hard, Natalia would have walked out, Jack was sure. She still would.

Around midnight, Jack got into bed to read, but the arson book had lost its appeal. Jack looked over the bookshelves on Natalia's side of the bed. A section of feminist stuff. Galbraith, not tonight. Kafka, no. *The Unquiet Grave* was more like it. Jack pulled out the slender paperback. Natalia had marked a few things with tiny angles at the beginning and end of sentences or paragraphs in her older and stolen copy, Jack remembered. She had talked about the book before they were married. Natalia had already marked the new paperback with a few little right angles.

The reward of art is not fame or success but intoxication: that is why so many bad artists are unable to give it up.

Cyril Connolly's two pages under WOMEN Jack remembered reading before. Natalia had again marked:

In the sex-war thoughtlessness is the weapon of the male, vindictiveness of the female. Both are reciprocally generated, but a woman's desire for revenge outlasts all other emotions.

Jack pondered this. Hard to imagine Natalia being vindictive toward ex-boyfriends, or toward him if they ever broke up. But then Natalia wasn't like most women; she had more sense of humor than most, more logic as well as insight, he thought, maybe therefore more objectivity. At any rate, primitive she was not. He remembered her remark on feminism: "A lot of girls like to be sex-objects while they're young and pretty, when they've got a job and all, then they're not prepared for being dropped when they're thirty-five or so, married or not." It had gone something like that. Natalia meant that they were often dropped by their boyfriends or divorced by their husbands who often married a woman of the same type, but younger. Natalia had no patience with "angry females" aged thirty-five and forty, who had decided that men were their enemies.

Now Jack was sleepy, and he put out the light.

The faint clunk of the apartment door closing awakened him. He heard Natalia tiptoeing, hanging her coat by the hall light.

"Hey," Jack said as loudly as he dared, not wanting to awaken Amelia. "You don't have to pussyfoot."

"Hi, Jack. Did I wake you? Sorry," she whispered, gripping the doorjamb.

She looked a bit tipsy and tired, and Jack adored her when she was like this, because she was usually in a quiet good humor and made revealing remarks sometimes. He looked at his watch. Five past 3. "Doesn't matter," he said.

Jack heard the toothpaste tube fall into the basin, and smiled. The shower gushed, but not for long.

Natalia came in naked, groping for pajamas or nightgown—she wore both alternately and unpredictably—then she put out the bathroom light and fell into bed. "Gosh, what a night!"

Jack waited. "He's not talking about—death and stuff."

"No-o. Well, not directly." She reached for the last cigarette, maybe the last, from the pack that was nearly always on her side of the bed, along with a cricket lighter and an ashtray.

Jack had a glimpse of her profile in the lighter's glow, her strong and rather thick nose, blond hair damp around her face.

"You don't mind if I stayed so late with him, do you? After all, he's not going to be here long." Her tone was apologetic, with the accent on long.

"Of course, I don't mind, honey."

Silence. Then she almost laughed as she said, "There was a

man with a little monkey in the bar. A little gray monkey, very lively. He—"

"A real monkey?"

"*Yes!*" she said through an irrepressible laugh. "The man was teaching him how to pick people's pockets. He was taking things out of men's—jacket pockets."

"That should've cheered Louis up."

"He was cheerful enough. Told me a couple of good jokes. I can't remember them now, but I will tomorrow." A very long silence, long enough for Natalia to put her cigarette out. "Louis has Weltschmerz. It's as if he's standing on a height somewhere, looking down on life—or the world and noticing certain things. Windmills—white horses—running boys on a beach somewhere."

"You haven't asked about Elsie."

"Oh, Elsie," she said in a happy, lingering tone. "She phoned just as I was leaving the gallery. Sounded happy as a clam! Louis spoke with her too. He's very fond of her, you know?"

"I know," Jack said, eyes closed, enjoying the warmth of Natalia's body though they were not touching each other, enjoying her soft, sleepy voice most of all.

"Elsie was wondering whether you liked her new girlfriend."

"I especially do, matter of fact."

Natalia gave a great sigh. "Oh-h, Jack, wake me up in time tomorrow."

It might be a Fernet-Branca morning, Jack thought, Natalia's favorite hangover cure, but he had seen Natalia much drunker and tireder, and she'd always made it if she wanted to.

21

IN early March, Ralph Linderman took a job at the *Hot Arch Arcade* on Eighth Avenue in the 80's. He hated the place, but the pay came out to thirteen dollars more a week than he had been earning. His hours were 8 p.m. to 4 a.m., busiest time for the arcade, which was open "24 hours day & nite", as a sign proclaimed in yellow lightbulbs under the arched name of the place, also in yellow lights, above it. As arcades went, and this meant video games, slot machines, candy and pop-corn machines, air-rifle range, juke boxes, the Hot Arch was smallish, having a long and narrow form, but by the same token intimate and crowded, with people often elbow to elbow. Incredible the number of idle young men and girls at 2 in the morning, and from the look of them they had been idle all day too. The dregs of humanity, Ralph thought. For a few days, he told himself that he had made a mistake in opting for this site to do his guard work, but gradually—even at the end of the first week—he realized that he relished the atmosphere in an odd way. He told himself that he was learning ever more about people. Though what he was learning was depressing, it might prove useful, might be the kind of lore that would protect him in future. Worst for Ralph to endure was the nonstop music, not plain noise, not merely one banal and blaring song, but two or three mixed. Even this had a bright side, if he looked at it the right way: the mingling made it cacophony, relieved it of the label of music, which Muzak still had, music with a beginning and an end. This was insane mankind piling disorder upon disorder. If it deafened and killed people, more people were born every day. The cacophony never had to stop, because machines created it.

And the hookers! The variety surpassed that of 8th Street. Red coarse lips, high heels most of them, but some wore oversized blue jeans, army camouflage uniforms, circus gear with black tights, white boots and short jacket straining over bosoms as big as footballs. And the hair! Wigs or blown-up yellow or white mountains of stuff that looked like spun glass, or black hair so lacquered, it looked like freshly laid tar. Then there was a skinhead hooker or two with no hair at all, scalp daubed with pink and blue. The very thin girl in the camouflage uniform was a skinhead, and she looked like a young boy prisoner of some kind at first glance, sad-faced too. The Arcade had a bouncer or shover-awayer at the door, a burly fellow in a mussed white shirt, bow-tie and dark suit, but mostly he chuckled and even greeted the hookers, let them come in and wander around. Why not? They attracted customers for the Arcade.

Ralph sat inside the doorway on the right as one entered. The cash register was opposite him on the other side of the entrance, some twenty feet away. Many articles such as T-shirts, postcards, and toy animals and dolls had to be paid for at the cash register. Drunks or drugged people often protested over "a mistake" at the cash register, but that was the bouncer's affair, if things got rough. Ralph was to watch out for hold-up attempts, and he had a bell behind him that made a noise and also alerted the police. Also behind him, six or eight photographs of wanted people and known pickpockets and muggers were thumbtacked to the wall. Ralph was to watch out for them.

> . . . *and when we do it do it do it* . . .
> *you'll make me* . . . *yeee-oooo—do it do it*
> *do it do it* . . .

Eight hours of such "music and song" Ralph had to endure daily. The theme was sexual intercourse, the music always the same, a monotonous tempo, *poing-poing-poing-poing* of electronic tones, apes-in-the-trees stuff intended to bring out the primitive. Ralph imagined the apes blacks, sexually obsessed, crouching in trees and maybe masturbating, or ogling one another in an effort to call attention to their private parts. A dyed blonde worked the cash register most of the nights Ralph was on duty. This woman was heavy-set and tough, her mind strictly on taking in the cash.

One cloudy afternoon, when Ralph was giving God a walk, a long walk that would take Ralph yet again through Minetta Street to Macdougal, then to West Third Street, he saw Elsie walking toward him with a suitcase.

A paralysing shock of surprise went through Ralph, and he stopped where he was. Fifteen or twenty yards away from him, she turned and hopped up the front step of the house where she had used to live, and where Ralph thought she lived no longer. Was she moving back? Ralph crossed Minetta Street and advanced until he was opposite the house. The third floor, he remembered, and there was light at the window, because the day was so overcast. After a minute or two, he saw two figures and Elsie's, a bit shorter, drew back and turned, and disappeared to the left. Ralph moved on a little in the direction of Minetta Lane and stopped again. Nothing could have torn him away. He knew where Elsie was, at this moment, she was not thirty yards from him!

Ralph waited.

Then he felt another jolt, not so great as the former, as Elsie opened the front door and came out, carrying the suitcase, and over her other arm a coat. She put the case down in order to shut the front door, twice, as if it did not close properly, then picked the case up and walked. Ralph stood close by a house wall and looked toward Minetta Lane and Macdougal, not wanting her to see him now, dreading the possibility of her seeing him and visibly hurrying, fleeing from him. She turned in Minetta Lane toward Macdougal, and Ralph, on the other side of the street, waited, not sure if she had glimpsed him or not, and then he followed her.

At Macdougal, Elsie turned right, with an air of looking for a taxi. She kept walking downtown and reached the Bleecker Street crossing, where a taxi stopped for her. If Ralph had seen another taxi, he would have grabbed it, gladly have paid extra for taking God along, but there wasn't a taxi in sight. Elsie's taxi moved downtown on Macdougal, and Ralph got across Bleecker and followed for half a block until the taxi disappeared. She must live in this direction, and she had gone back to Minetta Street to pick up some things she had forgotten. From now on, Ralph would not bother with Minetta Street, he decided, but look downtown.

Ralph Linderman's concern for Elsie—he never gave his feelings a name—had been stimulated by the Minetta Street sighting of her, but in the days afterward his sense of deprivation and isolation from her grew more acute. Where in that mess of SoHo, even perhaps the East Village, should he begin to look for her? If she had taken her last belongings from Minetta Street, she wouldn't be coming back. He might see her going to or coming out of the Sutherlands' Grove Street house, of course, but he would have to follow her all the way home to learn where she lived now, and with whom, and that was what interested Ralph. Once he had thought he had seen Elsie coming out of the Sutherland house, wearing a hat, which was why he had not been sure, and high heels, as she sometimes did, and a nice new coat. It had crossed Ralph's mind that she was having sexual relations with Sutherland, and that he was paying her something. On that day, the figure in question, Elsie or not, had walked quickly westward on Grove. Ralph had been on Bleecker, carrying groceries and with God on the leash. He had not followed the girl.

Ralph turned a dangerous and desperate idea over in his mind for two days, and at last came to a decision: he would telephone John Sutherland and ask about Elsie, maybe even ask where she lived, but certainly inquire about her health. No one by any stretch of the imagination could believe that he meant Elsie any harm, or if any misguided person believed that, time and the facts would prove him wrong. When he telephoned at 11 one morning, Ralph was braced for either Sutherland or his wife.

John Sutherland answered.

"This is Ralph Linderman. How are you, Mr Sutherland?"

"All right, thanks. And yourself?"

"Well, thank you. I'm calling you about Elsie. I wonder if you know if she's all right?"

"Far as I know," replied Sutherland.

"Because I haven't seen her around lately.—You've seen her not so long ago?"

"Mm-m—couple of weeks ago, I think. She's fine."

"Where is she living now?"

"She's moved—I can't tell you where, sir, because I just don't know."

"You don't have to call me 'sir'," said Ralph with a chuckle. "South of the Village somewhere?"

"I really don't know."

"I've seen her coming and going from your house. Don't you know if she lives downtown from here, for instance?"

"No, I don't. She's moved a couple of times."

Ralph did not believe him. "She's got a job?"

"Yes. Doing nicely. Modeling now."

"For painters? Artists?" Ralph at once saw her naked. "In artists' studios?" he asked, frowning.

"No, no. For photographers. Fashion. Very high-class stuff. Got to say good-bye now. Got some people here today."

That was that. Well. Photographers, taking pictures of Elsie in nice clothes. Maybe in clothes. Were they any better a batch than artists for whom she would pose nude? It was still her face, her body they were interested in, wasn't it? Of course it made money. Vulgarity always did.

22

JACK had just got back to his worktable, when the telephone rang again. Linderman had thought of something else.

"Hello?"

"Hello, Jack. Louis here."

"Oh, Louis! You just missed Nat by about ten minutes," Jack said. Louis and no one else sometimes called Natalia Nat.

"Well, I thought that. The thing is, I'm really calling you. I wondered if I could come by."

Jack was surprised. "Now?"

"Yes. I'm at Saks. I'll take a taxi. I wanted to talk with you. Unless of course you're busy."

"I'm not that busy. Sure, Louis."

"See you. Quick as pos." He hung up.

Most unusual, Jack thought. Jack glanced over the living-room, as if orderliness mattered, which it didn't. He went back to his workroom. This afternoon at 4, he was due to show his latest twenty drawings, five of which would be quite new to Trews, in Trews' office at Dartmoor, Aegis. Today, thirteenth of March, would be a winding up, a finish day, Jack hoped.

The doorbell rang, and Jack buzzed Louis in.

"Brought you this," Louis said as he came in, extending a Saks Fifth Avenue shopping bag to Jack.

This was the Saks "white box" of mixed chocolates, Louis explained, and he said everybody loved them.

"Thanks very much, Louis." Jack opened the box and offered it to Louis, who declined.

"I won't take much of your time, Jack," Louis said earnestly, standing in the middle of the living-room. He had removed his overcoat. The crown of his bald head shone, his large brown eyes blinked. "It's just that I—somehow—wanted to see you alone for a few minutes. You know? I don't think we've ever seen each other alone." Louis laughed suddenly.

"Maybe not. No.—Want a coffee or anything?"

"No, thank you, Jack. May I sit down?" He sat on the sofa. Jack took the green armchair, as he usually did.

"I want to tell you—how much I appreciate your wife. She is—something special. Unique!" Louis spoke slowly. "If I'd been in any position to do so, I'd have married her."

Jack slumped in the armchair and laced his fingers over his chest. "She probably would have refused to marry you, because it would've been too perfect."

"Exactly! Ha-ha! That's Natalia to a *T*!—By the way, don't tell her I came to see you this morning, would you? She might think it odd. Well, it is!" Louis laughed briefly, showing big square teeth in his narrow face. "Nobody knows. Don't tell anybody. It's our secret," Louis drawled with feigned boredom. "I don't have to tell you Natalia's the most priceless thing in my life. Even more than Bob, I think. Different way, of course, but still." Louis laughed in a soft way that was like Natalia's laugh sometimes. "You've no reason to be jealous and you never were, never showed it, anyway."

"I never was jealous. Cross my heart." He watched Louis gazing at him, Louis with his long hands one upon the other on crossed legs. "Except that—you may understand Natalia better than I do."

Elegantly Louis waved this idea away, and gazed toward the windows for a few seconds. "Another thing that's important to say today is that I'm glad Natalia married you. A person like you. Well, *you*. You're the only person I can think of or imagine that she could stand."

"Thank you.—I mean, I'm glad to hear it."

"She also thinks you're sexy," Louis said solemnly. "But not in a pushy way, you know. You're her sex-object and that's important, but of course she'd never *say* it in so many words."

Jack pressed his palms against his face for an instant. "Well, well."

"I'd love to smoke, unless it bothers you.—Thanks. I shouldn't, but I do. The hell with it." Louis took Natalia's jade lighter from the coffee table and lit up, the gold-rimmed lighter that Natalia seldom took out of the house, because she was afraid of leaving it somewhere. Louis handled it and looked at it as if he knew it well. "And what's the news of our little friend Elsie?"

"Elsie? Going great guns. She called us up last night. Making money hand over fist, I think."

"Isn't that just great? Isn't she an *angel*—like something that fell from heaven! *Oh*, I'd like to see her five years from now, when she'll be the ripe old age of twenty-five! Ah-hah-hah-*hah!*" Louis laughed wholeheartedly.

Jack had suspected, now he knew, that this was Louis' good-bye visit. Jack cleared his throat and said, "Elsie borrowed a couple of books from us. Saves her buying them for her class."

"Oh, yes, her school. What books?"

"A Scott Fitzgerald and a Saul Bellow."

"*The Victim*, I hope. Or *Mr Sammler's Planet*. But *The Victim*—that's the essence of Saul Bellow with its paranoia, you know? A masterpiece. Don't you think?"

Louis talked on about Bellow, how good he was, and Jack's mind wandered a little, as his ear picked up phrases like "good and proper" or "on the tiles" (in regard to Elsie), that reminded him of Natalia's speech, reminded him that Natalia had known Louis so much longer than she had known him. One of Louis' rather large feet in a well-polished black shoe dangled from a slender ankle. A funny life-work he had, Jack thought, selling houses and apartments, doing up shabby houses, waiting calmly at home, or so Jack imagined, until the telephone rang, and Louis suddenly made a tidy sum.

"Elsie might be in danger how?" Jack asked, in response to something Louis had said. "I sort of like her new girlfriend."

"Marion? Oh, so do I. They've been over to our place a couple of times. No, when I said danger, I meant this sudden success. It can change a person's—character, almost, since Elsie's so young. But maybe it won't hers after all. She's awfully direct—simple, blunt, even. Don't you think?" Louis looked at Jack. "She'd say good-bye to Marion in a flash, if she got a little tired of her.— Hope she doesn't soon. Elsie's full of ambition, and just now it's modeling, fine, and she doesn't need a course in literature and English grammar for that, but she's preparing for her next step."

"And what's that, do you think?"

Louis looked at the ceiling. "Television acting? Film? Wouldn't surprise me.—Oh, Jack! Anything new about the old fellow who was following Elsie?"

"No. He's lost her, thank goodness, since she moved down to Greene. He did call me just before you did today."

"Really? Called *you* here? What did he want?"

"Elsie's address." Jack gave a laugh. "I said I didn't know, because she'd moved. The trouble is, he's seen Elsie coming here a couple of times. Or he knows Natalia knows her. He spies, you know."

Louis looked thoughtful. "Unmarried, isn't he? Lives alone?"

"Yes. He's been married, he told me. His wife left him years ago."

"I don't know what's worse, a solitary creep or a married creep. You know, these rapist-murderers who always take so long to get caught, they turn out to be married men with a couple of kids and a steady job. Then of course there's the *so* creepy, nobody would marry them, and they hate women anyway."

"You never saw this old guy, did you, Louis?"

"No, but Natalia described him. She's seen him on the street. This type hangs on. He's probably dying to rape Elsie, but he couldn't. So he'll attack her or something."

Jack smiled uncomfortably. "I really can't imagine that," Jack said, realizing that he wasn't sure, however, because he didn't understand Linderman completely. "He thinks—I know this much—he thinks women are born seducers, and make-up and high heels are for leading men astray. Temptresses, he calls women."

"That's a classic," Louis said in an impatient and worried tone.

"Well—since he's lost Elsie's whereabouts, I'm hoping he latches on to someone else soon."

"Yes." Louis stood up. "Jack, my dear, I must blow. I thank you very much for letting me crash in. And I haven't even asked you how the yak book's going."

"Okay, thanks. I have the final—um—showing of my stuff this afternoon. I'm taking the last drawings in to the art editor, I mean."

"My good wishes go with you."

"A quick nip, Louis?" Jack asked as Natalia might have done. "A stirrup-cup?"

"A Fernet-Branca," Louis said with a broad smile. "Natalia would like that. A thimbleful, please, Jack."

Jack poured it.

"Not you?"

Jack poured a small Jack Daniel's, so he could lift a glass with Louis. "Cheers!"

"Cheers!"

As Louis was putting on his overcoat, he noticed Jack's exercise rings that hung from the hall ceiling. "You still working out?"

"When I feel like it."

Louis was smiling again. "Can I see you do something?"

Jack was not in the mood, but he took a deep breath, seized the rings and stuck his feet high in the air, flipped down and backward, forward and up again, weight on his hands, so his head was near the ceiling, but not so near as his feet had been.

"Marvelous. Oh, lovely," Louis said softly, with admiration. "Bless you, Jack. Good-bye and thanks again."

The door closed.

23

JACK did tell Natalia about Louis Wannfeld's surprise visit, since he wanted to and saw no good reason why he shouldn't, but Natalia was at once so on edge that Jack wished he hadn't told her. This was on a Friday evening, and Natalia remarked that she was glad that tomorrow was Saturday and she could beg off going to the gallery, because on Saturdays came the public, not the buyers, and Isabel would not mind too much.

"It means he's going to die soon. Or he thinks he is," Natalia said to Jack.

"Does he know—about how long?"

"No. I'm sure less than a year. Maybe a lot less. He's on a strict diet now and can't drink a drop."

Jack had noticed that Louis was thinner.

"Let's take the car and go somewhere tomorrow," Natalia said. "I think I'll go mad if I stay here."

Jack was a bit disappointed, because he had wanted a weekend at home. Trews had liked his drawings. Jack had wanted to laze around the house, make line drawings of Amelia as she played, or slept, or stood in front of him talking to him. He had a thick, blank-paged book half full now of Amelia since she had been a baby. He found that people laughed more at his drawings and were certainly more interested in them than in photographs he might have taken of the child.

By 11 the next morning, they were off in the Toyota, with Amelia in the back seat, and pajamas and toothbrushes for all of them in a duffel, in case they stayed the night somewhere. Natalia drove. She was a good driver, with quick reflexes, but she professed to hate driving. In the mood she was in now, driving would get rid of her nervous energy, Jack knew, which was all to the good.

"How's Elsie?" Jack knew that Natalia had called her up that morning, and talked quite a while.

Natalia smiled suddenly, close-lipped, looking straight ahead through the windshield. "Worried about her income tax now! I said, 'Sweetie, if that's all the worry you've got!'"

Elsie didn't know how to fill out her form, because she had never paid an income tax before, Natalia said, but Marion was going to help her.

Up the Garden State Parkway they went in the cold spring afternoon. They bought a cake somewhere, telephoned, and invited themselves to tea at the house of a cousin of Natalia's mother who lived in Saddle River. Jack had met her once before. This was a change of atmosphere, and a fulfilment of duty, even if unasked, which lifted Natalia's spirits a little. After that, Jack drove, and they stopped for the night at a motel of Amelia's choice. The décor was awful, but had amusement value. Natalia had brought her bottle of Glenfiddich. The motel people put a cot up in the room for Amelia.

When they got home Sunday afternoon, the telephone was ringing. Jack was nearest to it.

"Where've you been?" asked Louis' voice.

Natalia took the telephone, talked for ages, and at last reported to Jack that Louis had invited them to a party next Saturday night. It was a come-as-you-are party, and Natalia said she had asked him if he meant opposite-sex clothes, and Louis had said no, just old clothes or whatever one liked. Lots of people were coming, it seemed.

On the following Saturday evening, Louis Wannfeld opened the door to Natalia and Jack, wearing a long black garment that glistened with tiny gold lights like stars twinkling in a night sky. He wore sandals. "I'm a mandarin tonight," said Louis. "And you?"

"Me? Nuffin," said Natalia.

Jack noticed that Louis would have kissed her on the cheek, but that Natalia evaded it. Natalia was not fond of cheek-kissing.

"Greetings, Jack! Come in—and lose yourself," said Louis.

Louis' and Bob's apartment looked as crowded as at the pre-Christmas party, and the people seemed louder and more informal. The come-as-you-are idea had provoked some weird responses. Jack's eye was caught by a devilish male figure in black tights with red horns on his cap and a whip in his hand. One

162

woman and apparently her mate had come as butterflies in dia-
phanous gowns over leotards with spotted wings supported by
delicate wire frames. Jack saw Elsie, a figure in black, black ruffled
skirt neither long nor short, broad white belt, black high-heeled
shoes. Her fair hair was pulled back from her face and fastened in
back with something, and hung now below her shoulders. He
found his eyes lingering on her, returning, as if to a point of
energy amid the mostly older crowd, but Elsie was not in action
at the moment. She was standing and talking with a long-haired
young woman whom Jack recognized as Genevieve, Elsie's former
girlfriend.

Drinks. And hellos. Isabel Katz wore ancient jodhpurs and a
pink shirt. Louis' garment was a Chinese dressing gown, Jack
saw in better light, and he had an elegant white silk shirt with
black bow tie under it, evening trousers, and patent leather
evening slippers. Half the people Jack didn't know, or they were
too thoroughly disguised for recognition. Several wore masks.

"How that takes me back! And you can still get into it!" Louis
was saying to Natalia. "It looks the same as ever! *Just* like yourself!" Despite doctor's orders, Louis was a bit high tonight.

Louis' words were in praise of Natalia's outfit, which was
simply an old suit, a black skirt with fine orange stripes down it,
and a long-sleeved black jacket which hugged her body and
stopped at the waistline. Earlier that day, Natalia had dragged it
from the depths of some closet, its hanger folds not too severe,
but she had given it a pressing. She had worn this often, she said,
a couple of years before she had met Jack, and had always been
too sentimental about it to chuck it. Jack couldn't see its great
charm, but Louis gushed over it like a lover re-living evenings
with his beloved.

"Ardmore . . . Fifty-second Street . . ."

Jack had to smile. He drifted over to Elsie, and said a word of
greeting to her and Genevieve. A Beatles record or cassette played,
but not too loudly. It was *Sergeant Pepper*.

"Oh, Jack," Elsie said in her soft voice. "*Oh*, I'm glad to see
you!" With a small turn of her head and shoulders, she seemed to
detach herself completely from the stolid Genevieve and focus on
him.

Jack's smile broadened. "Are you? May I say you're looking
gorgeous tonight?"

"But I'm so tired. You wouldn't believe it."

No, Jack wouldn't have. Elsie was saying something about having been kept up till all hours by—what? It didn't matter. It was difficult to hear anything.

"*Fran!*" said Genevieve, extending a hand to get someone's attention. "Want you to meet Mr Sutherland."

Jack faced a sturdy young woman with short light brown hair, thin lips, and slightly worried or shy eyes. "How d'you do?"

"Fran Bowman," said Genevieve, or so it sounded to Jack. Fran was in trousers and dark blue shirt with a string of pale blue beads that hung down to her waist. She was bullet-headed and singularly unattractive, Jack thought. He remembered Marion saying that Genevieve's former girlfriend was a tough cookie, or some such. Elsie was watching him, and she gave Jack a smile that looked simply amused, like a child's smile. Her glance said, "Let's move on."

Jack nodded to Genevieve, and drifted with Elsie only six feet or so away, but this meant people between them and Genevieve and her friend. "Where's Marion tonight?"

"She's coming later. She has rehearsals tonight."

"And how're you doing with the income tax?"

Elsie gave a laugh. "It's done. Marion did most of it. It's just that I have no steady salary. It's very hard to figure."

"I know." Jack did know. He didn't know what next to say to Elsie, but he didn't want to leave her. "Feel like dancing?" He held out his hand.

She did not touch his hand, but they began to dance. The music wasn't *Sergeant Pepper* now, but something else that sounded especially pleasant and good for dancing. Male voices sang about good vibrations.

"That's the Beach Boys," Elsie said. She danced gracefully, turning full turns, the rows of black lace whirling.

Who was leading? It didn't matter. People were watching Elsie. She danced effortlessly, as if she floated in another element. The music changed, the beat was faster, and Jack moved in his own style and Elsie followed, responded as if they had rehearsed. Smiling, happy, Jack found himself leaping on every fourth beat, and Elsie did the same. People moved back to give them room. Jack's vision blurred except for the glow of Elsie's head. His pleasure was the same as that he experienced when he swung himself into a refreshing sweat on the handrings, and he felt he could go on all night, or forever. He wore jogging shoes, comfortable trousers and a T-shirt. He was himself now. Some of the people in the circle around them clapped their hands with the beat. Jack caught a glimpse of Natalia standing beside Louis, both watching Elsie with fascination, and not far from Natalia, Fran, thin lips compressed as she stared at Elsie, and murmured something to Genevieve. Jack and Elsie circled each other at a distance, and Jack had the feeling that he floated in air. Then the orchestra faded, the beat faded, and Jack realized that he held Elsie in his arms, that her hands were on his shoulders, lightly. He kissed her cheek, inhaled deeply as if he would devour her, and felt her breath as she laughed.

"More!" someone shouted.

Jack was slow coming back to reality and gravity. He stood on two feet again, looking at Elsie. She moved away toward the others in an odd near-silence that had fallen over everyone, as over an audience when the curtain drops and before applause breaks out. Then some applause did break out, laughter, murmurs, and a "Bravo!" or two. *It's Elsie's power to bewitch*, Jack thought. He went in quest of a drink.

Bob Campbell stepped into his path. He wore a black gown and a dog-collar, or God-collar, like a preacher. "Jack, you may enter the kingdom of heaven, I've decided. Elsie's already there. We love her, love her!" Bob spoke with fervor. "Is it a drink you're after, dear Jack?" Bob led him to the drinks table, remembered his favorite and poured a generous measure. "Don't you think Louis is looking well tonight?"

Jack didn't. He thought Louis looked yellowish, but he returned a polite, "Yes, indeed."

"He's wearing a Chinese robe we bought on our round-the-world trip five years ago. Louis hardly ever puts it on, but he was keen on it for tonight—a special night. D'you notice all our old friends are here? No coke tonight, at least not from us. Tonight's an old booze party with maybe a slight hangover tomorrow, something to nurse on a cozy Sunday at home, with Bloody Marys and eggs Benedict. Yum-m." Bob was in ebullient good humor.

Jack wandered off, looking for Elsie, and saw her with Marion near the hall door.

"Hello, Jack!" Marion said warmly. She put a thumb under

the shoulder strap of her blue overalls, under which she wore a checked shirt. "I am not as I am tonight. These are rehearsal clothes."

"Oh? And what're you rehearsing?"

"A couple of skits with music. For a bar in the Chelsea section."

They went to the drinks table to get something for Marion. Marion asked what he thought of Elsie's "big job," modeling a diamond ring for a full page in *Vogue*, and was surprised that Elsie hadn't mentioned it. Jack poured tomato juice for Marion. Elsie had vanished suddenly.

"My God, there's Genevieve," Marion said quietly, looking across the room.

"Yes. With her old friend, I think. Elsie introduced us."

"You don't mean that awful Fran?"

"I think that's her name. So they're back together?" Jack asked in a tone of mock interest.

"No." Marion shook her head. "Fran's willing but Genevieve isn't, I heard via the grapevine. Maybe Genevieve's carrying a torch for Elsie. I couldn't care less.—Fran ought to join the Mafia. Matter of fact somebody told me she's a dealer—in the really hard stuff, you know? Nobody likes Fran, so some awful stories get around."

Depressing, Jack thought. He glanced toward the wide doorway to the living-room, and saw Elsie and Natalia in the hall beyond, talking with each other, Natalia gripping Elsie's hand, then they kissed, and a second time, quickly and on the lips, before they walked into the room, Natalia a bit ahead. Jack saw that Marion was looking at him with a slight smile.

"I don't mind," said Marion. "Do you?"

Jack swallowed the sip of drink he had been holding in his mouth. "Not at all."

"Elsie adores Natalia."

"Oh? More than she does you?"

"I dunno," Marion said with a shrug. "But what can I do about it?"

"Lots of people," Jack remarked, "get attached to Natalia.— Louis, for instance." And Jack recalled a time shortly after they had met the Armstrongs, when Max Armstrong had had more than a crush on Natalia for weeks, but had had the good sense not to press his case too hard.

166

"Lots of people fall in love with Elsie too," Marion replied. She added with a laugh, "Quite a problem, these girls, you know, in bars—They just come right out with their passionate declarations."

Jack could imagine.

Suddenly Elsie was beside them again, and Natalia back on the sofa with Louis. It was after 1 o'clock, Jack saw to his surprise when he glanced at his watch.

"Now I really am getting tired," Elsie said more to herself than to Jack. "And hungry too."

The canapés on the drinks table had almost vanished, and if Louis and Bob were serving anything more substantial, there was no sign of it yet. "Let's go down to my place," Jack said. "Like before. Want to?"

"With Natalia?" Elsie asked.

Jack shook his head. "You can't tear her away from Louis for hours yet. Want to bet? Want to try?" He smiled.

Elsie didn't, and Jack went over to Natalia and told her he was taking the girls down to their place for bacon and eggs, and did she want to come?

"No, I'll stay on a while," Natalia answered.

"You can't have her yet, Jack," said Louis, as if he had an absolute right to keep her.

"Okay. See you later, darling.—Good cheer, Louis. And thank you!"

The three of them found their coats and departed. Jack felt happy. He loved playing host to Elsie and Marion. On Grove Street, the apartment was quiet, with Amelia asleep, and Susanne, Jack knew, asleep in the spare room down the hall beyond his workroom. Susanne had left one light on in the living-room. Jack told the girls of Susanne's presence, and asked them to be on the quiet side.

"Can I put on one cassette if it's very low?" Elsie asked.

Jack found it impossible to say no to Elsie. "If it's really low," he whispered.

Jack got to work in the kitchen on the menu of Canadian bacon, English muffins and scrambled eggs. Marion helped. Jack ground coffee with a couple of dishtowels over the machine to smother some of the noise. He heard faint music, and to his surprise it was Vivaldi's *Four Seasons*.

"Can you tell me why, Elsie," Marion said as they were eating, "that Genevieve bore got invited tonight? And why she brought that hood with her?"

"*I* didn't do it.—Maybe Bob decided to invite everyone who was at that last big party. The one before Christmas."

Marion exchanged a glance with Jack. "Embarrassing even to know the names of people like that."

"You don't have to rub it in," Elsie said. "Sure, I admit I brought Genevieve to that party before Christmas. But Bob told me they keep a list of invited people, so they can ask them again when they're giving another—"

"Or not, I hope," Marion put in.

"I'm sure it was like that, Louis or Bob inviting Genevieve, and Genevieve dragging along this Fran—just to be nice to Fran." Elsie spoke in the earnest way she had sometimes, when the circumstances didn't really warrant the earnestness.

Elsie was probably ashamed of ever having been a close friend of Genevieve's, Jack thought, but he had noticed tonight that Elsie had seemed quite cool and collected on seeing Genevieve again and had also talked with her. Jack poured more coffee. "True, Bob keeps a list. Come on, it's not important."

They got through the meal without waking up Amelia or Susanne. Again Marion lent a helpful hand with the clearing away, and Jack told her to leave the dishes.

"Tomorrow's Sunday," he said. "Today's Sunday."

Dawn was coming at the windows. Jack turned off a light.

"Elsie?" Marion said, looking into the living-room. "Gone. Wonder if she's conked out somewhere?"

Jack smiled. "I'll find her." He went to the bedroom.

Elsie lay face down with her head on his pillow. She had pulled the counterpane halfway back. In the dim light, she looked as if she were flying in space, the black skirt flaring, arms higher than her head around the pillow. Jack felt pleasantly high, or tired, or both. He knelt by the bed, and had an impulse to kiss her cheek to awaken her, but something stopped him or made him afraid to. Her eyelids flickered, and she saw him.

"I love you," he said.

Elsie smiled suddenly, like a child awakening from a good sleep. "Was I here long?"

168

"Maybe half an hour."

Jack went out with them to look for a taxi. They hadn't wanted him to phone for one, despite the crazy hour of a quarter before 6. They walked toward Seventh Avenue.

"There he *is*!" said Jack in almost a whisper.

Linderman, in the morning's gray haze, stood some ten yards away on Bleecker in his old overcoat and hat and with God on the leash. He stared at them as they crossed Bleecker. The sight of them might have stopped Linderman in his tracks.

"That's the old *guy*?" asked Marion.

"Yes!" said Elsie. "Walk faster and don't look at him!"

Suddenly the humor of it struck Jack, and he put his head back and laughed. Old Linderman was probably thinking that he had spent the night with two girls, one of whom was Elsie, the second an extra luxury.

Elsie bent, trying and failing to repress her giggles. "Hey, Jack!—I can just imagine what he's thinking! Ha-ha!"

Jack waved his arms in the middle of nearly deserted Seventh Avenue. He stepped out of the way of a truck. They had a taxi in about thirty seconds. Jack insisted on giving them a five-dollar bill for the fare. "Take it! No argument!" Jack said, and slammed the taxi door.

Jack stood for a moment on the sidewalk, looking down Grove Street, thinking Linderman's figure might appear, but it didn't. He walked homeward, and didn't glance into Bleecker when he crossed it, not really wanting to see even the back of Linderman and his dog. He went into the apartment quietly, and wrote a note for Susanne, which he put on the kitchen table.

Late night. Natalia is still out.

6 a.m.   J.

He put on pajamas and brushed his teeth. He thought of going into his workroom, putting on the light for a moment and looking at the three full-page photographs of Elsie which he had neatly cut out of magazines. But he had something better in his eyes, the image of Elsie's head on his pillow with her face turned toward him, eyes closed in sleep. *I love you*, he had said, in that tipsy and happy moment. Would Elsie even remember? Would it matter if she remembered or not? No. How many times a week did she hear the same words from fellows and girls? True, he was a little

169

in love with Elsie. But not only did she not want any boys or men at the moment, he had no desire to try to take her to bed. The fact that she existed made him happy.

And Elsie and Natalia? Now that was a surprise! What were they up to? Natalia had stayed out late a few evenings lately. Had she really been with Isabel Katz or with one of their art buyers?

Jack went to bed feeling happy, and fell asleep at once.

24

IF Ralph Linderman had been able to find a taxi on Grove or Seventh that Sunday morning, he would have taken it. He had seen John Sutherland passing some money to Elsie or the other girl. Naturally, he'd pay them off in a gentlemanly way, under cover of paying their taxi fare. Two of them! Ralph thought he had not seen this second girl before, a little taller than Elsie and in trousers, dark hair rather short and full around her head. Ralph had crossed Grove and concealed himself in a doorway, pushing God back against the door, but Sutherland had not glanced at the other side of Grove, just kept walking toward home, looking rather pleased with himself.

Ralph did not have to work that Sunday until 6 p.m. His hours at the Hot Arch Arcade were always changing. Now they were asking that he walk the length of the arcade and back every half hour. Bad enough to watch the scum of all races oozing past the entrance, but worse to see them in action inside, roughing one another up, not always playfully, falling asleep or passing out against the walls, groping one another and worse. Once he had stopped what he had thought was a gang rape, and the bouncer had only laughed at him. True, whores and their clients didn't need privacy any more. Privacy, even a desire for it, was a thing of the past. The changing hours threw Ralph's sleep off, and he was more irritable than when he had been working at Midtown-West Parking. He could sleep soundest between 7 a.m. and noon, if he had those hours free, otherwise he kept waking up every two hours.

He slept that Sunday morning, despite the shock of having seen Elsie Tyler after a whoring date with Sutherland. Ralph suspected now that Sutherland had lied about Elsie's modeling for fashion photographers. Fashion models made good money, and why would she be whoring if she earned enough? The pity of it! The sadness! If he knew where to reach Elsie, he was sure he could shame her into stopping this business with Sutherland. He would pay Elsie to stop it, give her half his salary, to keep her as she was. And Elsie would know from that, that he adored her, that he wanted nothing from her, unlike Sutherland.

Ralph awakened that dismal, drippy morning at a quarter of noon, rested but hungry, and with an appetite for some of Rossi's freshly sliced salami. He dressed and went out, without God. He bought some goat cheese too, and a length of Italian bread, and was walking homeward when a taxi went by on Bleecker—Ralph paused for it in crossing Bleecker—and he saw in profile Mrs Sutherland, leaning forward as she opened her handbag. The taxi was indeed slowing at the Grove Street corner, and Ralph walked toward it.

In his head, Ralph had nothing prepared. He might say "Good morning" if he were close enough. He realized that he burned to tell her that Elsie and another girl had apparently spent the night with her husband and left at 6 in the morning, but that would be difficult to blurt out on the sidewalk, possibly within hearing of a passerby. And had Mrs Sutherland, in fact, been out all night herself? Her hair looked more disorderly than usual, and she brushed it impatiently aside before she slammed the taxi door shut. Grove being one-way eastward, Mrs Sutherland now had a hundred yards or so to walk to reach her door. Linderman followed her.

She turned quickly left toward her house door, and Ralph had a glimpse of her rather pale and tired-looking face, her lipstick showing bright red in contrast.

"Oh, Mrs Sutherland!"

She turned and saw him.

"Good morning, ma'am." Ralph was still walking toward her. Then he saw her sudden frown, her parted lips that drew down at the corners in an expression of anger or horror, almost, and she pressed the bell. She had turned her back to him.

"Mrs Sutherland, one minute!"

Then the door buzzed, and she went into the house.

Ralph turned and walked back toward Bleecker. That had been a mistake, perhaps, and yet what harm had there been in it? Mrs Sutherland did look as if she had been up all night. She must know about her husband's infidelity, and no doubt it was making her unhappy. He recalled Sutherland saying, "I'm very happily married," or something like that. All false, a bald-faced lie!

But far worse was Elsie's involvement! Of all the girls in New York, the loose and willing girls and women, Sutherland was preying upon Elsie!

Ralph's thoughts were in some turmoil by the time he got to his apartment. He might simply ask Sutherland to desist. Or he could write a letter to him, and if Mrs Sutherland found it, so much the better! A polite letter as before, saying that he was aware of what was going on between Elsie and him, that what he had suspected had now been confirmed by his observation of the hours at which Elsie came and went, and did not Sutherland think that out of respect for his wife and small daughter, he should desist, leave Elsie alone? Ralph wished he had the address of Elsie's parents so that he could tell them what was going on, and give them Sutherland's name and address. Sutherland, a married man! And an artist, who probably made her pose nude before his orgies! How Elsie's parents would rally to his cause! How fast they'd come to find Elsie and take her back home! Elsie had told him enough about her parents to make him feel sure about this. Ralph recalled returning Sutherland's wallet, remembered how proud he had been to find Sutherland a *gentleman* who said thank you, and who gracefully offered him a reward. Well, Ralph would do the same thing, if he found Sutherland's wallet a second time. Principle was principle. And to slip once was the beginning of the end. And vice was vice.

Ralph began a letter to John Sutherland after lunch. He told himself that he did not have to send it, that he could reflect upon it after he had written it, but it did him good to write it and get it out of himself. He wrote a third page and a fourth. He might choose the best of it later, recopy it, and reflect again on sending it.

25

It was an odd Sunday at the Sutherland house. By the time Natalia arrived at noon, Susanne had taken Amelia to the American Indian Museum way uptown, and had also tidied the kitchen. Natalia showered, put on pajamas and dressing gown, and wanted "a little breakfast" plus a Fernet-Branca, before she went to bed. Awakened by Natalia's arrival, Jack had showered and shaved, dressed, and was feeling quite well. Susanne was back, but busy with Amelia, so Jack prepared Natalia's breakfast with fresh coffee, which never prevented her from sleeping, when she wanted to sleep. She looked disturbed, or annoyed, and conversation was impossible with Susanne present.

The weather had cleared, and light came through the front windows, sunshine through the back ones.

"I suppose I broke all records last night," Natalia said. She was eating an English muffin with marmalade. "Staying up."

Susanne was now playing a card game with Amelia at the far end of the living-room.

"No sleep at all?" Jack asked.

"Well, yes, around six o'clock in the living-room," Natalia replied. "Bob served marvelous clam chowder after you left."

Susanne came into the dining area and asked if Natalia wanted her to stay, and said she could either leave or stay, because she had brought some work to do. Natalia told her to do as she liked, because she was going to bed for a while.

"How *is* Louis?" Susanne asked.

Natalia seemed to close up, though she looked at Susanne and replied that he was looking pretty well, and had asked about her.

Natalia went off to bed with a second Fernet-Branca.

Susanne said she would silently steal away. "I can see Natalia's uptight about something," Susanne said to Jack.

"Oh? I think she's just tired."

Susanne departed in her raincoat, carrying the old brown briefcase, and she blew Jack a kiss before she closed the door.

Jack was a little sorry to see her go.

"Daddy?"

"Shush, honey," Jack said, walking toward Amelia's little figure, which sat spraddle-legged on the living-room floor, blond hair down to her shoulders and beyond, with some kind of game between her feet. "Your mom's trying to sleep a little, so you be quiet."

"Did you go to that party?"

"Of course I went to that party. But I came home earlier than your mom."

Amelia seemed to ponder this. "What's earlier?"

"Earlier!—Ten is earlier than eleven, for instance. Something earlier comes before something later." He drifted away, hoping Amelia would not call him again, and she didn't.

In his workroom, Jack looked at the three photographs of Elsie which leaned against illustration boards on his table—a fourth and latest was in a magazine in the living-room—and he heard his own words again, "I love you." That was crazy, airy, unreal, his words and his feelings even, as unreal as the Elsie he saw in the photograph in which her face showed largest: she wore a black evening dress with a single shoulder strap, she leaned sideways in an elegant chair, looking up at someone out of sight, and she held a glass of champagne that was about to touch her lips. Her hand that held the glass bore an expensive diamond ring on its third finger. Elsie had hands that could look lean and slender sometimes, strong and muscular at other times, both to the eye and in photographs. But the look in Elsie's eyes in this picture was the most amazing to Jack: she looked as if she could be nearly thirty, her upward glance seemed to hold the worldly wisdom of a hundred affairs, plus the knowledge of how to handle the man who had given her the diamond ring. The advertisement was for a jewelry company, and the discreetly small type below the photograph said: *Just* because *she has everything* . . . which made Jack smile now.

Another picture was a cover with the magazine's name across the top, Elsie smiling, lips closed, with most of the smile in her blue eyes. She might have been sixteen here, a naive teenager.

The third picture was of Elsie getting out of the taxi beneath the Hotel Chelsea's awning, looking as if she were laughing aloud, the skirt of her white dress blowing out, her eyes on the beholder. Jack remembered that freezing day.

He felt odd, different, as if he were in love, in a quiet way. He pulled out a big sketch pad of cheap paper. He was working on a composition for an oil, and he wanted to begin with the composition just right, even if the painting came out a bit different. He was still fond of the thin black outline for human figures and for objects too. In soft black pencil he had drawn a partial outline of a man seated in a comfortable armchair, though the armchair was not to look fat or overstuffed. Jack called the picture to himself "Puzzled Man". The slender man had his feet together, knees apart, and gripped his chin with one hand. Jack had sold a cartoon a few days ago, a one-liner: a dubious male customer was looking at a soft plaid hat the salesman was holding, and the salesman was saying: "Don't worry, sir, the *hat's* got the personality."

Jack jumped, his left hand rose from the sketch pad at the voice behind him.

"I'm going out for a walk, Jack. Sorry—if I startled you." Natalia smiled at his surprise. She looked better for her nap.

" 'S'okay, darling. Is it raining?" He saw that she had boots on and her raincoat.

"A little—I won't be long."

Then Jack heard the apartment door close. The telephone rang before Jack got back to his work. He answered it in the living-room.

"Hi, Jack, Elaine. How're you folks today?"

"Oh-h, not bad at all. I hear there was clam chowder after I left."

"Yes, and lots else. Wasn't that a party? Looked like forty or fifty, didn't you think? And that girl—the one you were dancing with—"

"Elsie."

"Elsie. I can never think of her name, because it doesn't suit her somehow. Lovely to look at—when she dances!—You said she's doing well at the modeling now."

"Indeed, yes!"

"I saw her on one cover, I remember.—Well, I just tried to

phone Louis and Bob to thank them, and nobody answered there. Maybe they're sleeping. So I thought I'd check in with you." Elaine gave a laugh. "We weren't home till nearly four. How's Natalia?"

"Out for a walk or I'd put her on."

"Let's get together soon, Jack. Love to Natalia."

When he hung up, Jack's eyes fell on the cassette that Marion had given him last night. Given or lent? Jack had forgotten. He would ask, and return it if she wanted it. It was labeled MARION GILL. NIGHT THOUGHTS. SOLO GUITAR. Jack put it into the cassette player.

The guitar began dreamily, as if the player were alone, strumming for pleasure. There were no words. The key changed. There were slow, wistful climbs into treble, then a flurry of notes, as if the player wanted to erase what he had played before. Jack sat down on the sofa, leaned back and closed his eyes. Amelia was in her room, quiet for the nonce, and Jack was glad. This was no song, no composition either, he supposed, just a rambling in musical phrases. The music was unpretentious, but it could create a mood, if one listened.

The telephone rang again. Jack bared his teeth with annoyance, and got up. He switched the tape off.

"Hello, Jack, this is Bob. Am I disturbing you?"

"No, Bob. We—"

"I'd really like to speak with Natalia."

"She's gone out for a walk. Are you home?"

"Yes." Bob sounded tense.

"She ought to be back in a few minutes. I'll get her to call you. No, hold it! She's just coming in." Jack laid the telephone down. "Bob's on the line."

Natalia shed her raincoat, and Jack took it from her. "Hello, Bob."

Jack saw her take the phone to the coffee table and sit down on the sofa.

"Oh-h.—Well, I thought—you know? I knew."

Jack hung the raincoat on a hanger in the bathroom, on the shower rod. Then he slowly crossed the back area of the living-room in the direction of his workroom.

". . . if you want me to come. Mightn't it be best?" Her voice sounded strained.

Jack drew the curtain of his workroom, and now his eyes did not seek out Elsie or anything else. Louis was dead, Jack was almost sure. Either a heart attack from last night's indulgences, or suicide in some manner. Jack shoved his hands into his back pockets, and walked back into the living-room. Natalia was still on the telephone, and he did not want to listen, but he walked slowly toward her, went behind the sofa to the drinks cabinet, and poured a Glenfiddich, took it to the kitchen for ice and water. He delivered the drink, and retreated again to his workroom. After a few minutes, he went out again, and there was silence in the living-room.

Natalia stood there with her drink, and looked at him.

"Something about Louis?"

She gave a nod, as if she were thinking about something else. "Yes. Sleeping pills. He—" She turned toward the front windows, and bent her head.

At that moment, Amelia rushed in with a loud, "Mommy!" She had something to show her mother, in her room, "a watercolor", and it was still wet and she couldn't bring it in.

"*I'll* be your first viewer, *I'll* look," Jack said, and followed his daughter into her room.

This effort was a large black and yellow butterfly, backgrounded by green trees proportionally much smaller. Again Amelia had kept spaces between the yellow border of the black wings, and the yellow dots on the wings.

"Admirable," Jack said. "Really quite nice. Simple and decorative." The watercolor lay flat on her low desk.

"When it's dry, I'll show Mommy."

"When it's dry," Jack said, and left the room.

Natalia was making another drink. "Bob doesn't want any help just now.—He's alone."

"What *happened*?" Jack whispered.

"Last night—this morning, Louis said he was going to his room to sleep. This was about nine this morning. They had two bedrooms, *comme il faut*, you know—as Louis always says. So Bob said this afternoon around three he went into Louis' room, and Louis was lying on top of the covers with his hands crossed on his chest, still in that Chinese dressing gown, and Bob thought he looked—Well, Bob couldn't wake him up." Natalia was whispering, frowning. "And he was even cool. A big overdose.—Bob saw the bottle—empty. That plus the alcohol, you know?" She drank some of her scotch. "So Bob said he spent the last couple of hours," she went on through a nervous laugh, "loading the dishwasher and straightening the *house*! He said it was the only way he could have survived. He didn't answer his phone and he hasn't told anyone but me."

Jack felt stunned, even though he had known. "Shouldn't he call the police?—Or a hospital? You mean Louis is just lying there in the bedroom?"

"*Yes!*—I told Bob I'd call the police, but he doesn't want me to." Natalia writhed slightly, a movement Jack had seen many a time when she was in a situation that she couldn't manage. She pushed her hair back, restless and tense. "Oh, he'll probably do it in the next hour."

But even Jack knew Bob well enough to imagine him pottering around the house in a daze for hours more, dusting the books maybe. "He can't just spend the night with Louis *there*, darling. It's five o'clock now!"

"I know. You're right." Natalia frowned at the telephone.

If she called Bob again, he wouldn't answer, Jack supposed, because he would think it was someone else.

Amelia walked in briskly with her watercolor. "Mommy!"

Natalia stared at it, then her eyes focused, and she saw it. "Nice, honey. Yes.—Can I have it? For my room?"

Amelia looked gratified. "*Yes*, Mommy."

The black and yellow butterfly reminded Jack of Louis' Chinese dressing gown. Natalia and Amelia went into the bedroom to set up the watercolor somewhere, and Jack waited, knowing that Natalia had to come to a decision. She came back and went to the telephone and dialed. After several seconds, she put the telephone down, and said to Jack:

"Doesn't answer. I think I should go up there."

"I agree. I'll come with you. That's—if you like."

"You don't *have* to," Natalia said, looking agonized.

"But I insist," Jack said quietly. Jack went closer, but did not touch her. "It's tough, darling. It's a tough thing.—Let's see if we can park Amelia at the Armstrongs', okay?"

He telephoned the Armstrongs. Elaine said it was quite all right, they were home all evening, and Jack said they would be there in about ten minutes. They found a taxi as they walked toward West

11th Street, and had it wait while Jack stuck Amelia in the door. Amelia seemed delighted to be spending the evening with the Armstrongs and their boy Jason. Jack said they'd be back to fetch Amelia before 10 probably, and if not, he'd telephone. Jack had thought of saying, "Sudden invitation for something uptown," but he said nothing by way of explanation, just turned and trotted back to the taxi.

Natalia had to speak with Bob's and Louis' doorman, who knew her, because Bob did not answer the doorman's call from downstairs.

"He doesn't know it's me," Natalia said. "He'll let us in. Come up with us if you want to, George."

The doorman went up with them, and Natalia called to Bob through the closed door, and Bob opened it a crack.

Bob was in shirtsleeves and trousers, houseshoes, and had a dishtowel in one hand. Jack let Natalia do all the talking. They had to telephone the police, that was the correct thing to do. And Bob agreed. Jack offered to speak with the police, but Natalia preferred to do it, and she did it. To Jack's relief, she did not ask to see Louis, nor did Bob ask her if she wished to. Jack knew where the bedrooms were, somewhere right of the foyer down a hall. Natalia would know exactly. Bob was trembling slightly, and he looked pale. Natalia put on more lights. Within fifteen minutes the police came, followed by some ambulance men. Jack barely glanced into the hall as they carried the covered body out on a stretcher. By this time, Natalia and Jack had persuaded Bob to spend the night at their house. Bob put some things into a carryall.

The doorman George, the one Natalia knew, was upstairs in the hall instructing the stretcher man, who used a different elevator, so that when Jack and Natalia and Bob got down to the sidewalk, it was just in time to see the blanket-covered corpse being borne out of the service entrance toward the ambulance, and to Jack there was something awful about that, as if a corpse was not to be seen by the happy living, the people who walked in and out of the main entrance. Jack thought suddenly of all the little items he had just seen upstairs, a gold pen which he knew belonged to Louis, a book with a place-mark in it on the writing desk, a photograph of Louis on a yacht with hair on his head, in white ducks and striped French sailor's blouse, a picture of which

Jack knew Louis had been proud. Natalia had squeezed her eyes shut and turned her head from the direction of the stretcher.

Jack got out of the taxi at West 11th, and said he would walk Amelia home, and he gave Natalia the keys, because she had not taken hers. When Jack got to Grove Street with Amelia at nearly 10, Natalia was cooking something in the kitchen. Bob was taking a shower, Natalia said. There was a shower and toilet off the spare room.

"Thank you, Natalia darling," Bob said when he came in, in pajamas and a cotton dressing gown.

They had a light snack. Bob declined a drink.

"Thank God, tomorrow's a working day," Bob said for the second time. His face still looked pale, his brown eyes lost and tense behind the round-rimmed glasses.

Jack got Amelia to bed, eased her into sleep by reminding her in a somnolent voice of the long, long day she had had, starting with a trip to the museum, long ago, that morning. Bob had retired. Natalia was tidying the kitchen.

"Bob told me Louis wanted no ceremony at all, just cremation," Natalia said. "All written in his will. And Bob doesn't want us to tell people—just now. He'll see that there's a little item in the *Times*."

Funny, Jack thought, though he said nothing. Awkward, too. The news of Louis' death would creep from friend to friend until everyone who cared knew it, he supposed.

"I think I'll try to see Elsie," Natalia said.

"Now?" Jack asked, surprised.

"She's another world. I need to escape this." Natalia went to the telephone. Someone answered at the other end.

Jack went into his workroom.

A couple of minutes later, Natalia said his name, and parted his slightly open curtains. "I'm off for an hour or so. Taking Elsie this." She held up a big art book. "De Kooning. She wants to borrow it. She's crazy about de Kooning. Funny, no?" Natalia's smile showed a trace of good humor that Jack was glad to see.

He nodded. "Give her my love."

26

THE next day Monday turned out to be as odd in its way as Sunday had been.

Jack had awakened before 7, and found the bed empty but for him, and had at first thought Natalia must be in the bathroom, but her part of the bed had an unrumpled look.

Then he remembered that Bob Campbell was in the house. And Bob had to get off to work, unless he had awakened early and gone off already.

Jack got up, and found the apartment silent. Amelia must be still asleep. Jack had a strong urge to jump into his track suit and trot around Bedford and Hudson for twenty minutes, but what if Bob woke up and found the house quite empty, save for Amelia? Jack had to laugh as he brushed his teeth.

So he put on a dressing gown and made coffee, set the table for four, in case Amelia and Natalia came in, and sliced some bread for toast, though Bob looked like the type who was always on a diet and had nothing but black coffee for breakfast. It was a beautiful day, with a promise of strong sunshine beyond the windows.

And what was Natalia doing now? What had she been doing? Had she had too much to drink at Elsie's and Marion's, and spent the night there because of exhaustion? Had she stayed because she wanted to? Had she slept in the same bed with Elsie? And where was Marion in all this? Jack could understand that Natalia had wanted a change of atmosphere, that waking up in another house, even if she'd spent the night uncomfortably on a sofa, was preferable to waking up and facing Bob over the breakfast table at an early hour. But why hadn't she telephoned, even late, last night?

Bob Campbell walked in from the hall, looking showered and

shaved and every inch the businessman, with his carryall in hand. "Good morning, Jack! Sleep well?"

"Yes, indeed! And you?"

"Pretty well, thanks. Natalia gave me a pill to sleep with, but I didn't even take it.—Can I do anything to help, Jack?"

Jack smiled. "Just sit down and tell me your breakfast order."

"Coffee and one piece of toast. Juice if you have it."

Jack poured coffee, then attended to the rest.

"Where's Natalia? Sleeping, I suppose. I shouldn't talk so loudly."

"Y-y—Sleeping—Probably she is, but she's not here. She went over to see Elsie late last night, Elsie and her friend Marion, you know, down on Greene Street."

"Really?" Bob sat, plump and alert on his chair and chuckled briefly, as if Louis weren't dead, as if it were any old morning.

"Yes," said Jack, glancing at Bob. Jack was curious to see Bob's reaction, and he found himself playing it just right, with the faintest puzzlement in his "Yes" that might lead Bob to say more.

Bob was sipping black coffee, staring at the sugar bowl. "I imagine I depressed Natalia terribly. The whole thing—yesterday. Louis—Of course she had to get away from it." He looked miserably at Jack as Jack sat down. "I want to thank you both again. I was a mess yesterday. Shattered. Natalia—She's the only person in the world I could've called on. So I did. Thank you both. And for putting me up." He finished softly, as if he had recited a prayer.

"Oh, not to mention," Jack replied. "Friends are friends."

Bob munched his toast, dutifully, without appetite.

"Have you been down to Elsie's place?"

"Oh, yes. We were there—twice, I think. Louis and I."

"Nice place?"

"Yes." Bob smiled. He had a small gold rim on a tooth behind an eyetooth. "High ceiling, all white, low couches. Marion has a nice way with things. Not too many guitars, maybe six." Bob attempted another chuckle. "Marion's good for Elsie, keeps her— Well, Elsie's like a kite going up, I feel sometimes, zooming anywhere. Marion sort of—"

Jack waited. Was Bob rambling on to avoid talking about Natalie and Elsie? Or talking to try to control his own grief? "Keeps her steady," Jack said.

"Yes. Something like that.—Got to push off, Jack," Bob said, standing up.

Jack got up too. "Bob, if you need us for anything—The Katz Gallery's closed today, so Natalia's here. In a while, she's here, I suppose," he added with a smile. "I'm here anyway."

Bob thanked him, and said that the crematorium, or wherever they took Louis, could reach him at his office. "I gave them all the necessary phone numbers last night. I'm supposed to go there at six today." Now Bob looked suddenly down, and drawn. "Got to brace myself—look good for the office. I'm not saying anything to anybody. That's the way Louis would want it. Bye-bye, Jack." He left the apartment.

Jack stood for a moment motionless, in the hall. Now he was out of the mood for his jog, now he would run into people hurrying for the subway or the bus. He put on blue jeans and a half-soiled shirt whose tails he left hanging out, tidied up the breakfast disorder to some extent, then Amelia came in, barefoot, in her pink nightie that nearly touched the ground. She looked like a cherub who had just quit a painting for a breather and a snack, in this case Shredded Wheat, her current favorite cereal. Jack served her a bowl of it, plus a glass of orange juice.

"They picking you up today?" Jack asked.

"Yep."

"You sure?"

"Yes, Daddy." Orange juice was all over her upper lip, and her tongue came out to lick it as she looked at him.

Maybe Natalia knew, but Jack wasn't sure. He called up the school. Yes, they were calling for Amelia, because they hadn't heard from the Sutherlands, and Miss Robles had just left, but she had two other children to call for first.

Jack had Amelia dressed in time for the doorbell, and he went downstairs with her. Amelia hadn't asked about Natalia, who was often asleep at this hour.

"Morning, Mrs Farley," Jack said. "Help you with that?" Jack held the house door wider.

"No. I'm fine, thank you, Mr Sutherland." Mrs Farley was again struggling with her shopping trolley, which hadn't much in it, but was always a problem for her on the front steps and stairs.

"Hang on a sec and I'll take it up," Jack said. "Morning, ma'am." He greeted the presumable Miss Robles, a dark-haired girl new to him. She had two other small children with her, a boy and girl, yelling at each other now on the front steps.

"This is Amelia?" asked Miss Robles.

"None other. I can pick her up at four," Jack said spontaneously. He could always call them if he couldn't. "Tell the school."

"Okay."

Jack had brought his keyring, and he opened the mailbox, grabbed two letters, then turned to assist Mrs Farley who was now in the hallway. Jack took her trolley in both hands. "Here we go!" said Jack cheerfully.

At least he made Mrs Farley's smile widen. "Thank you so much, Mr Sutherland," she said, a little out of breath as she reached her door. "That is most kind of you."

Jack went up to his apartment. One envelope was stampless and bore the all-connected handwriting which he recognized as Linderman's, and which he dreaded. The other was from Trews whose initials T.E.W. were typed on the back of the envelope above the Dartmoor, Aegis logo. Jack opened Trews' letter first, because good or bad news, it would be logical and therefore not disturbing.

Dear Jack,
Just to state that sales are 30% better than predicted on HALF-UNDERSTOOD DREAMS, and it is on the Editor's Choice list, number 6, in the next issue of Time.

Am dropping a note to Joel too.

Very best to you,
Trews
Trelawney E. Watson

P.S. *Are you thinking yet about a book on your own, maybe with theme but no prose?*

No, Jack wasn't, but Trews had twice mentioned such a project. Jack faced the second letter and opened it. There were two pages with writing on both sides. Jack read it rapidly, feeling increasingly vexed as he went on.

The gist was that his "continuing association" with Elsie was causing or must be causing his wife considerable pain and sorrow. Ralph Linderman professed himself disappointed that a man he had believed cultured and a gentleman could so betray his status as to "dally" with a young and innocent girl, perverting her character for his personal pleasures. "Elsie and others," was one phrase, and that meant Marion, Jack supposed, remembering the early morning—only yesterday morning—when Linderman had seen him and Elsie and Marion walking along Grove in quest of a taxi at Seventh. But Linderman devoted equal space to Natalia's "predicament" and also speculated on the effect of his behavior on his small daughter. He had seen his wife, he wrote, on the street, and tragedy and unhappiness were written all over her face.

Ah, Linderman! How little he knew! Little did he dream that Natalia and Elsie had spent last night—possibly—in each other's arms! In a way, the letter was funny, and in the old way sick-making, because Linderman was still on about his bedding Elsie. Jack had an impulse to burn the letter in the fireplace, but felt that this was old-fashioned and dramatic, and also he didn't want to see later the black ashes of it on top of the gray wood ashes now in the fireplace. So he tore the letter into little pieces, the envelope too, and dropped it all into the plastic garbage bag among wet orange peel halves, and gave the garbage bag a shake so the pieces would slide down.

Linderman had written that his conduct "merited being reported", and Jack recalled a word well crossed out here, as if Linderman might have had the police in mind. Well, that was amusing too. Get Linderman and Elsie up before the police and Elsie would assert in no uncertain terms that she was gay and what the hell was Linderman dreaming up?

Linderman hadn't really threatened to do anything, Jack realized. But Jack sensed that his frustration was mounting, because he did not even know where Elsie lived now, or Jack at least hoped that he didn't.

Jack put on the radio in his workroom, turned it from pop to a classical station, and got some soothing string quartet music. He turned the volume low.

An hour or so later, the telephone rang, and it was Natalia. She was still at Elsie's, she said.

"Bob got off to work this morning?"

"Yes. He seemed to be bearing up pretty well."

"Good.—I'll be home soon."

Natalia arrived around noon, arms full of things she had bought

186

at a deli, plus a bunch of daffodils. She arranged the flowers in a white vase. "Last night, I felt like collapsing, so I did."

Jack was then unloading bags in the kitchen. "I can imagine.—Could you sleep comfortably?"

"Out like a light. I didn't want to come back here and see Bob, frankly—talk with him, you know?"

"I do know. I understand, darling."

She straightened and looked at him, frowning a little. "Thanks, Jack." She said it as if she meant it. "I'll fix some lunch for us.—Any interesting mail today?"

"N-no. Well, a nice note from Trews about 'Dreams'. Show you." Jack got it from the coffee table. "Easier if you read it."

Natalia read it, and smiled. "Isn't that great? It is sort of a sleeper. Thirty per cent better! Not bad."

During lunch, Natalia didn't mention Louis or Bob, rather to Jack's relief. She talked about Elsie's pleasure in being lent the de Kooning book, of her pointing out the painting she was fondest of in the book last night, one Elsie had known and had looked up in the book. Elsie had voluntarily promised not to take the de Kooning book out of the house. Natalia talked, somehow, as if she knew the Greene Street place well, and it crossed Jack's mind that Linderman might follow her there one day. So while they had coffee, Jack said:

"I may as well tell you, I had an unpleasant letter from Linderman this morning. I hate even bringing it up."

"Lin—Oh, the old guy! What now?"

"The same thing. Except—" Jack had to laugh. "Now he seems to think I'm having an affair with Elsie, here in the apartment, and that it's making you very unhappy."

"*What?*" Natalia smiled, mirth welled up to her eyes. "You don't mean it!"

"I do. I threw the letter away. Tore it up."

"That's a pity."

"Well—I found it funny and not funny. He doesn't know where Elsie lives now, you know, and I hope he doesn't find out. Be sure he doesn't follow you down to Greene Street sometime."

Natalia seemed to take this seriously. "I'll watch out.—I didn't tell you, when I came back from Louis' yesterday, he happened to be on Grove and Bleecker, wouldn't you know. High noon. He came up and said, 'Oh, Mrs Sutherland!' and would've engaged me in a yack, I'm sure, but I pushed the bell and you let me in.—The nerve of him putting things on paper like that! You shouldn't have torn it up, Jack dear." Her voice kept its elegant control, but she slapped the edge of the table with her fingers.

"Why?" But at once Jack knew why.

"If we have to go to the police to get him off our backs, as Elsie would say—"

Jack was silent, thinking that he had made a mistake, though he could still put the letter together again. "Unfortunately, it probably isn't his last letter, so don't worry.—He saw me walking out with the girls yesterday morning. At 6 a.m., mind you." Jack smiled wryly. "So he thinks I'm dallying with the two of them. Paying them too, he thinks, because he saw me giving Elsie a fiver for the taxi!" Now Jack laughed.

Natalia shook her head. "It's too much."

"Why didn't you tell me you saw the old guy Sunday?"

She shrugged. "Because I don't like talking about him. I feel the same way Elsie does."

Jack saw in Natalia's face the same anger he had seen in Elsie's, though Natalia's anger at the moment was quieter. "As long as he doesn't find out where Elsie lives. I don't think he's got a clue now, but he did say, 'Is it south of the Village?' or something like that."

"Oh? He asked you that in the letter?"

"No, he called up here—once. I didn't want to tell you. He was asking how Elsie was and then where she lived, and I said I hadn't the faintest, because she's always moving, and he said, 'Is she living south of the Village?' or something like that."

"*Phoning* us now.—I'm sorry you ever lost that wallet. Even if you did get it back."

Jack frowned. "You know, if we got together, you, me and Elsie, and told the police about this guy's pestering—we wouldn't need any letter from Linderman to corroborate us." At that moment, however, Jack realized the weakness of their case. "The trouble is," Jack went on, "he doesn't use any dirty words and doesn't threaten anything. I wonder if the police would do something, or laugh? He's just a pain in the arse, after all." When Natalia did not reply, Jack got up, restlessly. "More coffee?"

"Yes, please, Jack."

Natalia changed the subject. This coming Thursday the Katz

Gallery was having an opening for the paintings of a young Austrian named Sylvester, whose work looked influenced by Hundertwasser, Natalia said, though his themes were more interesting. Elsie was coming and maybe Marion too. And Wednesday Elsie was posing in raincoats for a two-page spread in *Harper's Bazaar*. Natalia said that Elsie had turned down a five-thousand-dollar offer from *Playboy* to pose for a semi-nude pull-out.

"Elsie said, 'So these male creeps can masturbate better when they prop my picture up in front of themselves? No, thanks.' " Natalia laughed.

Jack realized that he didn't mind that Natalia was full of Elsie's news, because he was in love with Elsie himself. He wasn't even jealous of Natalia's being, maybe, in love with her, though logically Natalia's love for him would be thereby diminished. Wouldn't it?

"I'll clear the table," Natalia said, "so go back to work if you feel like it.—Got anything for the cleaners? I'm going in a while."

Jack had a pair of gray flannels to go, and got them.

Natalia said she would pick up Amelia at 4, too.

Some time later, the telephone rang. Jack was in the middle of a blue wash and went on with it, vaguely thinking Natalia was back and would answer. He continued covering the area he wanted to cover, because he couldn't add to it once it was dry. On the eighth or ninth ring, he moved.

The house seemed to be empty. He picked up the telephone in the living-room.

"Hello, Jack. This is Marion."

"Oh, Marion. Hi. If you want Natalia, she's doing errands just now."

"I didn't want to speak with her particularly, I wanted to speak with you," Marion said in her soft, precise voice. "It's about Elsie."

"Yes?" Jack anticipated a mild warning which he was supposed to pass on to Natalia, perhaps that Natalia might do well to keep her distance.

"I'm sure you know since Saturday night that Natalia's rather stuck on her. Maybe it's mutual just now." Marion gave the faintest of laughs. "Hope it doesn't bother you."

"No.—Not at all."

"Good. Because it doesn't bother me either. Nobody owns Elsie, not me, not anybody. That's part of her charm."

Jack smiled at the half-open window in front of him. "I know. I agree."

"Elsie picks people up and drops them—fast. So—"

"So?"

"That's the way to take her. Be braced for this being dropped, and enjoy her while it lasts. Since we're all seeing each other now and then, I wanted to make myself clear. No hard feelings on my part. Natalia knows that."

"Very nice of you. To say that."

Marion laughed a little, as if at his politeness.

Jack hoped that Marion wasn't being dropped. "Any message for Natalia? Want her to call you?"

"No. Oh yes! There's sort of a party at the Gay Nighties Friday night. I'll be playing for about fifteen minutes. Lots of other people performing. You're both invited. Remind Natalia."

"Where is it?"

"Down on Wooster. I gave Natalia the address."

Jack felt both jangled and a bit better as he returned to his workroom. So there was something rather real going on between Natalia and Elsie, or Marion wouldn't have troubled to make this call.

What did girls do? Jack's mouth twitched with a nervous smile. Natalia and Elsie had both had a little experience in the past, he mustn't forget that. An affair, he thought. Affairs were short by definition, with a few exceptions. Affairs weren't like marriages. Say nothing, play it cool, he told himself. That was not only civilized and polite, it was safe. He'd pretend not to see anything, or if he saw something because it was so obvious he couldn't possibly miss it, he would pretend not to care much or at all. And maybe his not-caring would be real.

After all, yes, he did want Elsie to enjoy life, to be happy. Hadn't he said that to old Linderman? It was Linderman who couldn't understand that. Jack didn't want to resemble Linderman in the least.

When Natalia came in a few minutes later, Jack gave her Marion's message about Friday. He and Natalia were going to the theater Friday evening, and Jack didn't have to remind her about that. Natalia said she supposed they could just as well look in at the place after the theater, if they felt like it, because the Gay Nighties show would go on until late, and Marion simply wanted them to put in an appearance to increase the crowd. It was the "opening" of the Gay Nighties.

"I'm going to try to reach Bob at the office," Natalia said. "I should've done it before.—Imagine going to the *office* today."

But Jack knew, they both knew that Bob Campbell had, for today at least, the day of the cremation, to carry on with a life-as-usual attitude or crack up. Jack had told Natalia about the cremation at 6 somewhere on Long Island, and she had been sure Bob wanted to go alone. Jack lingered, thinking it would be friendly if he said a word to Bob too.

"I see, thank you . . . No, no message." Natalia said to Jack, "Bob's left. I'll try to call him later tonight." Natalia had a pained expression, and was in one of her frequent states of vague unease. "I'd better call my mother. I've been putting it off."

To tell her about Louis, Jack knew. Natalia's mother Lily had always been fond of Louis. "I'll go pick up Amelia.—No, really I'd like a walk," Jack said, when Natalia offered to do it. He went out.

27

NATALIA took a dress and shoes in a shopping bag when she
went off to the Katz Gallery Thursday noon. The gallery was
closed all day until the opening at 6 p.m., because today she and
Isabel and a boy called Dan, who helped out, had to hang the
pictures. Natalia departed in old dungarees and sandals.

Yesterday she had had lunch with Bob, who had told her about
the cremation. Bob had waited for more than an hour on a marble
bench in a tomblike building somewhere in Long Island, until
Louis' ashes were brought out in a box. Then he had taken a
Staten Island ferry, and opened the box over the rail, and a man
had come up to him and said, did he have to contaminate the
city's waters further by emptying his lunchbox garbage into them?
Natalia had told Jack that a few of Bob's and Louis' friends, one
of them called Stew whom Jack vaguely remembered meeting,
knew of Louis' death by now. Bob had the idea that the death
would be less of a shock to people, if they learned about it two
weeks or a month later. Bob had gone to Philadelphia to see about
Louis' apartment there, and somehow the *Inquirer* had found out
and printed an article about Louis and his real estate work, his
saving of old buildings from the wrecker's ball and his efforts to
keep small neighborhood shops in business. Natalia had a
photostat of the article.

Jack arrived at the Katz Gallery before 7. The wide, white-
walled rooms were already rather crowded, and the hum of conversation reminded Jack of a well-functioning beehive, though the
wisps of cigarette smoke dispelled the bucolic. Some people had
drinks in hand. He looked for Natalia and didn't see her, and
glanced around also for Elsie.

"Hello! You're John Sutherland?" asked a smiling man of about
forty with round, friendly eyes.

"Yes." Jack took the hand the man was extending.

"Just wanted to say how much I admired your work in—in the 'Dreams' book. Lovely and different. Natalia tells me you don't use a pencil."

"Not when I can avoid it," Jack replied. The man still gripped his hand.

"I'm with Battersea Press. Harold Vinson's my name. Art director. Natalia knows me." He released Jack's hand. "May I telephone you if we have some work you might do?"

Jack smiled. "Yes, sure."

The man waved good-bye and drifted off, and his alert eyes lingered on Jack till he had to look where he was going.

Jack went into the big room and saw Natalia being the pleasant hostess far to Jack's left, laughing now, and the laugh was inaudible in the buzz. And the paintings? Jack could hardly see them. The ones he saw part of, their top corners, were full of dark squares of different colors, suggesting careless Mondrians. There was another of dusty yellow fragments coiled like a snail's shell, and this perhaps had made Natalia think of Hundertwasser. Sylvester's work would sell, Jack thought, because it had an elegance about it. The colors had style. He could not judge one single picture, because none was visible in its entirety.

And Elsie? He looked for her blond head and couldn't find it.

Jack went back to the foyer just as an elevator door opened and among five or six people, there was Elsie in a white sleeveless dress with a pale blue hat like a bellhop's cap on her head, a raincoat over her arm, and Jack's heart jumped. "Elsie!"

She had seen him at once too. "Hello, Jack!" She gave him her hand, pressed his, looked at him for an instant, then turned her eyes to the surroundings.

"Where's Marion?"

"Not coming," Elsie said. "She's got work just now."

"You look good this evening." Other people thought so too, Jack saw from the heads that turned toward Elsie. "Glass of wine or something? The drinks're here." He meant the table at the back of the foyer.

"No, not now."

"Want to go in? Natalia's in there—on the left."

They went into the main room, which bent around the corner of the building to the right. Now Natalia wasn't where she had been. Elsie wore black patent leather pumps and carried a black patent leather bag. Best of all, Jack noticed, was that her make-up had improved, the lipstick was the right red, the mascara was just enough to set off the blue of her eyes. And she looked utterly sure of herself, years older in her poise than at that first party at Louis', for instance. Jack saw her eyes light up and her lips part before she said:

"There's Natalia."

They moved through the crowd toward Natalia, Elsie preceding him. "Were you working today, Elsie?"

"Yes. And I don't own this dress!" Elsie replied over her shoulder.

Natalia's soft greeting to Elsie was "Hi, sweetie," that maybe no one but Elsie heard, that Jack heard only by lip-reading. Had Natalia's heart jumped as his had? Absurd for him, Jack told himself. He could recall five or six girls who had made his heart jump in the past, and where were they now? Faces and names half-forgotten or completely forgotten. But Natalia could still do it to him, often.

Elsie moved away from Natalia and tried to look at the paintings. She bent, she stretched to see them. Jack avoided being introduced to Sylvester, a young man with a reddish moustache, sturdy, shy, and looking as if he had put on his Sunday best for this occasion.

Isabel came over. "Hello, Jack!—Have you seen Louis yet? I invited them both."

"N-no, I haven't," Jack replied, and felt for an instant awful, as if he were personally guilty of a deception. Was Bob here even? "Excuse me, Isabel, I'll check with Natalia." Checking with Natalia could mean anything, checking if Natalia had seen Bob, for instance.

Natalia told Jack that she ought to stay on another half hour. It was nearly 8.

Jack couldn't bring himself to warn Natalia that Isabel had asked was Louis here. "I thought Elsie might like to have dinner with us—out somewhere," Jack said. Elsie was a few feet away then, but quite out of hearing. "Or maybe you and she want to have dinner together? In which case, I'll take off, I think."

"Together? No.—Sure, Jack, I'll ask her," Natalia said.

But Natalia was busy and Jack asked Elsie, who somewhat

ungraciously reflected, then said, "I could, if it doesn't get too late. I have to be somewhere at nine tomorrow morning."

Jack went and told Natalia that he and Elsie were going down for a drink at the bar around the corner, a bar Natalia knew, and they would wait for her there.

The bar was quiet and darkish, and so full they had to stand at the counter. Jack ordered a Jack Daniel's and Elsie said she would have the same. A man gave Elsie his stool to sit on. Jack, keeping a certain distance from Elsie, though very little because of the press of people, lifted his glass to her before he drank, but Elsie didn't see it. In fact, Elsie seemed to avoid his eyes, might have been having her drink alone, Jack thought. The yellowish light from behind the bar fell on the crisp white band that crossed her shoulder, on her bare arm below, an arm not yet suntanned—could Elsie acquire a tan?—rounded but not at all plump. A question occurred to Jack: *Did it annoy you that I said I love you?* It was the kind of question a teenaged boy asked a girl, hoping like mad that his declaration had annoyed her, upset her, delighted her. If he had asked the question, Elsie would probably have replied casually, *No, why should it?* with maybe a glance at him, maybe a blink of her perfectly mascaraed eyes.

Jack saw the eyes of the barman, who was polishing glasses, lingering dreamily on Elsie. Jack cleared his throat and said, "What're you doing tomorrow morning at nine?"

Elsie looked at him with attention. "It's what the professor calls a midterm exam. Like in high school. It's an hour-and-a-half exam on English and American literature."

"Oh!" Jack laughed. "I was thinking you had a modeling job! Are you worried?"

"Yes. Plenty." She was still looking at him. "I can write on and on, sure. I know what *I* want to say about those books, but is it right? Is it what the professor wants?—I want to pass that course."

"What books, for instance?"

"Dostoievsky's *The Idiot* is one.—Natalia helps me a lot. She's *read* all this stuff. I know what I want to say, that it's all emotion and very sincere but a little bit naive. *The Idiot*, I mean. And Natalia made me laugh Sunday—" Elsie sat straight, tipped her blue-capped head back and continued, facing Jack. "She said last Sunday, for all of us, was like the characters in *The Idiot*, when nobody goes to bed, and Prince Myshkin goes visiting everywhere in the small hours, and it's still light almost, because it's summer, and they have these long conversations sitting on benches out in somebody's garden! Ha-ha!" Elsie shook with mirth.

Jack grinned, happy, ecstatic, and not knowing why. He too remembered the innocent and half-dotty Myshkin, hung up on a girl who wouldn't have him, talking, talking. "I love you, like an idiot—like Myshkin, I think," Jack said, just loudly enough for her to hear. "Nothing to worry about. And I'm sure you're not worried."

This made her laugh again, a little shyly, though she seemed quite at ease, not afraid to look at him, genuinely unaffected by what he had said.

It was odd to feel so elated, happy in her company, Jack thought, when there were absolutely no sexual currents flowing from her toward him. He might feel some in himself. Or did he? But from her, nothing. She might have confided her exam anxiety in the same manner to an old uncle, another girl, or to her brother.

Elsie's loquacious mood continued at dinner, but it was focused on Natalia. From the instant Natalia had walked into the bar, she and Elsie had had something to talk about, the exam, then a photographer Elsie had posed for today. Natalia wore sandals with her black dress, having this morning put high-heeled shoes that weren't mates into the shopping bag to take to the gallery.

They went to a Hungarian restaurant up on Second Avenue, where the food was good but the service slow. Jack didn't mind. He listened. Elsie sat next to him, Natalia opposite them, her back to the center of the restaurant. Natalia preferred to face people she was talking to. Goulasch with noodles finally arrived, and cool rosé. Elsie ate with her usual gusto, which Jack found attractive, maybe because it was healthy. Back to Elsie's exam tomorrow. Elsie did not like Hemingway.

"Why not?" asked Jack.

"He isn't thick like the others," replied Elsie with a glance at Jack.

Jack knew what she meant. Hemingway was not full of details. He noticed Natalia's amused face.

"For instance," said Natalia.

"When he says in—*For Whom the Bell Tolls* that the hero

puts his hand on the woman's stomach because she's pregnant—
he says something silly to the woman. Like a little boy. And it's
supposed to be serious. It just made me laugh."

Natalia leaned back in her chair and smiled. "Just write that
you think Hemingway's a lightweight and tell them why."

"Should I?" Elsie's confidence seemed to come with the
question. "I will. A lightweight. That's the way I feel."

Natalia exchanged a glance with Jack.

Jack had to get up and hunt for the waiter to bring the bill, and
when he returned—having insisted that the waiter come with
him—Natalia and Elsie were in lively conversation, both leaning
across the table.

They took a taxi downtown, and went to Elsie's first. Jack
wanted to see her to her door, and said so. He was thinking both
of the possibly lurking Linderman and of Elsie's getting some
sleep tonight, though he mentioned neither. Elsie's and Marion's
place was in a large dark building on the east side of Greene
Street, four or five storeys high. Elsie had a key, and Jack, on the
sidewalk, watched her push open a tall, heavy-looking door.

As he got back into the taxi, Jack vowed to himself not to make
a comment in the next days or weeks about Natalia's fondness for
Elsie, but to let Natalia say something, if she cared to, and if she
didn't, so be it. "Now we go to Grove Street, please," he said to
the driver. "Go up Bedford and stop at the corner, if you will."

The taxi moved off and made a left turn into West Houston.

"Isn't she coming along!" Natalia said.

Jack smiled. "By leaps and bounds. Even the way she talks—
She doesn't slur things any more. Maybe Marion's influence.
Marion practices—"

"*I* told Elsie to say introduce instead of innerduce," Natalia
interrupted. "Doesn't take much effort to put a 't' in things."

When they got home, it was still early enough for Susanne to
catch a bus up to Riverside. Susanne had been reading at the
white table, an empty coffee cup stood beside her book. All was
well.

Natalia got under the shower, and Jack after her. He much
wanted to make love to her tonight, but doubted that she'd be in
the mood after a day like today. Jack was wrong. In bed, he kissed
her good night on her cheek, her lips, and held one of her breasts
gently as he often did, and things went on from there. And Jack

was proud of his performance, giving Natalia two climaxes to his one. Did Elsie excite them both? Jack didn't think so, at least not in regard to himself. Natalia was real and solid, he knew the slight roughness of the skin on her hips, and loved it. They had created a child together. Natalia was not unexplored territory, not a young larva that might or might not turn into a beautiful butterfly.

"You're my bread," Jack said softly, as Natalia lit a cigarette.

"What d'you mean?" she asked through a laugh.

Jack lay on his back with his hands behind his head. "Real." He turned his head, then his body toward her but he did not touch her. "Staff of life, you know?"

28

THE *Gay Nighties* looked like just that: nightgear waved in the breeze all over the façade and from over the doorway, flimsy nightgowns, striped sleepsuits, short nighties, some looking from the thrift shop. Jack and Natalia had come from a show in midtown, and it was now after 11. People stood outside, a few with glasses in hand, all rather weirdly dressed.

Natalia pushed calmly through the doorway.

The place was a ramshackle bar and art gallery, there was a small podium where Jack saw a man seated, dreamily strumming a guitar despite the lack of audience attention. Jack glanced around for Elsie, or Marion, and didn't see either. Natalia said "Hi" to a couple of people who greeted her, and whom she may or may not have seen before, Jack thought. Getting a table was hopeless, a drink at the bar might be possible. The artwork on the walls was of the kind Jack detested and at the same time was amazed by, kindergarten stuff in heavy oil with crude black outlines, depicting car crashes, explosions, or sexual activities. Amelia's efforts had grace and design by comparison, and certainly affection. The odd thing was that this crap on the walls was bought by some people.

"Hi!" It was Marion suddenly beside them. "We're over here." She pointed to a side wall. "Want me to get you a drink?"

Jack offered to attempt the drinks, but Marion said she knew the bartender.

"*Jonathan!*" she yelled.

They got scotches, nothing for Marion, and Marion forged a way for them to a table where Elsie sat, dressed again in white, and in conversation with a young man whose back was to the wall. A candle, stuck to the table's surface, had nearly burnt down in a messy pool of wax.

"Ludo," Marion said, indicating the young man, who looked Italian or Spanish, and who barely glanced up.

Elsie looked up calmly, and greeted Natalia and Jack in a hardly audible voice. She was often so, manifesting none of the pleasure people were supposed to show, out of politeness, on seeing each other. Jack sat as far from Elsie as possible, the better to see her. Natalia, rather out of necessity, had the corner of the table, next to Elsie.

"How'd the exam go this morning?" Jack shouted to Elsie.

Elsie smiled suddenly, her eyes brightened. "I thought it would be *long*. But it seemed short. An hour and a half. And I write fast.—I don't think I failed it."

Jack smiled. "Good."

Marion told Jack that she had already played tonight and had stuck her guitar in a safe place, she hoped. "I don't get a bang out of playing in dives like this—tonight," she said, tapping a cricket lighter on the table top nervously, idly. "Too many people for anybody to listen and nobody called for order."

Natalia and Elsie, because they sat next to each other, were not having to shout their conversation.

"Oh, I did want to tell you," Marion said, leaning toward Jack, "this morning I saw that old guy, you know, with the dog? I was just going home with groceries, a friend was with me, and I forgot to look around till I was at the door, and then I saw him on the opposite sidewalk, walking along slowly. So I went back *down* the front steps and said to my friend, 'Let's walk on, don't ask why,' and we went around the corner to his place for ten minutes or so.—I hope he didn't recognize me, but I dunno."

Jack recalled the Sunday morning when Elsie and Marion had been walking together from his house.

"I mentioned it to Elsie when she came home today at noon, and she was all upset and angry for a few minutes, because—" Marion glanced at Elsie. "—I hadn't looked around first. Elsie always looks around before she goes up the steps, even though she's never seen him in our street.—F'Chris' sake, you'd think he had nothing else to do with himself but *follow* people!"

Maybe only Elsie, Jack thought. He was aware of a slow wave of depression. The Greene Street house might have been spotted, connected with Elsie.

"So Elsie went off by herself this afternoon," Marion continued, "up to the Cloisters to get it off her mind, she said. And I feel like a dope!"

"Oh—" Jack shrugged. The Cloisters. Jack realized why Elsie and Natalia had been talking about tapestries a couple of minutes ago. The unicorn. He sipped his drink, and looked around at the crowd, which was mostly young, white and black. Some were homosexuals, some affected punk gear and hair-dos. Elsie was laughing now. And Jack for some reason still felt depressed. Electronic music started up with a deep beat, Elsie's style.

Jack reached for a little blank pad in his jacket pocket. He had a black ballpoint pen with him. He started with a lantern-jawed fellow who leaned against a wall and looked as if he might hold still for a few seconds. Jack didn't like his effort, flipped the page and switched to Elsie, got her hairline and cheek and eyes in the minimum of lines, hesitated until her lips were still, then drew her mouth in two lines, then another line for the white collar of her shirt. He turned the little page. The magic was working. He felt less depressed.

They were clearing the floor for dancing, some people had to move their chairs and tables back. Figures began twirling in the center of the floor. The boy called Ludo, who had been quiet as a mouse, stood up and extended his hand palm upward toward Elsie. Elsie got up. A black sash divided her white shirt from the loose white trousers below, trousers so loose that her hips looked fuller than they were, and the effect was charming.

I don't want to watch, Jack thought, *because Elsie's going to fall on the floor.* But she'd never fallen, and why should he think she would now? Jack put his palms against his face for a moment.

"You all right, Jack?" Natalia asked. "Hot in here, isn't it?"

"Yep. I'm okay."

Natalia wanted another scotch, and Marion stood up and got Jonathan's attention. The drink was brought by a girl in record time, and Jack took the opportunity to order a beer. Natalia was watching Elsie on the dance floor. The boy seemed to be a break dancer, and his action near the floor was mostly out of sight. Elsie danced around him. Jack did not want to watch except for a second at a time, to catch glimpses of a white figure in motion, like snapshots that he took when he opened his closed eyes. He overheard Marion saying to Natalia:

". . . told me she used to dance at home in her room with the lights out, danced naked till she was sleek with sweat. I believe her!"

Jack looked as the boy lifted Elsie by the waist and twirled her, nearly horizontal. The boy's body looked thin, and Jack could see sweat gleaming on his face.

Then Elsie walked toward them, calm, looking at no one, lips a little parted. Elsie took a cigarette, and leaned toward the boy who offered her a light across the table. She did not even look at the boy's face, didn't thank him for the light. She gave a big smile to Natalia.

Jack drew his sketch pad from his pocket again. He began drawing a sinister-looking pair of gay girls, who seemed frozen with diffidence, though they feigned unconcern as they leaned against a wall. Then Jack realized that one of them was the tough cookie named—Fran, wasn't that it? The bullet-headed former girlfriend of Genevieve. The girl with her was not Genevieve but a short-haired brunette wearing an oversized evening jacket and apparently nothing under it. Jack made a cartoon of Fran because he found her spectacularly unattractive. Her short but wide jaw looked capable of taking a heavyweight's punch, her eyes in his drawing came out like those of an evil pig, with intense dots for pupils, and the mouth was an ungenerous slit. Her eyes reminded him of the eyes of Linderman's dog God, but the dog at least had that good-natured, apologetic smile when he looked at people. Jack laughed to himself.

"Can I see?" Marion asked, smiling. "Or do you hate that?"

Jack shook his head. "Not just now, Marion. Another time, I promise." He had his beer and he drank. How to make Elsie laugh? Jack licked the beer from his upper lip. "Elsie?"

She turned from Natalia to him. "Yes?"

"Do you still love me?" he asked wistfully.

Elsie laughed, laughed again, as if the laughter substituted for words. Had her cheeks grown pinker or was he imagining?

Natalia heard him and barely smiled, indifferent.

At home, Jack didn't say anything about Linderman's having turned up on Greene Street. If Elsie had mentioned it to Natalia, Natalia might tell him, but she didn't, at least not that night. Natalia said that three of Sylvester's paintings had sold, one of them for three thousand five hundred. And Elsie was going away for Easter to a friend's house somewhere in New Jersey. Marion was invited, but wasn't going with her.

"For a week or so? Good idea," Jack said.

Natalia was undressing. She wanted a shower. "Yes, and I think it's Marion's idea. Elsie needs a break, and that school has a break at Easter, of course." Natalia disappeared into the bathroom.

Susanne was staying the night in the spare room, they had seen from the three books neatly stacked on the white table. Jack removed his trousers, peeled off his pale blue T-shirt, and reflected lightly on the vision of Natalia and Elsie opposite him at the table in the Gay Nighties. Their conversation had been earnest, but without any hand-holding that Jack had seen. They might have behaved the same way, he thought, if they had been alone on the sofa here. Tapestries and the unicorn. Sharper in Jack's eyes were the images of Elsie in the air as she danced, Elsie with eyes lowered as she listened to Natalia, red-nailed fingers propping her head. As ever these bright memories jolted him with pleasure, and at the same time were without sexual stimulation for him.

29

'DAMMIT to f—" Ralph Linderman restrained himself and shook a fist at the empty air in his hall. He was barefoot and in pajamas, gripping the knob of his apartment door.

"Ah—wah," was the reply of the tot who had just reached the top of the stairs. It wore little blue shorts over a bulging diaper, and nothing else, and it lived downstairs and had no business up here.

"Or-r—wee!" shrieked the second, even smaller, on its way up on all fours.

"You live downstairs! Both of you! *Down!*" Ralph made shooing motions with both hands.

A shrill female voice cried out in Italian from below.

Ralph gripped the stairpost and shouted to the floor below: "Madame! Can you kindly get these kids down? The stairs're dangerous for them!"

"Ah, you mind your own business, Mr Linkman. With your yellin' it's worse!" But she was coming up the stairs to collect the brats.

"I'll get the police if this keeps up," Ralph told her. "You've got no right disturbing the peace like this!"

"Who's the loudest? *Who?*" The burly young woman, who was new in the house, threw the smaller of the tots over one shoulder and took the other by the hand.

"Just keep your *door* shut! That's all I ask!" Ralph entered his apartment and shut the door with a bang. "Damn the bastards, damn them!" he muttered.

This was the second week of it for Ralph. The trouble had begun when the old lady who lived below and whose door was in the middle of the hall passage, died after a couple of days in a hospital, and her grandson and family had come for the funeral,

204

and were now apparently staying. Since one family, plus a detached brother or uncle, already lived there, all grown-ups, there was plainly not enough room for a new couple with two small children and probably another on the way, and it had occurred to Ralph to report this situation to the housing authorities, because there was surely a law about not more than a certain number of people in a three-room apartment, but he suspected what the authorities would say: if they are related, and so on, they could live like that. And the new family with the two babes would of course say they were not staying long, just visiting after a funeral.

But Ralph hadn't had four hours of unbroken sleep in the past many days because of the little creepers who seemed to be up all day, wailed at 6 p.m. and also at 6 a.m., and so it seemed to Ralph they existed on no sleep at all, which he could not. In these last days as his nerves had worn thinner, he had yelled and cursed in the halls himself, and made himself more disliked, he realized. He knew he was considered an eccentric, maybe even unfriendly, though he always said "Good morning" or "Good evening" when he encountered anyone in the house, even a rude and sullen youngster. Now because of his yelling at the babes, Ralph feared that the rest of the people in the building might be ready to band together against him. That was the incredible thing, that the other people in the building seemed to be able to stand the noise, maybe it was just like home to them, just like Italy or wherever they came from. But they didn't have to get their sleep in the daytime, didn't have to earn their living by night. Half of them didn't go out to work, anyway, simply didn't work.

In his small bedroom, Ralph lay down again and tried to compose himself. It was half past 4 in the afternoon. He had been trying to get to sleep since around noon. He had to leave for work by 7.10, and his alarm was set for 6.30.

"Ah, God," he said, addressing the dog who lay with his chin on his paws, gazing at him, "forgive me."

Ralph closed his eyes, forced himself to breathe slowly, to relax. The image of Elsie's house came to him, dark and gloomy-looking by night, four storeys high, its doors looking as strong and impenetrable as those of a bank, and this vision depressed him utterly, even stirred in him a scared or defensive attitude. Into that building the delicate and fair little figure of Elsie had gone and vanished one evening at 6. He had to erase that vision, or he would never sleep. Elsie was of course not in the telephone book at that address, nor was Marion Gill, though her name was pencil-written above another name downstairs outside the big door, and he had not troubled to look up this name in the telephone book and had now forgotten it.

He sighed, and settled his cheek in his pillow.

Rap-rap-rap!

That was a knock right on his apartment door. "Who's there?" he yelled.

"Sartori!"

Ralph pulled his bathrobe on, shoved his feet into house-slippers for decency's sake. He opened the door about six inches.

"Hi. Listen, I warn you to cut that yellin' out or—"

"I have the right to peace and quiet on this floor!" Ralph recognized this black-haired fellow as the father in that new family below.

"You say you got a right, we got a right not to have no screamin' maniac in this buildin', see?"

"Then shut your door downstairs!"

"It's hot and we were cookin'. People have—"

"Yes, and it stinks! Try opening your window!" Liver stench tonight and the inevitable tomato sauce, Ralph smelt from where he stood.

"If I catch you layin' a hand on one of those kids—" Sartori pulled his right fist back menacingly. He was in shirtsleeves, black brows lowered.

"Sacred cows," Ralph sneered. "Rest assured, I don't care to touch them! Scum of the earth! Crawling everywhere like roaches!"

Sartori's eyes flashed, and he looked about to launch his fist. "Man, you're nuts! What about that filthy dog of yours, piss—"

"What's my dog done?" Ralph stood his ground. "Not even barked! You leave God alone!"

"Oh, man," said Sartori, backing, shaking his head. "You're for the nuthouse." He was leaving.

Ralph shut his door. It locked automatically, but he slid the chain bolt as well. God stood on four legs looking at him, puzzled and tense. "It's all right, my friend. Sh-h," Ralph said, trying to reassure the dog as well as himself. And the Pope preaching against birth control everywhere on earth! Madness!

Useless to try to get to sleep for a mere hour or so now. Ralph shaved at the bathroom basin, and cut himself. He applied a styptic pencil. Then he opened a can of mushroom soup and heated it, adding a can half filled with milk, half with water, and sliced bread from a hardening loaf. When he reached for the soup, he struck the pot handle with the back of his hand, and the whole thing went on the floor.

"*Tum-tee-tum*," he said to himself as he began to clean it up with a floor rag, and he forced a smile that was like a grimace, he realized. He always made himself smile in the face of small mishaps, in order to try to keep his sanity, when he was angry enough to tear the throat out of somebody, in this case Sartori, the cocky and insolent progenitor of the two little sacred cows. Ralph munched some bread, and promised God his meal and his airing.

Ten minutes later, Ralph was down on the street with God, Ralph keeping his head high, determined not to look at Signor or Signora Sartori if he encountered them, not to look ever again at the remains of that family, the old brother and the uncle or whatever, who lived in the apartment still. A sharp hunger bit at his stomach, but no matter; it would keep him on his mettle. He could grab a frankfurter at the Hot Arch Arcade at any hour. Dismal eight hours, dismal part of his life now, that arcade, that cesspool, and now Elsie, gone the way he had feared she might, and with John Sutherland. The expression on Mrs Sutherland's face before she entered her house that Sunday haunted him. And then the time—had it been a morning or afternoon?—when he had seen Elsie and Mrs Sutherland walking along Seventh Avenue arm in arm, then Mrs Sutherland had quickly clasped Elsie's hand as she spoke anxiously to Elsie, begging her probably to leave her husband alone. What madness, what wrongness in the world! And now Elsie in a finer apartment, or so he imagined it, financed by payments from John Sutherland and maybe from others too. Elsie had become a prostitute, she lived with a prostitute, the young woman with short brown hair whom he had seen with Elsie and Sutherland at 6 in the morning that fateful Sunday. The young woman looked older than Elsie, who in fact could look like a child of fifteen sometimes. The young woman, who was probably called Marion Gill, no doubt took a cut of the money that Elsie earned.

And Sutherland had not had the decency or the courage to answer his letter!

Abruptly Ralph turned and tugged God toward home. Frowning, Ralph recalled his polite understatements in his letter in regard to Sutherland's newly found pastime, reminding him in the gentlest of terms of the irreparable damage he was doing to Elsie. Ralph had suggested the possibility of speaking to the authorities, meaning the police, but even that he had put in calm words. Elsie at twenty might be of "the age of consent", but a police inquiry would cause Elsie to give her parents' name and address, the police might contact them, and this Ralph wished, because he was sure her parents would—

Ralph's thoughts faltered. He felt shy about going to the police. Wasn't the age of consent even sixteen for girls? Couldn't Elsie even refuse to give her parents' address?

"Hi, loony," said a boy of about twelve, bouncing a tennis ball in front of Ralph's house.

Ralph paid the boy no mind.

A few minutes later, when Ralph was walking from his house toward the Christopher Street subway station, he saw John Sutherland. Sutherland was walking toward him, and greeted him with a big smile.

"Evening, Mr Linderman, how're you?" Sutherland asked, looking muscular and fit in his blue jeans and V-necked sweater. He carried a bottle-shaped object in a brown paper bag.

"Very well, thank you, and yourself?"

"Fine. By the way, Elsie's moved way uptown on the *west* side. I thought it was east before. She's doing well and she's going out of town for a month or so. Vacation.—I think there's a young man in the picture."

Here Ralph saw Sutherland wink an eye. Sutherland shifted from one foot to the other in his running shoes, as if he were eager to dash away. "A young man?" Ralph asked.

"Young man she met at the school where she goes. Nice fellow, I heard.—See you, Mr Linderman!" He ran off.

"Where uptown?" Ralph called after him, but to no avail.

Sutherland was trotting now, nearly out of sight.

Ralph didn't believe him.

30

JACK was still smiling when he reached his front door. What an act he'd put on, beaming with good cheer! He'd had the idea a couple of days ago, to give Linderman a bum steer as to Elsie's whereabouts, the next time he saw Linderman on the street, and to throw in a boyfriend for good measure. Linderman had looked awful, dark around the eyes and with a bad shave that had left him with stubble and a couple of cuts.

The last week had brought Jack a few pieces of good news. His drawings for the yak book had been finished and approved, and he had sold between thirty and forty new spots. And Jack's father Charles had to some extent "relented", and Jack could not attribute it to anything except the *Dreams* book, the favorable impression it had apparently made on his father. Uncle Roger had informed Jack of his father's pleasure in receiving a copy. Jack had inscribed it to his mother and father, of course, and his mother had written him a letter. Then his father had written a shorter letter stating that he was *sincerely* (underlined) glad to see a "fine complete job" by Jack, and he had added that Jack's drawings looked as if he were sure of his style now, or something to that effect. The next pleasant item was that he and Natalia had decided to go to Yugoslavia and Greece in late June. Natalia loved both countries. Jack hoped to gather some happier experiences in Yugoslavia than he had at twenty-two in their prison.

By early May, Elsie had been away for more than a week in New Jersey, staying in a house with at least six other people, it seemed. She had sent two postcards addressed to Natalia and him, telling of swimming and horseback riding, and of "cooking out in the backyard". Then a horse blanket had arrived, a "housegift" Elsie called it, yellow-and-green-checked and leather-bordered. Natalia loved it. Jack referred to it as "the stiff throw", because it was so thick, it scarcely bent, and stuck out at the sides of their double bed. One Saturday afternoon, Natalia drove up to New Jersey to see Elsie, and returned late Sunday night. Jack didn't ask if she had stayed the night in the house where Elsie was. He had the feeling they had gone to some nearby motel.

Jack felt cheered by his father's friendlier attitude. Jack liked to tell himself that he could live without family closeness and moral support, but his father's stance after the Yugoslavian prison episode had wounded Jack. "Absence of discipline" had been his father's cry, his phrase of scorn. Never again had Jack sniffed any coke, even for fun, even when his father wouldn't have known, or got tipsy as some people did now and then, and he'd stopped smoking. If he had ever mentioned these reforms to Uncle Roger, he had not to his father, to whom he hadn't written, except for Christmas cards, during those seven or eight years until the present, when he had sent the *Dreams* book. Jack remembered a theory he'd had after stopping smoking: people didn't need drugs, it was possible to think oneself into another or happier state, possible through music or looking at paintings, possible while working sometimes. It didn't work in the same way that coke did, to be sure, but there was something in that theory, Jack believed still. Jack was sure that he could stand, even at an open window, and think himself into a fainting state by imagining a car accident, someone's crushed skull, disembowelment against the steering shaft. He had never cared to carry that experiment far, lest he really faint.

Could Elsie, with her enthusiasms, do the same? ". . . not just New York, everything's like a big surprise sometimes. Music, especially when I wake up . . . Sure I think of the hydrogen bomb, not every day, though. Then I look up and see that the sky's still clear. But I can imagine the cloud hanging up there." Jack remembered her talking in this vein once, remembered her naive and earnest voice.

Elsie telephoned a couple of times from Connecticut, once when they had both been home, once when Jack had been out and Natalia had told him that she called. Then Elsie was back, and Natalia went over to see her the same evening, on Greene Street. Natalia asked if he wanted to join them, but Jack said he had to work. Natalia, Elsie and Marion were going out to a restaurant in the neighborhood for dinner. Elsie was a bright pink from the sun, Natalia reported, and added that Elsie had lots of work ahead, judging from the letters she had received and the messages her agent had taken for her.

From what Natalia said about such evenings, all seemed amicable among the three of them. Was Natalia trying or not trying to take Elsie away from Marion? Was Elsie already taken away from Marion, and merely sharing the apartment with Marion now? Jack really didn't believe the latter. More likely, Elsie was the casual one, so casual that she could easily handle two girlfriends. And Natalia was sure of herself, as always, and could afford to play a slow game, knowing that she would win in the end. Jack half expected Natalia to ask if he minded if Elsie came along to Yugoslavia and Greece. In fact, Jack wouldn't have minded. He could imagine himself sleeping in Elsie's hotel or pension room now and then, while Elsie spent the night with Natalia. The idea made him smile. They were going to rent a little house on a Greek island for three weeks. But it seemed that Elsie had too many jobs and commitments ahead this summer. As Natalia had remarked, Elsie Tyler was ambitious.

Jack and Natalia discussed the matter of Amelia's next school, as Amelia would be six in late June, and Natalia wanted to take her out of the kindergarten atmosphere, as Natalia called it, of the Sterling Academy on West Twelfth Street. They consulted with the Armstrongs, whose boy Jason was a year older than Amelia, and found that the Armstrongs had opted for a parochial school. "If the parents want the child to sleep at home and want a civilized atmosphere," Elaine Armstrong said, "parochial's the best. No problem if you want to avoid the religious instruction, and they're serious about standards." So Jack and Natalia put this on their agenda, to look into parochial schools, and there was one in their neighborhood.

Bob Campbell may have been right, Jack thought, in not announcing Louis' demise at once. The news had leaked through their friends and acquaintances, but weeks after the event. Bob said he had received some telephone calls from people, but few letters of condolence that he had been obliged to answer. Jack remembered that Natalia had informed Elsie about Louis, and it seemed that Elsie had written a letter to Bob, such a touching letter that Bob brought it along, one evening when he came for dinner, to show to Jack and Natalia. Natalia had perused the letter and, Jack thought but was not sure, her eyes were wet when she handed it back to Bob. "Louis would've liked that, yes," she had said. Once in a while, on a Sunday or late in an evening, Jack felt a change in Natalia, an absentness when, or so he imagined, she was thinking that if Louis were still here, she could call him up and they might meet somewhere, and talk until the small hours.

Elaine Armstrong telephoned to ask if they were going to the Christopher Street Arts and Crafts sale on the coming Saturday morning. Jack and Natalia were going, and they met the Armstrongs at the northwest corner of Bleecker and Christopher, as agreed upon. They had brought their offspring, and Max gave firm orders to Jason not to get lost or else, and Jason said he could find his way home if he did. Jack preferred to keep Amelia's hand in his. Finally Jack carried her piggy-back style. Christopher Street was a mass of people strolling past or lingering at pushcart displays, at goods propped up on planks. There was pottery, some rather good and some awful, and wooden everything from butter molds to articulated dolls.

"Human *rights*! C'mon, folks, let's see some *money*!" a gypsy-like female yelled from behind a counter of change purses and money belts.

"I'm already thirsty for a beer," Max said to Jack. "I'll be back in a second." He had spotted a deli.

Natalia bought a string of dried something, which looked dreadful and not even clean. "You soak it first in water," she said, putting it round her neck now like a garland.

"What are they, peppers?" Jack asked, but got no answer because Natalia hadn't heard him.

Max returned with two cans of beer, and gave one to Jack.

Elaine, dressed this morning in a blue-and-white culotte suit, bent over a quilt display, and discussed with Max the purchase of a pink and green double-bed-sized quilt for a hundred and twenty dollars. Max professed not to have that much with him, but Elaine said that he did have his credit card with him, didn't he?

Jack went up a comparatively clear stoop to get out of the press for a minute. Natalia was just below, looking at wallets and handbags, and he was sure she wouldn't buy any, though Jack had just seen one in white leather with yellow leather stitching that had made him think of Elsie.

"Daddy, I smell—*sausage!*" Amelia yelled into his ear, and kicked Jack with both heels as if he were a horse.

"I smell six kinds of sausages, all awful," Jack replied. "Wait for lunch." Suddenly he saw Elsie across the street, about thirty yards away. "Hey, Natalia!—Elsie's up there!" He pointed. "With Marion—across the street!"

"Yes?" Natalia came up the steps and stood beside Jack. "Hey, *Elsie!—Marion!*"

Elsie seemed to turn in response, she did turn, but judging from the calm way she spoke with Marion, she hadn't heard their call, and no wonder in the general din. A hurdy-gurdy and also a juke box contributed to the low roar of voices.

"*El—sie!*" Amelia cried shrilly, and waved.

"We'll never reach her in this," Natalia said as they watched Elsie move through the crowd with Marion in the Sheridan Square direction, away from them. "Pity. We could've asked them to have lunch with us."

"Yes." They were going to have lunch somewhere with the Armstrongs.

"I want down now," Amelia said. "And I'm awful hungry!"

Jack put her down. "I could see Elsie's suntan from here," he said, smiling. "It really is pink."

"You should've seen it a week ago!" Natalia went down the steps. "She posed for a swim suit ad a couple of days ago. Fortunately she's got an all-over pink at the moment."

They had lunch at a busy corner place called The Front Porch on West 4th and 11th Streets. Elaine had her pink and green quilt with her in a big plastic bag.

31

JACK was painting the curve of an armchair in dusty-pink oil, when the telephone rang. He let it ring five or six times, until his brush was nearly empty of paint. Natalia had taken Amelia out to some uptown galleries this afternoon.

"Hello?" Jack said.

"Hello, *Jack!*" said Marion's voice, breathless. "Can you come? *Now!* Please?"

"What's the matter?"

"Elsie's been hurt and it's pretty awful!"

"Where is she?"

"Here! Greene Street!"

"What happened?—Did you call a doctor?"

"N-no. There's—" Marion sounded choked.

"Marion, call St Vincent's! Or do you want me to do it?"

"Just come!"

"I will. But call the hospital, would you?"

Jack grabbed his keys and wallet and ran out. Had Elsie knocked herself out, falling from a ladder? Or had she been attacked in the apartment? Jack trotted south on Bleecker, keeping an eye out for a taxi.

If he saw a taxi anywhere, he'd race and get it, he swore to himself. But if that were true, couldn't he outrace a taxi all the way? He adjusted his running and his breathing with this in mind, and planned his pedestrian-dodging yards ahead, shifting from sidewalk to street when he had to.

At Houston he headed east and crossed at a run when a red light suited him. He almost knocked over a baby carriage, because the woman pushing it tried to dodge him, but the carriage was really only jiggled a little, and Jack yelled:

"I *am* sorry!"

"You *insane*?" screamed the woman.

At last Jack pressed the bell beside the name Gill which was pencilled in above another name, and Jack remembered that Marion had been lent this apartment.

The release button sounded, and Jack thrust the door open into a small square foyer, and the next door into the hall was unlocked.

"*Jack!*" Marion called from somewhere up the stairs.

"Yep!" Jack took the wide stairs two at a time.

"What the hell's going on here?" This came from downstairs left, where a door had opened.

Jack had a glimpse of a scowling middle-aged man standing with his hand on his doorknob.

"Jack, Jack, come *in*!" Marion said, hunched and shaking.

Jack went through another tall door to the right of the stairs.

Elsie lay on her back on the floor, with a pillow under her head. There was blood on the top of her head and down her face.

"My God!" Jack said. "What the hell happened?"

"She was attacked downstairs! I heard her yell—then I went down and somebody ran out the door. Elsie was falling, but she was still—I swear she was alive when I dragged her up the stairs! She *said* something to me!"

Jack pressed his thumb against Elsie's wrist, which felt coolish to him, but he was boiling hot. Her half-open eyes scared Jack. "You phoned the hospital? St Vincent's?"

"Vince did. Guy downstairs.—You think she's dead, Jack?" Marion was trembling.

Jack concentrated on finding a pulse. He could not find any. He laid his sweaty forefinger against her upper lip, and could not detect any breathing. Jack pushed her white jacket aside and was shocked to see more blood at and below her waistline on her left side, under the blue cotton trousers. "Jesus!—Get a blanket, Marion!"

Marion pulled a blanket from a bed somewhere, returned trailing it, and they covered Elsie to the neck. "Jack, do you think she's *dead*?"

"I dunno. F'Chris' sake, who was it down there? Could you see?"

Marion shook her head. "I saw the door closing—White pants—I think. Elsie was falling—sort of *up* the stairs. Then

215

Vince—the fellow downstairs—came out and helped me get her up. We thought even then she'd just been knocked out! We thought, just a cold towel!—I even told Vince to leave, then I called you, and then Vince came back, and I told him to phone St Vincent's. He's probably waiting down on the street now to show the ambulance people which apartment."

"My *God*," Jack whispered. He suddenly realized that the top of Elsie's head looked even a bit indented. Some blood had darkened, some was still bright.

"It's a horrible wound on the head! You think it might just be a coma, Jack?"

Jack didn't. He thought she was dead. He heard the moan of an ambulance, ominous and tired-sounding.

"They're here," Marion said.

"Who the effing hell—You couldn't see who ran out the door?"

"I couldn't see for sure, Jack, I swear. I suspect that fucking Fran. I swear to God!" Marion looked at him with wide, horror-stricken eyes. "Who *else*?"

A second or two later, there were men from the hospital in white uniforms bending over Elsie, and a policeman, still another man or two, suddenly filling up the huge room, asking questions. Jack did not exactly hear it, but Elsie had been pronounced dead, the attitude was that she was dead. Everyone had to stand back, while a man took photographs, first with the blanket, then when the blanket was removed. Marion Gill, as occupant of the apartment, was asked her name, relationship to "the girl here", and her name, and her nearest of kin and address. Marion had to go look somewhere.

"She was supposed to be home around four," Marion said. "No, I just know somebody ran out downstairs. I think someone in white pants. I saw the door closing."

A man was sent down to query the people who lived on the ground floor.

Amid the confusion of several voices talking at once, Jack heard in the next seconds that a brick or "a hunk of cement" had been found on the hall floor downstairs.

Then Jack was questioned. He had identification in his wallet, corroborated by Marion, who said she had telephoned him at just after 4 and asked him to come over here. Both Jack and Marion were asked if they had any idea who might have attacked the girl, and Marion said after a hesitation, "No," and Jack simply shook his head.

Shoes scraped across the floor. They were carrying Elsie's body away on a stretcher.

Marion followed the stretcher, into the hall, and Jack stood by her. Jack was afraid she might faint, but she stood straight and rigid. Below, a man was photographing the stairs, and a policeman was talking with four or five men and women who Jack supposed lived in the building.

"The fat one with the moustache," Marion said to Jack. "He never shows his face unless it's to come out and yell at somebody. Always taping something, so he hates any noise around. Why didn't he come out when Elsie was being—" She broke off.

Jack saw that she meant the middle-aged fellow who had asked him what the hell was going on when Jack arrived.

"I swear Elsie said something to me when I grabbed her," Marion went on. "I swear she said, 'Help me up' or 'My head—'"

Jack could not believe this, not after having seen the dent in Elsie's head. He took Marion by the arm and steered her into the apartment, which for the moment looked empty. And Marion wilted suddenly, her shoulders bent. "Sit for a minute, Marion." Sweat dripped from Jack's forehead, and his T-shirt was soaked. He saw blood, a dark wide splotch, on the turquoise-colored pillow that had supported Elsie's head, and he quickly turned the pillow over. Blood had soaked into the teal blue stone or cement floor, too, but was less conspicuous than the pillow. The blanket lay mussed on the floor. "Got a drink in the house, Marion? Or hot tea? Hot tea'd do you good."

"Hot tea!" Marion laughed bitterly. "You bet I've got a drink in the house. Upper right. Pour it, Jack."

She meant the cabinet over the sink. Jack got down the Cutty Sark, poured some into two glasses, and handed one to Marion.

Marion took a sip. "She was just *here*!" She sat up straighter on the sofa, then stood up.

"No, sit down again." But Marion walked, and Jack with difficulty led her toward the next possible sitting place, a double bed in the corner.

Marion sat down on the edge. "They're coming back. They're not finished."

"Who?"

"The police."

"Of course they're coming back. They'll get whoever did this.—Marion, do you want to call someone? Want to come home with me? Us?—You can't stay here alone.—Drink that."

She took a big gulp, her reddish-brown lashes closed, them she looked at him more steadily. "I'm okay."

Jack looked up at the high, white ceiling, saw guitars hanging on two walls, and three or four paintings by the same person which were not bad at all. "Where was Elsie this afternoon?"

"She had a job at two at a studio on East Thirty-eighth. Said she'd easily be finished in an hour or so, and she'd be home by four. Well, she was—She—" Marion's voice trembled.

"Come home with me, Marion. Or call up a friend. I'm not going to leave you alone here."

Marion rubbed her forehead. "I'll call Myra, okay."

"She's someone in the neighborhood?"

"Yes." Marion started to get up, nearly fell back again, then straightened and stood up like a soldier before Jack could reach her. "I'm really okay, Jack. And I'm going to get the son of a bitch who did this. I swear!"

"Never fear. We will."

Marion telephoned, and Jack wet his face at the sink in the kitchenette, slopped water over his ribs under his T-shirt. He heard Marion saying, "Okay, so let me in, will you? . . . In a couple of minutes. Five minutes."

They locked up, and went down the stairs. A man and woman were still in the downstairs hall, talking.

"Your friend's *dead*?" the woman asked. "Is that true?"

"Yes." Marion pulled back from the woman's outstretched hand.

"The police still up there, Marion?" This came from a tall blond young man in jeans and black T-shirt, with an earnest expression on his face.

"No," Marion said. "Thanks, Vince, for phoning."

"Phoning! 'S nothing!—Jesus, *Elsie*!" he whispered. "I was afraid to come up in case the police were still talking with you. Coming back tonight, Marion?"

"Not sure. I'm at Myra's."

"Okay, we're home. Keep in touch."

They walked south. Marion said Myra's place was two blocks away. Jack held her arm, lightly, maybe unnecessarily, but it helped him to hold her arm, and maybe she derived a little comfort from it too.

"Why do you think Fran might have done it?" Jack asked.

"She's such a sick creep, and she so hated Elsie. I dunno, Jack, but I *think*."

Jack got a bang on his thigh from the handlebars of a kid's bike, and the kid yelled something hostile back. "But you didn't say that to the police."

"*I'm* not going to get myself in trouble with the fuzz. False accusation? Ha! They'd think I was hysterical! Gay in-fights, maybe.—Plenty of time to mention Fran. Let's see what they come up with."

They turned a corner, left.

"You don't think Linderman?"

"Lin—The old creep? Na-aah, I don't see it." Marion sounded her level-headed self suddenly. She glanced at Jack. "I don't see it, really.—Here we are. Or I am." She was ready to climb a stoop of four or five steps.

"I want to be sure you get in," Jack said, and saw Marion smile weakly before she climbed the steps and pressed a button. "We're home tonight, Marion. We'll be home. Phone us if you want to. But you don't have to."

"Thanks, Jack." Marion's voice was clear and strong. A buzzer sounded, and she went into the house.

Jack turned uptown, head down, walking, breathing faster, looking ahead of him only enough to dodge anyone who might be coming toward him. His mind was full of curses, astonishment, disbelief, anger, and his eyes began to sting, which seemed the only normal or understandable fact at that moment. Tears, yes, clearing his eyes of dust, tears that hurt his eyes in a real way.

What was Ralph Linderman doing at this moment? Jack was heading for Linderman's abode, which had been his intention since he had poured the Cutty Sark in Marion's apartment. Ask Linderman a couple of questions. Of course he might not be in.

Jack looked at his wristwatch. 5.37. Now he was on Bleecker and he began to trot, trotted when he could without bumping into people. He wasn't sure of Linderman's house number, but he would recognize its entrance, its little stoop with its black door battered with use. Now a diapered baby sat on the stoop landing, a couple of boys were tossing a dirty tennis ball, and they stared at Jack as he walked between them, and watched him as he pressed the Linderman bell. The front door had been unlocked.

"That bell don't work," said one boy, and giggled.

Jack didn't know whether to believe him or not.

"You wanna see the ol' bananas?—Go on up!"

A shriek of laughter from both boys.

Jack tried the second door, which was also unlocked, and started up the stairs. Voices and cooking smells, age and dust. In the heat, every apartment door seemed to be slightly open. All the way at the top, Jack remembered, and the door back left. Jack knocked.

Footsteps approached. "If that's *you* again, I'm not opening this door!"

Jack rapped more firmly. "Sutherland here!"

A pause. "Sutherland?"

"That's right, Mr Linderman," Jack said, standing with feet apart. He wiped sweat from his eyes with his forearm.

Linderman opened. He was half-shaved, lather on part of his face, safety razor in hand. "What's the trouble?"

"Can I come in?"

Stiffly, Linderman stepped aside and let Jack in.

Someone below was yelling in Italian, and the voice was not entirely shut off when Linderman closed his door.

"Excuse my appearance," Linderman said, "but there's been disturbance in the house all afternoon, and I'm getting ready to go to work."

Jack nodded. Linderman was in trousers and undershirt. The black and white dog nosed against Jack's legs and wagged its tail half-heartedly. Linderman walked in houseshoes to the back of the apartment to turn off running water somewhere.

"What's the matter?" Linderman asked, coming back. "You've been running? In this heat?"

"No." Jack did not take his eyes from Linderman.

"Want a glass of cold water?—Why're you looking at me like that?—I suppose my letter annoyed you."

Jack felt as if his torso, his face, were a furnace. The sweat ran down him. "What were you doing this afternoon?"

"Hah!—Trying to sleep! A new wop family's moved in just below. Kids crawling all over the place, up these *stairs*!" Lin-

220

derman pointed. "I'm on duty at eight. Have to get my sleep. If these were *work* sounds, I always say, I wouldn't get so mad, but these are unnecessary noises! Kids screaming, *people* yelling!"

A *thump* sounded nearby, Jack jumped like a nervous cat, and he looked at the door.

"That's habitual! That's their ballgame—against my *door!*" Linderman spoke with sneering contempt. He still held the safety razor. "They do it deliberately, of course."

A child's voice squealed in the hall.

"I'd love to train God to clear 'em off this floor, but then they'd complain about my dog and *win!* Nobody cares about peace and order any more."

"Where were you around four o'clock today?" Jack asked.

"Four?" Linderman looked surprised. "I was here."

"When was the last time you aired your dog?"

"Aired God? This morning around noon. He's got to go out again before I go to work." Linderman shifted, almost touched his lathered cheek with his free hand, and didn't. "'S matter, Mr Sutherland? Have you had a house robbery? A break-in?"

Trotting toward Linderman's house, Jack had so easily imagined Linderman following Elsie as she walked home, Elsie saying something rude to him over her shoulder, and Linderman picking up the first thing to hand, some kind of brick from the gutter, having suffered the last straw of rejection from Elsie, hitting her on top of the head after she'd opened her door with her key, hitting her perhaps twice more while she screamed, then dropping the brick and fleeing when he heard Marion opening the door above. Now here was Linderman angry with his neighbors, saying that he'd been in all afternoon, and maybe he had been. Should he believe Linderman?

"Mr Sutherland—"

"No, no break-in," Jack said.

"Something happen with your little daughter?"

"No."

"With *Elsie?*" Linderman looked more concerned.

"No, no."

"Good. Well—if you'll excuse me just two minutes—You could sit down. I've got to finish this face-scraping, then take the dog outside for a minute." Linderman gestured toward his armchair, and retreated to his bathroom somewhere to the right of the two windows.

Jack walked toward the open door through which Linderman had gone. He saw an unmade bed in a small room, heard water running again. The bed did look as if Linderman had just got out of it, but couldn't he have got out at 3 this afternoon? Jack turned and walked toward the apartment door, then noticed above the door a square card edged in brown with black lettering: PREPARE TO MEET THY DOG. Linderman had pasted DOG over what must have been GOD. It was one of the cards that sold at souvenir shops.

"Ha-ha," said Linderman, returning. "My latest addition. 'Prepare—'"

"Where're you working now, Mr Linderman?"

"Ah. Something called the Hot Arch Arcade. Broadway and Eighty-first. Bread and circuses for the masses. Open day and night. I don't think you'd like the clientèle.—Mr Sutherland, you're looking pale now!"

"Pale?"

"Minute ago you were red as a beet, now you're pale! If you want to talk about—what I wrote to you about Elsie—Won't you—" Linderman extended a hand as if to escort Jack to a seat.

Jack edged back and moved toward the door. "Thank you, I'll be off. Sorry to've bothered you." Jack went out.

Then Jack was down on the sidewalk in the sun again, walking at a normal pace, and the air was cold on his body. He reached for his keys.

Natalia and Amelia were home, Natalia in the kitchen.

"Hello, Jack! Guess what we—What's the matter, Jack?"

"Nothing."

"You look beat!—Where've you been?"

Jack realized that he was shaking slightly. Was it a chill? He suddenly remembered Elsie's chill, here, in February, hadn't it been? He pulled his T-shirt over his head. "I think I'll take a shower." He went and turned on the hot water in the shower.

Natalia followed him. "Jack, what happened? Did you get into a fight somewhere?"

"Fight, no!" Jack almost laughed as he stepped under the hot water. The water felt marvelous. He let it run onto his head, his upturned face, hot as he could bear it. His teeth stopped chattering.

"A hot shower.—Want a cold drink?"

"I'd love some hot tea."

"Really?"

"I mean it."

Jack put on a terrycloth bathrobe and took his tea into the bedroom. He had beckoned to Natalia. "Sit down." He meant on the bed or on a chair. She didn't want to sit, but he insisted with a gesture.

"All right." She took the straight chair that always stood near his side of the bed.

"Elsie's been killed," he said softly.

Natalia started. "Killed?—What do you mean?"

"This afternoon. Marion called me. This was around four. I went—"

"Killed *how*?"

"Somebody hit her head with a brick." Trembling again, Jack lifted his teacup.

"Where was this?"

"It happened right in the entrance to her house. Marion heard her scream and—went down and got her upstairs. But she was dead. The police were there and—the hospital people from St Vincent's. Marion thinks—"

"I can't believe it!" Natalia whispered. "Do you think that Linderman creep—" Natalia had stood up. "Did Marion see anything?"

"No. She said she saw someone running out, someone in white trousers, she says, but really she's in a state of shock, Natalia darling, and she might not be right about that."

"It's unbelievable!"

"I just went to see Linderman," Jack said. "He says he'd been in all afternoon, and I swear it looks as if he has.—Marion mentioned this girl Fran. You know? That dikey type?"

"Fran, yes."

"What's her last name?"

"I forgot.—My *God*, Jack—you saw Elsie?"

"Of course. Yes. I ran down to Greene Street when Marion phoned me. I think she thought Elsie was just hurt—knocked out, but—" Jack did not want to describe Elsie's wounds. "Marion suspects Fran.—Oh, the cops'll get onto Fran, Linderman, question them, I'm sure. But how many other toughs were hanging around Elsie? *I* don't know. Do you?"

Natalia might not have heard him. She was frowning, head down, but not weeping. "F'Chris' sake, *Elsie!—No!*" she yelled suddenly at the thumping knock on the closed door.

Amelia opened the door a little, wanting something.

"I'll be back," Natalia said, going out. "No, honey, your daddy and I have to talk about something. For five minutes.—Yes, about the trip. We . . ." Her voice faded out of hearing.

The Yugoslav trip. They were leaving at the end of the month, flying to Belgrade via Vienna. A couple of suitcases, open and closed, lay in corners of the hall, and some packing had already been done.

Natalia was back with a Glenfiddich.

In the next five minutes or so, Natalia extracted every detail from him, the time, where Elsie had been wounded, what Marion had said, where Marion was now (Natalia had met Myra but was not sure of her last name, Jackson or Johnson), and what the police had said or asked, and what Linderman had said.

"I'm going to go and see her," Natalia said, putting a cigarette out.

"Who? Marion?"

"*Elsie.*"

Jack couldn't dissuade her. Natalia was going to go to St Vincent's, and then to the morgue, wherever Elsie was.

"Then I'll go with you," Jack said, getting up, ready to dress.

"I don't want you to. I'll do it."

Something in Natalia's determined voice, and face, made Jack pause. She really preferred to go alone.

"Don't let Amelia watch the box tonight. Something might be on it, you know? An announcement." Natalia had whispered.

Jack got dressed as soon as he heard the door close. He put on cotton trousers and a shirt that hung out. In the bathroom, he picked up his levis, still dark with sweat at the waist.

"Dad-*dee*! The Nebu—koo!" Amelia cried from the living-room.

"The what?" He saw his daughter on the floor, propped on an elbow, long hair flowing down.

"It's here!—I can read it! What is it?"

Jack leaned over the Yugoslav map which Amelia had spread on the carpet, not seeing a thing except the big rectangle of the paper. "It's a place. What else?"

"Are we going to see one?" Losing patience, Amelia said, "It's not a place, it looks like a tent! At the edge here. Look!"

Light, daylight fell on Amelia's fair hair from the windows behind her, and Jack thought of Elsie. This was the last light of the sun of the last day for Elsie. Jack closed his eyes and turned away. "Got to see about dinner. Aren't you getting hungry?"

"No," said Amelia, being perverse. "Where is Mommy?"

"Went out for a while. She'll be back."

Natalia had started dinner, so there wasn't much for Jack to do. The telephone rang while he and Amelia were eating. A man's voice said he was Police Officer So-and-So, and would it be convenient for him to come over and have a word with Jack?

"Of course. Now?"

"In about ten minutes."

Jack tried to get Amelia to bed. She suspected something, and consequently kept trying to fool him. Yes, she was going to bed, no, she wasn't, because someone was coming.

"Sure you can stay up," Jack said, trying homeopathy. "It's going to be a party. Cops 'n robbers."

Amelia's golden eyes widened. "Who's coming? How many?"

"It's a pajama party. Get those on!"

The doorbell rang.

Two policemen, both in uniform with blue short-sleeved shirts came up the stairs. Jack recognized one as the cop who had spoken to him in Marion's apartment.

"Mr Sutherland?"

"Yes, sir," said Jack.

They introduced themselves, and Jack showed them in and offered chairs.

Amelia came in barefoot and in pajamas and showed every sign of wanting to join them.

"Amelia, honey—Got to leave us alone for a few minutes." Jack tried to steer her back to her room.

"You said it was a cops 'n robbers party!"

"The robbers aren't here yet," said Jack.

"I won't!" Amelia said, squirming.

"Sorry," Jack said to the policemen, one of whom was smiling. "My wife's out.—Maybe we can go in the bedroom?"

Jack hated the idea, but he didn't want to lock Amelia up in her own room. Jack brought another chair into the bedroom. The policemen followed. Jack closed the door on Amelia, saying, "We've got to talk for a couple of minutes, honey!" knowing his daughter would be listening at the door. Or would she?

Reluctantly Jack sat on the foot of the bed.

"You were a good friend of this girl?" asked the policeman who was new to Jack, the one who had announced himself as Homicide Squad.

"Good friend—not a close friend," Jack said.

"How long have you known her?"

Jack reflected. "Nearly a year."

"And how'd you meet her?"

Jack glanced at the bedroom door whose key he had turned, though he had not heard any sound from the other side. "She was working in a coffee shop down on Seventh Avenue. I made a sketch of her on the back of my check there." He shrugged. "She was living in the neighborhood then, Minetta Street. We said hello on the street."

"And then?"

Jack felt uncomfortable, wanting to avoid the Linderman part right now. "Then—she met my wife and—my wife recommended her to a photographer. As a model. So she was getting some fashion model jobs that way."

"She certainly was," said the Homicide man, a sturdy fellow in his mid-thirties with straight brown hair that looked freshly washed and cut. "You ever heard of any enemies she had? In that business? Jealous people maybe? Jealous men? Angry men?"

Jack shook his head slowly. "Her friend Marion Gill might know—of people. I don't know any." As both the cops wrote on their pads, Jack asked, "Did you speak again with Marion?"

"Oh, yeah, just now," said the other policeman. "She checked in with us and we went down to see her. Very cooperative young lady."

Jack thought of Fran. "I hope you've got some leads by now?"

"We never know," said the Homicide cop, blandly.

Jack saw the door handle move and tried to ignore it. Though it wasn't warm, he felt sweat on his forehead again. "What was the weapon? I heard something about a brick—in the downstairs hall."

"Yes. It was a red brick with a little cement stuck to it," said the Homicide man, looking at Jack. "Weighing two and a half pounds."

226

Jack could imagine what it looked like.

"What're you thinking about, Mr Sutherland?" asked the Homicide man.

Jack took a breath. "Two things. That a man must've—Well, it took some strength—those blows. And I was wondering where the brick came from." Jack still spoke barely audibly, hoping that Amelia was not listening. "I suppose it doesn't matter much."

"We know where it probably came from. Just about ten yards from the door. Couple of ashcans there with débris on top of 'em."

"In which direction?"

"Direction?" asked the Homicide cop.

"From the door of the house."

"Oh, downtown. South," the Homicide cop replied. "The ashcans were downtown direction.—Mr Sutherland, have you any idea—suspicions who could've done this?"

Jack wiped away sweat with his palm. "No. I don't know her crowd. Her circle. I'd like to help. My wife and I were very fond of Elsie." Jack stood up nervously, impatient with what struck him suddenly as close-mouthedness in the two, a sudden blind-alley atmosphere.

"We'd like to speak with your wife," said the Homicide cop. "You know when she'll be back? Or where she is now?"

Jack didn't know how much to tell them, or why he should hold back, or if he should. "Exactly where she is, I don't know."

"She knows about this?" asked the other cop.

"Sure." Jack said in a near whisper, "I told her around—" He thought of his Linderman visit. "—when I got home from Marion's this afternoon."

"But you don't know where she went tonight? Maybe to Marion's?—She knows Marion?"

"Yes." What had Marion said about Natalia? "Matter of fact, she went off to see—to see what she could find out about Elsie," Jack said, still softly. "She went to St Vincent's first."

"Did she?" said the Homicide man. "Your wife's very concerned then."

"Yes. Everyone loved Elsie. Everyone." Jack did not sit down again. He wished they would leave, get on with the business of finding the killer.

"You saw a lot of her?" said the Homicide man.

227

"No-o. My wife and I invited her to a couple of parties we went to."

"Were you in love with her, Mr Sutherland?" The question from the Homicide man was in a flat and polite tone.

"No," Jack said.

"Easy to be, I'd think," said the other cop to his colleague, smiling.

"Will you—" The Homicide cop pulled a card from his clipboard. "—get in touch with us when your wife comes back? You expect her tonight."

"Oh, sure."

They were getting up. Jack opened the door. Amelia was not in sight. The Homicide cop gently closed the door again, almost, so they were all inside the bedroom still.

"There was a lesbian relationship between the victim and the girl Marion. You knew about that?"

"Oh, yes, I'd heard," Jack said.

The Homicide cop started to put his cap back on and didn't, then opened the door, and they all went out.

"You work here?" asked the other cop, looking around as if for the first time.

"Yes," Jack said.

"Dad-*dee*!" Amelia was suddenly out of her room, but now it didn't seem to matter. "Where're the robbers?" She advanced toward Jack. "Have you got a lot of parking tickets?"

One cop laughed. The other cop wanted to see Jack's workroom. They all went down the hall, the cops commenting on Jack's handgrips, asking him how he reached them, and Jack obligingly jumped for them and brought them down to convenient height for turning flips, though he didn't turn one.

"You keep in good form," said the cop who was not Homicide.

Jack pulled back the half-parted curtain of his workroom. There was his painting-in-progress, not on the easel but on his work-table, because he preferred the light there sometimes. His brush lay to the left, pink paint drying on it. The smell of turpentine hung in the air, and Jack poured a bit of turps into a tin can and stuck the drying brush in.

"Workin' on something?"

Jack gestured. "This was when the phone rang. Marion." He led the way out.

"Isn't that—" said the Homicide cop, going toward the two or three photographs of Elsie thumbtacked to drawing boards on the right side of his table. "That's the girl, isn't it?"

"Yes," Jack said.

"She's a beaut. Was," the non-Homicide cop said, shaking his head.

Jack scowled at this cop and wagged a finger near his lips. Amelia stood in the hall, listening, and Jack wondered how soon she would pick up what had happened. He sensed his little daughter's antennae all out.

"Thank you, Mr Sutherland," said the Homicide cop firmly at the doorway. "Your wife can call us any time tonight—if we don't see her first." He smiled a little. "You going away somewhere?" He had glanced at the suitcase in the hall, its lid propped against the wall.

"Yes, in a week or so. My wife and I.—Yugoslavia," said Jack, thinking of the tickets in his passport case. Would Natalia still want to go?

When the door closed, Jack reproached himself for not having asked them some questions. Had Marion mentioned Fran, for instance? Jack pressed his hands against his damp face, then went to the kitchen in quest of cool water.

"Have you got parking tickets, daddy?"

"Lots of 'em!" Jack said. "But the cops were very nice about it."

"You have to pay a lot of money." Amelia said it as if it were a fact.

"Yes. Yes, that's true."

"How much?"

"They haven't even figured out yet." Jack shook his head sadly.

Amelia ran off.

He heard the TV set come on, and went into the living-room. 'No TV tonight, honey. Cut it off. Time to go to bed."

"It's not even *ten*!" Amelia had a Swatch wristwatch.

"No argument. Brush your teeth and let's go. *No* foolin'!" He took her hand firmly.

His firmness worked.

Jack went into his workroom and cleaned all the pink out of his brush, because he didn't want to see the pink tomorrow. Then he looked around for something to read, knowing he would not be able to sleep for a long while.

The telephone rang an hour later, when Jack, after another shower, was lying atop the sheets with a book. He picked up the phone on Natalia's side of the bed.

"Hi, Jack, this is Marion," said Marion's voice calmly. "Natalia's here. Want to speak with her?"

"Well—she's okay?—What's new?"

"They've got Fran. They're talking with her."

"Really!—You're sure? The police're sure?"

"Oh, she's got some half-assed alibi." Marion sounded a bit slurry, either tired or a little drunk. "One of her shitty friends called up *here*—threatening *me*, the fuck."

"The police are charging her?"

"I don't know about that, but they're interested."

"Good," Jack said, feeling a surge of satisfaction. "What's Natalia doing?"

"Natalia's been wonderful.—She's sitting on the bed—having an iced coffee. Christ, what a night! It's not over."

"When is she coming home? Or is she?"

"I don't know. You'll have to ask her.—Natalia?"

Natalia came on. "Hello, Jack . . . Oh, I'm all right, never mind," she said in a tone of impatience. "*Yes*, I saw her . . . Just by asking," she said in response to Jack's question.

Jack heard the cool self-assurance that could cover fury in Natalia, and which he had seen make strong people cringe. "Marion says they're onto this Fran. What's her last name?"

"Dillon. She uses a couple of names."

"Are they really holding her?"

"Could be. I gather they've got her at some station, and she's full of POP or something tonight."

"The cops said that?"

"M-m—implied. And one of her girlfriends called up Marion tonight, pretty high on something."

Jack gathered that Marion had gone back to Greene Street around 7, after the police had seen Marion again at Myra's, as Marion had given the police Myra's number. So Natalia had been able to reach Marion at home. Then "a thug chum" of Fran's had called up to curse Marion out, because Marion had given Fran's name to the police as possible killer, and Marion had been able to name a girl at whose house Fran might be staying, and Fran was. Then the police had come to see Marion again, and had left just ten minutes ago—whether the same pair who had visited him, Jack couldn't tell and didn't ask. Natalia said that she and Marion had also telephoned Elsie's parents in upstate New York.

"The police had already told them," Natalia said. "They're coming tomorrow morning."

"Christ!—That must've been awful!" Jack said.

"The father sounded pretty steady, the *mother* was upset.— Well, my *God!*—I got a hotel room for them for tomorrow."

Natalia was staying the night at Marion's, she said, because it would be awful for Marion to be alone here, and the police wanted to know where she was, and were giving her some protection, a guard on the street. And both of them were exhausted.

After he hung up, Jack lay with his eyes open, staring at the corner of white walls and ceiling. *Genevieve called up*, Natalia had said at the last. *It's on the radio and TV. In the papers already. Don't buy any, it'll make you sick.* In the papers. He supposed the papers would seize on the fashion photos of Elsie.

Around midnight, Elaine Armstrong called. They had just been to a movie, and they had seen the headlines when they came out. Did Jack and Natalia know? Yes. Natalia was with a friend of Elsie's now, Jack said. And no, they weren't yet sure who had done it, but they had a suspect. Who?

"Some hoodlum," Jack said.

32

AT about the same time, Ralph Linderman, on duty at the Hot Arch Arcade, and standing to the right of the entrance, inside, caught sight of the tabloid held by Willy Shapiro across from him on the other side of the wide entrance. The girl in the big photo on the front page resembled Elsie, and Ralph at once moved toward it. Yes, *Elsie*, with her blond hair pulled back, her full underlip, black dress in this picture, and the bold black headlines above said: MODEL SLAIN!

Ralph seized one side of the paper, open-mouthed.

"Hey, Linderman, what the hell're you—" Startled, Willy Shapiro yanked the paper back.

"That girl! I just want to see the—"

"Well, *ask* to see it!" Willy yelled. "'S matter witcha, heat's gotcha?" Willy, a half-owner of the Arcade, a plump, balding man much shorter than Ralph, got off his stool, defending his newspaper, which Ralph had already torn.

"I know that girl! I want to know if she's dead!" Ralph yelled back, furious himself.

"This one? You know *her?*—*Says* here she's dead!" Willy again swung the paper out of Ralph's reach.

Ralph had a longer reach and got the paper, had just time to read Elsie Tyler's name below the big photo of her with earrings and a champagne glass near her lips, when he felt a punch in his abdomen. Ralph bent for an instant, more with shock than pain.

"*That* for your goddam rudeness!" cried Willy Shapiro, scowling with defiance and pride at having hit a bigger man. "You're cracked, Linderman! You're a nut!"

"Go back—" Linderman gasped "—back to Israel, you greasy little kike!"

"I never was in Israel, you fuckin' Nazi! An' you're fired! You

232

hate this place anyway, and as of this minute, you're fired!"—
Hey, Eddie! *Eddie!*" Willy Shapiro's voice blasted down the
Arcade, louder even than the juke boxes, arresting for a few
seconds the human din around them. "*Eddie!* Give this guy the
bum's rush and pronto!"

"What d'y'mean?" Eddie was a taller fellow than Ralph, a
gangling man who emptied the slot machines for Willy and was
therefore able to take care of himself with his fists.

"He's fired and I want him out! Now!"

"No sweat," Ralph said to Eddie and to Willy. He added to
Willy, "Bye-bye, Artful Dodger."

Unknown attacker . . . multiple blows with a brick . . . were some
of the words Ralph had just glimpsed below the picture of his
lovely Elsie. In his state of shock, the image of John Sutherland
came—and his wrath gathered. He got his jacket from his locker
in a room behind the cash register. Eddie hovered, looking not so
much hostile as puzzled, but Ralph said not a word to Eddie.
Ralph moved steadily, doing what he had to do, signing himself
out at oo.22 in the book. Ralph quit the Hot Arch Arcade without
a word or a glance at anyone.

He bought a copy of the tabloid Willy Shapiro had been reading
from the next vendor on Eighth Avenue, and read it under a
streetlight. It had happened in the afternoon around 4. In the
very doorway of her apartment house on Greene Street! In broad
daylight! . . . *fractured skull* . . . There were two more photos on
the inside pages. Beautiful she was, shining like a light! Ralph
trembled.

The wily Sutherland had come to see him just minutes after
the deed, and in a sweat of guilt! Sutherland asking *him* where
he'd been in the afternoon! Asking him in order to try to nail the
crime on him! Plain as day, Sutherland's tactics! Sutherland was
in love with Elsie, and either jealous of another man whom Elsie
preferred, or afraid that Elsie would tell his wife the extent of
their—their doings, maybe. Had Elsie refused to marry Sutherland? Or to go away with him somewhere? Had she possibly
been pregnant? Revolting thought!

Oh, the price she had paid for her loveliness!

He would tell the police about Sutherland. And maybe the
police knew already, maybe they had Sutherland at this minute.
Which police station should he speak to, the one in the Greene

Street area or the one nearest his place of residence? Ralph was then walking toward the subway entrance, but seeing a policeman on the sidewalk, he veered toward him.

"Excuse me, officer. I want to report something in regard to a murder. This murder, this girl." Ralph pointed to the front page picture on the tabloid. "Or do you know if he is already caught—Sutherland."

The youngish cop shook his head. "I don't know."

"Can you take the name down? He's the man who killed her!"

The cop looked uncertain, even uninterested. "Where d'you live, mister? Got a fixed address?"

"Certainly. I live on Bleecker Street."

"Well, you go to your nearest precinct station down there and tell 'em what you have to report. Okay?" The cop walked on.

Ralph rode homeward on the subway, a raincoat over his arm, a bulging plastic bag in hand with muffler and rain boots and the sandwich and fruit that he had brought for his snack around midnight or 1 a.m., a sandwich he had made before Sutherland's visit, and which he intended to throw away. He saw at least three other copies of the same tabloid being read by passengers in the subway car, and more on the platform where he switched at Seventy-second Street to an express train. At Fourteenth Street, he took a local to the Christopher Street station, then walked straight to his house. His nearest precinct station was at Tenth Street and Hudson, he saw in the telephone book.

Ralph dialed this Sixth Precinct number, and heat rose again to his face as he envisaged policemen calling on John Sutherland on Grove Street in perhaps less than a quarter of an hour from now.

The station answered, and Ralph gave his message: in regard to the murder of Elsie Tyler on Greene Street, he, Ralph Linderman, wanted to inform the police that John Sutherland, and Ralph spelt the name and gave Sutherland's address, should be considered a number-one suspect as killer.

"We'll note it down, sir. If you want to come in and see us, you can."

"Thank you."

Ralph aired God first. God had been quite surprised to see him at this hour and had been leaping about, barking in his repressed way, nuzzling against Ralph's knees. God got a short but happy airing, and Ralph promised him a longer one later.

At the precinct station, Ralph repeated his statement, gave his own name and address, which the officer at the desk did not write down. The officer kept bumping the end of his ballpoint pen on the blotter in an absent way, and he looked as if his mind were partly on something else.

"I know this girl who was killed!" Ralph repeated. "This man Sutherland came to see *me* around five-thirty or six today—or yesterday now. He asked me what *I* was doing at the time Elsie was killed. Can you—can you—"

"Can I what?"

"Can you call up the people who're handling this? There must be a homicide squad, no?"

"Several."

"Can you please telephone the one who's handling this and ask them if they've talked to Sutherland? Maybe they have him already! I'd like to know."

"Are you any relation of this girl who was killed?"

"No."

The man moved, but slowly, as if he were debating whether to pick up the phone. He dialed, spoke to someone in unintelligible monosyllables, asked Ralph his name again, then said "John Sutherland," much to Ralph's satisfaction.

Long wait.

"Uh-huh. Uh-huh.—I see.—Yep. Well, it's something!" Here he laughed. "Yep, thanks, pal." The round, tanned face of the policeman looked up with more interest. "Yes, they know about John Sutherland. They've been in touch with him."

"Then you've got him?" Ralph's brows concentrated, his lips were ready to smile in triumph. "He's in jail?"

"Well—I was told Sutherland was called up by this girl's friend just after the girl was killed. Right after." The cop nodded. "Thanks for your information, sir. We're handling it."

Ralph stood motionless. "You're fooling me, because it isn't proven yet. All right, but—"

"No, sir. Now look, I just went to the trouble to check this out. Sutherland was called up by the girl who lives with the—the murdered girl. Now get that through your head. G'night, sir."

"Good night. Thank you," Ralph said with a cold politeness. He left the station, unconvinced, and went in quest of a *Times*, though since the crime had occurred around 4 in the afternoon yesterday, he doubted that the *Times* had reported the events on Greene Street.

Ralph got his *Times* and bought also the 4-star *Daily News*, and looked first at the *Times* under an inadequate streetlamp, found on page two a short item headed *Young Model Slain*.

Elsie Tyler, 21, died minutes after being assaulted by a person or persons unknown on the doorstep of her apartment house on Greene Street. The young woman whose family lives in upstate New York had been a model for fashion photographers in the last months. Police are following leads on suspects.

Ralph looked down Seventh Avenue, thinking of the spot of light on the left side of the avenue, out of sight from where he stood, the coffee shop where Elsie had used to work. She had risen in life, to be sure, she had started to earn more money, and for how many months. Six? Maybe only four? She had glowed like a comet—or like a yellow rose—and someone had smashed her!

Who else but Sutherland?

At home, Ralph perused the tabloid, looking for police leads (none, the account was brief, with nothing at all about a suspect), looking for anything about the kind of life Elsie had been leading. There were no details, but the phrases "strikingly attractive" and "popular model of young women's fashions" and "the sophisticated young siren who made it" implied a fast life to Ralph. He could imagine.

He imagined Elsie in the Sutherlands' circle, moneyed people, the leisure crowd, the jet set, people who would keep Elsie up all night and ply her with drink and drugs.

Ralph convinced himself that he should lie low for another twelve hours, wait for more news from the radio (he had no TV and wanted none) or newspapers. He ate his salami sandwich and banana after all, while slowly pacing his living-room. God watched him, looking uneasy, hoping for another walk. Yes, he would wait for more details, little things that might point to Sutherland, and if he found them—Sutherland would be clever in trying to wriggle out, of course, but there was too much against him. Sutherland was a good runner, and could have done the murder and got back in time for the telephone call from Elsie's friend Marion, if that telephone call was to be believed. Or were Sutherland and Marion in cahoots? That was a possibility that

Ralph would keep in mind. The latest tabloid had said that "another young woman" with whom Elsie shared the apartment had telephoned a hospital and then "a man friend" for assistance, but the victim had died within seconds of the fatal blows. Ralph imagined attacking Sutherland with a similar weapon, just a brick maybe, smashing *his* skull, and though he himself might be caught for it, the price he might pay—several years in prison—would be well worth it. Yes.

Ralph did air God again, walked him west on Grove (the Sutherlands' lights were out) and through Bedford and Barrow to Bleecker again, to Seventh and down to the coffee shop where Elsie had used to work, and which was now shut and dark as if in mourning. He went on downtown to Houston, but did not cross it. To walk past Elsie's house on Greene Street would be too horrible. And maybe journalists, "the press", would be standing around outside, photographing, trying to extract titbits from neighbors.

He went to bed at nearly 4, exhausted by his thoughts, though he could not sleep. He did not have to go to work tomorrow, he'd been fired. Good! Ejected from that filthy hole run by a pair of two-legged rats who sucked money from the depravities: prostitution, drug-dealing, gambling, idleness, and the pickers of pockets. Good riddance to Shapiro and company! Let them give him a "bad reference" too! Ralph felt sure of his ground, *ground*, sounder than that of the Hot Arch Arcade! He turned and twisted. He could sleep tomorrow as long as he liked, he reminded himself. That was small consolation.

The ringing of the telephone awakened him. It was just past 8, Ralph saw. "Hello?"

"Hello. Am I speaking to Ralph Linderman?"

"Yes."

"This is Police . . ." The rest of the statement was lost on Ralph.

The important thing was that they wanted to talk to him. "Yes, I am home. Yes—*sir*."

"Good, because we're just around the corner."

Ralph dressed in haste, and closed the door on his small bedroom. His living-room looked presentable, so Ralph started making his coffee. Then his doorbell rang, and Ralph answered at once with the buzzer—necessary or not, he never knew in this house. And what would the people in the house think of cops traipsing up? They could just as well think he'd summoned the cops to complain about the noise, as that the police had come to get after him about something!

There were two policemen. Ralph offered them chairs, but only one sat down, while the other looked around, looked also at the PREPARE TO MEET THY DOG card. Asked for his place of employment, Ralph gave the address of the Hot Arch Arcade, because that had been true until so recently, and the firing business was of no relevance, he thought.

"You were a friend of Elsie Tyler's?"

"I knew her as a neighbor," Ralph replied, "when she lived near here. Lived on Minetta Street for a while."

"When is the last time you saw her?"

Ralph thought hard. "Could be—six weeks—No, more than two months, I'm pretty sure.—Who told you to talk to me? Mr John Sutherland?"

"No, we—We're asking around everywhere, you know. We just talked to the people where the girl used to work—down here. They gave us your name."

Ralph barely nodded. He knew they meant the coffee shop. The people there, that female manager, had no doubt put in a bad word for him.

"How long've you known Elsie Tyler, sir?"

Again Ralph thought. "Maybe a year, a little more."

"She ever come up here to visit you?"

"Oh, no, sir! No. We just said hello to each other on the street sometimes—passing."

The cop wrote something on his tablet which had a big clip at the top. "The people at the place where she worked said you used to talk to her a lot when you came in there. Coffee shop."

"I talked with her. Not a lot."

"They said the girl tried to avoid you."

Ralph felt annoyance, a bitter amusement. "I warned her against associating with the wrong people. Yes."

"Such as who, for instance?"

Ralph smiled, thinking that he had seen a lot of wrong people with Elsie, but didn't know any by name. "The young toughs in the neighborhood. I don't know their names.—Such people as might have killed her—and did!" Ralph was aware that he

238

trembled, and pushed his hands into his pockets.

The cop looked at him. "No names to give us?"

"Excuse me!" Ralph got up because his coffee had perked over and put the gas out. He turned the gas off. "I don't know the names of these young hoodlums I used to see her with," he said as he came back. "But I told the police at the Tenth Street station last night John Sutherland should be considered." Ralph spoke calmly, and nodded for emphasis.

"We've talked with John Sutherland."

"And he mentioned me, I suppose. He gave my name?"

"N-no, I don't think he did." The policeman looked at his colleague, who was still strolling about and looking as if he weren't listening to the conversation. "You and Sutherland know each other? How is it you know him?"

Ralph suspected that this was a trick question. Just what had Sutherland said about him that the police didn't want to tell him? "I returned his wallet. He lost his wallet on Grove Street and I returned it to him."

"Really? When was this?"

"Last August. Ask Sutherland. His name and address was in it, so I called him up and returned it with the money in it."

"Did you?—And then?"

"Then?—Then I noticed that Elsie was visiting him. He got acquainted with her at that coffee shop. He was having an affair with her. He didn't tell you that? No, of course he would deny it!"

"No-o," said the cop with another look at his fellow cop, who had picked this up too. "You're sure of that, Mr—um—Linderman? An affair?"

"Yes. I'm a guard. A nightwatchman. I saw Elsie coming and going from his house. At odd hours."

The cop wrote on his pad. "When, for instance?"

Ralph was suddenly impatient. "The main thing is, they were *having* an affair! Or Sutherland was using her as a prostitute!" The policeman in front of Ralph seemed not human, but a robot that didn't care, taking down facts maybe, but not caring or thinking at all about what the facts meant. "Don't you see what I mean? The *wife* knew. Mrs Sutherland. They were both having affairs—with other people."

"Who?—When you say both—?"

Now the other cop was listening too.

"Mrs Sutherland with her men friends or man friend. I saw him once. Tall nearly bald man."

The cop looked up from his tablet with a slight smile, shaking his head in a way that Ralph felt was patronizing. "Mr Lin—"

"John Sutherland was here," Ralph interrupted, "*here*." He pointed to his floor. "Just minutes after he murdered Elsie. He'd run here, and he was pouring with sweat. He asked me where *I'd* been—yesterday at four in the afternoon. He was trying—"

"You're saying Sutherland was *here* yesterday?"

"Yessir. He didn't tell you that? No, he wouldn't! He's trying to put the blame on *me*, but he can't because he—"

"Sit down, Mr Linderman. Let's all sit down." The seated cop motioned.

The other cop and Ralph took chairs.

Ralph wiped perspiration from his forehead. "Yes. John Sutherland came here yesterday afternoon around five-thirty. I was in the middle of shaving. I'd been trying to sleep all afternoon. Just ask any of the people in this house, if you don't believe me!" Ralph gestured toward his apartment door. "They'll tell you I was complaining about the noise they make. It's a noisy house here, kids screaming, people yelling. I have to sleep in the daytime because I work at night. I had to go on duty at eight last night."

This seemed to make an impression, Ralph saw. The cop or detective with the clipboard was writing. He had removed his cap. He had very neat brown hair cut with a military shortness. He murmured to his colleague:

"Sutherland didn't say anything last night about coming here, did he? Didn't mention Linderman's name. I'd have had it."

"No, sir."

"And Sutherland's a runner, don't forget that," Ralph put in.

"What d'y' mean, a runner?" asked the other cop.

"He jogs. He could've covered that distance between Greene Street and here—oh, six minutes, seven. And he was covered with sweat yesterday. I thought he was going to pass out."

The short-haired cop sat back, smiling tiredly. "Around five-thirty he was here?"

"Between five-thirty and six, yes."

"How long was he here?"

"Maybe ten minutes. He didn't sit down. I asked him why he

240

was so upset, asked him if something had happened to his little daughter, or to *Elsie*, and he said, 'No, no.' I can hear him now! And he looked mad—angry, when he found out I'd been here all afternoon."

The short-haired cop shook his head with an air of sadness or tiredness. "Mr Linderman, we have it from Marion Gill—Elsie Tyler's friend—"

"Yes, I've heard her name, Marion Gill," said Ralph attentively.

"Well, she called up Sutherland right after the attack, Sutherland was home, and he went running to Greene Street. You can forget about Sutherland as the killer, Mr Linderman."

Ralph was still not convinced. "Then he can forget about me, too! I'd appreciate that!"

The other cop smiled a little.

Ralph hated the smile, hated the atmosphere suddenly. So Sutherland had really been home? "Is this Marion telling the truth?"

The short-haired cop wiped his brow. "Yes, sir. She was upstairs in the apartment when it happened. We—"

"How do you know?" Ralph had suddenly thought of another scenario: Marion jealous of Elsie, because Sutherland liked Elsie more than he liked Marion. Had *Marion* killed her?

"Let me finish, sir. Marion's account of this was corroborated by a couple of people in the Greene Street house. They heard the yells below, they saw Marion running down the stairs. Two people saw her."

Ralph bit his underlip, then said, "Sutherland was having an affair with both of them, you know."

The other cop leaned forward, grinning at the note-taking cop, started to say something, but the short-haired cop silenced him with a wave of his hand. The other cop gave a big, silent laugh, however.

What was funny, Ralph wondered.

"We check out the house here?" asked the second cop.

"Yep."

They moved, said thanks to Ralph, asked him where he would be today and the next days.

"Here. I live here," Ralph replied.

They departed, and Ralph closed his apartment door, and on

241

second thought slid the chain bolt. Coffee. He lit the gas again. Then he went back to his door, and listened with an ear against it.

Ralph heard a mumble of voices on the floor below, the shrill but still unintelligible yipping of the dumpy young woman—the new one—who detested him. She might hate him, but she'd be the first to swear he was home all yesterday afternoon, yelling at her kids and threatening to boot them down the stairs.

God looked up at him and wagged his tail, as if happy to see his master's smile. Ralph patted the dog's black-spotted head.

"We'll have the last laugh, God," Ralph said.

Ralph stood straighter as he went to watch his coffee. *Justice!* Not "blood revenge" as the Jews were always screaming, just plain old justice with proven facts, no revenge or tit for tat, because people got jail sentences now, not death. Ralph was convinced that Sutherland had something to do with it. Had he possibly hired a killer? Should he suggest this to the police while they were still here? No, best not, Ralph thought. It was a classic, guilty people trying too hard to pin the blame on someone else. He mustn't look guilty or anxious in the eyes of the police, not for a minute.

As he poured his coffee, Ralph remembered a vivid dream he'd had last night: a couple of small boys in this house had attacked God, grabbed him by the legs, stuck a knife into his belly, and Ralph had retaliated by kicking a boy in the abdomen, hitting the other boy on the front of his neck with a judo whack, and in his dream, he had killed them both. His reply to the judge or to someone in the dream who was questioning him was: "God is more important than these vermin!" Or had he said "My dog"? Anyway, he had meant his dog, not a god, but in the dream, the judge had looked puzzled.

33

JACK jumped at the sound of the doorbell, sure that it was Natalia. Hadn't she her keys? He smiled a little as he pressed the release button, and felt that his face cracked with the smile. It had not been a smiling morning. The telephone had rung at least four times, their friends asking in astounded voices what he knew about Elsie, if he knew who might have done it. And Natalia had phoned around 9 to say that she was meeting Elsie's parents that morning and would invite them to lunch, and that she would try to be home "in the early afternoon". Anyway, she had arrived.

"Hi, darling!" Jack said, and embraced her, held her tight. She smelt of her particular perfume, of clean but warm hair. She smelt delicious.

"I'm filthy—and plooped!"

"How was it? What's been happening?"

"I've got her parents into the only hotel I could find in a hurry that—"

"Have you been on a trip, Mommie?" Amelia stood at the hall entrance, staring.

"I haven't been away long!—A trip!" Natalia said with scorn.

By tacit agreement, Jack and Natalia spoke of Elsie as "she" and "her".

"Her parents're darling people," Natalia said. "Not at all what I'd expected. They're civilized—and not hicky." Natalia had washed her face and hands in the bathroom, and was now leaning back on the sofa, drinking a beer out of the cold can. "At first they seemed sort of against *Marion*. I had to convince them about *that*. And they're—they're—" She glanced at Amelia who was listening. "They're really bowled over, just knocked out by this."

"Christ," Jack said, imagining it. "How long're they here for?"

"I suppose—two days more, not sure."

243

"They have friends here?"

"The mother mentioned somebody, a woman here."

"Was the brother with them?"

"What brother?"

"She has a brother, older, I think."

"Oh, yes! No, he's working in Atlanta now, they said. Not sure if he'll come. But the mother—" Natalia gave a laugh as she lit a Marlboro. "She's just like—her. Same kind of hair, eyes, same— Well, what was it?"

"Really?" Jack sat on the edge of the armchair seat, with his second tentative smile of the day. "I don't believe it."

"Whose mother?" Amelia asked.

"Sweetie—" Natalia took a deep breath. "Your daddy and I have to talk for a few minutes. It's very boring like—income tax."

Sometimes the boring ploy worked with Amelia, sometimes not. Amelia seemed torn, and went to look out a window.

"Talk any more with the fuzz?" Jack asked, barely audibly.

"Yes, this morning. They're not sure about this Fran. They're asking Marion for more names."

"Oh?—Has she got any?"

"No." Natalia crossed her extended legs and looked up at the ceiling. She wore black cotton trousers and sandals with nearly flat heels. "She could reel off half a dozen names, probably. Mostly with no fixed address."

Jack frowned and whispered, "All girls? Surely not.—What's behind all this?"

"You mean——"

"The reason for it." Jack spoke softly and intently.

Natalia got up, and poured a smallish Glenfiddich into a glass from the bamboo bar. "Envy," she said after her first sip. "Jealousy. Maybe drugs. Some drugged kook, I mean, did it."

"But who?"

"Who is who?" asked Amelia, turning suddenly from the front window.

"Somebody at your mother's gallery, honey," Jack said. "Not someone you know." Jack suddenly recalled that they had told Amelia that Louis was away on a long trip to Japan. That was so far working. Amelia had asked a couple of times about him. Japan wouldn't work forever, of course.

Jack's statement seemed to have created the uninterestedness that they both wanted. Amelia drifted off to her room.

"About who," Natalia said, relaxing again on the sofa. "Marion can't come up with anybody except Fran who would've had the—brutality—"

"And the cops spoke to Fran." Jack still whispered, as if Amelia were present. "Marion said she had a half-assed alibi."

"Oh, yes! And she was high on something and the police finally let her go."

"Let her go?—You mean, after just talking to her a few minutes?"

"I dunno how long. Something about Fran being with friends in a bar that afternoon, and they could prove it. That's what Fran's present girlfriend said when she called up Marion this morning. The girlfriend sounded fuzzy, and she mainly wanted to scream at Marion for mentioning Fran's name to the police."

"But—could you tell what the police *think*?"

Natalia shook her head. "I couldn't, Marion couldn't, because the police aren't saying yet.—The police're probably watching Fran to see if she'll spill something on herself.—Oh! Something else new since this afternoon!" Natalia's face lit up. "Fran's disappeared—from where she's supposed to be living. Marion told me this. I phoned Marion from the restaurant just now. The police called up Marion to ask if she'd heard from Fran or if Fran had even turned up at Greene Street!"

"Not so loud, darling," Jack said with a glance toward Amelia's room. "They must suspect Fran or they wouldn't be so interested."

Natalia shrugged. "It's really only Marion's hunch." She pushed her hair back, and sipped from her glass. "I didn't mention Fran to the Tylers, by the way."

"Was Fran hanging around Greene Street—around Elsie and Marion?"

"She was never in the Greene Street apartment, I know that.—But Fran's got that old grudge, Elsie took Genevieve away from her." Natalia's face crinkled with suppressed mirth. 'That Genevieve! Ha!"

Natalia needed a laugh, Jack realized. He could smile, too, recalling poor drippy Genevieve who sold cosmetics somewhere. "And what was the half-assed alibi of Fran?"

245

"One version is that she was in the East Village. Of course some barman can say he remembers her being there around four, but he's not quite sure. Then there's her own girlfriend or apartment mate—who's supposed to be a sculptress, by the way, but both of them keep themselves going by selling coke and such—she says they were shopping together on Eighth Street and she's got some junk they bought to prove it.—But there's nothing concrete, Jack." Natalia got up restlessly and moved toward the radio, but didn't turn it on.

"What about the Tylers? You're going to see them again?—Are they—" Jack had been about to ask if the parents were going to see Marion. And their daughter's body. Jack felt suddenly weak, or shocked, and he stood up to get rid of the feeling.

Natalia said that the Tylers were going to some kind of funeral service tomorrow, which they had arranged with the help of the woman friend who lived in New York. The burial was tomorrow in Long Island, and no, she, Natalia, did not want to go to the burial, and had told the Tylers that. Natalia looked at him with something stern and brooding in her face as she said this, and Jack remembered that she had seen Elsie in the morgue, what was left of Elsie. Natalia said the Tylers had been friendly, they had heard all about her and Jack from Elsie's letters, and the father said he was grateful to them for introducing Elsie to people who could help her. "Nice older people, the mother said." Natalia smiled.

Jack was touched when he heard this. Maybe the Tylers had been thinking about Elsie's success as a fashion model for photographers. The people he and Natalia had introduced Elsie to had at least been harmless. Her killer had come from among the people Elsie had met on her own.

"They're a bit baffled by her," Natalia went on. "They said they'd had no control over her. The mother sort of understands." Frowning, Natalia took a cigarette from the coffee table, and poured another small drink. "You can see the mother must've been just like Elsie when she was younger. And really she's not old now! The mother's from Sweden. I remember Elsie said Copenhagen—deliberately, probably. The mother started out as a ballet dancer, and gave it up when she married, she said. The father's good-looking, but sort of a failed type, I think. I think he had greater ambitions. He owns a furniture store in their town.—Mind if I play some music, Jack?' she asked in a tone that sounded as if she were sure Jack wouldn't mind.

"I'd adore some music. Whatever you want."

Natalia put a Beach Boys cassette in the machine, listened as she drew on her cigarette, turned it off. She looked for something else on the shelf of cassettes under a front window.

"And what about the trip? The twenty-ninth?"

Natalia dropped a cassette in. "Yugoslavia," she said. "I want to go just because I don't want to."

Jack understood, perfectly.

Natalia had chosen the "Country Dances" of Respighi. She stood near the window. "The police were good last night. Kept the journalists away from the front door.—And they were still questioning people all up and down the street, Marion said—about what they'd seen, you know?"

Jack listened, and waited.

"We took the phone off the hook for a while to get some sleep."

"While I think of it, Bob called up this morning. And Elaine last night.—And Isabel this morning too."

Natalia acknowledged this with a slight nod. "Did you buy a paper this morning?"

"No. Sorry. I frankly didn't want to face it."

"I did. Didn't bring them with me, of course," she added with a glance toward Amelia's room.

Jack moved closer to her. "How well did Amelia know Elsie? Did you take her around—"

"Couple of times, yes. I remember one afternoon, we walked around Washington Square—went and had ice cream somewhere." Still frowning, Natalia smiled a little, as if she remembered it pleasantly. "She'd know Elsie's name—recognize the pictures."

Jack thought of the morgue, and decided not to ask about that.

"You loved her too, didn't you, Jack?"

"Well, in a different way, maybe. When you say love—"

"Different way?" Natalia finished her drink. She turned toward the window.

Had he seen tears in her eyes? Then the telephone rang, and Natalia, being nearer it, picked it up. Jack could tell from the tone that the caller was a man, and from Natalia's words that he was Bob Campbell.

Jack went into the bedroom, not wanting to go to his workroom, because he was restless, and because Elsie's photographs plus his drawing of her were still in view there ... *incredible that it happened in broad daylight* ... Which of them had said that? *Elsie had been pretty good about writing and phoning her parents. She only told people she didn't want to keep in touch* ... Jack went out of the bedroom, and saw that Natalia had finished her telephone conversation. She was lying on the sofa on her back, hands behind her head.

"I think I'll go for a walk," Jack said. "Do we need anything? Milk?"

"Milk?" Natalia said vaguely. "I dunno. Look."

Natalia at least sounded like herself. Jack looked into the fridge, and found himself not caring if there was milk enough or not. He went out with his keys. Natalia must be shattered, he thought. And what about himself? Jack felt that he had to keep his emotions to himself. He felt that he was still suffering shock, as if he were a windowpane cracked into little pieces, still within a frame, but difficult to see through.

On the street, he looked far enough ahead not to bump into people, but in a way he saw nothing around him. He walked uptown, turned back before Twenty-third Street, and picked up some milk and the usual big bottle of Coca-Cola for Amelia when he was near home.

Natalia had news. The police detective McCullen had telephoned, because Marion's telephone wasn't answering, and he thought Marion might be at the Sutherlands'. McCullen said that a teenaged girl on Greene Street had said she heard some screams and then saw a woman run out of the building.

"She said it was a dumpy woman with short hair and light colored trousers, running in the uptown direction."

"Does he think it's Fran?" Jack remembered Fran's short hair, and her figure could certainly be called dumpy.

"He didn't say. But it fits Fran, doesn't it? A woman!" Natalia's face shone, as if the scent were getting stronger. "Nice of McCullen to tell me all that!—He wanted to know if we had a photo of this Fran, and I told him no. Imagine having one!" Natalia said with a laugh. "McCullen said they've both disappeared now, Fran and the girlfriend. The police broke into their apartment and saw signs of hasty packing."

"Really!—Where do they live?"

"East Village. Good for the drug business.—And they left the cat."

"Lovely pair." And how dumb of Fran, Jack thought, to try to disappear now, since the police had seen her drugged, and would surely want to see her in a more normal state at some point. "How about the girl on Minetta Street? She might have a picture."

"Genevieve. The police've been there. She hasn't any.—I can imagine Genevieve wants to keep out of it."

"I've got a little cartoon of her, matter of fact."

"Of Fran?"

"I did one that night at the Gay Nighties."

Natalia wanted to see it. Jack found the little blank tablet with its spiral top amidst the stuff on his worktable. There was the lantern-jawed fellow leaning against the wall, the over-sized-evening-jacket girl, then the slit-lipped Fran with the piggish eyes, and the jagged line of bangs on her forehead.

"Oh, Jack—that's great! Those eyes!"

And the awful jaw, Jack thought. He felt revolted now by the likeness done with his own hand.

"I'd recognize her in a flash—I bet the police could use this."

"You think so? They can have it." Jack's drawing showed an ample bosom under the round-necked T-shirt. Jack didn't want to see the cartoon ever again.

"We could make photostats. No, I'll let the police do that."

Jack took the little notebook from her, tore out the page and handed it to her. "My contribution."

Natalia went to the telephone.

Jack lingered in the living-room. Someone was coming over to pick up the drawing. Natalia had said just the right words, as usual. "What about the people in Fran's apartment building—or wherever she was. Didn't the police question them?"

"Clams, all clams.—Look at the girl on Greene Street—waits till today to say a *word* to the police, when she knew what happened yesterday, the whole neighborhood saw the ambulance and the stretcher coming out."

The police came half an hour later, in the form of a young officer, who was not McCullen, the Homicide detective.

"Yeah, hm-m," said the cop, smiling, looking at the cartoon. "Well, it looks clearer to me than a lot of Identikits I've had to work with."

"It's Fran Dillon—or Bowman to a T," said Natalia. "Don't forget she goes under a couple of names.—If she really is the one you want." Natalia was fishing, attentive.

"Dillon, yeah. We're looking for her all right."

"Do you work with Detective McCullen?" Natalia asked.

"Not directly, ma'am. I work with several. I'm just beginning." He declined a chair, and declined a cold Coke. He left.

"Just occurred to me," Jack said to Natalia, "could—the—the assailant," he went on more quietly, having just seen his daughter emerge from her room, "have been another model?"

Natalia had also seen Amelia. "Not likely. I never heard of any trouble there.—A dumpy model?" she asked with smiling eyes.

"Dad-*day*—was that more parking tickets?" Amelia asked. "Why was that policeman—"

"Yes—They're collecting 'em while they can before we flee the country!—But it's nothing to worry about. We'll make it."

The telephone rang, and Jack hoped it wasn't for him, but it was, and it was Joel. Natalia had answered. "Can you tell him I can't talk to anyone now? Tell him—You know."

Natalia knew, and Jack knew that she would think of a good excuse.

"Going out again for a while," Jack said when Natalia had hung up. "Won't be long. Maybe an hour."

Natalia understood that too, and asked no questions.

Jack walked to a flower shop at Seventh Avenue and Grove, and bought a dozen white roses, added six red roses on impulse, then took a taxi to the Mansfield Hotel on West Forty-fourth Street, where Natalia had said the Tylers were. The florist had given him a little envelope and card, but Jack did not write on the card until he got to the hotel, and borrowed a pen at the desk.

From another who loved Elsie.

Jack Sutherland

Then he wrote Mr and Mrs Tyler on the envelope, and handed the long box to the man behind the desk.

"I think they're in, sir. Would you like me to call them?"

"No." Jack shook his head. "Thanks." On Jack's left, an ele-

34

ON Thursday morning, Ralph Linderman saw the cartoon in the *Times* of Frances Dillon who was being sought for information in regard to the murder of Elsie, and his first reaction had been surprise that the newspaper would print such a drawing, which looked like a child's effort, and then when he read that it had been drawn by John Sutherland, Ralph felt a slow wrath rising within him. A clever little trick of Sutherland's to throw the police off his trail! What a convincing story Sutherland must have told the police about this Dillon woman—friend of Elsie's?—to inspire the police to start a search for her! Did she even exist?

Or could it be a double hoax, the police pretending to be believing Sutherland's story about Dillon, while they kept an eye on Sutherland? Had the police bugged the Sutherlands' apartment? Ralph hoped so. The conversation between Sutherland and his wife Natalia (her name was mentioned in the *Times*, and the Sutherlands were called friends of Elsie Tyler) would indeed be interesting, Ralph thought. Natalia Sutherland was bound to know the truth, and must be enduring agony now, knowing probably also that her husband had had an adulterous relationship with Elsie Tyler, and that he had fallen to such depths of evil as to kill the innocent girl rather than—Ralph suspected—let Elsie reveal that relationship to the Sutherlands' circle or perhaps to Sutherland's business associates. Or maybe Elsie had wanted to end their affair, and Sutherland hadn't been able to face that, and so had killed Elsie. No matter the details, Sutherland was a liar.

The fact that the police had seemed to clear Sutherland of guilt by saying that he was home when the girl called Marion telephoned him about Elsie, Ralph dismissed, because something was wrong there. Someone was off by ten minutes in the time. Or, for some reason, the girl Marion was covering up for Sutherland.

Sutherland could indeed have been having an affair with both of them. Ralph would never forget that early Sunday morning when he'd seen Elsie and Marion with Sutherland on Grove Street, walking away from the Sutherland house.

Marion Gill seemed not to be suspected at all, and yet she might have done it! Ralph had thought of this before, but now the idea had a new force. Sutherland could have been home for that telephone call. He and Marion might have a passionate attachment to each other, might have planned the murder. Did Natalia know about Marion too? Would Elsie have told Natalia about Marion?

Ralph, on the street with God at 11 in the morning, tried to compose himself, recalled that he wanted to buy a few things. He didn't want to go to Rossi's this morning, and because he had God now, he couldn't go into the Gristede supermarket on Bleecker. He went into a place on Seventh Avenue, and bought what he needed, including a thick steak, feeling still deep in thought, buried. He was not thinking about finding a new job as yet, or even about claiming unemployment benefits after the Hot Arch Arcade firing. It was only right and proper that a few days should pass while he thought of Elsie, days like a period of mourning, disturbed though they were. He had hardly slept last night, though he had anticipated being able to sleep at "normal" hours, when the damned Italians in his house were, it was to be hoped, more quiet. His sleeplessness was also a form of mourning, he felt, and to be expected.

On the warm afternoons and evenings, Ralph often lay in pajamas on his bed with books from the public library, and on the hour, he listened to the news on his night-table radio. There had been nothing about the Elsie Tyler tragedy for a couple of days, until one evening on the 7 o'clock news the announcer said that the police were still searching for Frances Dillon, twenty-six, one of a circle of friends of the young model, who the police hoped could provide information in regard to the killer.

Ralph got to his feet at this statement, and for a few seconds was oblivious of the babies' yelling beyond his closed door and on the floor below. If they found Dillon, was she going to be charged? Framed?

He stared at his telephone with an impulse to call up Sutherland and tell him what he thought, that he had seen the Dillon cartoon, and was on to Sutherland's trick. Yes, and that he was going to speak to the police again. Good idea, that last one, the police.

Ralph looked up the number of the precinct station on Hudson and 10th Streets.

The station answered, but Ralph was asked to wait a moment. He waited so long, that he put the telephone down finally. He got dressed. Warm as it was, he put on a tie and a summer jacket for this call on the police.

Ralph entered the station and spoke to a young officer at the desk. "My name is Ralph Linderman. I have some information in regard to Elsie Tyler—her slaying."

"Elsie—" The officer was not the one who had been at the desk on Ralph's first visit.

"The murder on Greene Street a week ago."

"Oh, that one. You can give your information here, sir." He reached for a ballpoint pen. "Your name again?"

Ralph gave it, plus his address. "I was here once before," Ralph said, with growing impatience, because this young man seemed even unacquainted with the case, or Ralph had that feeling. "The killer you are looking for is not the Dillon woman, it's John Sutherland who lives on Grove Street."

The young officer looked at Ralph more alertly, and rubbed his chin. "This case you're talking about—"

"The twenty-one-year-old girl! May I please speak with a detective or the—whoever's on this case?"

"Can you wait here a moment?" The officer disappeared into a nearby office whose door was open.

Ralph remained standing, watched by a cop guard who leaned against a wall behind Ralph. The young man was gone nearly four minutes, and reappeared standing sideways in the doorway, still talking to someone out of sight. He returned and said:

"Yes. Your information, sir?"

"The killer is John Sutherland who lives on Grove Street. I *know* some facts. I'd be glad to give them to the homicide squad or whoever's working on this. The reason I'm here is that this is the closest precinct station to my house."

"Yes, sir. But I just checked. Homicide knows Sutherland. They have some suspects now and they—"

"Sutherland is the man you *want!*"

The young cop took a breath. 'This case is very active, sir.—

What do you know about Sutherland?"

"I know that he's guilty. He was having an affair with the girl who was killed! Do the police know that?—I'd like to speak with someone who's working on the case and is familiar with—with the details up to now. May I talk to the man in the office there?" Ralph made a nervous move toward the open door.

"Oh, no, sir, you're not to go in there."

"And why not?" Ralph walked on.

The guard moved, the young cop moved.

Ralph was suddenly taken by the arms, and he relaxed with feigned tolerance.

"Never fear, I'm not violent," Ralph said, shaking his arms free. "I'm here—I am here to say that Sutherland is the killer and you're wasting your time looking for anyone else—like this woman the police found today, Dillon—F-frances!"

The two cops stared. One nodded, and said, "Right, sir," as if placating someone who was out of his head.

An officer appeared in the doorway of the nearby office. "What's going on, Charley?"

"He's still talking about Sutherland."

"Ask him what he's got definite," said the cop in the doorway.

"I *know*," Ralph said, addressing this man. "He's a good runner, did you know that? Jogger. He could've run between Grove and Greene in ten minutes! He had a relationship with that girl! With both of them, the one called Marion too! If you'd—"

"We have to have facts," the doorway cop interrupted tolerantly. "If you have facts—Were you a witness to this murder?"

"No, sir, I was home. On Bleecker Street."

"Well—" The officer shrugged.

Ralph began again. Suddenly all four of them were talking at once, and Ralph was being urged out, especially by the guard.

"But I *know*!" Ralph kept saying.

"Sutherland's not going to get away . . . married man with a fixed address! . . . Ha-ha! . . . Take it easy! . . . Tomorrow's another day . . . G'night, sir."

Ralph was suddenly alone on the sidewalk. Their voices echoed in his ears, though he felt surrounded by silence, as if he'd gone deaf. He started walking uptown, then turned around and headed east at the next corner. Sutherland and his fixed address! Yes, sure. But Sutherland was wriggling out day by day, with his clever little schemes and stories to protect himself, and of course the more he stayed home with his wife, the better he looked, the more innocent.

Ralph felt angry and nervous, and walking briskly relieved none of the feeling. He was suddenly at Sheridan Square. Then he did something he had not done in many years, entered a bar-restaurant with a green awning, a familiar fixture of his neighborhood, with the idea of buying a drink. He ordered a whisky, and was asked what kind he wanted. Of the many names the barman recited, Ralph chose White Horse. He felt torn up inside, miserable. He had tried, and failed. A drink was said to be a sedative. The cold ice in it tasted good. He was still thirsty, and ordered a glass of water and also a beer. Discreetly, not looking at anyone, Ralph undid his tie, rolled it up and stuck it into his jacket pocket, and removed his jacket also, which was dampish from sweat. The place was air-conditioned, pleasant. Ralph drank his beer slowly, happy to see darkness coming outside. The bar-restaurant was busy, all the people strangers to him. Had Elsie and Natalia ever come here together? Ralph began to feel better, cooler. He ordered a second White Horse, and paid with a ten-dollar bill, and left a dollar tip.

But he sat on, not having finished his second scotch, adding water to it from the glass. Sutherland breezing through! Sure. Perhaps threatening his wife, forcing her to silence with a blow even, perhaps even at this moment in the Grove Street apartment. Maybe the police had called up the Sutherland house a few minutes ago to make sure Sutherland was still there? Sutherland would be more uneasy after that, and his wife Natalia would be more hopeful that the net was tightening on her husband. Hardly a year ago, Ralph would have believed Sutherland incapable of such behavior. But so would he have thought it impossible, bizarre, that Elsie's life would be crushed out like this, so suddenly and brutally. To think that Sutherland had proven more vicious than any one of Elsie's hoodlum friends!

Ralph finished his drink, and went to the men's room. Then he walked home, hung his jacket, and put God on the leash. High time for God, he realized.

After walking God back home, Ralph pushed his wallet into a trousers pocket, and went out again. He could not bear his four walls now, he had to get out and move. He walked to Washington Square, and strolled around it slowly, thinking to derive some mental balance and tranquillity from the fact that this was a square, a civilized little *park*, or had been a couple of decades past, even in his lifetime. A tall male prostitute in blue jeans, thin as a wand, eyed Ralph briefly, and drifted on.

"Evening, miss!" said Ralph in a burst of peevishness, and he too kept on walking.

A broken whisky bottle lay where the sidewalk met a low metal fence. That whisky bottle might be somebody's weapon tonight. Who could face that? What man would stand up against that brandished by a thug determined to take his wallet?

Call Sutherland up and go to see him tonight, Ralph thought suddenly, confront him and his wife in their own house with the truth. Wouldn't Mrs Sutherland welcome that? On the other hand, Ralph was sure that Sutherland would refuse to let him come up, and would say—as he'd said at the very first, Ralph recalled, when he'd brought Sutherland's wallet to him—"I'll meet you down on the sidewalk." More likely, Sutherland wouldn't meet him anywhere.

Ring their bell and barge in, Ralph decided. Take a chance on being able to do that.

Ralph directed his steps westward toward Sixth Avenue, walking steadily, and collecting his thoughts. He would remind Sutherland, in the presence of Natalia, of the Sunday morning when he had seen Elsie and her friend Marion in Sutherland's company at 6 in the morning. He would present the Sutherlands with a lot of truths, and demand to know other truths from Sutherland himself.

Feeling more and more sure of himself, Ralph was a bit jolted to see Sutherland walking toward him on Grove Street. Ralph had just turned the corner from Bedford, having taken a longer route than necessary.

"Mr Sutherland," said Ralph.

"Ye-es.—Hello." Sutherland's silent steps slowed. He was carrying a white plastic sack.

"I'd like to say a few things to you. And to your wife. May I come up to your apartment for a couple of minutes? I'd like your wife to hear what I have to say."

Sutherland took another slow step toward Ralph in what Ralph felt was a hostile or at least unfriendly manner. Sutherland had been near his own doorstep when Ralph had seen him, and now they were drifting toward Bedford, Ralph along with Sutherland.

"Not a good idea to come up tonight," Sutherland said. "Late, you know. What is it you want to say?"

"Your wife has got to hear this too," said Ralph, stopping.

"My wife?—Just what're you talking about?"

"Does she know that you had those two girls to your house—Elsie and Marion—that Sunday morning early when I saw you? And I think Elsie saw me too?"

"Of course she knows. We'd all been to the same party.—What're you getting at?" Even in the darkness, Ralph could see Sutherland's brows draw down.

"That you are guilty," Ralph said, "and if you don't turn yourself in, I'll take the—"

"Oh, cut it out, Linderman! Shove it!"

"This *trick* with the cartoon in the newspaper! You think I don't know that's a trick? You couldn't put the blame on me, so you—"

"Your meddling isn't doing one damn bit of good. You've been a pain in the ass since—"

"I'm going to write your wife a letter—put it in her *hand*! She'll listen to reason!"

"You leave my wife out of this," Sutherland said with sudden grimness, moving closer to Ralph.

Ralph backed a little. Two people, a man and a woman, walked past on the sidewalk and glanced with curiosity at both him and Sutherland.

"You keep away from me and my wife," Sutherland continued in a lower tone, "or I'll get the cops onto you and pronto. You don't know how many times Elsie and the rest of us came near doing that already!"

"Hold it! I've got a gun here! I can settle the score here and now!" Ralph had his hand in his right side trousers pocket, where his wallet was, and the wallet's corner made a good show.

Sutherland glanced at the pocket. The light was not strong from the nearest streetlamp, but strong enough for Sutherland to see, and Ralph fancied that Sutherland turned white in a matter of seconds. Sutherland let the plastic sack slip to the sidewalk, and swung at Ralph suddenly with his left fist.

Ralph dodged the blow, though it scraped the top of his head. He hurled himself forward, at the level of Sutherland's waist, but he crashed against Sutherland's knees instead, and fell.

Sutherland had fallen too, Ralph got to his feet first, then Sutherland was up like a jack-in-the-box, and he grabbed Ralph's wrist and swung him toward a housefront. Ralph heard his own shoulder and head crack against brick. He managed to raise a foot—or a knee?—in time to catch Sutherland, who was coming at him again. Sutherland bent in pain, and Ralph struck him in the side of the head.

Both stood, a little bent, gasping. They were on Bedford Street now. A man veered away from them as if frightened, crossed Bedford and walked on.

"You will—turn yourself in," said Ralph.

"You'll get the hell *out*!" Sutherland seemed ready to tackle him again.

Ralph stepped back.

So did Sutherland step back, glanced at the sack he had let fall, but did not pick it up. Sutherland said more quietly, "Keep away, Linderman."

"*Hey*, down there!—*Cool* it, would you?" The voice came from an open window somewhere on Bedford.

Sutherland glanced up, waved a hand nervously, but Ralph did not glance up.

"Adulterer," Ralph said calmly, "and murderer."

Sutherland said just as calmly, "Piss off or I'll bust you wide open." He advanced with fists ready.

Ralph met them: he struck at Sutherland's stomach, but got a blow on the jaw himself. Ralph staggered—he was aware of that—and he did fall, rolled a very little, and got up again with some effort.

"Go on home," Sutherland said, grabbing Ralph by the shirtfront. "I don't care if you make it or not." He released Ralph with a shove.

Sutherland was walking off, swaying, Ralph could see that, bending his head, spitting once before he turned the corner into Grove, out of sight. Ralph stood on his two feet, scowling, hot. Two people a few yards away stared at him, sidestepped into the street, and walked past. Ralph went to the corner. He could see Sutherland, and he walked after him, taking great breaths of air. Ahead of him was Elsie's killer, half-conquered, wobbling.

"Sutherland—" Ralph started up the front steps as Sutherland stuck his key into the lock.

Sutherland turned, left fist ready—his other hand held the sack—and came down a step.

There were at least four steps, and Ralph on the second and third, fell against Sutherland in what might have been a tackle but wasn't quite. Sutherland shoved him, and Ralph was aware of a sharp pain in his shoulder as he struck the sidewalk. Suddenly the line of the curb edge, the darker hue of the street inches from his eyes, were very clear in the light of a streetlamp.

"C'mon, get up," Sutherland was saying, twice, in a tone of impatience.

And Ralph was trying, and of course he would get up in a matter of seconds. He got one foot under him, rose and swayed.

"Say, what's going on here?" said a strange voice. "Is this fellow—"

" 'S okay," Sutherland said. "Never mind."

Ralph wiped his wet mouth and chin with his forearm. "Officer—I'm glad to see you. This man—I've been—been to the local precinct station today—about *him*."

"Who?—Where d'y'live?"

"I live here," Sutherland said.

"Bleecker Street. Right up there."

"Is it you two been fighting? We had a call about a fight.—What's going on?"

"Nothing." Sutherland turned and put a foot on his step, then looked back. "He can make it home, I think."

The cop looked puzzled. "You got some identification on you?" he asked Ralph.

"Yes.—Yes, sure." Ralph reached for his wallet.

35

JACK stood at his door, watching. The cop was taking Linderman off, but in a gentle manner, talking with him, going in the direction of Bleecker Street. The cop was holding Linderman's arm to steady him. Jack went into his own house, climbed the stairs two at a time, but in a slow, plodding way.

"Jack, f'gosh *sake!*" Natalia was in the hall, whispering. "What was all that?"

They went into the apartment and closed the door.

"Your ear's bleeding. And your forehead!—Linderman started a fight? I saw some of it out the window."

"Don't worry." Jack was in the bathroom, washing his face, looking at the ear Natalia had mentioned, where oddly there was a nick such as a knife might have made. A knuckle cut was worse, and the forehead scrape kept bleeding. Jack pressed a cold wet facecloth against his forehead, and turned to Natalia, smiling.

She was frowning, puzzled. "He attacked you? Just like that?"

"Not exactly.—Don't worry, honey. Really—I think it's finished now."

A couple of minutes later, when Jack sat on the sofa with a Jack Daniel's on the rocks, he wondered about finished. Finished? Would Linderman ever be finished?

"Can't you talk to me, Jack? What was he saying?"

"Sorry, it's—I haven't felt as funny as this since I had a fight with my worst enemy—when I was twelve!" Jack laughed, moistened his lips and drank. The drink cut the faint taste of blood in his mouth. "Old Linderman put up a hell of a good fight—for a man his age."

"I hope that cop's putting him away for a while."

"No. I think the cop's walking him home!" Jack laughed.

"Linderman's accusing me again, that's all. I heard him tell the cop he'd been to the local precinct station today, and maybe that's true.—He thinks my cartoon of Fran is a trick—on my part."

"Do you mean he just came up to you on the sidewalk—out here?"

"Yes! He intended to come up to see us. He wanted you to hear the truth. You know."

Natalia was silent. She knew. "Gad, am I glad we're leaving town! Eight more days. They're bound to find out something definite in that time.—Don't you think, Jack?"

Jack was not at all sure, but he nodded. "Sure."

"You're sure you're not hurting or bleeding somewhere else, Jack?"

Jack took his knuckle from his lips. "No, I'm okay."

"Thanks for picking up my cigarettes." She had looked into the plastic sack. "Come in the bathroom, Jack. I'll put some Savlon on your forehead. I should've thought of it right away."

Jack went with her. The white cream felt good. Natalia's mother Lily bought it in England and kept the Sutherlands in supply.

The telephone rang, and Natalia went to get it. The telephone calls kept coming, like the short notes of sympathy about Elsie, as if Elsie had been a member of their family. Sylvia Kinnock's telegram of a few days ago had touched Jack:

... REALLY TRAGIC AND HATEFUL. AM STUCK IN ATLANTA OR WOULD BE WITH YOU. MY THOUGHTS ARE. LOVE, SYLVIA

Two days after Jack's fight with Linderman, he and Natalia heard on the 6 o'clock TV news that Frances Dillon had been found in The Bronx, and was being questioned by police in connection with the slaying of Elsie Tyler nearly two weeks ago. Natalia went out to get the late edition of the *Post*. The paper reprinted Jack's drawing, and said that Dillon had been recognized in a Bronx grocery store by a young man who had remembered "the woman's hairline at the forehead and her mouth from the cartoon". Dillon had been wearing sunglasses and had been in the company of a woman friend.

"Well, well," said Jack, pleased by the small success of his cartoon. He was not sure of Fran's guilt—she might have fled the East Village out of panic about her drug-dealing—and he was glad that Natalia took the news calmly too.

"Now we'll see," was Natalia's remark. "They'll hold her till she has some sober moments, anyway."

By an earlier arrangement, Susanne Bewley was away on a two-week holiday, and in Maine with her boyfriend Michael. She had telephoned when she had heard of Elsie's death. "I remember that girl so well," Susanne had said to Jack. And she had asked if Linderman was suspected, though she hadn't recalled his name. Natalia must have told her about Linderman. Jack wondered if Susanne knew how fond Natalia had been of Elsie? Not likely, he supposed, yet one never knew how much another person, especially the quiet Susanne, might pick up or intuit.

Jack felt a strange silence between him and Natalia sometimes. They were both on their feet a lot, going out on errands, preparing to close the house for a month, maybe longer. Amelia spent half her time at the Armstrongs', as Elaine's sister was visiting and could keep an eye on the kids. But what was Natalia thinking, and feeling, for instance when she looked into the deep freeze part of the fridge and said in a bored tone:

"Good God."

It still looked pretty full, Jack knew, even though they had tried to empty it, and he also knew that Natalia didn't give a damn about the state of the deep freeze.

"Susanne's coming right after we leave, honey. She can take it home to use."

In Natalia's eyes he saw either a vagueness, as if her thoughts were far away, or a hardness, as if he weren't Jack, her husband, but maybe somebody else. And was she possibly wondering how he felt? Or did she care? Had she been more in love with Elsie than he? And maybe in a different way? Natalia had been to bed with Elsie, of that he was sure, and he had not. But then he hadn't wanted to, he reminded himself. It hadn't been that kind of love. Or was it because he knew he would've been rejected by Elsie that he took this attitude? He'd been over all this before, he realized as he slid a drawing pad into the bottom of a suitcase. He had loved to admire Elsie from a distance, as if she were a good painting or a drawing. Yes, that was closer to the truth. What had Natalia hoped or expected from her relationship with Elsie, which Marion had seemed to accept? Or when in love, did one always expect anything more than the experience, the pleasant sensation of being in love? Jack wondered if he would ever ask Natalia about all this.

"Can you get that, Jack?" Natalia said from the front hall.

She meant the telephone. It was Marion. No, she wasn't at home, she said, but at her friend Myra's house around the corner, and she wanted to tell Natalia and him that they had got Fran.

"Oh, we heard that, sure, couple of days ago," Jack said.

"No, I mean she confessed! A cop on McCullen's squad called me up twenty minutes ago to tell me. Wasn't that nice of him? I thought you'd both like to know—*love* to know—the latest news."

"No kidding, Marion! It's *true?*' Jack asked in a cautious voice, unbelieving.

"My hunch was right. That pig!" Marion sounded quiet and grim. "That's what this city has, what this city does. I'm a realist. I'm not even surprised."

"They're sure she's telling the truth?" Jack meant, that Fran wasn't talking out a fantasy for some odd reason.

"The police sound sure of it. She said she saw Elsie and did it—on an impulse. It'll probably be in the papers later tonight. Tell Natalia."

"She's here. Want to speak with her?"

"No.—I couldn't face it. I mean—Sorry, Jack!"

Jack said he understood.

"Who was that?" Natalia called from the hall.

"Marion." Jack walked in her direction. "She said Fran confessed—confessed to it."

Natalia's eyes widened a little. "Really.—Good. *Good!*—That didn't take long. A day and a half?" Natalia went into the kitchen, absently picked up a dishtowel that lay over the back of a straight chair. Her fingers tightened on the towel. "Good. That beast! I don't even want to call her an animal. She's worse."

"Marion said—Fran spotted Elsie on the street and did it on impulse. Homicide Squad man called up Marion and told her."

Natalia pulled the dishtowel taut between her fists, then snapped the towel once like a whip, and dropped it again over the chair back.

When Jack next saw Natalia, a half hour later, she was lying on the sofa, looking at the ceiling. He saw her daub her eyes with a handful of paper tissues.

And what had he been doing for the past half hour? Almost the same thing in his workroom, wandering around with wet but somehow relieved eyes, not caring now if a couple of pictures of Elsie were still visible, not looking at them either.

Natalia saw him and pushed herself up on one elbow.

"You really loved her, didn't you?"

"Yes." Natalia looked at him. "Didn't you?"

Jack was silent for several seconds. "I suppose you went to bed with her."

Natalia shrugged and smiled. "Bed. Yes. That's not—everything, is it?"

How did Natalia mean that? He waited.

"And you?" she asked.

Jack gave a laugh. "Me?—I never tried!"

"But you wanted to?"

"Not really, no. Frankly, no."

Natalia was sitting up, forearms on her knees, smiling now.

In the amusement in her eyes, Jack could read a lot. Natalia realized all the things that were true: that he had been knocked for a loop by Elsie, that Elsie would have refused him if he had ever proposed making love to her, and that in fact the act of "making love" wasn't of great importance compared to loving, compared to caring.

With a quick nod, Natalia got up, and the nod seemed to say, "I understand, and you know that I do."

Neither Jack nor Natalia spent much time over the newspapers. They glanced through the paragraphs. There was Fran Dillon's unhealthy-looking round face as she sat in T-shirt and trousers, talking to the police. "I was jealous of her, sure. I hated her." Jack wondered if Fran was going to plead temporary insanity, insist that she had been "overcome by emotion", and he realized that he didn't care. The point was that they had her, and that the details she gave made her confession sound true.

More pleasant and satisfying, like a breeze from another and better world, were the contents of a manila envelope that came from the Tylers in upstate New York. It was addressed to both Jack and Natalia, there was a letter and a photograph of Elsie at about four, sitting on a pony—not a Shetland but a red-brown ordinary pony—in blue overalls and white socks, brown sandals, and hair so fair it looked white, grinning with the wide naiveté and joy that both Jack and Natalia had often seen in her face, blue eyes dazzled with happiness. Mrs Tyler had written the letter and signed herself Grace Tyler.

> *... our favorite picture of Elsie as a small child, but my husband had a copy made so we are not without it, and I thought you both might like to have it. How Elsie loved to ride around on that pony! It belonged to a neighbor who let Elsie and her brother ride it quite often until it grew faster than the kids did. In these sad days, we look sometimes at this picture and are grateful that we had Elsie with us for a while.*
>
> *Again our love and thanks to you both, and God bless you for your kindness.*

William Tyler had added a few words below.

Natalia propped the photograph up on the living-room book-shelf near the telephone, and smiled at it. It was like sunshine, Jack thought, like Elsie herself, back for a while, though he knew the feeling would pass, change. What he liked, what he was sure Natalia liked too about the Tylers' letter was that there had been no bitterness in it, no hint of a desire for revenge for what had happened to Elsie. Nothing but friendliness and good will.

"Her brother—" Natalia said, turning to Jack. "I didn't meet him, but Elsie's mother said he came to the service and sat apart from them. He was so broken up, he didn't want to meet any-body."

Elsie's brother. Jack didn't know his name, and maybe Elsie had never uttered his name, though she had mentioned him.

Jack straightened after peering at the photograph, and felt pain on both sides of his ribs. Which of them had won that fight? He hadn't hit Linderman as hard as he might have done (or so Jack believed), because Linderman was an older man. But still, who had won? It was funny, but after that fight with a boy when Jack had been twelve, either he had forgotten or he couldn't remember now who had won. He remembered only tensed nerves and muscles, and giving his all to that fight. Had Linderman won in his attitude to Elsie? She was an ideal, he had said, too young to know how to manage her life, still in the process of growing up— words like that Linderman had used, and looking at Elsie's photo-graph at perhaps four, Jack realized a new truth in Linderman's rantings.

36

RALPH had lain low for a few days after his encounter with John Sutherland, nursing his bruised shoulder, swollen eye and cut lip. He had fought well, Ralph thought, or at least he hadn't been wanting in courage, and that made him feel proud. Bleeding at the mouth, he had reiterated his story to the cop who had seen him home, and the cop had listened rather sympathetically and said he would check it out at the Sixth Precinct station to which Ralph had been, and to which the cop said he was attached. Ralph had been badly shaken then, and had not wanted to ask the officer to go with him again to the station. Ralph had understood that a policeman couldn't turn a blind eye to a fistfight between two men on a sidewalk, and Ralph had wanted to show a willingness to go home, had wanted to prove that he had a home by pulling out his keys. The cop had heard of Elsie's case. The cop had mentioned a suspect (maybe a couple of suspects), and Ralph had told the cop, for what it was worth, that Sutherland's cartoon, printed in the newspapers, was a trick to throw the police off his trail.

The girl Fran Dillon, found in The Bronx, did have the shadiest of reputations, according to the newspaper accounts, well known on the drug scene, habituée of bars frequented by addicts and prostitutes of both sexes, no fixed address and no employment. She had not been a friend of Elsie Tyler, but was acquainted with people who knew the slain model, and admitted to having seen her on several occasions in the company of other people. Well, just what did that prove, Ralph wondered, except that Sutherland had been able to present a cartoon of an underworld character and with the help of Marion Gill concoct a story that a figure looking like Frances Dillon had run out of the Greene Street apartment house? How convenient that Sutherland would have made a sketch on an earlier occasion, and Marion Gill would have seen the same person running from Elsie's corpse!

Ralph had enjoyed a few days when nothing happened, when he toyed with the idea of going to an employment agency on East 14th Street to get a job, and put it off one more day, when he sat on a bench in Father Demo Square with God, getting some sun on his face and his healing lip, browsing in a book he had brought. On such an afternoon, on the way home, he had seen the headline: FRAN ADMITS GUILT! And another was SUSPECT TALKS! Ralph bought both papers, and walked directly home to read them. The same phrases were used in both the *Daily News* and the *Post*. Frances Dillon said she had had no intention of killing Elsie Tyler when she had left a bar on Wooster Street and walked uptown through Greene Street on her way to her East Village apartment. Then she had seen Elsie Tyler approaching her, and had had an impulse to hit her, and had picked up a brick that she had happened to see, followed Elsie up the front steps as Elsie let herself in, and struck her on the head, struck her "several times", said Frances Dillon, though she also said she could not clearly remember doing it, and that she must have blacked out. It seemed to Ralph that she was going to plead, "Pity poor me, I'm just a drug addict, not responsible for what I do, and besides I was jealous of Elsie because she was so pretty and popular." The jealousy element came out in both the newspaper accounts. In fact, a mess of emotions was implied, as the Dillon woman was called a lesbian, and it was projected that Elsie Tyler might have spurned her advances. Sick-making! Just as bad, even worse, was what criminals got away with these days, just by pleading diminished responsibility due to drink or drugs or some invisible brain defect, which could never be proved, of course, and which had led them to do this or that. But those cases, if won by the accused, required an expensive lawyer, and Ralph doubted that Fran Dillon was going to come up with one.

The woman Dillon had been living with, Virginia something, had said that Dillon admitted days earlier what she had done. Still another woman, Genevieve something, who had been questioned immediately after the murder because she was an acquaintance of Dillon, had said that she knew Dillon detested Elsie Tyler.

Elsie! It pained Ralph every time his eyes fell upon her name in the newspapers, yet he devoured every sentence, hungry for information. Could it really be that Frances Dillon had done it? Surely not all these women—and some men were quoted too, the bar-keep at the Wooster Street place where Dillon had been until nearly 4 p.m. that afternoon—all these people's statements tended to point to person and place. Ralph listened to the radio. And as early as possible that evening, he bought a *Times*, in which he read the same thing over again in more restrained but all the more convincing prose. The *Times* gave no hint that Frances Dillon's confession might be an hysterical one, might be any kind of fantasy.

The morning of the next day, another edition of the *Daily News* reported a bid of $300,000 for Frances Dillon's life story and of her slaying of Elsie Tyler, from a New York magazine that Ralph had heard of but had never bought or read. That kind of money could pay for a slick lawyer to get her off on a "temporary insanity" plea, just as if she were the daughter of a rich family, Ralph thought. Dillon's confession might be true. However, the Hitler diaries had been a hoax, and a lot of money had been paid for them.

Still, the grip of anger against Sutherland that had seized Ralph was easing a little. It was a relief to him mentally and physically, though he was not at once aware of the cause of the easing. He went for the second time in his period of joblessness to the Museum of Natural History up on Seventy-ninth Street. He adored this museum. There seemed always to be something new in it, because it was too big to take in on any one day, and he also found pleasure in looking at things that he had seen before. He could forget for half an hour at a stretch who he was and everything about his personal life. That day, Ralph found himself staring at a primitive drawing or marking on a clay slab made by American Indians. The face of one of the stick figures reminded Ralph of Sutherland's drawing of Frances Dillon—except that this little face was cheerful, the figure dancing even. He must have seen this exhibit before, but now he saw it with new eyes, as it were, and he looked eagerly at other human figures depicted on slabs and on the scaled down models of mountainsides.

"What're you smiling at?" a treble voice asked him.

The voice had come from a boy of about five on Ralph's right.

Ralph hadn't realized that he had been smiling. "These. These little figures," Ralph replied, pointing.

"Eddie—" said the man with the boy, probably his father. "You mustn't bother people—talking to them."

"Wasn't bothering me," Ralph said, but the man and the boy were moving off. A polite man, Ralph thought. Nice to know there were still some polite people in New York.

Ralph bought a *Rolling Stone*, because it had an exclusive interview with Fran Dillon, according to its bold headlines. With this four-page story plus photographs, Ralph had a deluge of details, names, even incidents—Elsie flirting with everybody, male and female, according to Fran. Ralph knew this to be untrue, because he had had a chance to observe Elsie, when she had worked at the coffee shop down on Seventh. How much else was untrue? And yet, the details piled up, as if Fran Dillon were deliberately trying to amass justification, in her eyes, for what she had done. She told of blackouts. Small wonder, Ralph thought, considering that she admitted to taking all kinds of drugs. "A sophisticated couple" on Grove Street was mentioned, and it was said that they had introduced Elsie Tyler to "a different and more worldly group", and Fran Dillon had actually attended a couple of their parties, invited not by Elsie Tyler but by a friend of the slain girl. Ah, poor Elsie, it came down to the fact that she had associated with the dregs!

He took another day to digest all this, and in an odd way was afraid to think hard about it. Sutherland then was not Elsie's killer. Not Elsie's killer. Ralph had wanted Sutherland to cringe, or at least flinch, when he had said he was pointing a gun at him. But Sutherland had not.

It was time he got himself to the employment agency. It would look better, if he didn't let too many days or weeks go by without a job, without trying. For this occasion, Ralph shaved himself neatly, and put on a clean shirt and a tie. A jacket wasn't necessary, he thought. It was another warm day.

By mid-morning, he was walking east on Fourteenth Street toward the employment agency. The sun bore down, and the summer air, wafted into his nostrils as a bus swerved to the curb, stank as usual of car exhausts, grease, vague filth of all kinds. Ugly people shuffled toward him, slowed by the heat, overweight people with shopping bags, tired, bored, but still moving, slouching toward some destination. And of course the inevitable kids were with them, some hardly old enough to walk, some being pushed in collapsible seats-on-wheels, one peeing in the gutter this minute while his mother waited.

Suddenly Ralph slowed, almost stopped, and someone at once bumped against his sore shoulder from behind.

He'd seen Elsie! She was several yards ahead, blond head lowered for a second or two, then up again, and the distance between them narrowed fast. Elsie with her quick tread, not looking at but somehow dodging all the hideous figures before her. Ralph blinked. *"Els—!"*

In an instant, and it was like a gunshot, he realized that the girl wasn't Elsie, that this girl was taller, that this girl held her head more down, yes, and was an all round larger girl. And the fair hair was not really blond but dyed, phony.

Ralph stood motionless as the girl swept past him. He was oblivious of the people who jostled him, of the mumbled complaints in foreign tongues and accents against his blocking the flow of human traffic. No, there wouldn't be another Elsie. Not ever again on earth, not ever.

37

"WE kept the newspapers out of sight, but Jason either found them—or overheard something Max and I said. Maybe both," Elaine Armstrong said to Jack on the telephone. "Anyway, he told Amelia. I am sorry, Jack. And we've had a TV shutdown here too."

Jack said he understood. His daughter would recognize Elsie's photograph, and she could read. Jack remembered Natalia saying that she and Amelia and Elsie had once had ice cream together at some place in the Village, and how many other meetings had there been? "Don't worry too much about it, Elaine. We wouldn't have done any better, probably.—What time's convenient for me to pick her up?"

"I could walk her down. Now, even." Elaine said she felt like taking a walk, and Amelia's little suitcase wasn't heavy at all.

In less than five minutes after she got home, Amelia spotted the photograph of Elsie on the pony on the living-room bookshelf. "That's Elsie—when she was little!" Amelia said, and her face lit with pleasure. Had Elsie given it to Mummy? Was Elsie coming back?

"Coming back," Natalia said with a troubled frown. "Well—"

Jack was nearby, and like Natalia didn't know what to say.

"No, she's not coming back, honey," Natalia said. "But we have this. It's nice, isn't it?" She meant the photograph. "I think she's even smaller than you here." Natalia threw a dismal glance at Jack, as if to say, "Oh, *Chr-rist!*"

"*Why* isn't she coming back?" There was in the question not only naiveté but a challenge.

"Because she's dead—now. Elaine told me you knew that, Amelia.—We're all sad and sorry. But it's true."

Amelia had locked her little fingers together and was bending them backward, looking at them. "But *you* didn't tell me.—She was dead when I went away."

Natalia sighed and slapped her forehead.

"Because it was very sad news, Amelia, hon." Jack put his hand against the back of Amelia's head, ruffled her hair gently. "We didn't want to tell you sad news like that. You know?"

"But it's true, though," said Amelia.

"Yes," Natalia said.

"Somebody hit her." Amelia looked from Jack to her mother.

"That's true," Jack said. "We were going to tell you when you came back home. But—"

To their relief, Amelia walked away, rather erectly, toward her room. But in the next hour or so, as they added to their note in progress for Susanne on the typewriter, took showers, and went out somewhere for a snack, Amelia's questions continued in the same vein. It was as if she had to have it confirmed over and over again by her parents: Elsie had really been killed, she would not be coming back again, she had been hit by another woman, and it had killed her. Amelia even knew the name Fran, and startled both Jack and Natalia when she uttered it.

Jack had an unpleasant vision of his little daughter poring over the newspapers, the tabloids, staring at photographs of Elsie, of Fran, of the Greene Street house where perhaps Amelia had been, understanding probably more than half of what she read. Jason, a year older, might have latched onto the papers when his parents weren't looking, and shared them with Amelia. Jack would never want to ask Amelia or Jason about that.

The next morning, at some time between 9.30 and 10, Jack and Natalia and Amelia descended the stairs with their luggage, aided by Max Armstrong who had called up and come down to lend them a hand. It was a Saturday morning, and Max didn't have to go to the office.

Max found a taxi—they had been shy about ordering one for a specific time, lest they be delayed by something—and as Jack was walking toward Bleecker with a bag in each hand, he caught sight of a blond girl walking toward him and his heart almost stopped. The sun was behind her, glowing on the top of her head, she walked with light steps that seemed hardly to touch the ground, head high and with a smile on her lips.

She's still alive! Jack thought.

276

But no, this was another girl, a different girl, and Jack shut his eyes as she passed him, nearly brushing his shoulder. His heart began to beat again, after a stumbling start. Amazing, that resemblance at a distance! Amazing, that lift, that shock of dazzlement at the sight of this girl, a total stranger!

"Jack!" Natalia called from the corner where she stood with a taxi door open.

Jack felt a clout on the left side of his face and forehead that made his ears ring, made him dizzy for a second. He had walked smack into a lamppost!

Up at the corner, Max and Natalia were laughing at him.

Winnie's War

Winnie's War

Jenny Moss

WALKER & COMPANY
NEW YORK

First published in the United States of America in 2009 by
Walker Publishing Company, Inc.
Visit Walker & Company's Web site at www.walkeryoungreaders.com

For information about permission to reproduce selections from this book, write to Permissions,
Walker & Company, 175 Fifth Avenue, New York, New York 10010

Every effort has been made to trace the copyright holder of the historical jacket image, and we
apologize for any unintentional omission. We would be pleased to insert the appropriate
acknowledgment in a subsequent edition of this book.

Library of Congress Cataloging-in-Publication Data
Moss, Jenny.
Winnie's war / Jenny Moss.
p.   cm.
Summary: Living in the shadow of a Texas cemetery, twelve-year-old Winnie Grace struggles to
keep the Spanish influenza of 1918 from touching her family—her coffin-building father, her
troubled mother, and her two baby sisters.
ISBN-13: 978-0-8027-9819-0 • ISBN-10: 0-8027-9819-5 (hardcover)
[1. Influenza—Fiction. 2. Epidemics—Fiction. 3. Family life—Texas—Fiction. 4. Texas—
History—1865–1950—Fiction.] I. Title.
PZ7.M8533Wi2009   [Fic]—dc22   2008023233

Book design by Nicole Gastonguay
Typeset by Westchester Book Composition
Printed in the U.S.A. by Quebecor World Fairfield
2 4 6 8 10 9 7 5 3 1

All papers used by Walker & Company are natural, recyclable products
made from wood grown in well-managed forests. The manufacturing processes
conform to the environmental regulations of the country of origin.

For John and Christine

Hope is the thing with feathers . . .
Emily Dickinson

Winnie's War

1

October 12, 1918
Coward Creek, Texas

*W*innie, stop playing with those forks," said my grand-mother.

I looked down at the silver forks I'd been polishing for her snooty ladies' tea coming up on Tuesday. I'd placed the forks perfectly side by side: the outer tines of one just touching the outer tines of another. They looked so pretty there, all lined up. In my mind, everything had its place and all was right when things stayed in their place.

When she was a young wife, my grandmother ordered her flatware from the Manchester Silver Company in Rhode Island, right before my grandpa lost everything he owned. Marrying grandpa was marrying herself into Money, or so she'd thought.

"When you finish polishing one, Winnie, put it in the box. Don't leave it on the table."

I stuck out my tongue at her. Well, I did after she turned her back and started talking to Mama, who was peeling potatoes. A warm breeze drifted in through the screen window, bringing the smell of burning wood in with it. I held my nose. Papa was getting rid of the scraps left over from Lewis Locke's coffin. He said it was bad luck to keep them around.

"Aren't you finished yet, Winnie?" asked my grandmother, while she stood there doing nothing.

I kept on polishing. Usually she didn't need a reply. I could tell she just wanted me to leave anyway so she could talk about something I wasn't supposed to hear. I was staying put.

My grandmother, Clara Winifred Tucker, said me and my two little sisters had to call her Clara. She said she's way too young to be a grandma. The way I see it is that she is a grandma, so I think she's old enough to be one.

She bit her lip a bit, looking at me hard. The gray-streaked hair piled on top of her head like an old bird's nest swayed a little to the left side, and I cocked my head to see her straight. And waited. I knew she wouldn't be able to contain herself.

"Margaret, did you hear about Mrs. Wells?"

Mama didn't say anything. It was her way.

"Well," Clara went on, "she has got that flu. It's come to our town just like I said it would."

I shivered. Papa had read in the *Chronicle* that schools were closing in Houston. Nobody was closing schools here yet.

"How sick is she?" I asked, trying not to think about poor Lewis Locke lying in his coffin. He'd been the first Coward Creek boy to enlist, ready to fight the Germans. Instead, he'd died of the influenza up at Ellington Field. His mama and papa were burying him in his uniform and had asked Papa to build their boy a special coffin.

Clara reached across the table and messed up my forks. "Put them in the box, child."

All my forks jumbled up, going this way and that! How could anybody be so mean, and why did that somebody have to be my grandmother?

"What is wrong with this girl, Margaret? Have you seen how she folds clothes? It takes her a night and a day to get them folded just right."

Mama said nothing.

I placed my forks back into their line. Clara made a clucking noise like she was disgusted with me. She grabbed a wet dishrag off the washstand and pressed it to her forehead. It's not that hot out, I thought.

"Anyway, Mrs. Wells's fever is very high. It hit her like a ton of bricks. She was talking to Mr. Levy, and she started shivering and shaking and pressing her fingers over her eyes, saying they were burning. Mr. Levy helped her up the front steps and sent her boy to get Mr. Wells."

That sounded like Mr. Levy. He might be a little grouchy, but you could tell his true nature by his hands, as gentle turning the fine pages of a book as they were putting a squiggly worm on a fishing line. My papa had gentle hands, too.

"Is Clyde sick, too?" I asked. "He wasn't at school yesterday." And I'd been a little glad about that. Clyde liked to steal cookies out of lunch pails. Mrs. Wells only gave him healthy apples. He was also Tillie's sweetheart, always hanging around her. Tillie was Mr. Levy's granddaughter.

"No, he isn't sick. He stayed home to help care for his mama, like a good son."

Clara eyed me again. I thought she was looking at my forks, so I cupped my arm around them protectively.

Still looking at me, she said to Mama, "I don't like Winnie going over to play chess with Mr. Levy all the time. It's not right. A young girl playing games with an old man? And chess!

That's a man's game. What are people in town thinking about that?"

"Leave Winnie alone, Mother."

I smiled real big at Clara. Mama didn't talk much, but I liked it when she did.

Clara pressed the cloth against her thin lips. She looked out the window. "I don't like this flu, Margaret. I knew when I read about it in the papers that it'd sweep through Coward Creek like the big flood did."

Clara was always talking about the hurricane of 1900 like it'd just happened yesterday. But that was years ago. Mama was a child when it hit. Clara said that's when Mama turned even more inward. I didn't like when she talked about it because Mama didn't like it.

"That hurricane killed so many people."

Mama's back stiffened. I wished Clara would shut up.

"All those people in Galveston drowned. They were swept off the beaches, even out of the windows in their houses. Right off those sinning streets."

Oh, no. Here she goes again.

"God sent that hurricane to wash those sinners away, just like in Noah's day."

That was the stupidest thing I'd ever heard. But I was careful not to say anything. I knew I'd get my cheek slapped.

"That whole island was full of sin—"

Mama walked out of the kitchen.

I glared at Clara. Didn't she have any sense?

She hesitated for a moment. Then she looked over at me and pinched my arm, leaving a red mark.

"Don't look at me like that," she said. "No child's ever going to look at me like that. I know who I am."

I knew who she was, too. She was a mean old lady.

I dropped my eyes back to my forks, the perfect line of metal soothing me. If only life could be so orderly. If only I could line up my worries, side by side, and fix them one by one, cleaning up the first, putting it away, moving on to the next.

The first worry I'd tackle was living next to the cemetery. Dead bodies. Sorrowful hymns. And possibly ghosts, which maybe I believed in.

Another thing I fretted about was if the Germans were going to team up with the Mexicans and invade Texas.

And if my old best friend Tillie was ever going to be my friend again.

And the weak lungs of my middle sister, Mary. She was only one year younger than me, but was as frail as she was sweet. This Spanish influenza was a terrible thing. How could Mary fight it if she got sick?

I wondered if those germs could get into our house. When I was little, I thought nothing could get inside our house to hurt us. Papa had built it special for Mama. He'd made it sturdy, sure to keep out floods and high winds. People in town remarked on how fine a house it was and what a gifted carpenter my papa was, even if we didn't have much money.

But our home wasn't just a bunch of wood. There was something about it, like it was a living thing, with qualities a person might have. It was maybe a little sad, but had a kind of strength, too. Not the tight, upright courage of a soldier like Lewis Locke. More like a mama should be, with her arms open wide, letting her children run only so far before she scooped them back up. A mama should always scoop her children back up, protect them from things.

My mama couldn't do that.

I hoped I could someday.

2

I ran in the wagon wheel ruts right toward town, thinking about Mrs. Wells. If I was going to figure out a way to keep that flu out of my house, then I had to see what I was up against.

I wished I could go by Tillie's like I used to, but she'd been very put out with me since she became Lessie Craven's friend. Tillie and I had been best friends since we were nine years old. She wanted to be a motion picture actress and move to Hollywood. Sometimes we acted out scenes from stories, her favorite being *A Little Princess*. I was usually Becky, the scullery maid. Tillie made a perfect Sara Crewe.

And now she was mad at me. I had no idea why. I hadn't done anything mean to her. Just because I was friends with her grandpa didn't mean I couldn't be friends with her, too.

I reached down, ran my fingers along the tall yellow grass of the prairie. I liked the way the prairie stretched out toward town with a flat beauty, like the palm of God's hand, like He was holding us in it. At least I was hoping He was.

About a half mile up the road, the white-planked houses, stores, and churches of Coward Creek rose up out of the earth like crops in a field. Our growing town was right on the railroad tracks and had a promising future, my papa said. Cattlemen and truck farmers from all around brought cows and figs and strawberries to the depot to be shipped out to market.

They also sent mules and hay to our armies in Europe. Coward Creek was doing its part for the war effort and our boys Over There.

I thought Mama was glad Papa built our house by the tracks. When the train rumbled by, she looked off in the direction of the whistle, like she was wishing she was riding in a passenger car with plush red seats.

But me, I didn't want to live anyplace else. In that, I was like Papa, not Mama.

Billy Bill came barreling down the dusty road in his new Ford Roadster. "Hey, there, Winnie Grace!" he yelled.

I jumped out of the way, cursing him, but under my breath like a lady does. He took off his straw hat and waved it in the air as he went past. Clara said the U.S. Army wouldn't take Billy Bill because he was just sixteen, so the rest of us had to put up with him.

Papa said we didn't need an automobile, and I guess he was right because all we did was walk to town and back. When he bought our land by the cemetery for a real good price, he took a job with the undertaker, Mr. Coldman. Papa kept the grass mowed and the gate fixed. He made coffins and drove the hearse. Sometimes he was a pallbearer if the deceased didn't have many friends.

Most of the houses and stores in Coward Creek were on dirt roads laid out like a nine-patch quilt, just southeast of Creek Street. Main Street ran along the southernmost edge, crossing the tracks down by the train depot and the park. More businesses were on the other side of the tracks.

Clyde Wells lived to the north of Creek, closer to my school. I cut up Fourth and over to Spring Street.

The Wellses' house was a small two-story with a low fence around it to keep the cows out. All the windows were wide open because it was such a pretty day.

Mrs. Wells's second-story window, which hung over the porch, was open to all of Coward Creek. She stood right there, framed, like a woman in a picture. She looked out with her hair all straggly and stuck to her neck. Pulling at her earlobe, she was staring straight at me, her eyes wild.

It scared me so because Mrs. Wells was usually so prim and proper. You never saw her in Craven's Drug Store or the Missionary Baptist Church without her hair done nice and neat and her white gloves on. And here she was not looking so good.

She reached out toward me. It happened so fast, no sounds came out of my mouth at first. She stretched her hand out, through the window, then she just kept on coming.

"No!" I screamed, jumping over the fence in my dress, never taking my eyes off her.

I saw someone at her side, grabbing her around the shoulders. It was Mr. Wells. His glasses were askew, and he had his thin arms wrapped around her whole upper body, and that body was half hanging over the sill. Mrs. Wells was still reaching out to me.

Mr. Wells pulled her back inside, which was no small feat because Mr. Wells was a postmaster and just not that big. When they moved out of my view, who should I see standing there but

Clyde. He gave me a quick look that had none of his mischievous nature in it. Then he was gone.

I just stood there, looking up. My heart pounded like a trapped bird in my chest. I felt like a piece on a chessboard, not able to go forward or backward until someone else pushed me along.

This flu was not like any I'd seen before, attacking Mrs. Wells so fast like that. Two days ago, she'd been a lady with white gloves, and now she looked like a lunatic that the stuck-up Englishman in *Jane Eyre* might keep in his attic.

A bad feeling settled in my stomach. How was I going to keep this flu away from my mama and my papa and my two baby sisters?

Mr. Levy might know the answer. He'd been a teacher in Galveston and the principal of Coward Creek High School before he retired. I was also thinking it'd be nice to feel those polished chess pieces in my hand. Nothing could calm me like a game of chess, to have my mind on it and nothing else.

Flu germs were flooding out of Clyde's house, and I was breathing them in, so I took off down the street to Tillie's.

I stood outside, pacing back and forth, wondering if my one-time best friend would even let me in. Her father was the banker, and she lived in the largest house in town. Except for the Bills'. Theirs was bigger, but I didn't ever go there.

Ivy curled around the posts of Tillie's home. In the springtime, flowers popped out, looking so pretty. Mrs. Lawrence loved flowers. They spilled out of pots all over her porch. The ivy and potted plants gave her house a shaded look, a spot of green in our dusty town.

A flock of blackbirds flew over my head, *caw-caw*ing into the quiet of the street, sending shivers down my spine. A couple of blocks away, I could see two hatless ladies standing in front of Graves Grocery Store.

No one else was out, except for nosy Mrs. Craven peeping at me from behind her store-bought curtains. A lone cow ambled down the wide street. Probably he'd escaped from the pens by the railroad depot.

Out on the long porch came Tillie, looking down at me from the top step. "What are you doing out here, Winnie?" She twisted her brown curls around her finger.

"Well . . . I was waiting for you."

She folded her arms. "Grandpa's not home."

But then, he was standing beside her, the screen door banging behind him.

"Hello, Winnie."

"Hi, Mr. Levy," I said, waving my hand. I felt better just looking at him. If he'd let me in, I could settle myself down in his study with its warm wood and leather-bound books. I could run my hands over that smooth chessboard, breathe in the pipe smoke, and listen to his advice.

The screen door banged again. It was Tillie's mama. My goodness, was everybody coming out here?

"Hello, Winnie. Your grandmother just telephoned for you. She needs you at home." Her big blue eyes looked out of her square face with a kindness Tillie wasn't showing right now. Tillie took after her papa. I thought I resembled her mama more than she did.

"I don't know why she called when her voice can be heard clear across the prairie," I mumbled.

"What, honey?" Mrs. Lawrence asked in her soft, musical

voice. She'd left Coward Creek to be a singer in Galveston when she was young. But then she decided she'd rather get married to Tillie's papa.

"Nothing," I said, but I didn't move.

Tillie's mama played with her daughter's dark hair, running her fingers through it like it was cool pond water.

It must be so nice to have a mama who doesn't hide in the kitchen all the time. Such a mama could protect her family from something bad because she could see it coming.

"Winnie, you need to tell your grandmother the patriotic meeting is cancelled because of the flu. Mr. Ichiro has had it for over a week. He's a widower, you know. No wife to take care of him."

I felt that bird fluttering in my chest again. "Yes, ma'am." Mr. Ichiro was a quiet Japanese man who lived on a rice farm just north of town. How did the flu get up to him?

"I forgot to tell her when I was talking to her on the telephone."

"Yes, ma'am."

"Your grandmother does so much for our soldiers, Winnie. Last week, I saw her rolling bandages with the Red Cross ladies."

She does it to get into that social club, I thought, but I didn't say anything. Mrs. Lawrence wasn't a member either.

"I haven't seen your father at one patriotic meeting, though," she said.

"No, ma'am. He's busy."

"I suppose. Well, you better get home, honey."

I couldn't get my feet to move.

"Grandpa cannot play chess with you today," said Tillie.

Mr. Levy walked down a couple of the steps. His white hair was flying all around his head. "What's wrong, Winnie?"

He always seemed to know my mind better than I knew it myself.

I wondered if he knew what could keep us all from getting sick. But if he did, wouldn't he be telling everybody?

Tillie stepped forward to hear what I was going to say. Her mama was right behind her, resting her hand on the porch post and looking at me.

"I was just wondering, Mr. Levy. Is there anything we can take that would keep us from getting sick with the influenza?"

"Oh, we're not worried about that," said Mrs. Lawrence. "None of us ever seem to get sick."

Tillie looked at her mama in surprise. We all did.

But Mrs. Lawrence's gaze was steady. She must be a little like my mama after all, burying grief so it wouldn't haunt her. Thing is, it seemed to haunt my mama more, even though she buried it deep and silent.

"You want to come in and talk about it, Winnie?" asked Mr. Levy.

I glanced at Tillie. She grabbed her mama's hand and held it. I was sad we weren't friends anymore.

"No, sir. I gotta go home."

Mrs. Lawrence came down a step. "It was good to see you again, Winnie. Come back for a visit real soon. We miss you around here."

Without another word, Tillie went back inside, letting the screen door slam.

I walked very slowly in the wagon ruts, running my fingers through my hair and trying hard not to remember Mrs. Wells's wild eyes. I couldn't imagine what Clyde must be thinking, seeing his mama like that.

3

I saw the two flatirons on the top of the cookstove and knew why I'd been called home. A thick blanket was spread across the kitchen table. A small bowl of water and a stack of wrinkled napkins were on the counter. Clara had found something else for me to do for her tea party, of course.

Without a word to anyone, I sprinkled the linen with water and rolled it. I shoved the wooden handle onto one of the irons and carried the heavy thing over to the table. I'd use the other iron when this one cooled down.

Clara hovered over me while I worked. I wondered why she just didn't do this herself. I was getting warm from the heat of the cookstove and her hot breath on my neck.

"You need to be faster than that," Clara said. "You'll scorch that fine napkin."

I snapped. "I don't need your help!"

"Winifred Alice Grace! Don't you *ever* talk to me that way."

Mama looked up from her mending. "Winnie knows how to iron."

That took the steam out of Clara. She clamped down her lips

on whatever she was about to say next. Clara treated Mama differ-
ently than she treated the rest of us, like she was afraid Mama'd
break right into little pieces if she talked too harshly to her. My
grandmother turned on her heel and was out the door.

And just like that, the black cloud over my head disappeared.
I took a deep breath and got back to my ironing. I glanced at
Mama. I was glad to have her all to myself.

I never knew if she would stick around, though. She might go
polish all the windows in the house or head to the backyard to
tend her vegetables or someplace else besides here talking with
me. Mama was always busy doing something for us. Her hands
were never still. I hoped chattering at her would make her stay.

I tried to think of things she might want to know about. I
knew I couldn't ask her what she thought about or if she ever
thought about me.

My youngest sister Miranda was outside sitting on the
ground, playing the fake piano-on-a-board Papa'd made her. Her
fingers moved over the painted keys. She sidled up to the window
and pressed her small face into the screen. "Joseph's digging Lewis
Locke's grave." She pointed. "See the dirt flying, Mama?"

Mama nodded at her. "Yes, I see it."

Miranda stayed at the screen, her fingers on the mesh. Her
nails were dirty, and her cheeks were smudged. I wondered where
Mary was. I knew *she* wasn't playing in the dirt. Miranda didn't
mind getting messy or not combing her hair or what others might
say. She was always watching, with lots of thoughts on her face.

Her staring seemed to make Mama nervous. "I'll do the ironing, Winnie. Come over here and darn these socks."

Miranda's face fell. I guessed she wanted to be by Mama, too.

I picked up Papa's sock. Miranda wandered back to her silent piano playing.

It wasn't like our mama never said anything. She would smile and talk sometimes, if it was a quiet evening and the work was done and we were all sitting in the parlor together. And she did talk to Papa a lot. I noticed how she relaxed when he was there, as if his presence made everything all right.

But she wasn't like other mamas, those who liked to be around their children. I really wanted to know *why* she wasn't like that.

Nobody ever talked about what happened to her in the 1900 storm. I couldn't help but think on it. There might be some answers there. I wondered did she lose a baby brother. Maybe she forgot to hold his hand and his little body got washed into the creek and I lost the only uncle I'd ever had. And then Clara tore up all his pictures and nobody ever spoke of him again.

"Ouch." I'd stabbed myself right in my thumb with the needle. I should've had my thoughts on the task at hand. I looked up. Mama was intent on the ironing.

I sucked the blood off, careful not to get it on Papa's sock. "Tillie's going to California next year on the train with her Aunt Cora, Mama. She's hoping to be cast in a motion picture and be a star like Lillian Gish."

Mama put her hand against the small of her back and stretched. I wasn't sure she was listening.

"At least, that's what I heard from Effie Becker," I said all in a rush, hoping Mama might look up. "Tillie's not talking to me."

I bit off the thread, putting down Papa's sock and picking up a shirt. I found the hole in the elbow he'd pointed out.

"Tillie's friends with Lessie Craven now. Lessie's mad at me because I beat her at the literary contest last year. She said I must've cheated because nobody two years younger than her could beat her at anything." She'd also spouted off that no coffin maker's daughter would know George Sand and George Eliot were lady writers.

Mama hadn't attended the literary contest. Papa'd been busy making a rosewood dining table for Mrs. Bill, so he wasn't there either.

Clara had come, though, decked out in an old silk dress specially designed for stout women. She sat in the front row, just a few feet away from the stage, and frowned at me when I stopped to think who wrote "I felt a Funeral, in my Brain." A vision of my mama came into my head as I ran over the lines, so I faltered and couldn't remember who the poet was.

I still won the contest, though.

Miranda tapped on the screen, bringing me back to the present. "Nolan's here to see you."

"Where?" I asked, setting my darning aside.

Nolan Field and I were destined to be married, though I wasn't sure he knew it yet. We were like two young lovers haunting the moors of England, except we haunted the creek by my house.

"He was out there in the pecans awhile, looking at the house. Then I saw him go to the bridge."

Mama kept ironing. She didn't care much when I ran off with Nolan.

But Clara did. I slipped out the door quietly just in case her ears were perked up listening for grandchildren trying to do something fun.

I sent our flock of chickens flying and took off down the road skirting the cemetery, my bare feet hitting the cool dirt. I waved at Joseph walking away with his shovel. It looked like he was finished with Lewis's grave.

I didn't like the thought of sleeping when just out my window was an open grave in the cemetery and an empty coffin in the barn. Dark dreams tonight, I was sure. On the nights before funerals, I stared at the ceiling, my eyes wide and sleepless.

Coward Creek was clear and wide and never quiet. The birds and insects made sure of that. I even saw a whistling swan the other day. I told Mama about it because she had a soft spot for birds, always throwing out bread crumbs to them, talking to them like they were dogs or cats.

I asked her if she'd ever seen one of those swans before. She shook her head. Mama liked birds, but she didn't like the creek. She hated the water.

I ran on the wood planks, looking through the cracks to the water below.

Right in the middle of the bridge sat Nolan, with his dirty feet dangling, throwing rocks. He offered me a smooth, flat one, but I took one of the bigger stones. I liked the cold weight of it. I threw the rock, watching it arc, waiting for, then pleased by the deep *plunk* as it hit the water.

A train rattled by on its track not far from us, black smoke billowing out of its stack. I counted the boxcars.

Nolan didn't say anything until we saw the conductor in the red caboose. Then he stood up and shouted out, "Hey there!" Nolan either wanted to be a farmer, a soldier, or a conductor.

One of our favorite things to do was to be here on this bridge together. Sometimes we'd fish. Maybe try to spot a gator. Or wave at the finely dressed fellas and their girls traveling in automobiles back and forth from Houston and Galveston. Coward Creek was a small town, only about five hundred people, but lots of folks traveled through it.

"Did you know Mrs. Wells has the influenza?" I asked, taking another stone.

He nodded.

"I read an article in the *Galveston Daily News* today," I said. "People are in a panic."

The crickets were loud, welcoming dusk.

"We gotta think of some way not to get sick, Nolan."

He didn't reply. Nolan thought about things for a while before he said them.

I dropped my voice to a whisper, out of habit, always careful of what might worry Mama. "Mr. Coldman said people in Philadelphia are leaving their dead in the streets to be hauled away. It's like the bubonic plague from hundreds of years ago."

Nolan slid me a glance. His eyes were deep blue like the way-out sea must be. "I bet old Mr. Coldman was wishing he was in Philadelphia."

He was wrong about that. Mr. Coldman might be the undertaker, but he wouldn't wish death on anyone, especially a death as vicious as a flu death. Folks were either dying fast or lingering on for a month before the breath finally went out of them.

"Mr. Craven has something that'll keep it away," Nolan said.

"Well, what is it?"

"Vicks VapoRub. You stick it up your nostrils every day."

My nose twitched when I thought of that strong-smelling goop. "You sure that'll work?"

"That's what the advertisement in the *Chronicle* said."

If the paper was printing it, it was probably true. Finally, some good news. We didn't have any Vicks ourselves. Last winter, we'd used up the last of Mrs. Hayward's when Mary had been sick with a chest cold. Mary was always getting sick. Her weak lungs, Clara said, were from Papa's side of the family.

"Is Mr. Craven selling it?" I asked.

"He's all out, he *says*," he said, slapping a mosquito on his arm.

"All out! Can we get it from someplace else?"

"Everybody's out of it. Craven's ordering more."

"There's got to be someplace else that has it. There's got to be!" All of a sudden, I was desperate to get some VapoRub. The more I thought about it, the more I had to have it.

Nolan skipped a stone across the surface, one, two, three. "When I was asking Mr. Craven about flu medicine, he kept glancing under the counter, like he was guilty about something."

"You think he's got some?"

"I'm going to sneak in after dark and see what's in there."

"You're going to steal it?!"

"People are dying from this flu, Winnie."

"No one's died in Coward Creek, yet."

"They just buried Edna Bloom two weeks ago, right over there," he said, pointing to the cemetery.

"You know she was a nurse in Galveston," I said, glancing toward the graves and quickly back. "Her mama and papa just wanted her buried close." Close to my bedroom window, it seemed.

"And Lewis? What about him?"

"He was at Ellington Field. Everybody's getting it in the army camps."

"Well, Craven shouldn't be hoarding the stuff."

"It's still stealing," I said, hitting my cheek too late. I wiped the blood and black mosquito parts on the railing.

Nolan's mouth set down in a hard way. He rolled the stones around in his hand, not looking at me. "You know how the Cravens embarrassed my mama."

I blushed. Mrs. Field had been banished from the Missionary Baptist Church because Mrs. Craven had said she wasn't walking in the Christian way.

The preacher hadn't wanted to do it. But Mrs. Craven, with her little eyes and fat fingers, had argued at the church meeting it wasn't proper. She told Mrs. Field to her face she had wicked hips.

Nolan's mama was so humiliated, she stopped coming to town. I rarely saw her off their property anymore. She was always so sweet to me, braiding my hair in long plaits and tucking wild-flowers in the folds, making me feel like a flower princess.

Jimmy Craven tried to tease Nolan about his mama at school, walking around the hall with swishy hips. Nolan socked him in the nose. Blood spurted out, and Jimmy sobbed, but his nose wasn't broken. Nolan got tanned for that one, but Jimmy didn't ever say one more word about it.

Lessie, Jimmy's older sister, was always calling me "wild" for going out with "that Field boy" whose family got banished from the Baptist Church.

I shrugged it off, not respecting Lessie as much as I did one of our hogs.

Clara was not pleased with me for the trouble. Mrs. Craven was treasurer of the ladies' club she was dying to get into.

"You can't steal it," I said to Nolan, "even if you have cause to be mad at them."

"Aren't you worried about your family getting sick?"

"Yes, I am."

"Well, the Cravens aren't."

"Promise me you won't, Nolan."

He dropped some stones in my hand and closed my fingers on them. His hand felt soft and warm on mine and gave me a sweet shiver. He shrugged a shoulder and nodded.

I nodded too, but couldn't help but wonder how we'd get into Mr. Craven's store if we needed to.

4

*T*ombstones, and black suits and skirts. That was mostly what I saw as I leaned over the sill of my bedroom window.

And men in uniform with their knee-high boots and wide-brimmed army hats. Lewis Locke would've liked all these folks at his funeral. Half the town had turned out, following the marching soldiers and the wagon carrying the flag-draped casket all the way over from the Presbyterian Church.

Now they were all gathered together, some under the shade of the only graveyard tree, singing "The Old Rugged Cross." Edna Bloom's fresh grave was a bit away from Lewis's. I noticed the mourners kept their distance from both graves, probably because they were worried about catching the influenza.

Tillie stood by Lessie Craven, their hats touching. I was sure they were whispering and not singing.

I knew it made Tillie feel special to be Lessie's friend. Lessie was fourteen and liked by half the school. That would be the boy part of the school.

Clara had jostled for a spot next to Mrs. Bill, the principal of our school and the richest woman in town. Funerals were a perfect place for a lady to make a good impression, Clara said. No public wailing or carrying-on. Just a dab at the eyes with a clean white handkerchief.

Some people thought the Grace family should be at all the funerals just because we lived next to the cemetery. And because Papa made coffins and worked for Mr. Coldman.

Clara would plead with Papa and Mama, but they wouldn't go. I'd try to go missing on funeral days, but Clara usually found me.

My earliest memory was in the cemetery.

Singing hymns by an open grave.

The smell of turned-up dirt in my nose. Cold, deep dirt that smelled different than the dirt on top.

The whole idea of death didn't seem right to me. It didn't fit. How could someone be alive one day, breathing the fresh air, laughing, talking, and then turn up cold and stiff the next? Nothing orderly about that. God messed up something there, I thought.

But here I was, hanging out the window, trying to see what was going on down there. Dead people and funerals pulled at me at the same time they scared the good sense out of me.

I was partly scared because of the ghosts. If I was sure a body would just stay in the ground where it was put, then I probably wouldn't have been so worried. The thought of them coming out at night and hovering over their tombstones sent shivers down my spine. And if they wanted to haunt some humans, we were the closest ones.

Just now, I imagined I saw Lewis's face, wispy like a ghost's, floating above his open grave. He had a little smile, like he was amused by me, like he always was when he wasn't dead.

I remembered seeing him at the train station, grinning at his mama even though he was fixing to be shipped off to fight the Germans. He'd looked so handsome in his uniform. He'd given me just that same little smile. It made me feel a little weak in the knees even though I was in love with Nolan Field.

And now Lewis was dead. He hadn't even made it to Europe.

Folks flooded out of the cemetery. Tillie and Lessie linked arms and came my way. They wore black gloves and dark dresses. Lessie tried to pull Tillie toward the dirt road, but she sauntered over to my window.

"Hey," I said.

"Hi," she said. She took off her mourning hat, which had a crepe tail streaming out the back of it.

Tillie glanced back at Lessie, who I could tell was giving me a look of pure venom, even though she was pretty far off. "Don't you like Lessie's wool serge dress? Her mama bought it from a shop in Houston."

"It looks too hot for a sunny day."

"You didn't want to come to the funeral? I thought you liked Lewis."

"Yes, I did like him, but I didn't want to come."

Tillie gave me a look. She knew I didn't like funerals. "I haven't seen you at the house in a while," she said. "I mean, before yesterday."

I shook my head, confused. "It didn't seem like you wanted me there."

"I would if you wanted to see *me*," she said.

"I do, Tillie."

Tillie always had to be in first place in everybody's hearts: her mama's, her papa's, her grandpa's, her school friends', and mine, too. She was always everyone's favorite, but nothing seemed to be enough to fill some empty hole inside of her.

"Come on, Tillie!" yelled Lessie. That girl was impatient.

Tillie ignored her, watching me instead, pulling at her dark curls. We both had brown hair, but hers was the color of a dark brownie and mine looked like muddy creek water.

I'd actually become best friends with Tillie at a funeral. We'd been nine years old. Old Mrs. Straw had died during one of our freezes. Almost all of Coward Creek had crowded into her musty-smelling parlor with its heavy curtains and dark furniture. It was a cold January. Ice had crunched under our feet as we walked to her house.

Tillie and I had slipped out during the mourning and moaning. We perched on the fence, swinging our stockinged feet, her stockings being made of thick fine silk and mine of cotton with holes in the toes.

I had been glad to be out in the cold air, poofs of my breath coming out, reassuring me I was alive and not dead like old Mrs. Straw. And Tillie said, "It's so ugly here."

Her voice was as flat as a pancake. She'd looked out over the prairie, one hand on the fence, one pushed into her fox muff. Such an unhappy feeling drifted from her to me. So I told her a funny story about two mockingbirds fighting, which made her laugh.

I studied her face now, looking up at me from below my window. She still had that same look in her eyes, like something was missing. I knew she thought that missing piece wasn't in Coward Creek.

"Lessie has a relative," she said to me, "who works in the motion picture industry."

I knew the truth about that, but Tillie looked so hopeful, I couldn't bear to tell her.

"Winnie, do you think you're smarter than me? Because that's what Lessie says you think."

I thought for a moment. "You know more about movie stars and Hollywood than me."

She smiled. "I do, don't I?"

"Yes, you do."

"And did you say I'd never be a movie star?"

"No, Tillie. I never said that."

She gestured toward Lessie with her hat, its black veil swaying to and fro. "Lessie thinks I'll be one."

I nodded.

"Well, what do *you* think, Winnie?" She looked like she was about to cry.

"You will, Tillie."

She sighed, like she was relieved, and a flicker of a smile came to her lips. As if me saying it meant it would happen.

I wanted to tell her I missed her. And she looked up at me like she wanted to tell me something, too.

She put her hat back on her head. "Is it on right?" She must like her new hat. I thought she might be fishing for a compliment.

"It's pretty," I said. "Hey, maybe I'll borrow it from you sometime." Then I realized I'd only be wearing it to a funeral and blushed for saying such a silly thing.

She laughed. "I can't see you in a hat, Winnie."

I shrugged a shoulder. "No, I can't either."

She glanced back toward Lessie, who was red in the face. "I'd better go. Billy Bill invited Lessie and me over for angel cake."

I waved a hand at her. "Bye."

"Bye, Winnie."

I watched Tillie and her new best friend walk away.

There are worse things than losing a best friend, but just right then, it didn't feel like there was.

hid in my room for a while, but Mary found me. I looked up from my book, irritated. I had known Clara would give me something to do, even though it was supposed to be a day of rest. But it turned out Clara wasn't the one looking for me.

Papa wanted me to get tablet paper and a pencil and meet him in the yard. I knew what that meant. It was not welcome news. Papa could read well enough, but numbers were tricky for him.

Barefooted Will Frazier was out by the hog pen, talking to Papa. I walked over to them slowly. Ooh. I couldn't tell if it was our hogs that smelled so bad, or Will. I took a couple of steps back. Will was in Mary's grade at school. She was the only one who would sit in the desk beside his. Those Fraziers didn't take to bathing.

"I need you to come with me, Winnie," Papa said in his serious somebody-has-died voice.

Will rubbed his red eyes and leaky nose. I backed up a bit more, wondering if he might have been exposed to the influenza. Papa frowned. I took a big swallow, trying to push the fear down my throat.

"Where's Mr. Coldman?" I asked.

"His services aren't needed on this one." Papa put his hand on Will's shoulder. "Let me get my stick."

I watched Papa walk away. Will didn't say anything, just sniffled and looked off toward the creek. I didn't know the Fraziers very well. Will's father worked for the railroad company, off and on. He'd moved his family to Coward Creek at the beginning of summer. Will had a little sister, Mae. I hoped she wasn't the one who had passed.

"Let's go this way!" Papa yelled from the barn door, waving us toward him and the railroad tracks.

He carried the dead stick, which is what I called it. Papa forbade me to say that in front of anybody else.

The dead stick was several inches taller than Papa and had marks on it, at the top for the length of the body, and at the middle and the bottom for the children and the width of the shoulders. There were names beside the marks. That one stick was a record of all the coffins Papa had built.

Papa took us away from the road. I knew he was avoiding all the staring eyes and questions of the townspeople. We crossed one set of railroad tracks and walked through the prairie grass. Looking to the west, I could see the poles and tracks of the electric train in the distance.

The Fraziers lived in the Coward Creek Hotel, which was a two-story boarding house owned by the Painters. The hotel was positioned between two sets of tracks, so the Painters could rent to travelers coming in on the steam train or the electric train.

Will was really crying now.

"Will," Papa asked, "did I hear you almost got ate by a gator?"

Will's head jerked up. "I don't think she was going to eat me, Mr. Grace. She was protecting her babies."

"But she chased you?"

"No, sir, she didn't chase me. But she opened her mouth and snapped."

Papa kind of laughed. "How many babies did she have?"

Will wiped his nose with the back of his hand. "She had thirteen babies!"

"Thirteen! I've never seen that many gators in one place." He looked over at Will askance. "You sure it was thirteen? You're not pulling my leg, are you?"

"It was thirteen, Mr. Grace. Zeke and I counted all the gators."

"Are they still there?" Papa asked.

"Oh, no, sir. They're gone."

"Well, I'm sorry to have missed them."

Papa was trying to get Will's mind off the death in his family, for sure. It didn't work for me, and I doubted it worked for Will.

My stomach felt queasy. I again wondered who was dead and what they died of. I thought of Zeke and Anna Painter, black-haired twins who went to my school. If someone in their boarding house had the flu, they could have it, too. My hands felt all sweaty holding the pencil and tablet. I wiped my palms on my dress.

I tried to think calmly. I didn't know if this *was* influenza.

We went into the kitchen through the back door. I watched Will run off around the side of the house. Papa nudged me with his hand on the back of my neck to get me through the door. I told myself the body in here was no different than those dead bodies at the cemetery. But those dead bodies scared me, too.

Mrs. Painter greeted us. "Come in, come in." The kitchen was a mess, with dirty bowls and raw vegetables strewn about. Something good was cooking in a big pot on the cookstove. Mr. Painter might own the boarding house, but everyone knew it was his wife that ran the place.

Mrs. Painter had the same dark hair and eyes her twins did. She wore a pretty silver crucifix around her neck. "You just missed Reverend Patch. He went out the front." She poured Mrs. Frazier a cup of coffee. Steam rose up from the mug. I wondered where Zeke and Anna were.

Mrs. Frazier was sitting at the big table. One of her arms was wrapped around her daughter, pulling her in close. I was so glad to see Mae. She went to the younger kid's school with Miranda.

"Come this way, Mr. Grace," said Mrs. Painter.

Papa nodded at me and followed her, holding onto the dead stick. I stared at the closed door for a moment, thinking about the body in the parlor. I took a breath, sat down at the table, and pulled out my paper.

I wished Papa had told me who had died. It was probably Mr. Frazier, with the way all his kin were acting. But it would be a terrible mistake on my part if it were another boarder instead.

I plunged in. "Do you have any special wishes, Mrs. Frazier?" It was best to keep things general at first.

She wasn't taking me in. There was a nothing look in her eyes. She pulled Mae in closer and looked out the window. Mae's lower lip was pushed out. She buried her head in her mama's shoulder and put her small hand on her mama's chin.

So I put down my pencil and looked out the window, too. The Interurban, the electric train running between Houston and Galveston, went by. Even after it was gone, we kept looking out over the prairie. The sun was big and orange and low in the sky.

Papa came back in with Mrs. Painter. He leaned the stick against the wall. I couldn't tell which mark was Mr. Frazier's because there were so many of them.

Mrs. Painter lit the coal oil lamp in the middle of the table and cleared off some dirty dishes. She put a cup of hot coffee in front of Papa. "Do you drink coffee, Winnie?"

"Yes, ma'am," I said, "but—"

"Let me get you one then." She bustled over to the cookstove without looking back. My stomach felt too sour for me to drink any coffee. I didn't tell her that because I thought she just wanted something to do. She gave me a mug that looked just like Papa's.

"Thank you," I said.

Papa looked at the blank piece of paper in front of me. He took a sip of his coffee.

"He came home sick two days ago," said Mrs. Frazier to Papa, her voice lonely and empty. "I've never seen the flu act so fast."

Oh, no. This was not what I wanted to hear. My foot started tapping until Papa put a hand on my knee to slow it down. Mae looked from me to Papa, her eyes so sweet and young. I felt ashamed. Here I was worrying about myself, and little Mae had just lost her father.

"Otis was a large man," Mrs. Frazier said, squeezing Mae so tight I saw the girl wince. "Healthy. A big eater."

"Yes, he was," said Mrs. Painter. "He always had second helpings, sometimes thirds."

"How does my Otis get the influenza on Friday and die on

Sunday?" Mrs. Frazier looked so lost I wanted to answer her. But I couldn't think of anything to say. Mrs. Painter could, though.

"Doc Fox said it works on some people fast and some people slow." Mrs. Painter sat at the table with us and took her boarder's hand.

Mrs. Frazier pulled away. "It's usually the old and the young who die. Not the healthy ones."

"Look at all the soldiers who are dying of it. Strong young men, like Lewis Locke. This influenza is different."

Things got quiet except for the sound of Papa sipping his coffee and the stew simmering on the stove. I held the hot cup in my hands, feeling the heat of it on my fingers. I heard footsteps up above us and then on the stairs. A man I didn't recognize was at the door of the kitchen, with a suitcase in his hand.

"Why, Mr. Horn, where are you going?" asked Mrs. Painter.

He glanced at Mrs. Frazier. "I'm not staying here."

Mrs. Painter hustled him out the door right quick. We could hear their voices in the hallway: his insistent, hers a little angry.

Mr. Painter stumbled through the kitchen door, the smell of liquor on him. He was unshaven, and his suspenders were off his shoulders, dangling at his sides. "What'sss with Otissss?" he asked, his words all slurred and sloppy.

Papa stood at once and took him out the door. Everybody in town knew Mr. Painter and Mr. Frazier liked to drink together, which was why Mr. Frazier kept getting fired from the railroad company. They always hired him back, though.

"We have our own wood," Mrs. Frazier said to me.

I nodded. It was all right for her to give us the wood. But I knew Papa wouldn't be able to use it for Mr. Frazier's coffin because the burial would have to be in a day or so. It took Papa several days to make a coffin from scratch. In order to get it done on time, he'd need to use his own already-cut wood. He'd just stack up Mrs. Frazier's wood to use on someone else's coffin later. No need to tell Mrs. Frazier that.

I could hear Mr. Painter yelling at the boarder. Then a door slammed.

"We have it in my brother's barn. Pine."

"Okay," I said. Sometimes people supplied their own wood.

Papa came back in and sat down. Now Mrs. Painter was yelling at Mr. Painter. I poured some more coffee for Papa. Mrs. Frazier hadn't touched hers.

"They have their own wood, Papa."

"How much is it going to cost, Mr. Grace?"

I sat back down and picked up my pencil. I figured she wasn't going to be able to pay for Mr. Coldman's hearse. "There's the cost of digging the grave—"

"No," said Mrs. Frazier. "The railroad company said they'd take the body to Galveston. Otis's mother wants him buried down there."

"Okay," I said, feeling sad for Mrs. Frazier. I wondered if she minded that her husband's grave would be so far away. Maybe I just felt that way because our cemetery was so close. "Then there's just the cost of the labor."

Her brow wrinkled up. "I might have trouble paying you right away, Mr. Grace. But I would like a nice coffin."

Papa nodded. I could see him thinking. I knew what he was thinking about. It was hard to figure out what Mrs. Frazier could trade. Why, they didn't have anything. They didn't own any land or furniture or family heirlooms or chickens. But there was one thing Mrs. Frazier could do better than most anyone else.

"Papa," I said, "you sure do like custard pie. Mrs. Frazier, didn't you win the pie contest on the Fourth this year?"

I remembered because Lessie's mama had been more than a little put out. She usually won the pie contest. But this year, much to my delight, Mrs. Frazier swooped in and took the top prize from Mrs. Craven.

Lessie had been as mad as her mama. She couldn't believe a newcomer had won. Someone not even from Coward Creek had stolen away first place, Lessie had said. A stranger.

It wasn't like Mrs. Frazier didn't have kin around here. Her brother lived on a farm somewhere over in Friendswood. But Lessie talked like she wasn't even from Texas.

"Mama's a good baker," whispered Mae.

"You do make a fine pie," said Papa. "I bought a piece at the picnic."

"I can make you a custard pie," Mrs. Frazier said. "But that's not enough for two days' work."

She was right about that.

"I guess you don't know how much I loved your pie," said Papa.

"All right, Mr. Grace." She looked relieved. "We'll be leaving soon to go live with my brother and his family. But I'll make you one before I go."

"There's no hurry," he said. "Friendswood is close by."

"All right then."

Papa stood. "We'd best get home. Can your brother get the wood out to me?"

"He'll have it to you tonight." She kissed the top of Mae's head.

We left Mrs. Frazier and Mae alone in the kitchen. We walked back along the tracks. Papa poked the dead stick in the ground as we went, not looking too worried about being exposed to the influenza.

I couldn't understand why Papa was so carefree. Not much bothered him. Not even hurricanes. In the last twenty years, two bad hurricanes had come to Coward Creek. I wasn't around during the 1900 storm. But I was nine years old during the hurricane in 1915.

I remembered Papa wouldn't leave the house. Mama was screaming as loud as the wind. And I kept thinking about the new brick schoolhouse for the older kids and how that might shelter us better. Mama was yelling it was the same kind of storm as the one in 1900. But Papa said we had to stay in the house. Everything would be fine, he said.

We had been fine, except for the part where Mama screamed.

Coffin building never troubled Papa either. I thought he enjoyed it even. Maybe he was used to death because he made a living around it.

My stomach still felt queasy. I wondered if I had a fever. I put my hand to my forehead. It was a little warm and sweaty.

Papa laughed a little.

"Papa, what's so funny?" I asked. It was no time for laughing. Things were dire. If big old Mr. Frazier could die of the influenza, I was sure my papa could, too.

He just shook his head.

"Tell me, Papa."

"Well, I was just thinking about something Mr. Craven said to me yesterday, how sad it was that I had three girls and no sons." He glanced over at me like he expected me to say something.

"I don't see what's wrong with girls."

"I don't either," he said.

I studied Papa's calm face. I couldn't help but think he just didn't understand about things, how bad they could get. I knew, even if he didn't, that someone else was going to die of the influenza. It wasn't through with us yet.

6

*R*ipples stood on her back cat feet, her front paws swiping the air, watching me milk our cow. She wanted a drink. I took a quick look out the barn door. No Clara. So I squirted some milk at her, hitting her just south of her mouth. She dropped down, her pink tongue out and flicking at her chin. Cassie looked back at me, mooing loudly, unhappy with my fun.

I put my cheek on her side, welcoming her warmth in the coolness of the morning. "No more playing, Cassie."

She munched on her grain while I finished milking. The sun was coming up, coloring the sky pink and orange.

"Winnie!"

I saw Papa coming from the privy. I stood.

"You're going to be late for school," he said, holding a *Chronicle* in his hand. His eyes were tired. He'd been up a long time already, working on Mr. Frazier's coffin.

"Papa," I said. "Does the paper have any news about the influenza?"

He *pshawed* at me. "You just had the flu last spring, and you seem to be fine."

Mr. Frazier wasn't fine, I thought. But I wouldn't say that to

Papa. He might be a calm sort of person, but he didn't like his daughters sassing him.

Ripples followed me and the bucket of milk into the kitchen. The smells of frying ham and baking biscuits greeted me. Coffee was boiling on the cookstove.

"You've just now finished, Winnie?" Clara fussed. "I guess it's up to me to strain the milk. Sit down for your breakfast."

"I don't want to go to school, Clara," said Mary, her gray eyes as big and round as two moons. "I don't want to get the flu."

Mary was the only one of us who got Mama's pretty looks, although Mama's prettiness was sad and tired these days.

I'd seen pictures of my mama when she was my age. We didn't have any of her when she was younger than twelve. Those had been washed away in the 1900 storm.

Mama as a girl could have been Mary staring back at me. Except Mama's eyes in the photographs seemed to have the same inward look they had now.

The boys already hovered around Mary. Her face was perfectly shaped, like an egg. Her hair was dark and curly. Such a sweet happiness radiated from her that you broke into a smile when she smiled. She hated the freckles sprinkled across her nose, but I liked them.

"You're going, young lady," Clara said to Mary. "Winnie, you're to come right home today. I need to get this house spick-and-span ready for my tea tomorrow."

I squinted at Clara while I ate my ham, thinking about her standing by Mrs. Bill at the funeral yesterday. I knew the real reason Clara was making us go to school. It had nothing to do with us learning something.

"What, Winnie? What?" Clara demanded.

Even though Mrs. Bill was rich, she was real nice. She loaned me lots of books; the last one was *Wuthering Heights*. That was a good one, all about how much Catherine loved that wild gypsy boy Heathcliff. I expect Nolan had a touch of Heathcliff in him.

"Nothing," I said, still chewing on my ham.

"What do you mean, *nothing*?"

"I mean I have nothing on my mind, *ma'am*."

I was lying. I had a whole lot of stuff on my mind, and all those thoughts were banging into one another. Maybe Nolan was right. The Cravens were no-good rascals. Maybe we should steal the medicine. But just the *thought* of breaking into that store made my stomach feel tied up in knots.

"Margaret," Clara said, looking over at Mama smearing butter on steaming biscuits. "I declare! You're raising your number-one daughter to be rude!"

Clara was always declaring something.

"Answer me straight, Winnie!"

How did I get put in the same family as her? Even Mrs. Bill would look at me and say, "How are *you* Clara's granddaughter?" From the way she said it, I knew it was a compliment.

"Answer me!" yelled Clara.

"I was just wondering why we were going to school when there's flu raging through the country and if it had anything to do with Mrs. Bill being the principal and the mother-in-law of Queen Bea."

"You will not call young Mrs. Bill that! Do you hear me?"

I stared hard into Clara's eyes, telling her all sorts of things with my hunched-over eyebrows and my pushed-out lips. Like:

I know you would sacrifice your entire beloved family just to please Queen Bea.

Queen Bea was the president and founder of the Coward Creek Ladies' Club, setting it up for the mutual improvement and betterment of the backward women in the town. She was married to Billy Bill's older brother, Tom Bill.

Clara'd heard Queen Bea was a do-gooder, at least as far as the war was concerned, so my grandmother became the most patriotic woman I ever saw. She knitted more socks and scarves than anybody in town. I could only feel sorry for the soldiers because surely her clicking needles had twisted grumpiness into the yarn.

"Margaret, are you going to let her talk to me that way?"

Mama kept buttering. Clara left the pail of milk on the washstand and stormed out of the kitchen. Good riddance.

The first time we met Queen Bea was on Declaration Day, about one year back, May 1917. Declaration Day, the day we honored the dead, was held in the cemetery. All the women dressed in white and wore their best hats. Nobody noticed what the men wore.

Tom Bill had driven up in his father's shiny black touring car, interrupting our singing of the *Battle Hymn of the Republic*. We all huddled around to see his new bride. Puffed up with pride, Tom Bill held out his hand to help Queen Bea down. She had the longest eyelashes I'd ever seen and hair the color of kernel corn. I hated kernel corn.

But Clara, she wanted into Queen Bea's club something fierce. Nothing, and I mean nothing, meant as much to her as those town ladies.

I smoothed back Mary's silky hair. Not even us, for sure.

Sometimes I thought everyone in my family went around with closed eyes. It was so frustrating to be the only one who knew bad things were coming. I glanced over at Mama's back. Or at least knew they were coming and would do something about it.

I had to talk to Nolan today. I was getting desperate.

7

Nobody in my house would watch out for us but me. Papa never worried. Clara was too set on moving up in Coward Creek society to think about anything else. Mama wouldn't come out of the kitchen.

I needed advice straight from the horse's mouth and that horse would be Dr. Fox. He was a Quaker, and a deep thinker besides. Although, he was one of those thinkers who always seemed to be thinking about something other than what you wanted to talk about. So there was no telling if talking to him would be of any help.

I leaned across the aisle at school and whispered to Effie Becker, "I need to talk to Dr. Fox after school. You think he'll be at the hospital?"

Dr. Fox's hospital was on the second floor of Effie's house. Her papa rented the space to the town. The upstairs was haunted from when it'd been a hotel, so Mrs. Becker wouldn't live up there.

Effie said to never let them put you in Room 2 because that's where the little girl clutching the eyeless doll lived. She died in the cholera epidemic in 1900 and had never left.

Effie leaned away from me. "Are you sick?"

"Oh, no," I said, thinking Effie was looking a little pale herself until I remembered that was her usual color.

"Well, I don't think he's going to be back for a while. Mrs. Fox told my mama he was in Friendswood. There's lots of flu cases over there."

That sent a ripple of fear through my insides. I glanced at Nolan's empty desk. Where was he? His absence only added to my sack of worries.

"I heard you went with your papa," said Effie, her eyes wide, "to measure Mr. Frazier for his coffin."

"Yes, I did go with my papa."

"Did you see . . . Mr. Frazier?"

"No, I didn't, Effie."

She nodded. "Did he die of the influenza then?"

"I'm afraid he did."

"Miss Livingston?" asked Jimmy Craven, sitting right behind me. Jimmy had an almost perfect face until he opened his mouth. Then all that handsomeness just turned ugly and you wondered what God was thinking to waste it on him.

"My daddy says that German spies are spreading influenza germs in theaters and in churches. They came here secretly in their U-boats right into Boston Harbor."

Eddie Payne pushed Jimmy's shoulder. "The Germans are getting it, too, you idiot."

"My daddy says they had it first, and now they're bringing it over here to infect Americans."

Now Eddie Payne was looking at Jimmy like he believed him. Eddie was no coward. I'd seen him kill a water moccasin. But I guess you can be afraid of one thing and not of another.

"We're all going to get that influenza and the Germans are going to start winning the war," said Jimmy to the quiet class. He had cast a spell over us with our own fear.

You had to feel sorry for Jimmy, though. His papa was a sour-faced man who would stare at you when you went into his store. A couple of months ago, Mr. Craven had to go to Judge Long's court on account of him being cruel to animals. He got mad at a cow and stuck it with a fish spear. The judge made him pay twenty-one dollars and thirty-five cents.

"The Germans are most certainly not spreading the influenza," said Miss Livingston.

I liked Miss Livingston, her big blue eyes, and the way she held her little Yankee hands together in front of her when she talked. She turned back to writing the poem "Ghost House" on the blackboard: *I dwell in a lonely house I know.* I noticed the chalk was shaking a little as she wrote the words.

Jimmy's whispering was close to my ear: "Your friend Mr. Levy's a German, ain't he? Not to mention a Jew. I bet he's spreading the flu. My daddy said he was the one talking to Mrs. Wells when she keeled over."

Tillie was sitting right in front of me. She must've heard because her ears turned pink. I whipped around. "Mr. Levy's Dutch, not German. He was born in America, and he's not spreading the flu!"

I hadn't realized I was yelling until I saw a slow grin crawl across Jimmy's face. Turning back around, I was confronted with all the wide eyes of the half-empty class and of Tillie and of Miss Livingston.

Tillie gave me a thank-you smile before straightening in her seat. I was so pleased I almost forgot I was about to get into trouble for disrupting the class. But Miss Livingston just nodded at me like that was the last word on the subject and began writing the poem again: *That vanished many a summer ago.*

"Winnie, I know why you're defending those Germans," Jimmy whispered, sounding angrier now. "Your daddy's a spy."

Again losing my head, I turned on him quick. "Papa's not a spy!"

"My daddy said he hasn't bought one Liberty Bond!"

"He has too!" Papa was trying to pay off one bond. We didn't have as much money as some folks, but Papa wouldn't want me to say so. I thought Clara should sell all her pretty dishes and things so we could buy more bonds. But she'd never do that.

"And he doesn't attend the patriotic meetings. Why's that? I'll tell you why. He's in cahoots with the Germans."

"Leave her alone!" yelled Tillie.

Now it was my turn to give her a smile of gratitude.

Jimmy set his jaw like he might say something more, but he didn't. Tillie's father had bought more Liberty Bonds than anyone else in town, even the Bills.

"Quiet," said Miss Livingston, but handling an unruly class wasn't one of her strengths. I planned on being a teacher one day. But I was going to have my class in order. I'd send someone like Jimmy Craven running home to his mean old papa, with me switching his behind the whole way.

"There are enemies among us, my daddy says. Those Germans are cunning and vile."

"That's enough!" said Miss Livingston, pressing her fingers to her forehead. I knew how she felt. He was giving me a headache, too.

Vile. Jimmy was too stupid to know what that word meant. He probably didn't even know how to spell it.

I saw his eyes slide over to Effie Becker. He stared at her hard and mean. Then he moved over to an empty desk away from her. She had her head down.

I put all my anger into my eyes and shot it right at Jimmy. Effie's brother was off fighting in France. Nobody could say anything bad about the loyalty of that family. Anyway, Jimmy's concerns didn't seem to keep him from gobbling up the sweet apple strudel from the Becker's bakery.

Jimmy's face was set into that same mean look his papa always wore. But I also saw something else there. He looked scared. Seeing that made me scared, too.

In the middle of all this, Mrs. Bill walked in, her heels *tap-tap-tapping* on the wooden floor. We all got quiet real quick. Her back was all stiff and straight, just like Mama's.

She gestured for our teacher to move away from the blackboard. Miss Livingston, her raised hand still gripping the white chalk, cast a sad look at the ghostlike words of Mr. Robert Frost's poem. Like she was afraid she'd never be able to finish writing it. She grabbed the side of her desk, and the chalk dropped to the floor. What was wrong with her?

Mrs. Bill didn't seem to notice. Taking a breath, she said, "Clyde Wells has the influenza."

I heard Tillie gasp. Then the class seemed to all stop breathing at once.

How could it be? I thought of Clyde's face in his window.

"Students," continued Mrs. Bill, "the school is closing for now. We'll let your parents know when it reopens."

Miss Livingston collapsed into her chair. Mrs. Bill turned to her, surprise on her face. "Are you all right, Lena?"

Our teacher held her stomach. "I feel a little ill." She closed her eyes. "I'll be all right."

I was frozen with fear. Miss Livingston had the Spanish influenza.

8

I leaned against the brick wall at the top of the steps, waiting for Mary. Pulling open the heavy door, I peered down the hallway. It was pretty quiet. Not many had come to school today. Those that did seemed to be out here on the steps or out in the yard.

My poor teacher wasn't anywhere to be seen. Neither was Mrs. Bill, who had gone to her office to telephone her husband. She wanted him to pick up our sick schoolteacher in their automobile and take her home.

Miss Livingston lived with her father in a house close to the park. It was just the two of them. He worked at the bank and played the horn in the town band. Everyone liked him. He was the kind of person who just came on in and made himself at home, no matter where he was.

I looked down the crowded steps. Huddled together at the bottom like a pack of hungry coyotes were Lessie Craven, her brother Jimmy, and two boys from Lessie's class who were sweet on her. They were laughing, not looking at all concerned about Miss Livingston.

Tillie was down there with them. She liked being with the

older kids. Now that she was Lessie's friend, she was asked to picnics in Kemah and even to Billy Bill's big birthday party. A twelve-year-old girl shouldn't be around a sixteen-year-old boy. I knew that even if her mama didn't.

Lessie glanced up at me, her haughty chin up in the air. I had the feeling she was waiting for me. Lessie was a girl bully. Boy bullies hit you in the nose. Girls like Lessie picked on the soft-hearted with cruel words. She didn't bother me. But there wasn't a girl with a more sensitive nature than my sister Mary.

The doors flew open. My heart started pumping.

But it wasn't Miss Livingston. It was Anna and Zeke. Mrs. Painter shouldn't have let them come to school. They'd been exposed to the influenza. I wondered how long it took before symptoms started showing up. I heard you could catch it quick.

"Hi, Winnie," said Anna.

"Hi," I said, moving down a step. "Is Mary coming?" I always had to wait for my sister. Her classroom was upstairs, and she liked to visit with all her friends.

"I'm not sure—"

"She was," said Zeke. He stuck his hands in his pockets and looked down, being shy.

"Did you see my mother's peanut butter candy recipe in the *Coward Creek News*?" Anna asked, stepping down beside me.

"What?" I couldn't believe Anna wanted to talk about candy.

"The paper got it wrong." She moved closer to me to let a couple of older girls go by.

"Anna, aren't you worried about Mr. Frazier?" I asked, scooting closer to the ledge. I looked over my shoulder at the dirt below. "He died of the flu, you know. And now he's lying in your house."

"Winnie!" she fussed. "It's disrespectful to speak of the dead like that."

I went back over my words in my head, trying to figure out what I'd said wrong. Lessie looked up at me, cupped her hand, and whispered something to Tillie.

"Anyway," said Anna, "it's only supposed to be a half a cup of cream, not two and a half cups." She shook my arm. "Are you listening?"

I pulled out of her grip. "Yes, I am. One cup of cream." Where was that sister of mine?

"No! Not one cup. It's supposed to be a half a cup. You need to tell your grandmother."

"Okay."

"Mama's so upset," Anna said with a sigh.

"I'm sorry, Anna." It must be hard to run a boarding house with a dead man in your parlor.

"She's worried everybody'll think she's a terrible cook."

The door swung open again, and there was my sister. Thank goodness!

"Does Miss Livingston have the flu?" Mary asked me. "Someone said she fainted while teaching class."

"No, she didn't faint," I said. "Come on. We have to go."

But she was looking at Zeke, who gave her a shy smile.

"Zeke," Mary said, "are you really going to learn to fly those biplanes you were talking about?"

"One day I am," he said, his eyes on the ground.

"You're just eleven," said Anna.

"I'm not going to fly them today," he said, turning red in the face. "But when I'm older, I aim to be one of those pilots up at Ellington Field."

"Mama's never going to let you get in one of those things."

He scowled, but his face softened when he looked over at Mary. She could put anybody in a good mood, especially Zeke.

"Let's go, Mary," I said. But she didn't budge. I followed her gaze down the steps.

Lessie stared up like she was just daring us to come down. Mary leaned in closer to me.

"Those Cravens," said Zeke. He might have been shy and quiet, but he was a fighter. The boys used to make fun of him because of his drunk papa and because he was a twin to a girl, but he beat a couple of them up, so they stopped.

"Mrs. Craven told my mama she couldn't be in their social club," said Anna.

I wondered why anyone wanted to be in that club. All those women did was gossip. Nobody, and I mean nobody, was safe from their mean tongues.

Next to Queen Bea, Mrs. Craven had put herself as the social leader of Coward Creek. And for some reason, people let her be it.

Some said it was because Mrs. Craven was descended from one of the Old Three Hundred, the first settlers in Texas. She could boss folks around because she'd been here longer. She was better than the rest of us.

I'd decided it was because the ladies knew she'd gossip about them if they didn't do what she said. Her daughter Lessie had the same hold over the girls as her mama did the ladies.

Everybody turned to look as Mr. Bill drove up to the front of the school.

"I'll go tell Mrs. Bill," said Anna, disappearing through the door.

"Well, we have to go get Miranda at her school," I said. "We'll see you later, Zeke."

Mary didn't notice that Zeke nodded at her. She was still staring at Lessie. I squeezed her hand as we took the steps. Mr. Bill was coming up as we were going down. He had on a gray three-piece suit. I rarely saw him in anything other than fancy clothes. He was looking at his gold pocket watch and mumbling to himself.

"I hope Miss Livingston is all right," said Mary, although her eyes never left Lessie.

"Me, too," I said, watching Mr. Bill enter the school.

"Where are you going, Winnie?" asked Lessie.

I walked right on by, pulling Mary behind me, shaking my head at Tillie for standing there with Lessie.

"What a *sweet* bow, Mary," Lessie called out. One of the boys laughed.

Mary's hand went to her hair. She flushed.

I whipped around. "You leave her alone, you hear me?" I felt Mary's grip tighten on my hand. Jimmy stepped toward me.

"Winnie's grandmother thinks she's good enough to be a member of my mama's social club," Lessie said, her face right in my face.

"Don't you start with me," I said to her.

"Come on, Winnie," said Tillie, pulling on my sleeve. "Let's go get Miranda."

Lessie turned on Tillie, right then and there. "Where are *you* going?"

Tillie kept on walking, pulling me and Mary behind her.

"You will never leave Coward Creek, Tillie Lawrence!" yelled Lessie.

"Don't look back at her," Tillie said, her lip quivering.

I didn't think I'd ever seen Tillie act so brave.

9

*T*illie twisted one long ringlet tighter and tighter as we stood on the corner of Main and Prairie Street under dark rolling clouds. Gusts of wind blew our dresses here and there. Dust from the road swirled. Mary and Miranda had their heads together, their long hair flying, examining a black marble they'd found in Mr. Straw's yard.

"Don't go over there, Tillie," I said. She wouldn't look at me.

Mr. Straw watched us as he rocked on his front porch. He wore his tattered Confederate uniform left over from the Civil War. Today must've been the anniversary of a battle he'd been in, but I couldn't remember which one. I was sure it must've been bloody and left lots of brave young boys dying on the battlefield.

Mr. Straw stood up, thin and twisted like a bent stick. "Is that you, Sam?"

"It's me, Mr. Straw," I hollered. "Winnie."

"He's crazy," Tillie said real low, which wasn't necessary since Mr. Straw couldn't hear very well and the wind was picking up.

"He just thinks I'm his little brother Sam."

"Sam's been dead for fifty years," she muttered, sliding her eyes over at Mr. Straw. She was acting strange. Tillie usually tended to old people, knowing all the proper words to say.

Mr. Straw sat back down. He scooped up his white-toed cat and put her in his lap.

"He's seeing ghosts," said Tillie, her forehead all wrinkly.

I picked a stick up off the ground and broke it, over and over, into even pieces. "You can't go over to his house, Tillie."

"I thought you were supposed to go home," she said, changing the subject. "To help your grandmother."

Miranda looked up, eavesdropping again. "Are we going home?"

I shook my head. I hadn't sent my sisters home yet because I didn't want Clara to know our schools let out early. But I was also worried about them being exposed to the flu. I didn't want them going anywhere they could catch it. Not over to the boarding house and not to the Wellses'.

Effie walked by and patted Miranda's hair. Miranda clutched her painted piano closer and narrowed her eyes. She didn't like to be touched, except by Mary.

"Can we go to the bakery, Winnie?" asked Mary, her eyes following Effie.

Miranda nodded. "I want a cinnamon roll," she said, licking her lips.

"With what money?" I asked.

"Yours," she said, pointing at me.

I dug some pennies out of my dress pocket and dropped them in Mary's hand. I'd been saving them up, but I didn't know it'd be for a bribe. "Don't go home right away, okay?"

Miranda grinned. She always knew when I was doing something I shouldn't.

"But don't go anywhere else but the bakery," I ordered.

"So," said Miranda, "we can't go home and we can only go to the bakery. What are we supposed to do? Stay at Mrs. Becker's all day with just four pennies?"

"Would you just go, Miranda?"

My sisters walked off, with Mary holding Miranda's hand, listening to her talking up a storm about who knows what. Mary was good at listening, especially to Miranda. Those two were 'specially close. I turned my attention back to Tillie, who was looking off in the direction of the Wellses' house.

I'd never been able to understand what she saw in Clyde. But I was sorry he was sick. The other day, when he'd looked into my eyes, I'd felt close to him in some kind of way. I didn't tell Tillie about it because I didn't want her to be jealous.

"You go on to my house, Winnie."

That's exactly what I wanted to do. I had to see Mr. Levy.

Tillie knew I wanted to do just that. "I don't understand why you like that stupid game," she said.

"The Indians played chess a thousand years ago," I said, hoping she'd be impressed.

"The Cherokees?"

"Not the Cherokees, Tillie. The real Indians, from India."

"I suppose," she said, sounding like her mama.

Just then, Mr. Bill drove by in his black Cadillac. He didn't look our way. His eyes were hidden by the tilt of his hat, but I could see the grim set of his jaw. Miss Livingston was in the passenger seat, her head in her hand. They went by so slowly I couldn't help but think of a funeral procession. Mr. Bill probably didn't want to jostle Miss Livingston around too much.

"She'll be all right," said Tillie.

I watched the back of the motorcar moving away from us. "You *can't* go see Clyde. He's sick."

"I'm just going to walk by his house."

I studied her for a moment. Well, she was her own person. I couldn't tell her any more than I already had.

"I don't think you should, but if you do, don't go to the door. And whatever you do, don't look up to the second floor window."

"You're not to tell Mama where I went," she said.

"Okay, then." We were friends, again.

She mumbled something.

"What?" I asked.

"Winnie, I'm sorry about . . ."

I shrugged. Seeing how much this apology was taking out of her, I tried to walk away.

"Lessie only wanted to be friends with me because I'm going to be a movie star."

I thought it had more to do with the Lawrences' money. In that way, Lessie reminded me of Clara, always craving to be around people who had money. "It's all right, Tillie."

"She doesn't like you."

"Well, why do I care?"

"I know you don't, Winnie. But I did. Care, I mean."

"Why do you? She's just a mean old girl who'll grow up to be a mean old grandmother."

"I'm not like you." She shrugged. "We're different."

"You're not like her either."

She nodded. "I guess she won't be introducing me to her famous relative now," she said with a kind of sad laugh.

"Is it her cousin?"

"Uh-huh."

"He's a movie projectionist in Alvin."

Her hand went to her hip. "Are you sure?"

"Yes, I am."

"Is his name Martin?"

"Yes, it is."

She let out a long breath. "I don't know why I believed her anyway."

I didn't either, but I didn't say it.

I watched her walk away, thinking I should stop her, but I didn't.

10

*M*rs. Lawrence wasn't happy when I arrived at her door.

"The school's closed? Where's Tillie?" She clutched red flowers in one hand and an etched glass vase in the other. Mrs. Lawrence had a maid, so she was always doing things ladies do and not things mamas do.

"She went for a walk, ma'am." That was the truth, but not exactly.

She opened the screen door, looking off down Main Street. "Come on in." She placed her hand on my head as I went by. "You're getting so tall, Winnie."

"Yes, ma'am," I said.

She smiled. "Mr. Lawrence has been asking about you. Don't stay away so long next time."

"No, ma'am, I won't," I said, smiling back at her. Tillie's mama looked right at you when she talked to you, like she really was glad to see you.

"Papa's waiting for you, I'm sure. Go on in."

I entered Mr. Levy's study like it was church. It smelled of sweet pipe smoke and musty books. The wind blew through the open windows and fluttered the papers on the dark mahogany desk. Mr. Levy always seemed to be reading or writing on those papers. He was a great scholar.

"Well, hello, Winnie," he said.

"Got your nose in a book again, I see," I said.

"It's a good book, too."

I settled myself in one of the two large wooden chairs surrounding the table with the chessboard.

"Ready for a game?" Mr. Levy asked from behind his desk.

"Yes, sir."

The board was already set up. My royal couple and their court stared across the checkered field of battle. I picked up a bishop, just to run my fingers along its smooth curves. Nothing in life was as perfect or as wonderful as chess.

Mr. Levy had taught me to play when I was about Miranda's age. After that first game, chess and Mr. Levy became a regular part of my life. A still part. A place offering some answers to the thoughts stirring up in my head.

Today, I started us off by moving a pawn, which was my favorite piece. Small, but real important to the outcome of the game. Mr. Levy told me a French fellow said the pawn was the soul of chess. I liked that the smallest piece could make such a difference.

Outside, the wind was whipping up. I should've probably been worried about getting the girls home before a storm. But I felt safe, playing chess in Mr. Levy's study. I didn't want to think about Miss Livingston clutching her stomach or Mr. Frazier's dying of influenza or Mrs. Wells being sick or Tillie walking down there or why Nolan wasn't in school.

I ran my hand down the dark wood of the wall beside me. "This house is built well. Just like our house."

"Your father built a mighty fine house," Mr. Levy said, pushing his black pawn up to meet my white one.

"We got water in it during the 1915 storm."

"I remember that," he said. "It's your turn."

"But we went upstairs and the house held together."

"Yes, I remember that, too. Still your turn."

"Mama didn't do so well that night," I said, placing my pawns shoulder to shoulder.

He was quiet.

"She screamed at Papa," I said, looking up to see how he would take that. "I'd never seen her like that. She said she'd never wanted to stay in this miserable town, but he'd made her."

Mama wanted to get out of Coward Creek because she was afraid of living by the water, and Tillie wanted to get out because she was afraid she couldn't be happy living on the prairie. Why couldn't they just be still?

Mr. Levy settled back in his chair and looked at me straight on. "I can't exactly remember when your papa began courting your mama, Winnie. They were always together, even as children. They lived in their own world, not letting others in."

"They're still like that."

"I know that. So, you wouldn't think anyone would be surprised they married, but I was."

"Why was that?"

"Everyone knew your mama didn't want to live here."

"She's afraid of the storms," I said.

"Have you ever wondered why she stayed?"

"Because of papa?"

"That's what I think."

"She blames him, though," I said.

"Maybe not all the time. Maybe just during the 1915 storm. It was a powerful hurricane, Winnie. You remember."

I'd been afraid of that storm. But not as afraid as I'd been when Mama screamed at Papa. But at least I knew what happened during *that* hurricane. I remembered the howling wind, the creek flooding over, Mama screaming, Papa calming her down. And then it was all over and we were left with mud and mess for a while.

But nobody would talk about what happened during the other storm. I lived in a house of secrets. That made it just as lonely as the house in Mr. Robert Frost's poem. Secrets were our ghosts.

I scooted some of my pawns together and lined them up like soldiers. "You were here during the 1900 storm, too?" I asked.

"Yes, I was."

"There's something about that storm I don't know," I said, pulling another pawn into the line. "Something about my mama."

He nodded. "I believe something did happen, Winnie. There was a child who was at your mama's house all the time. She died in the storm. I always thought Jane's death was a part of your mother's sadness."

"Who was she?"

"Well, she didn't come to school, but she was young, maybe five or six. Her mother was gone. Her father kept to himself."

"And she *died*?"

"Many people died in that hurricane. It was a great tragedy." He looked off, like he was remembering. "Jane's father moved away after it was all over. I heard he went to Kansas. He had kin up there."

"So you think Mama changed after that little girl died?"

He nodded. "But your mama was always a quiet child. After that, though, she wouldn't leave her house very often. Clara had a time getting her to come back to school. A few of the children were that way after the storm."

Just then, a memory came to me. I was sitting beside mama on a sofa. She was telling me Clara used to brush her long hair when she was a child. Did she have her hand on my head while she talked? I ached to find the memory, but it was gone. I felt sure it was before the 1915 storm. We lost more of mama then.

Mr. Levy put some books on top of his papers. The wind was really blowing now. The swing on the front porch knocked against the side of the house every now and then.

I can't explain it, but just looking at Mr. Levy made the spinning inside me slow down. I wouldn't say he was all soft-hearted kind, like our preacher's wife was. Mrs. Patch would put her arm around you and pull you in close and say everything was going to be just fine. Mr. Levy didn't do that, but he was kind all the same.

I took a deep breath. I guess you have to face what you're scared of sooner or later, whether it's ghosts, dead people, or the Spanish influenza. "Mr. Levy, what do you know about this flu?"

"It's serious."

"Do you know how to keep from getting it?"

"I don't think anyone knows. Doctors are working on a vaccine, but they don't have one yet. In San Francisco, people are wearing gauze masks over their faces to keep the germs from spreading. I guess the best course of action is to stay away from those who have it."

I thought about Tillie down at Clyde's and stood up. "I have to go." I could hear the telephone ringing.

"You haven't finished the game!"

The grandfather clock started chiming. It was twelve o'clock. How could it get here so fast?

"I'm sorry," I said, running out the door. I had to find Tillie and keep her from going into that house.

Mrs. Lawrence was talking into the receiver. Clara's harsh voice spilled out into the hallway.

Looking back over my shoulder at Mrs. Lawrence, I ran right into Tillie, who was coming through the front door.

Her face was flushed, her brown eyes bright. "He's all right, Winnie," she whispered. "I talked to him through his window. He's not as sick as his mama."

I was glad she was home, but I never should've let her go down there.

11

*I*n the middle of Main Street, in front of their family's grocery store, Catherine and Helen Graves jumped rope, spraying dirt into the air. When I got closer, I heard their song:

I had a little bird, and its name was Enza
I opened the window, and in-flew-Enza.

I knew they were just celebrating being let out of school early, but their singing made me uneasy. The dark sky and the chill in the wind didn't help.

Mr. Benigni, who drove the grocery delivery wagon, stopped his horse right in front of them. He opened his mouth like he might yell at them in Italian like he did sometimes with kids. But instead he started singing along. His accent made it funny and not so scary.

He took off his black hat and nodded at me, still singing, his gray moustache wriggling. But as he was singing, I started wondering, *Does he have the flu?* I looked over at Catherine and Helen. Did they have the flu?

Bakery smells drifted into the street. Fresh bread. Strudel with the last of the season's apples. Sugar and flour mixed up with butter and cooking in Mrs. Becker's oven. So delicious. How could anything bad happen when the street smelled like sugar and apples?

I didn't see Effie when I went through the bakery's door. She probably was in the back, hiding from the meanness of Lessie Craven, who was licking her fingers while eyeing my sisters.

Miranda stared right back over her cinnamon roll, white icing on her nose. Mary looked lost, her hand up on her face, rubbing a cheek, as if there were a smudge there she had to clean off.

"Good afternoon, Winnie," said Mrs. Becker, in her German accent. She stood behind the glass counter of goodies, biting her lip. Her hair was piled on top of her head in a loose bun, strands of it wisping down around her face.

"Hi," I said, smiling at her.

Mrs. Craven didn't look up. She was counting cookies in a paper bag, to make sure she hadn't been cheated. That family didn't trust anybody.

"Clyde's not as bad off as his mama," she said, still looking in the bag, "but he was coughing a lot, I hear."

She went on and on. I wanted to cover my ears and sing church hymns so I wouldn't hear anything about the influenza. But although I didn't want to hear it, I couldn't stop listening to it, either.

"I need to tell Jimmy not to go down toward the Wellses' house. That family needs to stay inside their home so they don't get the rest of us sick, too."

"Oh, my," said Mrs. Becker, her face drawn. She'd been a cheerful woman until her son went to fight the Germans.

"Mrs. Becker, I hear we're pushing the Germans out of France," I said. "It won't be long now before the war is over and Peter can come on home."

"I hope so, Winnie," she said. "I hope that is right."

"It is. My papa read it in the newspaper. The kaiser's boys are on the run." I sniffed. "Is something burning?"

"Not again!" she said as she ran to the back.

Clara said Mrs. Becker had the cleanest floors and shiniest windows of any storekeeper in town, even if she did burn the bread now and again. Effie told me her mama prayed on her knees every day for one hour because she was so afraid her son was going to die.

Mrs. Craven turned to me. "Hello, Winnie."

"Hi."

I tried not to rock back and forth on my heels. Not only was it unladylike and would spoil Clara's chances of presenting us as a family worthy to have a member in the Coward Creek Ladies' Club, it also might signal I was nervous. So I kept my feet planted on the floor.

Lessie's eyes narrowed again like the snake she was. She was livid, I could tell. Tillie had chosen me over her.

"Come on, girls," I said, startling Mary when I put a hand on her shoulder.

Miranda took another bite of her cinnamon roll. "Lessie said Mary would be pretty as our mama except for her ugly freckles."

Mrs. Craven gave Miranda a quick look.

"Lessie also said our mama wasn't even pretty anymore."

"My Lessie never said such a thing," said Mrs. Craven.

Miranda's cheeks flushed. "Well, gosh! Can't you hear? You were standing right there when she said it."

"Why, you little liar," said Mrs. Craven. "I need to wash your mouth out with soap."

That was too much! Clara surely wouldn't want us to put up with this. I stepped forward, but didn't have a chance to speak. A voice, quavering but not halting, came from behind me.

"Miranda's not a liar. I know her heart, and it is good!" Mary was beside me, shaking all over.

Miranda popped the last bite of the roll into her mouth while Mrs. Craven stood there sputtering. Mrs. Becker came back into the room, her eyes on Mrs. Craven. She gave me a quick look with her eyebrows raised, trying to figure out the trouble, I was sure. But she didn't say anything.

"I have to get y'all home," I said to my sisters.

Mrs. Craven shook her fat finger in my face. "You—you need to tell your grandmother what that child said to me. I'll be asking if she was properly reprimanded." She was getting worked up, her fleshy cheeks jiggling as she bobbed her head. "You children don't get any manners taught to you down there by that grave-yard."

Oh, that made me mad. I was ready to bust.

The door opened, and there stood Queen Bea, with her painted face and her high-cut shoes. Why didn't Mrs. Craven get *her* kicked out of the Baptist church?

"Why, hello, Bea," said Mrs. Craven, stepping back from me.

I took Miranda's sticky hand and pulled her toward the door.

Bea smiled, her blue gaze curious and drifting from one to the other of us, like a cloud floating in the sky. "Winnie," she said finally.

Then of course Jimmy Craven walked in, just so I could have

my three least favorite people all right here in this one room
with me.

Wait a minute, I thought. What was that smell? It was coming
from Jimmy. His shirt was damp on the front.

And what was that on his nose?

He leaned back from me, but I knew what it was. I declare, it
was Vicks VapoRub!

"Winnie," Queen Bea said again.

I tore my eyes off of Jimmy.

"Is your grandmother still having her tea tomorrow?"

"Yes, ma'am. She is."

"Even with the influenza? That railroad man died of it. Mrs.
Wells is sick with it, too."

"So are Miss Livingston and Clyde Wells," said Jimmy, his eyes
shining. "It's spreading fast."

"Is that right?" asked Queen Bea. "And Clara is still having her
tea?"

"Yes, ma'am," I said cautiously.

"*Tsk, tsk,*" said Mrs. Craven.

Queen Bea laughed. "She must really want to see us."

Jimmy smirked at me, his nostrils all shiny with Vicks.

I couldn't believe that this scoundrel was getting flu medicine
when my baby sisters weren't. Mary had weak lungs and was the
sweetest person I'd ever known. It wasn't fair.

"I'm glad to hear it, Winnie," said Queen Bea. "Clara has some
backbone, not to be afraid of a little influenza, which we get every
year anyway."

I would've felt gratitude toward her, but she'd probably only
said that to needle Mrs. Craven. I thought we shouldn't have a
party, but nobody asked me.

"You'd better get your sisters home, Winnie," said Mrs. Becker, "because of the storm."

"Yes, ma'am." I shooed them out the door before anybody could say anything else.

But I wasn't going home.

12

*T*he rain pounded against the tin roof of Nolan's barn. He and I sat in the hard-packed dirt, cutting up a burlap sack with a knife. I leaned against a stack of hay, breathing in the cold fresh air the storm had brought. Turned out, he wasn't sick. His papa had needed him to work on the farm.

I liked being stuck in the barn with Nolan. I was worried Clara would hunt me down again. That woman was persistent. I was sure she'd be calling over at the bakery, so I shooed my sisters' sticky faces home before the downpour started.

I doubted Clara would find me at Nolan's. The Fields didn't have a telephone. Knowing her, she'd send somebody after me. But not in this storm. Just keep on coming, rain, keep on coming.

"What will your papa say about you cutting up one of his fig sacks?" I asked.

The Fields started their fig farm when their orange orchard froze three years in a row. They were new to Coward Creek, only living here about five years now.

Nolan shrugged. "He only uses them for the smashed figs."

I hoped our idea worked. We'd come up with it together.

Nolan reached out toward me, stopping before he touched my shoulder. "You okay, Winnie?"

I stared at his hovering hand. He saw me looking and dropped it. Sometimes Nolan held my hand at the creek when nobody was looking. But today, it was just us two alone in the barn. Things seemed different.

I suddenly thought about how Clyde had kissed Tillie last summer. She hadn't shut up about it for weeks.

"A kiss on the cheek?" I'd asked her. "Isn't that like a great-aunt kissing you?"

"No!" she'd said. "It's not like that at all. But it's hard to explain to someone who hasn't experienced it herself."

I was thinking now I was ready for the experience.

Nolan was good with a knife, very careful. "Go get that twine," he said, waving the knife toward the corner of the barn.

It was on top of a pile of rusty farm tools. I unwound some of it and wrapped it around my head. "I think this is a good length, about a foot and a half?"

Nolan took the twine from me. I stacked up the squares of burlap in a pile.

Shadows gathered in the corners of the barn, but Nolan had set up a lantern to work by. A night owl hooted from up in the rafters, hiding from the rain. Blackie, the dairy cow, glanced over at us. The horses were gone, probably caught out in the storm somewhere with Mr. Field, but their smell had stayed behind.

I watched Nolan's hands. He had a farmer's hands, strong and square-shaped. His fingers moved fast over the twine, measuring it out and taking a swipe with the knife to cut off equal lengths of it. He gave the pieces to me. I wove the rough rope through the holes in the burlap, making knots so it would hold.

Everybody in town knew what a hard worker Nolan was. On Saturdays, he picked figs from sunrise to sunset and carted them in his papa's wagon to the canning factory. But not many folks knew about the stillness inside of him.

"What kind of knots are those you're tying, Winnie?"

"Well, on this side, I tied a bowline knot to keep the twine secure. But, over here, I put in a couple of half-hitches so the person who wears it can get a good fit."

"You tied those real good. Who taught you?"

"My papa. When he was a boy, he worked on Mr. Blackwood's four-mast schooner, taking tourists from Houston out into the bay. Mr. Blackwood taught him all these fancy sailor's knots."

Papa'd loved being out on the lake or in the bay, but knew that Mama would never put up with a life living off the water.

"I bet you learned that fast," said Nolan. "You're quick at learning."

I felt a smile twitching at my lips. "I don't know about that."

"You'll make a good teacher someday. Though I never could understand why you like school so much."

These were a lot of words for Nolan to say, so I was hanging on every one. I wanted to write them down later in my journal. I could show them to Tillie.

"I like numbers," I said. "And words, too."

He cut off another piece of twine.

"But I tell you, I'm not a great lover of science," I said.

He nodded.

"For instance, take the reason the sky's blue. Mr. Levy explained to me about how the blue part of the light gets splashed out over the sky. I just can't wrap my mind around it. All I know is that God picked a real pretty color for the sky and I don't care much how He made it happen."

"Uh-huh."

"And germs. How is that we can breathe each other's flu germs, but we can't see them?"

Nolan glanced over at my pile of finished masks. "How many do we have?"

I counted. "Enough for your family and mine."

"Do you think we should make some more?"

"Well, I'd like to give Tillie one and Mr. Levy one. Maybe Dr. Fox would want some to give out to his patients?"

Nolan's eyes shone in the lantern light. "Mr. Craven might want them for his store. We could sell them to him."

I didn't understand this about Nolan: how he could want to steal from Mr. Craven one day and want to sell something to him the next.

"I don't know, Nolan. I'm not sure that would be the right thing to do, with people getting so sick and dying and all."

He shrugged.

"Doesn't seem right," I said.

"Winnie," he said, his hands quieting down. "I've made up my mind about the medicine in the Cravens' store."

"Well—"

"I'm going at midnight tonight."

"Nolan—"

"Nothing you can say will change my mind. So don't try."

He stared at me, then.

"Don't get caught," I said.

He grinned. "Want to try the masks out?"

We each put one on and stared at each other. Nolan's hair hung down over his eyes.

As quick as a bird swooping for a fish, he leaned over to give me a peck. The burlap scratched my lips when he pressed his mask against mine. My stomach flip-flopped.

My face went hot. I hoped Nolan couldn't see me blushing. His eyes smiled at me over his mask.

I couldn't wait to tell Tillie. I'd gotten a kiss on the lips, not on the cheek, even if it was through fig-smelling burlap.

13

The loud bangs of Papa's hammer stirred the evening air. I hovered in the doorway of the barn. I wasn't going in. Not with what he was doing.

I put my hand to my face, touching the scratchy burlap instead of my lips. I thought about my first kiss and couldn't help but smile like a foolish girl. Like irritating Amy in *Little Women*. What was wrong with me? Jo wouldn't act so silly over a kiss. But a sweet feeling burst inside of me. I wanted to talk and talk about it.

But not with Papa. That would be plain awkward. I wondered if he could tell by looking at me that I'd been kissed. I was glad I had the mask on.

I wished I could talk to Mama about it. But she wouldn't even hear me if I told her. That would ruin everything. All of a sudden, clear out of nowhere, anger washed over me. Why couldn't my own mama listen to me?

Papa looked up and wiped the sweat from his brow. Two lit lanterns hung over his long worktable, even though it was not yet dusk. I'd come sloshing home when the rain stopped. I knew better than to be stuck out on the prairie in the dark.

"Clara's been wanting you." He gave me a look that said, *You're in trouble and I'm glad I'm not you.*

"I was at Nolan's." My feet were wet, muddy, and cold. I thought about the long wool socks tucked under my pillow; Mama had knit them for me last Christmas. They'd feel warm on my feet.

Papa picked up a few more nails and stuck a couple in his mouth. He positioned one on the pine board in front of him. Papa liked the smell of pine. Said it was fresh and new. But cut pine always smelled like death to me. An ending of something, not a beginning.

I played with the splinters sticking out of the door. The rectangular box was already put together. Papa was working on the lid. He was a good carpenter, building things fast when he needed to. But he wasn't that fast. I knew he'd use some planks he'd already prepared.

Had he been expecting more death? I felt sick to my stomach, sicker than when he made Lewis Locke's coffin. How many more people would die of this influenza?

Papa banged away at the nail. It disappeared into the wood. He glanced up at me as he took the nails out of his mouth. "What's that on your face, Winnie?"

"It's a mask." I lifted my hand, showing him the rest of Nolan's and my handiwork. "You want one?"

"Not right now," he said, lining up another nail. He didn't ask me what the masks were for. I could tell he wasn't going to ask me that or anything else.

I had to talk to him about Mama, though. It was just too much on my mind lately. It wasn't right for my papa and my mama to keep things from me. We should get sadness out in the light of the day, instead of burying it and hoping it would disappear.

"Papa?"

I watched him run his long fingers across the wood. Some might've thought a carpenter shouldn't have such pretty hands, but I liked the look of them, always so calm, just like the rest of him. His hands never shook, his foot never jiggled. He never chewed on his lip or rubbed his chin.

Papa wasn't a worrier. But I was, just like Mama.

He still hadn't answered me, so I tried again, desperate to know the answer, but asking all in a rush: "What happened to Mama in the storm of 1900, Papa?" I wanted to ask if it had anything to do with Jane, but I couldn't bring her name to my lips.

He looked up. "That was a long time ago, Winnie."

I played with the splinters a minute more. "Something bad happened, right?"

"Yes," he said, "but it's over now."

My heart raced, but I couldn't stop asking questions. "Does Mama not want us? Me and the girls?"

There was a pause. "Come here, Winnie."

I walked over to him, worried about what he was going to say. He squatted down and grabbed my shoulders. "Your mama feeds you, doesn't she?"

I nodded.

"She makes your dresses? Bought that fancy journal for you?"

"Yes, Papa."

"That's her love, Winnie. That's the way she shows it to you."

I thought about how Tillie's mama sometimes held her face when she talked to her. I couldn't imagine Mama looking at me like that—really listening to me, cocking her head to hear me talk, to hear what I might say. It filled me with such a longing.

"But she's not like other mamas," I said.

"She does what she can," he said, letting go of my shoulders. "Now if I were you, I'd be trying to figure out how to hide from Clara."

"Night, Papa," I said, edging my way back around the coffin.

I jumped a puddle, running, wanting to get away from the banging.

Coffin-building on one side of me and a cemetery on the other. Death was too close. Secrets seemed to make it closer, squeezing me in, taking my breath away.

"Winnie!"

I turned around, seeing Papa coming toward me. He had his hand out. "Let me see one of those masks you made."

I picked out the one I meant for him and gave it to him.

He studied it. "Who did these knots?"

I smiled, feeling the burlap rub my face. "I did."

"These are good knots, Winnie." He handed the mask to me. "Would you keep one for me?"

"Yes, Papa, I will." I watched him disappear into the barn.

Miranda sat on the top porch step. On her lap was her fake piano. Her long fingers moved over the keys. Her lips were moving, but no sound was coming out. Beside her was a rat in a cage, his little nose sniffing the air.

"Where'd you get him?" I asked, leaning down to take a look.

"Out on the prairie."

He picked up a piece of carrot with his paws.

"He sure is busy," I said. "Why'd you want a rat anyway?"

"I thought we'd put him in our house. If he dies, then we know he's got the flu."

I looked at her, amazed. "Well, that's a good idea, Miranda."

"I know." She tapped the top of the cage. "His name is Britches."

"You shouldn't have named him. It's not good to get too attached."

"Mary named him."

We looked at each other. Mary was sensitive about living things. She once cried when she'd accidentally squashed a doodlebug.

I glanced at Miranda's bare feet. "Clara won't like it that you don't have any shoes on," I told her. "It's too cold out. You're going to get the flu running around like that."

"What's on your face?"

"It's a mask. To keep the flu away."

"I want one."

I gave her the smallest mask and helped her get it right on her face. She gazed at me over the burlap. I tucked a strand of her hair behind her pink ear. "You're safe now, Miranda."

"Clara's mad at you."

"I know." She was always mad at me.

The lanterns were on in the house, tossing light out the windows. As inviting as it looked, I knew better than to walk right in. Clara was put out, for sure. She'd been fretting about this tea for weeks and counting on me to help. I might've felt a little guilty if I wasn't so anxious. The only kind of person that could frighten me more than Clara was a dead one.

I watched Miranda's fingers move from key to key. Just then, the night held two kinds of sounds—the loud banging of Papa's hammer against the coffin wood and the silent music of Miranda's fingers, so like Papa's, running up and down the piano he'd made for her.

I looked back at the lantern-lit barn, feeling Papa's presence all around me, in the house he'd made, the toys he crafted, the sounds in the air.

I remembered once I was dusting in the parlor and he was outside on the porch talking to Mrs. Bill. Their voices had drifted in to me.

"Winnie's a good student, Mr. Grace," Mrs. Bill had said. "She could be something beyond what this prairie town holds for her."

There was a long pause, while I held my breath and I imagined Mrs. Bill looking up at my tall papa, waiting for his reply.

"Well, ma'am, I don't know about that. But, my Winnie, she's the salt of the earth."

I wanted to be that for my papa.

14

I left Miranda to her silent piano playing and snuck around to the back door. Quietly I opened it, slipping into the hallway and up the stairs. I passed Mary, who was up on a step stool looking in the mirror in Clara's room. On her tiptoes, she peered at herself and clutched a half a lemon in one raised hand. She squeezed juice onto her cheeks and rubbed it in. The smell was sharp and made my mouth go sour.

"Winnie!" she said, as excited as if I'd returned from a long trip.

"Shh," I whispered. "Don't talk so loud."

"Clara's looking for you. You should go hide because she's going to give you a whooping. Miranda wants to pick the switch off the spanking tree." She looked at me like I was headed off to the gallows.

"When she sees you wasting one of her lemons, she's going to be switching you, too."

Mary pulled in her lips, looking so scared I regretted my words. "Don't tell her, Winnie," she whispered. "It's the only thing that'll make the freckles go away."

"Did Lessie Craven say something to you about your freckles?"

"She has such pretty skin, doesn't she?"

"You do, too, Mary. Don't believe anything that mean old girl says."

"And her hair is so blond, like the sun gave it a kiss." She played with her dark waves. "I wish I had blond hair like that."

I wished I could make her wishing go away.

"Did Clara make you work real hard today?" I asked her, pulling back her hair and looking at her in the mirror.

"I swept out the whole house. Miranda dusted all the furniture."

"Well, we don't have much furniture, so I suspect that didn't take long."

"What's that on your face?"

"A mask to keep germs out. You need to wear one when those ladies come over tomorrow. They'll be breathing on us all morning."

I heard Clara before I saw her. My heart plunged into my stomach. There she was: in the hallway with her hands on her hips.

"Winifred, I'm going to tan your hide."

Mary tucked the lemon behind her back and ran out the door.

The switch lay on the windowsill. Clara hadn't used it yet. She wanted me to stare at it some and think about what I'd done.

I didn't have long before she was done with her bath. We'd partitioned off one side of the parlor with hanging sheets, and covered all the windows. Miranda and Mary had carted in pails of hot water. We all had to take a bath tonight, even though it was a Monday.

The kitchen was hot from the baking, so I opened the window

to let in some cool night air. The crickets sang high and soft. The light from the coal oil lamps cast shadows about the room.

The smell of the lemon cookies lingered, even though I'd taken the last batch out of the cookstove a few minutes ago. My mouth watered, but these cookies weren't for us. We couldn't be taking sweets out of the mouths of the ladies coming for tea. Those ladies needed some sweetness.

Mama washed the cookie dough out of the big blue bowl. I loved that bowl. It looked like the prairie sky. It had been her grandmother's, about the only thing they had left of hers. Clara had found it in the mud behind what used to be their house, after the 1900 storm was over.

"Nolan and I made these masks, Mama. Do you want one?"

I didn't think she heard me.

"I bet you were wondering where I was this afternoon," I said. "Well, I was over at Nolan's, making these masks. The flu germs won't be able to get through the burlap. I was talking to Mr. Levy and that's what he said." It wasn't actually what he said, but close enough.

Mama dried the blue bowl, taking her time about it, handling it like it was something real special. I thought it was best not to tell Mama about Miss Livingston. I hoped Clara wouldn't mention it to her. She was always blurting out things she shouldn't.

"Will you wear one, Mama?" I asked, holding up a mask.

She glanced over her shoulder at me. Too quick of a look to see her eyes. I knew the color, though. Smoky gray, like storm clouds.

She turned to her side now, her hip against the table. "That's fine, Winnie," she said to the inside of the bowl. Then she looked out the dark window, a deep wishing on her face, like she wanted to fly away from here.

"I'll pick one out for you." I laid the masks on the table, arranging them by size.

Papa came in, his face sweaty, his shirt covered with wood chips. He gulped down the glass of water Mama gave him.

They stood side by side at the washstand, their backs to me. Papa whispered in Mama's ear. She put her head on his shoulder, leaning into him, not minding the coffin dust. I was sure Papa had forgotten all about those words Mama had yelled at him during the 1915 storm. Or else how could he be so tender to her?

I was very still. I didn't want them to leave. We could stay just like this. Or maybe I could squeeze in between them, and have one on either side of me. Feel my arms against theirs.

I thought about how it would be to work side by side with my mama, like washing the dishes together. Feeling the cool water on our hands. Laughing about Clara. Mama might rest her head on the top of my head. I wondered what that would feel like. I pretended for a moment and held that warmth inside of me.

The screen door slammed against the wood frame when Papa went back out to the barn to finish the coffin. Mama reached to put the bowl back up on the shelf.

"Winnie!"

Clara. Probably out of her bath.

With my hands full of masks, I ran onto the back porch and around to the side of the house. The barn stood right in front of me, with dots of lantern lights swaying and lighting up Papa's huddled-over shape. Clara'd find me there, for sure. I fought the urge to hide by the creek. Water moccasins didn't mind the dark.

Dodging muddy puddles, I ran around the house and up the front steps.

I slipped past the hanging sheets and up the stairs. I closed my door oh so quietly and dropped the hook into the eye of the lock.

Bang. Bang. Bang.

"Winnie, I know you're in there! You come out of there now."

"I'm sorry, Clara. I can't. My clothes are all muddy, so I had to take them off."

The door rattled. I was afraid the puny latch wouldn't hold.

"Clara, I'm naked!" I screamed, although I was standing there in my sweaty dress and muddy shoes.

The banging stopped. "When you come out, you'd better get yourself ready for a whooping and a bath."

"Yes, ma'am. I will."

She gave the door one last hit before she left.

15

*I*s your behind sore?" asked Miranda.

"Put your mask back on," I told her as I fixed my own. "And go to sleep."

I shifted to my side in my narrow bed. I might've deserved the switching. Still, I held on tight to being mad at Clara.

I was mostly worried about another matter: Nolan sneaking out to the Cravens' at midnight. The thought of it filled me with a restless feeling.

"Mary won't stop snoring," Miranda whined.

"Be quiet!"

"Well, can't you hear her?" she asked. "Gosh!"

"Go. To. Sleep."

"I'm hot!"

"Get out from under those heavy blankets, then!"

I wished I had a room to myself just like Tillie did. Of course, Tillie's baby sister died when Tillie was three. I shivered. That wasn't anything to wish for. I wondered if you had to have something bad happen to you to have something good happen to you. Like, did you have to have your baby sister die to get a room all to yourself?

"Why'd you close the window?" asked Miranda. "I think somebody's afraid of ghosts." She giggled.

I threw back my covers and ran across the wood-planked floor.

Miranda hid.

From under Mama's hand sewn crazy quilts, a muffled voice said, "I'm going to sleep now."

"You'd better," I said, trying to sound mean like Clara and sending Britches scurrying in his cage. At least he was still alive. No flu germs in this house.

Looking down at my sisters, I felt a heavy burden on my shoulders. What if they got the influenza like Miss Livingston? What if blood clogged up their lungs and they drowned?

Mary's mask covered one of her ears. Her hands were flung over her head. Out of her nose came old-man snorts. I didn't know how she could make such awful noises at night.

I put my head to her chest, listening. It sounded clear. I rolled her to her side and straightened her mask. It wasn't fair that Jimmy got Vicks and Mary didn't.

Miranda peeked at me with one eye. She would never be quiet until she got her way.

I cracked the window open, feeling the damp air creep in. I wished I could see flu germs, like pieces of dust in the air. That way I could tell if they floated in right now.

The thin trees separating us from the cemetery shivered. Just beyond them, tombstones rose out of the earth. Who ever thought of decorating a grave with a tombstone? So hard and cold. I'd like one of those crosses made out of sticks before I wanted an ugly piece of granite.

A body couldn't have any peace in eternity with a tombstone planted above it. Being put in a box and lowered into the earth was bad enough. I figured that's why there were ghosts. They didn't want to stay in the cold ground with an ugly piece of rock for a pillow.

I couldn't imagine what it must be like to be dead. Reverend Patch said our souls flew to heaven, but all I could think of was being in a casket under shovelfuls of dirt. I wanted to make sure I had in my coffin one of those strings that would ring a bell above the ground. Everybody could come running if they buried me alive by mistake.

I'd read all about that in an essay I'd found in Mr. Levy's library, written by Edgar Allan Poe. Such dreadful stories about people who were thought to be dead but weren't really. One young French woman was put in a coffin, what Mr. Poe called a narrow house. Her lover wanted a lock of her hair, so he dug up her grave and found her very-much-alive eyes wide open and staring at him. Lucky for her.

That was one good thing about living next to the cemetery. Papa could hear the bell if I rang it.

I settled back down in bed, my head on my chicken-feather pillow, my eyes staring at the ceiling. Thunder rumbled in the distance, the storm a long way off. Mama was probably wide awake, listening. Whatever happened to her in the hurricane must've been terrible. That would explain why she couldn't be a normal mama.

Sometimes I got mad at her for not being more like Tillie's mama. I squeezed my eyes shut, trying to push those thoughts away. She couldn't help being afraid, could she?

People were scared of all sorts of things. Like being a soldier, for one. Jimmy's cousin had fled to Mexico, and he didn't know a soul down there and didn't know one word of Spanish.

And Mrs. Becker was frightened for her boy.

Tillie was afraid of being stuck in Coward Creek her whole life.

Mr. Wells had looked so scared pulling his wife back in the window.

Clara was a different story. The strongest woman I'd ever seen, but deathly afraid of those ladies in the social club. That was a fear I didn't understand. My goodness. She was poor now, not the rich young bride she used to be. She just should get used to it.

I had asked Mr. Levy what he was afraid of. He didn't reply. I guess some folks like to keep their fears to themselves.

And me, I was afraid of the dead people in their graves and of the flu getting in my house and making me or somebody I loved one of those dead people. I was afraid of walking across the prairie in the dark when the ghosts were out. Mostly, I was afraid of being like Mama and being scared all the time.

If I was Mama, and this was my house, I'd put my foot down and say, "No, Clara! We're not having a ladies' tea when the flu's raging through the country and my children could get sick." I'd do what needed to be done to keep my children well.

And just then I knew what I had to do.

The girls were soon asleep. All I could hear were crickets chirping and Britches scratching in his cage.

I was out the door for a midnight walk across the prairie.

16

*I*t was the little girl following me, I just knew it. Ghosts were quiet, but I could tell she was back there.

She was a lonely thing. She'd washed up on shore twice in her glass coffin after the Kemah graveyard was flooded. Once during the 1900 storm, and once during the 1915 storm. Finally they'd buried her in Coward Creek, to get her away from the bay.

Most of the time I didn't believe in the glass-coffin girl, who was said to be clutching a palmetto leaf in one of her hands. But right now, out on the prairie at midnight, it seemed real possible she was back there, rustling in the prairie grass.

I started walking faster, my eyes on the wet road, its mud splattering my dress. I couldn't see very well, even with my lantern. Only about half of the moon was out. I looked over my shoulder, my heart catching in my throat. What was in the deep dark of the grass?

Way off in the distance, a light shone in town. I was glad someone was up this late. It would give me a point to walk to. How did thieves and cow rustlers make a living when they had to work out in the dark?

Pulling my sweater closer around me, I wondered if there were any people who weren't ghosts on the road tonight. Was that the whinny of a horse or just the whining of the wind?

I took off running.

My lantern bobbed up and down, hitting against my body. I kept my eyes on the muddy road, trying not to trip. My heart was beating hard in my chest.

I didn't stop when I reached Mrs. Hayward's house. I rounded the corner to Main and kept going, not caring if I woke anybody up.

Someone grabbed my arm. I screamed.

I knew it was Nolan as soon as my mouth opened, but I couldn't stop the sound from coming out. A light went on at Tillie's house. Nolan blew out my lantern and pulled me behind a skinny tree. Because that's all there were on Main: skinny trees and a few bushes. Surely we could be seen.

I felt like someone was looking out the window. Maybe it was Tillie's papa, Mr. Lawrence.

We waited there in the dark, looking up at the light for the longest time. My legs hurt from crouching down, but I didn't say a word. Finally the light went off, but still we crouched there, not speaking. I could hear Nolan breathing. I could hear myself breathing.

"What are you doing here?" Nolan whispered.

"I'm here to get some of that medicine for Mary."

"I'll get it. You go home."

"No, I won't."

He didn't say anything else, just looked off toward the Cravens'. The street was dark. All the houses and stores were shut down and quiet.

Even the little bit of moonlight was worrying me now. As we crossed the street, it seemed to light us up as bright as the sun.

We pushed our backs against the planked walls of Mr. Craven's store, holding our breath in case Mrs. Craven was awake and listening.

Nolan scooted over in front of the window. He looked up and down the street, but no one was moving around at this hour. This town was so dead, I wondered if we could rob the bank and get away with it.

It was too dark to make out the face of the soldier grasping the bayonet on the Liberty Bond poster in the window. But I knew the words across the front of the yellow placard said, "Come on!" I felt a pang of discomfort every time I saw it. Maybe I should try to earn some money so I could buy a bond myself.

Nolan pulled a match out of his pocket, struck it, and lit the wick of the lantern.

"You think the window's open?" I asked.

Nolan nodded and stood up.

"What if it's not?"

He dropped back down and gave me an exasperated look.

"I'm just asking, Nolan."

"I unlocked it today."

"How did you—"

When I saw the look on his face, I shut up. It was hard not to talk. All this nervousness in me had to come out.

I went over to help him as he slid the window open. He crawled in and put out his hand for me. I threw a leg over, holding my dress close to me.

The store was spooky, the lantern casting shadows on the walls.

Two long counters ran down each side of the room, closing us in like the sides of a coffin. My breath seized up inside my lungs. Looking around, I could make out the stacks of cans and boxes on the shelves going up to the ceiling. They were so neat and orderly it calmed me down to see them.

I stood by the soda fountain stools, watching Nolan make his way around the counter. He knew right where he was going. So much so I wondered what I was doing here, standing in the middle of the Cravens' store. I could have seen him do this from the window.

I kept trying to breathe. I didn't feel any excitement about breaking into a crazy man's store. I didn't feel any satisfaction I thought a thief might feel. Suddenly swimming before my eyes was the face of Clara, like she was right here in front of me.

Was I actually standing in the Cravens' store in the middle of the night about to steal some Vicks VapoRub?

It was taking Nolan too long. Something was wrong.

I thought I heard some noise above me. Was that Mr. Craven getting out of his bed? He probably kept that fish spear under his pillow.

I tiptoed over to Nolan, who was pushing aside jars as he looked on the shelf below the cash register. I grabbed his hand to get him to look at me.

"We have to go," I said, my voice squeaking out.

He gave me a look that said a lot of words and some of those words had to do with him not budging until he got what he came in here for. I figured he wasn't here only for the medicine. It was revenge, too.

"Go on." He moved farther into the store.

I was faced with a choice. I didn't want to be stealing medicine after all. I may not be able to talk any sense into Nolan, but I wanted out of this store.

I was almost to the window when a clatter erupted behind me, loud enough to wake the dead. I whirled around, my heart thumping in my ears. The nicely stacked cans on the counter were now rolling all over the floor.

"Go!" Nolan shouted.

My hands trembled with the lock, but I undid it and flung open the door. I took off running down Main, my shoes squishing in the mud.

I heard Mr. Craven yelling. Someone fiddled with a window above me.

I ducked behind the Marsh house. Their dog Clay barked until he saw that it was me. Then he ran toward me with his tail wagging. Light poured out of his owner's windows, giving me a path to Mrs. Hayward's.

My feet flapped one after the other on Creek Street, the road to home. Once, I tripped and tumbled facedown into the mud. I got up and wiped the muck off my face as I ran.

The glass-coffin girl didn't enter my thoughts.

Next thing I knew, I was on my porch, gasping for breath, looking at all the lights on back in town.

My eyes burned.

I'd left Nolan back there all alone.

17

*B*awk. *Bawk.*

The chickens fussed at me for waking them up, the big mean one pecking at my fingers and ruffling her brown feathers at me. I put the eggs in my basket, feeling the weight of each like guilt in my hand.

Jimmy barged into the henhouse, a big grin on his face.

"What are you doing here?" I asked. "Get out!" The chickens started squawking and jumping around the coop.

He stepped back out into the yard, but he was so excited he could barely talk. "My daddy caught Nolan stealing from us last night."

I hid my face behind my hair as I reached for each new egg. Each one so warm and smooth.

"Didn't you hear what I said?" Jimmy asked.

"Go on home, Jimmy!" said a voice I recognized.

I left the chicken coop. Miranda was leaning against the fence, her feet crossed casually one over the other. She tended to turn real brave when she was in her own yard.

Jimmy ignored her. "There was somebody with that thief."

Our rooster crowed. I glared at the fat bird, thinking he was trying to make me feel as guilty as Peter.

"My mama thought she might've recognized who it was."

I dropped an egg then, splat on the ground, watched the yellow running out into the earth. I felt bad, like I'd killed a chick.

I backed out of the yard, dodging Jimmy's grinning face.

"You sure are quiet, Winnie." He stepped closer, the smell of Vicks coming off of him. "Aren't you surprised to find out your sweetheart is a no-good thief?"

It was the beauty of his face that did it. I just snapped. Angry, I think, that God had given a lowlife such a nice-looking face.

I balled up my fist and slung it at him as hard as I could.

Thing is, he dodged it, and I ended up in the dirt. I was just a girl who didn't know how to fight. At least that was what Jimmy said I was when I went down.

"Winnie!" yelled a voice I didn't want to hear.

Lying in the dirt, all I could do was stare up at the blue sky and wish I was someplace else. Clara yanked me up, gripping me hard by my upper arm, and set me down on my feet.

I couldn't see her eyes because they were just slits. Her face was red. Her lips contorted in six different directions. Not a word came out of her mouth. She stomped off. Another whipping tonight, I was sure. My behind was still sore from the last one.

Jimmy ran off, laughing.

"All the eggs broke," said Miranda.

I looked down at the mess of yolk running in the yard.

"I'll clean it up," she said, taking my hand.

I knew I should tell of my part in the break-in, to make the world right again, but I also knew there was no way Clara was going to get into her social club if I did. And maybe I was afraid of telling her, too.

Poor Nolan. Did Sheriff Milroy have him down at his house, holding him until he could take him to the county jail? Oh, I couldn't think about it. Clara's tea was in a couple of hours.

I'd confess, after.

18

*W*innie!" Clara screeched.

"I'm right here," I said.

Clara was in bad shape. Drops of sweat rolled down her cheeks. Her gray hair was damp. She was going to have to change that fine voile shirtwaist of hers if she couldn't calm her nerves.

"These napkins you ironed are wrinkled." She pressed two into my palm, hard. "Do these again."

The white linen was so pure-looking in the mess of emotion this morning. Clean and simple, like life should be. But life was messy. Nolan was caught, and here I was setting up a table for some stuck-up women.

"There's no time to redo them." I put them back on the dining table covered with bone-white china, plates of lemon cookies, and a small pitcher of cream. The aroma of tea drifted in from the kitchen.

Clara twisted my arm. "What's this?!" She snatched my mask off my face, scratching me with the burlap.

"Ow!"

"No, you don't, young lady," she said. "And look at your face. It's all red and irritated from the burlap. You look a sight!"

She fled into the kitchen, barking orders at Mama.

"I need that, old woman," I muttered, rubbing my cheek.

How could we be having a tea at a time like this? The government closed down the school and the motion picture show and even the churches in Galveston, but we were still going to have a meeting of the Coward Creek Ladies' Club. Three of the ladies had called to say they weren't coming. But that didn't stop Clara.

I had seen Papa and Mrs. Frazier's brother load up the coffin in a wagon early this morning. They'd be shipping Mr. Frazier off to Galveston for burial. At least he'd be out of the Painters' parlor.

The women came two by two, walking across the prairie, like Noah was saving them from the flood. I was sure the town's flu germs swarmed around them like invisible deadly flies, clinging to their coiffed hair and Sunday best. Once they were in our house, I held my hand over my mouth until Clara jerked it down.

"You'll sleep in the cemetery tonight, child," she whispered hot in my ear.

My stomach went to ice. She'd do it, too, if I ruined her day. And I had this terrible feeling I just might.

The ladies' hems and shoes were muddy, but Clara had thought of that. Rags were ready on the front porch.

When big-boned Mrs. Craven came in, she was already talking about the break-in at her store. She eyed me while she talked, like she was trying to figure something out. I broke into a sweat.

She wasn't forthcoming with any details. She wanted to carry on about it first. The ladies stood in the doorway, listening, wanting to hear all about it. I could tell Clara was staring at me, hard, but

I looked off and tried not to chew my lip or rub my hands together or do anything that made me look guilty.

"I heard it was the Field boy," said Mrs. Stone.

Mrs. Craven opened her mouth. But Clara said, "Oh, look, it's Bea," and pointed out the window.

I was glad to see Bea driving up in her touring car.

Of course she'd arrived last. When I opened the front door for her, she looked at me like I was a slimy slug clinging to her silk skirt. She wore high heels, and her outrageous hat with the ostrich plumes made her look even taller.

"So pleased to see you," said Clara in a sweet voice.

Mama gave Queen Bea a quick nod. "Good morning."

I thought Mama looked pretty. Her cheeks were flushed pink from the heat of the kitchen. Strands of brown hair curled around her face. I didn't know why she didn't fix herself up more because she looked so nice when she put her hair up and wore a dress not soiled with pig lard and bits of bread dough.

Our snooty guest gazed with ice blue eyes down at my thin, short mama. "Hello."

I'm sure Mama didn't even know she was being snubbed.

Queen Bea sat straight as a board on one of the high-backed wooden chairs Papa'd made. The other ladies tried to politely nudge each other out of the way so that they could claim the coveted seats beside her.

Jimmy's mama and surprisingly, quiet Mrs. Stone, won out. Although small, Mrs. Stone did win the mouse-killing contest last year at the Fourth of July celebration, although some complained that she took off before the whistle.

"Well," said Queen Bea as I gave her a cup of tea. "Do you like it here, Clara, living with your daughter and her children?"

She said it like Mama wasn't standing two feet from her offering everyone cookies she'd sweated over the night before. My hand shook, like it did when I was angry but couldn't speak my mind.

Hold your tongue, Winnie. I had to keep reminding myself to be ever-vigilant, on account of my bad temper that would just pop out of me.

Queen Bea eyed me like I was that slug again, but one with a hot cup of tea hovering over her lap.

"Yes, I do," said Clara, who gave me a hard stare. "Although, it's not the same as when I was a new bride living with my husband in Galveston. Those were grand times."

"Yes," said Queen Bea, as if she'd lived them, too.

Even plain Miss Pearl nodded and looked off like she was remembering old times that happened before she was born.

I heard a whistle blow and braced myself for the noise of the train on the tracks. I felt the vibration in my toes and it wasn't too bad, but Queen Bea grabbed the edge of her seat. Mrs. Craven did the same. "Oh, my," said Miss Pearl.

Clara fiddled with the beads around her neck. "I do believe my son-in-law built his house a little too close to the railroad tracks."

I rolled my eyes and watched the train chug by. It spat out a long trail of black smoke.

Mama disappeared into the kitchen. I tried to follow her, but Clara grabbed the hem of my dress and yanked me into the seat next to her.

What? I mouthed at her. Surely she didn't expect me to stay here with them. I glanced toward the kitchen, but the door was closed.

Everyone waited.

Mrs. Craven burst out, "Our store was broke into, Bea. Just last night."

The queen looked a little put out at first. "Really," she said, as if nothing could be more boring. I liked this.

But Mrs. Craven was not to be shut up. "Yes, it was that Field boy."

I expected Clara to do something, although I didn't know what, but she sat there calmly drinking her tea, like it was of no concern to her. I was sure she knew that everyone knew Nolan was my sweetheart.

"Mmm," said the queen, clearly not impressed. She was from Dallas, after all. Robberies must have occurred all the time up there.

"Is Mrs. Wells still sick?" Queen Bea asked, peering at Mrs. Stone over her teacup. "You live closest to her, don't you, May?"

Mrs. Craven looked like a little girl pouting. She put down her teacup and narrowed her eyes so much they closed up. She'd been snubbed.

"I haven't spoken to her in a while," said Mrs. Stone.

Miss Pearl's hand fluttered to her throat. "I brought her some fresh cantaloupe from the farm," she said timidly. "Mr. Wells came to the door. He looked very tired." Deep lines ran back and forth across her forehead. "I heard Miss Livingston doesn't have the influenza after all."

I looked over at Miss Pearl, trying to understand what she was saying. She spoke so quietly I really had to work at it.

"She doesn't?" asked Mrs. Stone.

"It's a stomach ailment."

I sighed in relief. Finally something good had happened.

"People are dying in Houston and Galveston," announced Mrs. Waters, the organist at the Methodist Church. "Many are getting pneumonia. We've been fortunate only three people from Coward Creek have died. And Mr. Frazier came home with it on the train. He must have brought it into town."

"No, Mrs. Wells got it before that," said Mrs. Stone, shaking her head. "And Mr. Ichiro came down with it over a week ago. The railroad man didn't bring it to us."

"Well," said Mrs. Craven, sitting up in her chair, but still looking like a blob of butter. She had none of Jimmy's handsomeness. He got that from his papa's side. "I heard the Krauts are spreading this flu."

I pressed my lips together, tight. Those ignorant Cravens.

Mama came back in, clutching another platter of cookies. She offered one to Mrs. Waters, who smiled and nodded.

"My husband said the enemy's trying to kill our women and children," Mrs. Craven continued. "They have spies in our country. Spies!"

She had the largest hands I'd ever seen on a woman. When she lifted one to her face to rub the top of her nose, it covered her entire face. I watched that big old hand go up and down, up and down.

"How thrilling!" said Queen Bea, wiggling her shoulders. "Perhaps we have spies right here in Coward Creek."

The ladies giggled.

"Not the Beckers, of course," said Queen Bea. "They have a boy fighting."

"Hank thinks it's the Jews," said Mrs. Craven. "They did kill

Jesus, after all. They won't be happy until all the Christians are dead."

A rushing noise like the biggest waterfall in South America flooded my ears. Mama retreated into the kitchen. She didn't like that kind of talk, but she wouldn't say anything either. I squinted as fierce as I could at Mrs. Craven, but she wasn't looking at me.

"Yes, Clara," asked Queen Bea, "doesn't your granddaughter play chess with Mr. Levy? I heard he was the one who was with Mrs. Wells when she became ill. Winnie, what has Mr. Levy been plotting against the good people of Coward Creek?"

She smiled like she was making a joke. Jimmy's mama guffawed. Even polite Miss Pearl twittered. Mrs. Waters twisted in her seat and looked out the window.

I shot up, my fists tight. I'd be sleeping in the graveyard tonight, but I didn't care. Words flew around in my head like angry crows, but I couldn't get them out of my mouth.

Clara rose. Her head was a-shaking like the old preacher's used to. She put her teacup down on the side table. The cup rattled against the saucer.

Queen Bea smiled at Clara with a knowing look. There was something going on here I didn't understand. Some secret thing.

"I'd like to thank everyone for coming," Clara said.

That's all she said. She stood there, with her empty hand trembling.

Queen Bea's smile froze on her face. Her delicate hand put down that delicate cup. "Thank you for the tea, Clara."

They left one by one, taking Clara's hopes with them.

My grandmother stood there, not moving.

All the running around and polishing and cooking and fretting and planning and scheming for over a year and . . . it was over.

19

A house full of hush. Papa working in the barn with the wood he loved so much. Mama out there with him. No chattering from my sisters because they weren't home yet, banished to Mrs. Hayward's until after the tea was done.

Well, it was done, good and done. Mrs. Hayward would be watching those ladies making their way across the prairie, all on foot except for Queen Bea, who was driving her touring car the short distance to her house.

Clara was still in her room.

I cleared the table. Moved the chairs back. Hauled in some water from the well and heated it on the stove. I soaked the dishes in water and lye soap, then put them in cooler water to rinse. The water was soothing to the touch, but not soothing enough.

I knew what I had to do. I was putting it off.

The screen door banged. Miranda ran upstairs, and Mary sat down at the table.

"Can I have a cookie?" she asked, staring at the plate.

I nodded, a lot on my mind.

"Where is everyone?" she asked.

"I thought you wanted a cookie," I said, looking over at her. She had her head down on the table.

She mumbled something into her arms I couldn't understand.

Miranda came in. "Winnie," she said, leaning her head into Mama's apron I had on. "I need to tell you two things."

"What?" I asked.

"Well, the first thing is, Britches has black goop coming out of his eyes."

"The rat?"

"The second thing is, I think he's dead."

I didn't move for a minute, but then I dropped the white china plate *plunk* in the water and took the stairs two at a time.

The rat was lying on his side and stiff as a statue.

Oh, no, oh, no. Not the rat. Was it in our house? Was the flu in our house?

Mary and Miranda came in. "Did he have the flu?" asked Miranda.

"Stay here."

I picked up the cage and went downstairs. I grabbed my work gloves and the trowel off pegs in the kitchen. I went outside and walked all around the edge of the cemetery until I was farthest from the graves. I put the cage down and dug a hole deeper than I needed to. I told the rat how sorry I was that we'd sacrificed it for the influenza and then I placed it in the hole. As I patted the dirt, I wondered if it would be a little rat ghost haunting us because we'd gotten it sick. So I said another prayer.

I looked back at the house and found I didn't care about those dirty dishes. Not with the rat dying and me leaving Nolan alone to face the Cravens.

With Clara hiding away, no one would notice me being gone. It was usually her that kept track of my whereabouts, or at least tried to.

I went down to Dr. Fox's, thinking I had to get my questions answered before I made my confession. Could a rat get the flu? Does that mean we might get the flu? No one answered the door. I sat on the stoop for about a half an hour, hoping somebody would show up, but no one did.

I made my way to the sheriff's house. I stood in the wide dirt street, trying to figure out what I was going to say before I went in. Not coming up with anything, I went around to the side, to the alley between the feed store and the sheriff's, and sat down. Leaning against the side of the building, I closed my eyes, trying to still the thoughts in my head. I could feel my dress getting wet, the ground still damp from yesterday's storm.

"Winnie, what are you doing?"

The sheriff stood in the entrance to the alley, blocking the way out to Main Street. He was a tall man, almost six and a half feet. Papa said they must grow them that way in Alabama, that he'd never known a man so tall he could block the sun at noon.

I stood up, brushing the dirt off the back of my dress. "Nothing, sir."

"Come on out of that alley."

I had to get this over with. "I have a confession to make, Sheriff."

He studied me while he chewed on his tobacco. "You were with Nolan Field when he tried to steal that Vicks, weren't you?"

My mouth dropped open.

"Go on home, Winnie." He spat some black juice on the

ground. "And whatever you do, don't tell the Cravens. I've had enough of them for a while. Just between you and me, I think that woman's out of her mind. She reminds me of my mama, and I came a long way to get away from my mama. God rest her soul."

"How'd you know?"

"Mr. Craven heard Nolan talking to somebody. He thought it was Eddie Payne, but I had my suspicions it might be you."

Out in the street, I could see Effie Becker and Evelyn Marsh walking together, their arms linked, laughing. I wished I could be so carefree.

"Is Nolan in trouble?" I asked. The girls looked our way, and I took a step back into the shadows.

"Yeah, he is. He broke into Mr. Craven's store."

"But I did, too."

"Well, are you ever going to steal again?"

"I don't think so, sir."

Sheriff Milroy spat again. "Wrong answer, Winnie."

"I mean, no, sir, I'm not going to ever steal again. I promise. Still it doesn't seem right that Nolan got in trouble and I get away scot-free."

"Probably isn't. But I'm not talking to those Cravens again, so just consider this your lucky day. But I tell you, Winnie, if I ever catch you doing anything you're not supposed to do, I will go right to Clara and tell her everything. Now, go on home."

"What's going to happen to Nolan?" I yelled to the sheriff's back.

"His daddy didn't look too pleased," he said over his shoulder.

I was still smarting from Clara's whooping, but mine wasn't so bad compared to the one Nolan probably had got. I kept following the sheriff. He was up on his porch.

"Sheriff, you should make the Cravens share that flu medicine with folks around here. It's not fair they keep it all to themselves."

"Now, Winnie, I see you win the spelling bee and the arithmetic contest every year up at the school."

"Yes, sir."

"Why's a smart girl like you thinking that rubbing ointment on your skin is going to keep you from getting the Spanish influenza?"

I wondered for a moment if he was in on hoarding the medicine with the Cravens.

"Go on home, Winnie." He slammed the screen door.

I had one more thing to do.

No one answered my knocking at the Lawrences', so I let myself in. Mr. Levy stood on a small wooden stool, his long form all stretched out and his fingers reaching for a leather-bound book on the highest bookshelf.

His books were in alphabetical order, with their outsides pushed to line up with one another. I was the one who had arranged them so nice.

"Hi, Mr. Levy."

He mumbled something back and stepped down, looking at the cover of the book. I kept staring at those shelves, as I sat down.

"How was your grandmother's tea?" he asked.

I knocked my back teeth together, trying to think of what to say. To find out what I wanted to know I had to tell Mr. Levy about those things Queen Bea had said. I didn't want to hurt his feelings.

With book in hand, he settled himself into his leather chair. "I saw those fine ladies coming back across the prairie, not long after I'd seen them leave town for your house. Thought that was odd."

"I'm afraid it's pretty awful, Mr. Levy. I don't want to surprise you or anything, but there was some talk about—and it was mostly joking and not said in seriousness, but that doesn't matter, I know—"

"Winnie." I looked up. Mr. Levy's eyes were so blue against the white of his hair. "What happened?"

"Queen Bea . . . she wanted to know, were you plotting against the Christians of the town."

Mr. Levy put his pipe in his mouth.

"I stood up to give her a piece of my mind—"

"Did you, Winnie? Now that's not a surprise."

"But the thing is . . ." I was so ashamed, I didn't know if the words would come out. "I . . . I couldn't say anything. It was like I was struck mute. All the heated words in my head stayed right there, just getting hotter and hotter and going no place at all. But then . . . a strange thing happened."

I remembered the look on Clara's face—the anger right beneath the surface, threatening to bubble up if those ladies didn't do what she said—but her voice staying so calm.

"Yes?"

"It was Clara. You know how that old woman's—sorry, Mr. Levy, but you know how she can be—she's been scheming to get into this stupid club for months now. Sometimes I think it's the only thing she cares about . . ." I stopped, thinking about how small she'd looked after the ladies left, like she was some frail granny.

"Well?"

"Mr. Levy, it was Clara, not me, that stood up and faced that Queen Bea down. She said, 'Nice of y'all to come,' which everybody knew meant, 'Get the heck out of my house.'"

His white eyebrows shot up.

"Excuse me for cussing," I said. "But that's another thing so strange. I had all these mean words I wanted to say and I wanted to hurt them with those words and make them see sense and then Clara says her polite words in a polite voice and it seems louder and angrier than what I could've said."

"I can see Clara say it, too. It reminds me of when she was a young woman, always with a cause."

"And then Queen . . . what did you say?" I stared at him a moment, trying to collect my thoughts. "You knew Clara before she was a grandma?"

"You knew that, Winnie. I moved here as a young man to become the teacher at the school. That was before I'd met Tillie's grandmother. Clara was a student, very bright. Pretty, too."

"Oh, ugh, Mr. Levy. I don't want to hear anything like that."

"It's even worse than you think."

"What do you mean?" I asked, suspicious.

"I courted her."

"What?"

He laughed, which he rarely did. "I wanted to marry her."

I stood. "No more, Mr. Levy. Please."

"I don't know if Clara shared my feelings, but I believe she would have said yes if I'd asked her. She wanted to get out of that house. Away from her father. But he didn't approve of me."

I never knew my great-grandfather. He died in a streetcar accident in Galveston. "I don't think she liked her papa."

"I don't believe she did."

Clara said her father was a mean old man and if he'd lived long enough to see his grandchildren, she would never have let him around them.

"Your grandmother is more than you know, Winnie."

"But she's so, so. . . ." I couldn't finish.

"People are all sorts of things. Clara's got a good heart, a strong heart."

"A good heart? I don't think we're talking about the same woman." But then I thought about her standing up to those women at the tea.

"Everything belongs, Winnie. All things. Sometimes what a person's good at can also be what irritates everyone around him."

"Clara's got such strong opinions about how things should be done."

"Like someone else I know?"

I saw what he was suggesting. "I'm not like her!"

"I see her strength in you. Hasn't it been you and Clara looking out for your family?"

Tears popped into my eyes. What was I crying for? "I don't know, Mr. Levy. But I don't want to be like her."

He gave me his handkerchief. "It's probably not as dreadful as you think it is."

20

I walked into a quiet yard. No one was out on the porch.

Mama wasn't in the kitchen.

Following voices, I went upstairs. The girls lay in their bed, with wet washrags on their heads. They looked so small, swallowed up by covers. Miranda reached out for me, but Mama pushed me back. Mary's breaths were fast and shallow.

"They just have headaches," Mama said, her lips trembling.

"Okay." I glanced over at them holding hands in bed. I wanted to listen to Mary's chest.

"Do we have the flu, Winnie?" Miranda asked in a whisper.

"No!" Mama said, so loud Mary jumped. She drew back from Mama and reached out for me.

"Let's go down," Mama said, pushing me out of the room. "We need to make supper."

"Okay," I said to her. "Girls, I'll be right back up to bring you some aspirin for your headaches."

Mama pulled me down the stairs, her fingers digging deep into the flesh of my arm. Her hand was hot and sweaty. I wasn't used to her touch. All these years I wanted her to touch me, but now I just wanted her to let me go.

"Is Papa in the barn?" I needed him here.

Mama didn't answer.

We passed Clara's shut door.

Once we were in the kitchen, Mama grabbed a rag and wiped her face.

"Are you okay, Mama?"

She picked up some dirty carrots from the garden, dipping them into a pot of water, cleaning them, her hands moving very fast.

"I think we need to see about the girls, Mama."

Her hands moved faster. I thought about Mary and her shallow breaths.

"I need to get Clara." I wanted Mama's hands to stop. "Can we—"

Mama wheeled around, water flying from the carrots onto my dress. Her eyes, wild. Her face not the quiet face I knew.

"Would you hush, you vexing child?! Stop that *talking*! You're always going on and on about nothing, Winnie. Nothing! Can you just be quiet for once?"

There was no ticking clock in the room. No whisper of shoes on the wood floor. Not one insect sang, not one dog barked. Just a quiet deadness all around. And inside of me. I wondered if my heart would pump soon, and just then it did. A great big bump that hurt my chest.

Mama ran out, pushing past Clara standing in the doorway in her wrinkled dress, staring at me with the saddest look I'd ever seen.

We heard Mama screaming and ran upstairs. Standing in the doorway, I saw the girls tossing and turning in their bed.

Clara gripped my arm. "Go get Doc Fox."

I couldn't move.

"Winnie, go!"

As I ran down the stairs, I heard her say, "Winnie, don't come back here. Go to Tillie's."

21

I knocked loudly on Dr. Fox's door. Over an hour had passed since I was here last. I hoped someone was home. I stared at the flowerpot on the front step. The daisies were white and wilting. I banged again. No one came for the longest time.

The windows of the hospital across the street were shut. Any patients in there must be sweltering. I was not letting them take my sisters to that place. It was filled with sickness and ghosts.

The door swung open. There stood Mrs. Fox, wiping her hands on a rag. Black circles were like ugly bruises under her eyes.

"Is Dr. Fox home?"

She sighed. "He's sick, Winnie."

"With the flu?" I asked, my heart sinking.

"I'm afraid so. He's worn himself out and now he's gotten it. Who's sick at your house?"

My eyes burned. "My sisters."

"Clara will know what to do, Winnie."

"Yes, ma'am," I said. I should go home to be with my family, but Clara wouldn't let me in the house.

I cut through the yard of the hospital and over to Tillie's.

I stared at Olive Tell on the cover of *Photoplay* magazine, but my head was filled with thoughts of my little sisters holding hands in their bed. I should be there with them. Clara shouldn't have run me out. Nobody could take care of Miranda and Mary as well as I could.

"Olive's pretty, but I like Mabel better," said Tillie, holding up another magazine. Tillie does look a little like her, I thought, studying the big brown eyes and dark hair of Miss Normand.

Ragtime music danced up the stairs to us from the parlor. Mrs. Lawrence sure knew how to play the piano. Listening to the jazzy tune made me smile. I knew Clara wouldn't like it at all. Miranda would. She'd love to be banging out songs on a real piano.

Tillie's house had just about everything, even indoor plumbing, which I thought was the best. It sure must be nice not to have to run out to the privy or use the chamber pot at night.

"I want to get my hair bobbed, just like Irene Castle," said Tillie. "Some actresses are doing it."

She jumped up and held her arms out like she was dancing with a real fellow.

"Your mama wouldn't let you cut your pretty long hair," I said.

"Yes, she would," Tillie said, twirling around the room.

"Yeah, you're right. She would."

Mrs. Lawrence let Tillie buy all the *Photoplay* and *Motion Picture* magazines that she wanted. Clara wouldn't like it one bit that

I was looking at these scandalous people, who were spread out all over Tillie's floral woolen rug.

"Why don't you dance with me, Winnie?"

It didn't seem right to dance while my sisters were sick in their bed. "Not today, Tillie." I had phoned Clara to tell her about the doctor being sick. Just as I had thought, she wouldn't let me come home.

Tillie settled back down and picked up a magazine. "This one has a great article, Winnie. See here," she said, flipping the pages. "*Want to be a star?*"

"No, I don't," I said.

"No, Winnie, that's what the article's called. See, it says on the front, *Is your nose straight? Do your eyes match? Read about it, anyhow.*" She laughed. "Where is that article? I want you to read it."

Mary would like reading these magazines, I thought. I should bring her down here when she's better.

Something clutched at my stomach. I leaned back against Tillie's brass bed, staring at her light pink wallpaper, its stripes so perfectly lined up. Not one jagged one. Not one out of place.

"Are you all right?" asked Tillie.

"I think so."

"Mary and Miranda will be just fine," she said, patting me on the arm.

"They might not be. Life's not perfect, you know. It's not like your wallpaper."

"What are you talking about?" she asked.

"Things don't always end up like you want them to."

"For heaven's sakes! Why do you worry so much? I've never seen anyone fret over so much stuff."

"Aren't you scared of the influenza?" I asked.

"No, I'm not," she said. "And you shouldn't be either. Your sisters will be all right. Everybody gets the flu. You just had it last spring." She picked up another magazine, smiled while she looked at the cover.

"Why do you want to be an actress so bad?" I asked.

Her eyes lit up. "I don't understand why anyone *wouldn't* want to be a motion picture star. You get to live in California. Aunt Cora says it's the most beautiful of the forty-eight states. And you get to act in pictures. Play a part in someone else's story. You like stories, Winnie. You should understand wanting to do that."

"No, I don't," I said.

"And people read about you in magazines and you go to dances and parties."

"Sounds kind of crowded." Tillie might not be afraid of the influenza, but I thought she might be afraid of being alone.

"Well, never mind," she said. "Just look at the magazines then. Aren't the actresses pretty?"

I nodded, wishing Tillie would just stay here with me. "Why do you want to leave Coward Creek? Everything you need is right here. You live in this big house, almost the nicest in town. And it's a nice town, too. Not too big, but right on the railroad, which can take you to big cities, one of them north, one of them south of here."

"Coward Creek nice? Winnie, we've got to get you out of here to see other places."

"The people here are nice. The creek is nice. I think it's nice."

She started reading another article, ignoring me.

"And . . . you've got your mama and your papa and Mr. Levy. Your mama, she dotes on you, Tillie. You're the apple of her eye."

"Hmm," she said, her eyes still on the magazine. "That's not as important as you think it is."

She was wrong about that. It was the most important thing.

Maybe you had to not have something to know what a treasure it was.

22

That night, Tillie and I whispered in her bed, our heads huddled together on one soft feather pillow. Her cat, Miss Pickford, was between us. The house was real quiet and smelled of lavender. How could bad things happen in a house that smelled so pretty?

"Tillie, do you remember your baby sister?"

"No," she said, tickling Miss Pickford under her chin.

The Lawrences had a big plot at the cemetery. Only one tiny grave was in it now, and that was Emily Rose. She had died of pneumonia when she was barely one year old. Mrs. Lawrence had given her a birthday party with a pony, a real live monkey, and a white layered cake made by Mrs. Becker. Half the town had come to the celebration. Not two weeks later, everyone was gathered together again, but this time at the cemetery.

"If you could come back as something after you died," Tillie asked, "what would it be?"

"I don't know." I knew she was only asking me the question so she could tell me her answer. "What would you be?"

"A sparkling diamond. Ladies would put me on their fingers and admire me. Maybe even a movie star like Lillian Gish would wear me to fancy movie star parties."

"Uh-huh."

"What would you be?" she asked.

I looked out the window. "You'll just laugh."

"No, I won't."

I could see the stars.

"Tell me, Winnie."

"Well . . . I think I'd be water," I said.

"Water? That doesn't make any sense."

I should've known not to tell her.

"I just don't understand you sometimes, Winnie." She raised her arms and swayed them back and forth.

Maybe Mama was right. Maybe nobody ever knew what I was talking about. But I so wanted Tillie to understand me. I sat up in the soft bed. "Water's wonderful, Tillie. It's refreshing. Nothing's better than a tall glass of water on a hot day."

"It doesn't catch the light like a diamond does."

"Oh, yes, it *does*. Have you been by the creek and seen the sun hit it? It's like a sharp, quick brightness. The fish fly out and plunk back in. Water has great sounds. Like when you pour it. And when the rain comes down. What a sweet sound that is."

Tillie's arms kept swaying. "Until it comes down in buckets. Water's also hurricanes. And tears, too." She dropped her arms and looked at me. "And fluid in the lungs, like my baby sister had. Water is terrible things. Why'd you pick something like that?"

Tillie's breathing was slow and even, so I thought she was sleeping. I jumped when she spoke: "Are you asleep?"

"Nope," I said, looking up into the dark of the ceiling.

She grabbed my hand. I turned to look at her with her face on the pillow, her eyes on me. "You're the best friend a girl could have," she said in her best actress voice.

I flipped over to my side, facing her. "You're a good friend, too."

"Mama's right. I won't ever, ever find another friend like you."

"Yes, you will, Tillie," I said, pleased her mama said such a nice thing about me.

"Not someone like you—so loyal and true."

"You'll have lots of friends." People always swarm around girls like Tillie. "Especially when you're a motion picture star."

"I'm so sorry about Lessie," she whispered.

"That's all right."

"I was mad at you."

"Well, why ever for?" I asked.

"Sometimes I think you just want to be my friend because of my family and not because of me."

"No, Tillie."

"Well, you're always talking about my mama and how nice she is to me."

"She is nice to you."

"And my grandpa. You come see him as much as you come see me."

I chewed on my lip. I didn't want to lie to Tillie. I liked her, of course. She was my best friend. But I also liked to be here and see all the love around her. It made me feel like a part of it, even if I was mostly watching from a distance.

I didn't know how to explain that to her.

Tillie and Miss Pickford had fallen asleep. The wind rattled the windowpane, like it was trying to keep me awake, so I'd just lay there and worry about my sisters. It didn't feel right being here with Tillie. I should be in my own home, in my own room, with my sisters.

Miranda had a way of not wanting any attention until she was sick. Normally if you said something to her or about her, she'd fold her thin arms together and look off like an angry cat, like she didn't want anybody to know she was even capable of being mad; but being mad she was.

Mama wouldn't know how to take care of them. She wasn't like other mamas. She could cook for you, sew for you, but she didn't want to talk to you or smooth your hair back when you had a headache or rock on the porch with you. I didn't think it was her fault, really.

Once, Clara and I'd been down on our knees in the soil of our garden, planting potatoes. Mama was in her room, with one of her headaches. Before I'd come out to help Clara, I'd given Mama an aspirin and a cold washrag. That was after the 1915 storm. Mama spent a lot of time in her room that first year.

Clara blurted out, "Your mama was just born different. I'd never seen such a sensitive child."

I'd looked up, knowing there was more, wondering how I could get to the root of it. "She's worse since the hurricane."

"Your mama lets the past haunt her. Don't you be like that, Winifred. Do you hear me?"

"All right," I said, not really sure what she meant.

She wiped her forehead with the back of her hand, leaving a streak of dirt. "No, you're not like that. You're a strong girl."

I stared at her, waiting for the next thing.

"Winnie!" she fussed. "Where are those seed potatoes?"

And that was all.

I turned over on my side and tucked my hand under my chin

because it made me feel safer when I did that. I wished I could hear my sisters breathing.

"I don't feel well," said Tillie, waking me.

I tried to see her face in the early morning light. A breeze blew through. I could hear the train running through town.

"You're so hot," I said.

Her teeth were chattering. "I'm c-c-cold."

I bounded out of the bed, scaring Miss Pickford. "Mrs. Lawrence!" I yelled, running down the hall.

Their door was open. She sat up in bed in her white lace nightgown, turning on her electric lamp. Mr. Lawrence was a lump under the blankets at her side. "What is it, honey?" she asked me.

"It's Tillie."

She put her hand to her mouth and stared at me, not moving.

"What's wrong?" asked Mr. Lawrence, sitting up.

"Tillie has a fever," I said.

We were back in the hallway, me following closely behind them.

I climbed back in bed with Tillie while Mrs. Lawrence felt her forehead. "Cecil," she said. "Cecil, she's so hot."

Tillie coughed and turned her head. "Mama, my body hurts."

"Is it the influenza?" I asked Mrs. Lawrence.

"I'm so cold," Tillie said, her eyes only half-opened.

I wrapped my arms around her. "It's okay. I'll keep you warm." I rocked her a little. "I'll keep you warm."

Mrs. Lawrence sat on the side of the bed, stroking Tillie's hand, like you'd expect a mama to do. "Stay with her, Cecil. I have to get some things for her."

She ran out of the room, calling for her father.

"Winnie, you shouldn't be here," Mr. Lawrence said. He leaned over Tillie and pulled the covers up around her neck.

Mr. Levy appeared at the doorway, his white nightshirt to his knees. He placed his hand on Tillie's forehead. "It's all right," he said in a soothing voice. He pulled me off the bed. "Go to the Cravens' house."

"But—"

"Go, Winnie."

I whispered *bye* in Tillie's ear and slipped out. I saw her mama in the kitchen putting a pot of water on the stove.

I ran all the way home, fear ripping at my heart. I'd been so busy trying to protect my family from the influenza, I hadn't given a thought to Tillie.

23

I took the porch steps two at a time, threw back the screen door. Mama was screaming. Like it was 1915 again and the water was rising. But it was me she wanted, who she yelled for. "Winnie!"

Her voice came from her own room. I couldn't get there fast enough.

Clara, as strong as she was, struggled to keep wild-eyed Mama in her bed. Papa seemed shrunken down, huddled in the rocking chair by the window. He clutched a blanket around him, his red-rimmed eyes on Mama.

"Margaret," he said, real low.

Mama kept screaming. With her eyes focused on me, she lunged, trying to escape Clara's arms. "Winnie!" Her hand, opening and closing, sought mine.

I grasped it. It was slippery with sweat.

"No!" Clara tried to yank me from my mama. "You'll get sick, Winnie. Get out of here!"

I held on. "She needs me."

"She's talking out of her head."

"Mama needs me," I said, not letting go.

. . .

I stayed with her. Clara moved Papa into her room. She nursed him and the girls, who weren't as sick as Mama.

Mama's breathing was raspy and loud. I propped her up on two pillows, but she pulled them out from under her head and pushed them to the floor. Clara placed an old tea towel smeared with mustard plaster on the nightstand, the smell of it sharp in my nose. She pressed another towel into my hand. "Remember to put this down first or the mustard plaster will burn her."

"I know how to do it," I said. I'd made many a mustard plaster for Mary and all of her chest colds.

Clara hustled out of the room.

Mama lay still while I put the warm poultice on her chest. I stroked her hair. "Let that do its work. It will help you breathe."

She was quiet for a while. I pulled the rocking chair up to her bed, so I could be closer to her.

I stared at her in a way I didn't normally get to. Although my mama was not much more than thirty years old, she looked as old as Tillie's mama, who was over forty, having been an old maid before she married.

When Clara came back in, she put some aspirin in my hand and gave me a glass of hot lemonade. "Get her to take those. And make sure she drinks all the lemonade."

I put the medicine and glass down and pulled the pillows off the floor. I lifted Mama up as gently as I could, like she was a baby bird, and slipped those pillows underneath her.

Her eyes flickered open. "Is that you, Winnie?"

"Yes, Mama," I said, taking her hot hand. "I have some medicine for you."

"When did you get home?"

"I've been home, Mama. Don't you remember?" I picked up the little pills. "Here's the aspirin. Open your mouth."

"What's that?" she asked, looking suspicious.

"Aspirin, Mama."

I got her to swallow and sip a bit of the lemonade.

She slept some. Clara drifted in and out, fussing about the full glass of lemonade, bringing me a washrag and a bowl of cool water, throwing another quilt on Mama, asking me how she was doing but never listening for the answer before she left again.

I ran a cool cloth over Mama's flushed face. Her head rocked back and forth as she whispered things I couldn't understand. She might have been saying, "Papa," but I didn't know.

Her breathing slowed down. I ran a finger over her blue lips.

I didn't know if I could bear seeing my mama die. I wanted to tear out of the house and run to the bridge and jump in the creek and sink into that clear water, surrounded by the sights and sounds of *living* things.

Clara came back in when Mama started screaming.

"The wind is loud!"

Clara tried to push her back on the bed.

"We have to get out," Mama said.

"There's no storm, honey," said Clara, in a soothing voice I remembered her using when I was sick last spring. "Lay back down for your mama."

Mama lay back, her lips moving but no words coming out. I bit my own lip as if I could get her to stop doing that.

Clara stared at me, her gray hair loose out of her bun, hanging down over her shoulders. I hadn't known her hair was so long. "Oh, Winnie."

Miranda's voice called out from our room down the hall. "It's Mary! Come, Clara!"

Clara left us alone.

I looked down at Mama's white face. A quick fear shot through me. It was like I didn't know her, this woman lying on the bed. It was like she wasn't my mama after all. Like I'd never had a mama.

Trembling, I soaked the rag in the water and wrung it out. I pressed it to her forehead, looking into her eyes, which gazed past me.

It was like I was *her* mama, or maybe her big sister.

So I talked to her like I would to Miranda or Mary. I smoothed back her hair and sang to her.

"The water is rising," Mama said. "We have to leave."

I glanced over at the blue of the late afternoon sky. "There's no storm, Mama."

"Papa says we have to leave."

I looked back at the hall, even though I knew he wasn't there. "Papa's resting in Clara's room. He didn't say that."

"Who are you?"

"Oh, Mama, it's me, Winnie. Your daughter, your oldest."

Her eyes lit up for a minute. "I know," she said.

She tried to sit up. "The house was shaking. The roof flew right off."

"Lay back down against the pillow, Mama. The roof never came off our house."

"Not this house," she said, angry now. "My house."

So she wasn't talking about the 1915 storm. It was the other one. "Shhh, Mama. That's all over now."

"We couldn't find her."

"Who, Mama?"

"Papa buried us in hay bales in the barn. I had hay in my mouth, couldn't breathe."

"It's all over now," I said, starting to cry. All these years I'd wanted to hear about that storm and now I didn't. I just wanted her to stop going on in that raspy voice.

"We found Jane. All tangled up in barbed wire." She grabbed my hands. "All my doing."

"Shh, honey," I said, trying to use that calm voice of Clara's. "You hear me, Mama, you know it's me?"

She groaned, clawing at my hand. Then she was still. I wrapped my arm around her, listening to her breathing those awful sounds, much worse than Mary's chest colds. I heard a gurgling inside of her.

"Talk to me, Winnie," she whispered. "Like you do."

Just her knowing it was me, that right there, kept me going.

I told her about Nolan kissing me through burlap and how we'd stolen the Vicks VapoRub and how he'd gotten caught, but I hadn't. I told her that Mr. Levy had courted Clara, even though she probably knew that. I told her Tillie was sick, too.

As I talked, she got more peaceful.

I thought about how she'd told me I talked about nothing. But those same kinds of words, those nothing words, were calming her down. My words were both things to her, contradictory things, just like water being joy and sorrow, just like Clara being strong and mean. Both things. Did it all belong? Just like Mr. Levy said?

Her eyes lit up then, staring at the ceiling with a look like a sharp burst of love had pierced her. She pointed, but I saw nothing.

"Look," she said, with wonder in her voice. "Look."

"I can't see anything there, Mama."

"Look."

"I love you, Mama."

She was quiet and still. I think she heard me, though.

24

I couldn't get my legs to move. I couldn't yell out for Clara.

I just kept talking.

My mama wasn't in her body anymore. But I kept talking.

Clara came in and saw. The life went out of her face, draining it of color. She leaned against the doorsill, putting her head against the wood.

She took a breath and kissed Mama's forehead. "Go to your father, Margaret," she whispered to her. "He's waiting for you."

When I cried, Clara held me, like she'd been my mama all along.

25

_M_ama's funeral.

People came to the house. Cold chicken. Grits. Cakes. Even Mrs. Craven brought a pie. It was apple. But I didn't eat a piece. I didn't eat anything.

Papa and the girls were too sick to come out to the cemetery. Mrs. Patch stayed and tended to them while we stood out by the grave.

I can't remember a word Reverend Patch said.

I do remember Effie singing "Softly and Tenderly, Jesus Is Calling." Mama's favorite hymn. When we sang it at church, Mama would cry and whisper it was the loveliest thing she'd ever heard.

Tillie was still sick. But Mr. Levy came.

I saw Nolan at the edge of the crowd of folks, standing with his mama and papa.

Tears streamed out of my eyes as they threw dirt on my mama's coffin. The coffin Papa didn't get to make for her.

No ghosts whispered in my ear.

I thought of Mama's face when she pointed to the ceiling and told me to look. Such a light there in her eyes and in her smile.

Whatever that light was, that was where Mama was, not here in the coffin.

I felt like she was right beside me. Such a peace about her.

The wind blew.

Mama was gone.

26

"Winnie."

Mrs. Patch stood in the doorway of the kitchen. She wore Mama's white apron with the embroidery on the pocket.

"Yes, ma'am? Do the girls need me?"

I'd been looking out the window in the parlor. I longed to go sit on the bridge, but it wouldn't be right for me to leave. I probably should be helping with the dishes, but the kitchen was empty without Mama. I'd thought about going upstairs to Papa and the girls. But then I just kept on sitting.

"Isn't that Nolan Field over there by the hog pen?"

I looked. "Yes, ma'am, that's him."

"Why don't you go see him?" she asked. "He's been out there since the funeral."

"I need to tend my sisters," I said, standing. "I shouldn't be sitting here."

Mrs. Patch walked over and gave me a look of sad eyes. "Winnie. Go talk to that boy or he's never going to leave."

I stepped backward. I was afraid she might wrap me in a hug and I didn't want to be wrapped in a hug. "Okay, for a few minutes."

"Mrs. Hayward is upstairs with your grandmother. You take all the time you need."

It was hard walking out to Nolan. I didn't want to see another person. Everybody said how sad they were or how my mama was in heaven. I didn't want to hear that because it made me think about it real hard and I didn't want to think about it at all.

"Hi," said Nolan.

"Where's your mama and papa?"

"They went home."

"Your papa let you stay?" I asked. "Aren't you in trouble?"

"He said it was all right. I brought you something."

He handed me a jar.

"Nolan," I said. "Where'd you get this?"

"Well . . ." He looked kind of sheepish. "More people had it than we thought." He shrugged. "Miss Livingston's papa came by the house. He told Papa he was so glad Miss Livingston didn't have the flu he wanted to help somebody else out. So he gave us his jar of Vicks. He didn't want me doing anything else against the law."

"I declare."

"It's about half full," Nolan said. "Now you can use it so you won't get sick."

"I don't think it keeps you from getting the flu after all."

"That's not what the paper said."

"I don't know," I said.

"You don't feel sick, do you, Winnie?"

"No, I don't."

He let out a breath. "Good. That's good."

Then we both got kind of quiet. I guessed Nolan had used up

all his words. I was happy he didn't say anything about my mama. I didn't want to talk about her or about Papa being sick or the girls being sick or Tillie being sick or anybody being sick. I couldn't hold it all in my head or in my heart.

One of our sows grunted. She stuck her snout down into the mud. Then she lumbered over to the fence by us. Maybe she thought I was Mama coming to pour slop into the trough. I wondered if hogs knew voices. Would they be waiting for Mama's voice, not knowing why she didn't feed them anymore? Would the chickens be waiting for her, too?

I glanced up at the bedroom windows. I wished Papa and the girls would get better. The house was quiet and lonely.

I opened the jar and took a sniff. A sharp smell went up my nostrils and behind my cheeks. We were silly to think this would keep the flu away. I guess desperate folks do foolish things.

"I'm sorry, Nolan."

"Why?"

"The store. I ran away, leaving you there. And I never confessed to it. Except to the sheriff."

"You told Sheriff Milroy?"

"Yeah," I said.

"Why'd you do that, Winnie?"

"I couldn't let you take all the blame."

"It was me who came up with the idea."

"I went along with it. I broke into the store with you."

"I don't know why folks keep calling it a break-in," he said. "We just opened a window."

"You unlocked the window, though."

"Yeah, but I didn't break it." He grinned.

"Yeah." I didn't know why, but thinking of smiling made me want to cry. So I didn't do either.

"Did the sheriff tell Clara?" he asked.

"No, he didn't."

"What did he do?"

"Nothing. He told me to go home."

Nolan patted the top rail of the fence. "I like Sheriff Milroy."

"He shouldn't have let me go. I did a cowardly thing." I leaned over the fence, but kept my fingers away from our hog. She liked to bite. "Just running away like that. I did it because I was scared."

"You're no coward, Winnie."

"I left you all alone in Craven's store. Aren't you mad at me?"

"No, Winnie. You're my girl." He blushed.

I couldn't help but smile at that. He smiled back.

But then I remembered.

"What's wrong, Winnie?" Then he remembered, too. I could see it in his face.

"Will I always feel like this, Nolan? Like I won't ever be happy again?"

His face fell. He just stared at me, not saying anything, but looking like he wanted to. Reaching over, he took my hand like it was the most fragile thing he'd ever held. He threaded his fingers in between mine.

I looked down at our hands and felt a tinge of happiness. Even with my heart in little pieces.

27

*H*ow's Tillie, Mr. Levy?"

He was stooped over a little, his eyes tired. He looked like I felt inside. "She's very sick, Winnie. You'd better go home."

"Can't I see her?"

"It's not safe for you here."

I looked down, watching Tillie's cat crawl around my legs. I didn't want to backtalk, but I was with my mama when she died, and my papa and sisters still had the flu. I wasn't going to get sick with it.

Mr. Levy stepped out on the porch, closing the screen door behind him. I felt the slap of the door in my heart. I was being kept from Tillie, from her house, from her grandpa and mama.

Mr. Levy smelled of pipe smoke, coffee, and something else, a medicine smell. I noticed the black stain on his light shirt. The bitter taste of quinine filled my mouth, as if it was on my tongue. I wondered about that stain and the smells and then figured it out. They must have put the quinine in coffee for Tillie. But she wouldn't take it.

"Come sit with me," Mr. Levy said.

I picked up Miss Pickford, cradling the softness of her fur against my cheek. Tillie should have her cat with her. She should have her best friend with her, too.

I followed Mr. Levy over to the swing. It moved a little beneath us when we sat down. I peeked out behind the ivy clinging to the porch posts. Jimmy Craven and Clyde Wells were playing marbles out in the street, shouting at each other about something.

Clyde had recovered from the flu just fine. He hadn't said anything to me when I passed him by. Even Jimmy had looked the other way. Death makes people go quiet.

Mr. Levy and I rocked slowly. I waited for him to say something, to tell me that Tillie wasn't that sick. But he didn't. I tried to think of something else so it wouldn't hurt so much inside.

A screen door slammed. Mrs. Craven flew out of her house next door. "Jimmy!" she yelled, going out into the street.

He got to his feet. "What, Mama?"

"You shouldn't be playing with him. Clyde," she said, waving her big hand at him, "you need to go on home. You could be spreading germs."

"But, Mama—"

"Now, Jimmy! Get in this house! And with Tillie sick right next door and her windows open . . ." She'd finally seen us behind the ivy. I could tell by the way she was talking she didn't know there were any grown-ups about.

"Good afternoon," said Mr. Levy.

She nodded at him. "How's your granddaughter?" she called out.

Mr. Levy didn't answer.

"She's fine!" I said.

Mr. Levy took my hand. We rocked in that swing for almost a full hour before he took Miss Pickford and went back inside.

I sat there for a while, watching Clyde, who was still in the street, even though Jimmy had won all his marbles and gone back in a while ago. Clyde came to the porch steps and looked over at me. "Did I get Tillie sick, Winnie?"

His cap was on crooked, slanted over his eyes. He stepped toward me when I didn't answer. I wondered if we both didn't get her sick. I let her go to Clyde's house that day. I could've stopped her.

"Don't think on it, Clyde," I said. "It's water under the bridge."

He stood very still, and then turned and ran down the steps. I figured I said the wrong thing to him.

I went around to the back of the house, looking up at Tillie's window on the second floor. It was open, like Mrs. Craven had said.

I knew I should go home. I had to make supper. Papa and the girls were still sick. Clara wouldn't let me near them, saying I might still get the influenza and she couldn't lose me, too.

Just then, Tillie went into a coughing spell. It froze me in my tracks. I could tell the influenza was deep in her lungs. When her coughing stopped, I settled down in the patchy grass under her window and stared at the Graves's backyard. Helen and Catherine were jumping rope, their favorite thing.

From her bedroom, Tillie and I had watched the Graves sisters grow up, jumping rope, fighting, or trying to push their goat back into his pen. That always made us laugh. He was a stubborn goat, always getting into trouble, sometimes eating the lunches right off the shelves at Miranda's school.

Who would I laugh with if Tillie died?

Tillie's mama was singing to her in her pretty soprano voice. Tillie said her mama had been so good she'd been asked to sing at the opera house in Galveston. She decided to marry Mr. Lawrence instead. I wondered if that was why Tillie wished for stardom. Maybe she felt like she needed to finish something her mama never got to.

The words weren't clear, but Mrs. Lawrence's song sounded like something you sing to babies.

I was there under that window when she started screaming. I pressed my hand over my mouth and kept watching the girls skipping rope.

I didn't go to Tillie's funeral. I locked my door. Clara knocked, but I just stayed on my bed, my head buried in my pillow. I knew Tillie would leave me one day, but I thought it'd be to go to California.

I wondered, did her face light up like my mama's did when she died? If I'd been there, I could've held her hand while Mrs. Lawrence sang to her.

Through the glass of my window, I watched the mourners. Mr. Levy and Mr. Lawrence helped a figure all in black over to the gravesite. Tillie's mama could barely walk on her own. I touched the pane, wanting to comfort her.

Lessie Craven cried, but I didn't. I wouldn't let myself think about it.

It's cold out here," said Clara. "Why are you sitting on the ground? You need to come inside, Winifred."

I pulled my coat tighter around me, looking up at the naked branches of the lone graveyard tree and at the gray sky above. "I'll be in soon," I said, wishing she'd leave me alone.

She smoothed her dark skirts and sat beside me.

"What are you doing, Clara?"

"Sitting in the dirt with my number one granddaughter."

She patted the grave. Her lips were tight, tight, as if she were afraid to move them because something might spill out, maybe her whole heart would just tumble out into the dirt.

That's what I felt like. Like my whole heart was ripped out of my body and beating on that grave. Mama's grave.

Clara looked away.

I asked quickly, "Is Papa okay?"

"He's sitting up in the rocking chair. I told him to stay put. If I don't keep an eye on that man, he'll be out in the barn."

Clara's eyes were gray, like Mama's, but even in their sadness, they didn't have the lost look Mama's always had. They were strong eyes.

Papa was in a restless sleep. I sat down on the edge of the bed and took his hand. He had pneumonia, the doctor said. Dr. Fox had come down here, looking all white and frail himself. There wasn't much he could do for Papa. He said to tend to him with the home cures we'd used on Mama and the girls.

I leaned over and said real soft, "We need you, Papa." I said this to him every day.

Clara had told me to watch him while she cooked supper. I read to him from the pages of the *Houston Chronicle*, mostly war news. Folks were saying it'd be over soon. It was hard to know if Papa heard me. His eyes were closed, but he was more still when I read. Clara had told him about Mama, but I didn't know if he'd understood.

"Winnie," said a whispered voice. Miranda was in the doorway, her long nightgown brushing the dusty floor. Under her arm was her piano board.

"If Clara sees you out of bed . . ."

She glanced down the hallway. Even Miranda was scared of Clara.

"Papa needs some music."

I put the newspaper on the bed and waved her in.

We looked down at him, watching him breathe. Maybe it was our nursing, maybe something else, but Papa was getting better. His fever was down, and he was breathing easier. Clara said he'd come through the worst of it.

Miranda pulled up a chair and sat down. She positioned the piano on her lap. "Papa," she said, "I'm going to play for you."

Her ten fingers moved along the painted keys. I stood behind her while she played her silent song.

I didn't know how Papa'd struggled so long and yet was getting well. Mama had died so quickly. People in town said it was the way this influenza worked. Even the old-timers said they'd never seen anything like it. But I wondered if Mama had just been more willing to let go of life.

"He liked it." Miranda was looking up at me. Her hands were still.

"Yes, he did," I said.

"He's getting well," she whispered. "See the color in his cheeks?"

"Yes, I do."

"Has he said anything?"

I shook my head.

Sometimes Papa would mumble or open his eyes for a second, but he wasn't really with us even when he did that.

Miranda jumped when we heard a loud clatter in the kitchen. Her eyes got big and she ran out of the room with her piano. She was brave, but she wasn't stupid. Clara was fast for an old woman.

Mary's chastising voice drifted from the other room: "You weren't supposed to get out of bed, Miranda. Clara said."

Our house seemed to be healing no[w] voices echoed through it. Just now, they we[re] which we cut out of the Sears Roebuck catal[og] too, with little tabs at the shoulders so we co[uld] on the dolls.

You'd think with a mama gone and a papa s[ick] in the house would stop. But that wasn't the w[ay] went on for the living. I thought about Mama, t[hat] her life hadn't seemed to be able to go on after tha[t]

I didn't want there to be any more secrets. I pla[nned to tell] Clara about Mama when the time was right.

I glanced down at Papa. His eyes were open, and [he was look]ing right at me.

"Papa!" I shouted, grabbing his shoulder.

He blinked hard.

My sisters ran in from the other room. Miranda th[rew her] arms around him. "It was my song that woke him up."

I turned to see Clara at the door. "He's awake."

"I see that," she said, her eyes tired and pleased.

"The kaiser abdicated, Winnie," she said. "It was in the newspaper. This terrible war will be over soon."

"That is good news," I said. "Effie's brother will be coming home."

"All our boys will be," said Clara, in her no-nonsense voice.

I glanced over at Lewis's grave, thinking about how he'd died a month too soon. Too much death.

"Don't think about it, Winnie," said Clara, looking straight at me. "Put your mind someplace else."

I nodded and swallowed hard. But I wasn't good at just willing stuff away like Clara was. That wasn't the best way to be, anyhow.

But Clara's strength *had* taken care of us all these years, while Mama had looked no further than the fear inside of herself.

"Clara," I said, "I have to ask you something."

She narrowed her eyes.

"Mama talked about the hurricane when I was nursing her. The storm of 1900."

"Winnie . . . your mama couldn't take the hardness of life." She shut her eyes for a second before she went on. "Anything would've blown her over. I knew that when she was a child."

"But she was upset about someone named Jane."

Clara's face closed up tight. I could see her turning away from my words.

"Mama said it was her fault Jane died," I said.

Clara's eyes darted back and forth for a moment, as if she wasn't sure of something. "Jane was always at the house, getting under my skirts. She didn't have a mama, and her papa would leave her with me while he worked the chuckwagon. I told your mama to look out for little Jane that day while your grandfather and I got ready for the storm. Your mama lost track of the girl."

Oh, Mama, I thought.

"After that storm, your mama would sob whenever Jane's name was mentioned. So I forbade anybody to talk about it. No one was going to say her name in my house." Clara pressed her palms on the ground to push herself up. "Your mama needed to let that go. People should leave the past in the past."

I thought about mama living in the quiet of buried things. Maybe she'd been a little like me after all, wanting to talk. But I knew Clara couldn't do that. She might be able to handle the hard times, but she couldn't talk about them. She didn't dwell on unpleasant thoughts. But there were things I had to know.

"What was your papa like, Clara?" I asked.

Her mouth twitched as she stood. She pressed her hand to her lips. Her eyes were dry, though. She didn't look sad. Just angry.

"Don't give any thought to him, Winnie."

I nodded, digging in the dirt of mama's grave.

"Never again. Do you hear me?"

"I won't," I said, feeling the strength in her. But I had strength, too. I'd talk about him if I wanted. I'd think about him if I wanted.

"I mean it, Winnie."

"I heard you."

"What did you say to me?"

"*Yes, ma'am* is what I meant."

"All right, then."

I was sure Clara and I would have days of fighting ahead of us. She'd be on me until the day one of us died. But she'd always be there for me, too, in all the ways that mattered.

"You're not to stay out here too long," she said. "It's too cold. And not proper for a young lady to be sitting here among all these graves." She brushed off the back of her dress. "Not proper at all."

I thought it was all right.

"Winnie," she said.

"I'll be in soon."

I sat there for a while by Mama's grave. I still couldn't look at Tillie's.

I knew Mama had passed on. I'd been there when she took her last breath. But I wasn't so sure about Tillie.

30

We walked in a close huddle to school, ducking our heads when the wind blew. Such a cold day. Sometimes in December, we would get a long spell of warmth. Not today.

Mary grabbed my mittened hand. Miranda saw and grabbed the other, sending my lunch pail swinging. The smell of warm biscuits drifted up to me, and my stomach growled. I hadn't eaten my breakfast because I'd been so busy doing my chores and getting the girls fed.

Patches of fog hovered over the prairie, keeping us on the road. In the old days, I'd been worried the white mist was ghosts' breath. But Mama wasn't a ghost. She was in that place that lit up her eyes when she died.

"Why do we have to go to school on such a cold day, Mama?"

I felt a gripping at my heart. I looked over at Mary. She was growing fast, but still a head shorter than me.

"What did you call me?"

She hid her face in her worn red mittens.

"Don't call me that, Mary."

"You're like our mama," she said, gulping for air.

I held her as she cried. Miranda put her hand on Mary's shoulder, her own lip quivering.

"You can call me Mama, but just today," I whispered.

31

Ouch," Miranda said, grabbing her head.

"Sit still!" I twisted a rubber band around one ponytail braid.

"Well, gosh, I can't, with you pulling on my hair."

Clara turned around, her hands powdered with flour. "Sit still, Miranda, so your sister can finish those pigtails."

I glanced out the window. A cold blue sky. The rain we'd been having these last few days had finally stopped. No more gray clouds.

"I'm cold," said Miranda. "Why can't I sit by the stove?"

"You can have my place," said Mary, getting up.

Miranda stood while my hands were moving. The hair fell out of the braid. "Miranda!"

I sighed as Miranda switched seats with Mary.

I gazed out the window again, thinking of Nolan. He said he'd be down today. I hadn't seen him much these last few months. Things had been busy since Mama died. I'd had a lot of work to do before, but now my life seemed to be only about hauling water and cooking supper and taking care of two baby sisters.

"Get on out of the house, Winnie."

I turned back to see Clara looking at me.

"I have to finish Miranda's hair, and then I have to get the washing basins ready and—"

"Go on," Clara said, going back to her baking. "The washing can wait."

"Why does Winnie—" Miranda was cut short by a look from Clara.

I grabbed my coat off the rack quick before Clara changed her mind. When I went out the door, I heard her yell, "But you better not be gone too long!" in that voice that should've been calling hogs instead of grandchildren.

My first thought was to run down to Tillie's. I stopped short. Tillie wasn't at her house anymore. In fact, she was closer to me than that, right over in the cemetery.

I closed my eyes, feeling her so close to me. I crumpled down on the ground and cried. I couldn't put my mind someplace else, like Clara told me to do. It was right on Tillie, and on Mama, too.

Nolan found me. All of a sudden, he was just there, sitting beside me. He didn't say anything.

When my sobbing stopped, I wiped my eyes and nose.

"Race you to the creek," he said.

I jumped up and started running, feeling the cold air whisk by my bare ears and still-wet cheeks. I cut through the cemetery. Nolan passed me up at Lewis Locke's grave.

Out of breath, we fell onto the wooden bridge. We didn't say anything, just laid there, looking up at the sky and listening to the sounds of the water below.

I wondered if Tillie was a motion picture actress in heaven, with angels eating popcorn and watching her on the big screen.

I wonder.

32

I stood with the Baptists, watching the preacher and Nolan out in the creek. They weren't too far off the bank. The creek got deep toward the middle. Folks crowded under the few trees at this place on Coward Creek. It was a clear April day and already getting warm. A breeze cooled us off, rippling the water around Nolan.

Behind him was the bridge, our place. That was where we'd been when he told me what his papa was making him do.

Nolan looked nervous. He was quiet, but I could tell. I caught his mama's eye. We smiled at each other, sharing our caring for Nolan in a glance.

On a branch of the soapberry tree, just above my head, was a redbird, just chattering away. I wondered who she was talking to. She stopped when she caught me watching, cocked her head, and flew off, her wings a flash of red against the blue sky.

The graveyard was behind us. It seemed right to me now that we were baptized by where we were buried, that we lived by the graves.

I liked being close to Mama. I knew she wasn't in her grave, but I liked looking over and seeing the Grace family tombstone, with the pretty words on it that Clara let me pick out:

Hope is the thing with feathers—
That perches in the soul—
And sings the tune without the words—
And never stops—at all—

Mama would have liked it, I was sure.

Those words made me think of Tillie's mama. She'd turned inside of herself since Tillie died. Papa said he didn't think anybody could get her out. But I hoped she'd find her way back.

I visited her a lot these days. After a game of chess with Mr. Levy, I would bring her a glass of cold iced tea. We rocked on the porch, sometimes talking, sometimes not. I thought it gave her some comfort. I know it did me.

Five people in Coward Creek had died of the influenza. Mama, Tillie, Mr. Frazier, Eddie Payne's father, and Joseph's son, Jess, who'd just turned fifteen and had helped dig the graves sometimes. Edna Bloom and Lewis Locke were also buried here, even though they'd died someplace else.

Not many compared to some parts of the country. Galveston lost about a hundred or two hundred, I'd heard. But faraway places like Philadelphia and Boston, they'd lost thousands. I couldn't imagine all those people dying. I wondered if there were other girls like me who had to take care of their mamas when they were sick.

The memory of that day made my eyes burn a little, but I didn't swallow the thought. Sometimes you just had to let a sad feeling drift away on its own.

I felt a hand on my shoulder. Looking up, I met Mr. Levy's blue eyes.

"Hi!" I said, happy to see him.

Clara gave me a stern look. "Quiet, Winnie. Listen to what the preacher is saying." She looked up at Mr. Levy. "Hello, Henry. It's nice to see you."

"Good afternoon, Clara," said Mr. Levy, smiling at her.

Oh, no. This was just a little too much niceness between the two of them. "There's Mrs. Bill, Clara," I said, pointing to my principal, who had just arrived and was closer to the bank.

"Yes, there she is," said Clara, ambling down to be by the richest woman in town.

"Where were you yesterday, Mr. Levy?" I whispered. "No one answered the door."

"I took the Interurban to Galveston."

"Oh?" I asked in surprise. He rarely left his house. "Why'd you do that?"

"I went to *shul*."

"Huh?"

"I spoke with Rabbi Cohen."

"You have friends in Galveston?" I asked, watching Nolan. The preacher put one hand on the back of his neck, talking quietly to him.

"I do, Winnie," he said. "And I'll be seeing them more often."

"You aren't leaving Coward Creek, are you?"

Clara whipped her head around and glared at me. I looked up and pretended to be listening to the preacher.

"No," Mr. Levy said, squeezing my shoulder.

I nodded, relief washing over me.

Nolan pinched his nose with both hands. Reverend Lane clutched Nolan's wrists with his free hand and lowered him into the water.

Nolan was becoming a Baptist again. After the Baptists had

kicked his mama out of the church, the whole family had left. Mr. Field was livid about Nolan stealing the Vicks. First, he gave him a whooping. Then he said they all had to be baptized and start going to church again.

He worked it out with Reverend Lane. The preacher agreed, over Mrs. Craven's loud objections. Reverend Lane personally went out to the Field farm to ask Nolan's mama to come back. All the dying from the war and the influenza must've knocked some sense into the preacher's head. I meant no disrespect because he did the right thing in the end.

Nolan came out of that water, with it dripping all around him, with a grin on his face. It shocked me to see it there, with the water running down his mouth. He was enjoying all this.

The sun hit the water, and it glinted like a diamond.

Tillie was right, water was hurricanes and tears. But it was joy, too.

All of it belonged. All the broken parts, the whole parts, all of it. If we pushed something away because it was broken, then we wouldn't have much. Because everything had some of both.

33

It was hot out. I lay beside my mama's grave on the warm ground talking to her about what I thought would happen in the years to come. My plans were to marry Nolan and have four children, three girls and one boy. I thought I'd make a good mama.

But there was something else I wanted to do. I started thinking about it after mama died. It just seemed to fit. Clara would think it was a waste of my time. She'd never understand *why* I decided to do it. So I just wouldn't tell her.

The first day of school was two days away. I was ready to go back, even though it'd be hard to get all my chores done along with my homework. Mama sure had done a lot while I was at school.

The screen door slammed. Papa walked toward me, carrying two tall glasses. I sat up, wondering why he wasn't in the barn. He'd been working on Mr. Straw's coffin for two days.

Miranda's voice pierced the quiet summer day. That child could yell. I could see my sisters sitting on the bridge, the fishing pole rising above their heads. Mary wore Clara's wide-brimmed hat so she wouldn't get any more freckles.

Papa handed me a glass of iced tea. The glass felt good and cold in my hand.

"Thank you." I was so touched my papa would bring me some iced tea. I took a long gulp.

"It's hot in the barn," he said. His shirt was wet around the neck and down the front. He waved his tea at the girls. "What are they doing?"

"Miranda's giving Mary a fishing lesson." I put the glass up against my sweaty cheek.

He let out a chuckle. "If our little lady catches a fish, I guess anything is possible."

Mary didn't like the smell of fish or the look of their wet scales or the way they flopped around on the line. She'd probably squeal and drop the pole in the creek if a fish clamped down on her worm. Miranda would never let her forget it if she did.

Papa sat beside me. "I see Clara has a visitor."

My nose turned up before I could help it.

"You don't like Mr. Levy courting your grandma?"

"Courting! They're just talking on the porch, Papa."

His eyes twinkled. "They sure do talk on the porch a lot."

"They fight more than anything else. Rather, Clara fights and Mr. Levy listens." He even seemed amused by her. I took another sip of my tea, thinking how I didn't understand them at all. "Anyway, they're too old for courting."

Mr. Levy was on our doorstep the Saturday after Nolan was baptized. He didn't have a book or anything for me. But I was glad to see him. He settled down in a rocking chair on the porch, and I ran to get us some sweet lemonade. When I came back, Clara was rocking beside him. They were laughing about something.

I stood by her, clearing my throat.

Clara took both glasses. She gave one to Mr. Levy and kept the other one herself!

I'd stomped off. No one called me back.

Mr. Levy kept coming over, and Clara kept monopolizing all his time. Sometimes I would sit there, waiting for him to say something to me. And he would. But I thought he was more interested in having a conversation with her.

They'd reminisce about folks they used to know or things they used to do together. Back in the old days, Coward Creek had been nothing but a couple of dirt roads and miles of lonely prairie. Mr. Levy had left behind the busy city to teach in a one-room schoolhouse. He and Clara argued about whether or not it was fair he was paid more than the lady schoolteacher he replaced.

They talked a lot about politics. Texas had just become the ninth state to give women the right to vote in all elections. Clara was taking that right seriously. All the effort she had put into becoming a member of the Coward Creek Ladies' Club now went toward figuring out who to vote for.

Her arms flew around her head when she talked about it. I could see some of the old spark come back to her. She'd lost that when Mama died. Of course, that old spark was the same thing that made her so stubborn and hard to live with.

Mr. Levy didn't seem to see it that way. I felt left out of their fun.

I put my glass down in the dirt and wondered if this was how Tillie had felt when I'd come down to see Mr. Levy instead of her. "Huh," I said, my eyes burning at the same time a smile slipped out.

"Is something funny?" Papa asked, trying to look up into my turned-down face. "Or sad?"

"It's nothing, Papa."

He put his glass beside him and stretched out on the ground. His hands went behind his head, and he looked up at the sky. A warm breeze lifted the leaves of the water oak tree. They made a soft rustling noise.

"Papa," I said, "I want to be a nurse."

"I thought you were going to be a teacher."

"I've changed my mind."

"Why is that?" he asked, sitting back up.

"I'm not sure I can explain it well."

"Well, why don't you try?"

"It was when Mama died," I said. "I think I made Mama's passing easier for her by being there."

He gave me a quick nod.

"I got something from it, too, Papa. Something stirred deep inside of me, making me feel it all made some sort of sense, even if Mama was dying." It was hard to say the next words, but I did. "Seeing Mama go to her peace brought me some kind of peace, too."

Papa's gaze drifted to Mama's tombstone. Maybe I shouldn't have said what I did. Maybe he thought nothing good could ever come from somebody dying. He kept staring, so I looked, too. *Hope is the thing with feathers.*

"Papa, are you sad you didn't get to make Mama's coffin?"

"What?" He shook his head. "No, Winnie, I'm not. Your mama isn't in that coffin."

I was glad he knew that. I thought about telling him about

the light in Mama when she died. But I wasn't ready to do that yet.

Papa looked like he wanted to say something else. He patted his hand on his leg while his face looked all a struggle. I just sat there, waiting for him.

"Did you know, Winnie, your mama was as good a student as you are?"

I smiled.

"She knew all the answers, but wouldn't say them out loud. Her lips would move when the schoolteacher asked a question. And then she'd smile to herself when she got the answer right."

These words about Mama were like little gifts from Papa. "You were sweet on her, Papa?"

"Like you and Nolan."

I blushed and ducked my head.

He reached over and tousled my hair. "Of course I wasn't in school much. I had to help out my ma. We struggled to make a living on our farm. My pa wasn't that reliable."

He glanced up at a squirrel scuttling across a branch. I wanted that squirrel to go away and not distract Papa from talking. "What was Mama like?"

"She was the prettiest girl in school, and shy and quiet. I wanted to take care of her. Even though Clara thought I wasn't good enough for her."

"So you slipped off to get married."

He looked at me in surprise. "Who told you that?"

"Mrs. Craven."

"I bet she did." He smiled. "You think *you've* seen Clara upset. You should've been there that day. The whole town heard her."

"She came around, though, didn't she, Papa?"

"She and I do all right," he said. "She's helped out a lot, especially with you girls."

I met his gaze. "Because Mama couldn't, you mean."

He sighed. "Things just are what they are, Winnie."

"But I don't understand Mama."

"People aren't easy to figure out."

"She was my mama. I want to figure her out." I could tell he was impatient with my words, but I kept talking. "I think losing that little girl in the storm made her afraid to take care of us. But I don't know."

"Life's hard out here. People just do the best they know how." He stood, brushed off the back of his pants. He put out a hand to help me up.

I took it, knowing these were all the words I was going to get, for now.

"You'll make a good nurse, Winnie."

There was a shout down by the bridge.

Mary was fighting with the fishing pole. It swung back and forth with a long fish at the end of the line. "Look, Papa!" she yelled. Miranda pulled the line up so we could see the fish and grinned like she'd caught it.

"Hold on!" Papa called out as we ran over.

That silver fish was flipping and flopping. Mary held up the pole with something like wonder on her face.

Miranda jumped up and down, her arms flying. The bridge shook beneath our feet, and I glanced at the creek below. The water looked to be still, but I knew it was moving—toward the lake, the bay, out to the sea. Always moving, picking up dead sticks, fallen feathers, and broken weeds along with it.

I knew sad things weren't always washed away. Sometimes they stayed with you, alongside all the happy things. Mama didn't know how to let the good and the sad live side by side.

I think I know how to do that now.

AUTHOR'S NOTE

When I was a child, my family spent many holidays and summer weeks in my parents' small Mississippi hometown. My grandmothers lived down the street from each other in houses built in the early 1900s. My brothers and I took many a lazy walk to the downtown area, with our hands clutched around coins to buy candy or pop at the wooden-floored drugstore. On those trips, I thought about what it would be like to grow up there. As I got older, I continued to wonder. Eventually I created my own small town of Coward Creek, borrowing the name from a creek in Texas.

Still, what mostly drew me to this story was Winnie. She popped into my head just talking away, as if she had something to say and wanted someone to listen to her. *Winnie's War* became the story of a twelve-year-old girl trying to reach out to her troubled mother.

Most of *Winnie's War* comes from my imagination. But this very sad time in our history really did happen. What follows is a description of some of that history.

The Spanish Influenza

I don't remember when I first learned about the Spanish influenza. I'm not sure we even discussed it in my junior high and high school history classes. Perhaps my introduction to it was the moving film *1918*, the play and screenplay penned by the Texas writer Horton Foote.

The Spanish influenza was a mystery to me: how did so many people die of the disease, and yet this tragic time seemed to have vanished from our nation's memory? I wanted to know more about this pandemic, and in particular, how it affected the people living in the Houston/Galveston area, where I live now. Hence, the setting for Winnie's story emerged from my interest in the influenza and my curiosity about small towns.

The Spanish influenza of 1918–1919 killed at least 20 million people worldwide. In the United States, approximately 675,000 people died. It was the deadliest influenza pandemic in modern history.

There were three waves: spring and fall of 1918, and the winter of 1919. The mild spring wave brought headaches and fever, but most recovered in two to three days. The second wave began in August 1918, toward the end of the First World War. It was soon clear this was a much more dangerous virus than had been experienced a few months before. Most deaths would occur during the fall wave.

People had suffered the aches and pains of this illness for years, but the 1918 virus had unique characteristics. In years past, influenza preyed mostly on the very young and the very old. But this virus confused doctors. Healthy young adults, those in their twenties and thirties, were dying at the same, or higher, rate as the babies and toddlers and the elderly. Also, more influenza victims were dying.

In the story, Winnie's mama dies quickly after showing symptoms of the influenza, but Tillie lingers for a week before she succumbs. The virus did work in this way, with some victims dying in two or three days and others hanging on for a week or more. Many others would recover after a month or more of illness, as did Katherine Anne Porter, a Texas writer who almost died during the 1918 pandemic and wrote a famous book of short stories, *Pale Horse, Pale Rider*, based on that and related experiences.

The Spanish influenza hit some cities, such as Boston and New York, very hard. In Philadelphia, over four thousand people died in one week in October. The city morgue overflowed with bodies, which were piled one on top of the other in its rooms and corridors. The influenza did not kill as many people in the Houston/Galveston area, which is where I placed Coward Creek, but the losses were keenly felt. One small town in Galveston County lost five people to influenza or pneumonia in a little over six weeks.

Keeping the Influenza Away

People turned to home remedies to ease the symptoms of the influenza, as Winnie did with the mustard plaster compresses for her mother. They also used anything else they could find to keep from getting sick, resulting in some unusual choices. Mothers made children wear bags of camphor around their necks. Fearful people carried potatoes in their pockets, created homemade tonics, or ate large amounts of fried onions. None of these helped.

One common treatment was the use of Vicks VapoRub. Sheriff Milroy is right when he tells Winnie that Vicks will not prevent influenza. People used it as a treatment for the symptoms, but there is no evidence it helped. Advertisements in newspapers of the time noted a shortage of Vicks VapoRub. The earliest date for the notice that I found in the *Houston Chronicle* was October 27, 1918. In *Winnie's War*, Nolan sees the notice in mid-October. I moved up the date of the advertisement so it would fit into the story's time frame.

Some cities mandated that citizens had to wear masks. A photograph of the period shows people without masks not being allowed on a Seattle streetcar. In San Francisco, it was required by law to wear a mask, although these were not Winnie's scratchy burlap masks, but gauze masks medical personnel wore. In the end, the masks were not effective. They could not stop the tiny flu germs from getting into the nose and mouth, although they would keep out droplets of water that may have contained the flu virus.

Coward Creek

Coward Creek is a fictional town with fictional people. It is based on real towns in the Galveston County area of Texas. Like Coward Creek, these towns were populated by people of different ethnicities and faiths, e.g., Italians, Germans, Mexicans, Japanese, Baptists, Catholics, Jews, and Quakers. Many disembarked from ships coming into Galveston to begin their new lives in the United States.

Hurricanes

The hurricanes of 1900 and 1915 had a significant impact on the Galveston area. Of the two, the 1900 storm is the most well-known. Many books and stories have been written about this powerful hurricane. It is believed six thousand people died.

The 1915 storm was just as powerful, but by that time, the seawall had been built in Galveston. The loss of life was not nearly as great, but people remembered it as being a frightening storm that blew off roofs and flooded streets.

Galveston has had other hurricanes since that time, but none as destructive as the storms of 1900 and 1915.

Final Thoughts

Writers note the scant mention of the Spanish influenza in the journals and documents of the time and in history books today.

Most Americans know very little about the 1918–1919 influenza waves. Some researchers theorize the time was so terrible that people just wanted to forget it. Others say the pandemic got lost in the sadness of the war or that it was over so quickly people didn't have much time to absorb it.

More writers are focusing their attention on the Spanish influenza these days. There are many stories to tell. *Winnie's War* is just one—it happened only in my imagination but now lives on the printed page.

ACKNOWLEDGMENTS

Many thanks to:

My agent, Nancy Gallt, for finding the right places for my stories.

My editor, Emily Easton, for pushing me to see what Winnie needed.

The very patient Mary Kate Castellani for answering my newbie author questions.

My much-missed critique group, The Yellow House Writers, Mary Ann Hellinghausen and Bettina Restrepo, and our generous leader Joyce Harlow, for critiques of early chapters of the manuscript.

Amazing readers Ruth Baxter, Tim Crow, Rose Green, Barbara Holt, Pam Kinser, Millie Martin, Tamra Norton, and Christine Suffredini; to Deb Bryson for her encouragement; to Mary Beth Kelsey for believing in the book; and to Melissa Marr for her advice.

All the blueboarders, but especially Verla Kay for creating such a wonderful community of writers.

The librarians at the numerous libraries I visited in Harris and Galveston counties, but especially to Mrs. Simkulet, wherever you may be, my first favorite librarian, who taught me how to shelve books and about kindness.

My dear friends Heidi Clark, Norma Dempsey, and Sharon Reed, for introducing me to the writings of Richard Rohr, especially his book *Everything Belongs*, and for their wisdom.

Sally Barringer and David McKissack for always being available for a last-minute read, and Ken McKissack and my father, Howard McKissack, for anything else I might need.